Darque Legends:
Search for the Wyrdritch
Book Three

DERRIEN RELYEA

http://thedragonwarrior.com

ISBN 978-0-9905884-4-3 (print)
ISBN 978-0-9905884-5-0 (digital)

In Legend Song they'd praise our stand,
tell how we fought the End of Man.
Come with me now and you will hear
of how the Evil One drew near.
Too long the warnings were ignored.
With just a few left to stop the Hoard,
know 'tis the truth that you will learn,
when these pages you do turn.

'Twas a time of war. The Black had returned, his despicable Hoard gaining power with astonishing ease amongst those unfamiliar with their own history. Humans and the Magic bearing Races had drifted apart since the Last Holocaust, and many chose ignorance o'er facing the truth that the Evil One was rising once more. 'Twas no less so than with Lord Rohar, the royal leader of the Sprite Nation, upon the Island of Dreams.

While Darque and the Dragon Clan were entering the Black War, the 7th Egg mysteriously disappeared from the island, along with the Heir Apparent of the Sprite Nation, Kevon. The boy had been poisoned by the Sorcerer's Spell Sword and the only one who could heal him was Myrrdin's sister, Persephone. But she, along with the entire Wyrdritch, homeland of the Elves, disappeared at the time of the Last Holocaust. Did she yet live?

Framed for their abductions, 'twas up to Caleichante, Captain of the Sprite Elite Guard to make the treacherous journey 'cross Kadoor with the two Princes, chased by her own Guard and the Hoard, to find the Wyrdritch and Persephone afore 'twas too late. This was a race with more than one life to lose, a mission she could not afford to fail, for if Kevon died, if the Egg landed in Hoard hands, all the Races would once again be at war with each other. 'Twould be nowhere safe on all Kadoor.

Novels by Derrien Relyea:
- Darque Legends: The Black War Begins
- Death of Life (A Darque Legends novel)
- Search for the Wyrdritch (A Darque Legends novel)

Coming Soon:
- Battle of Winter's Edge (A Darque Legends novel)

In the works:
- Darque Ages: The High Races Counsel (a prequel series)

You can read some of the epic poetry which inspired the Darque Legends series, online at:

http://www.thedragonwarrior.com/

Table of Contents

THIS BOOK IS DEDICATED TO A VERY SPECIAL DRAGON LOVING FRIEND, ANASTASIA SEWARD, WHOSE COURAGE AND WISDOM FAR SURPASS HER AGE, AND WHO INSPIRED THE CHARACTER OF PRINCESS ANASTASIA OF THE ELVEN NATION

As Ana is not considered an adult, although she knew about the character's cameo in the second book, when she heard Anastasia would be featured in this one she was initially elated. Then she frowned, knowing she wouldn't be able to read any of them, at which time I felt compelled to make her a promise. I would publish the third book as 'Ana's version', which seemed to satisfy my young friend. However, I later learned that when speaking to her grandmother about it, referring to the fact that she loved series stories and that she hadn't read the first two novels, she declared, "But Grandmother, I won't know what's going on!" To which her grandmother replied, "I'll read them to you" (so that she could edit them along the way). Kudos, Linda, you are most dedicated, and an inspiration to me as well.

Creating Ana's version of this book has made me even more hopeful of my ability to not only edit the first two novels to YA appropriate, but to create a new YA series about Dragon Hunters, which I have in the works. The only sad thing about that now, is that I don't write for a living (although I still have hope) and have little time to devote to such. But knowing Ana's schedule, I am encouraged to keep trying!

DISCLAIMER

I am not your child's parent. You are. Only you know what your child can and cannot handle, what he or she should or should not be reading. There is no set age for maturity. Do not depend on others to make those decisions for you. You are responsible. Only you. Read what they are reading. Be aware. Be the parent.

Acknowledgments

Once again there are far too many people who are supportive of my efforts to name individually, but I send out my heartfelt thanks to you all. Special credit goes forth to Anastasia Seward, her grandmother and my long-time friend, Linda Senn, along with my awesome artist Lisa Dixon (http://lisadixonfinearts.com), and Ariel Frailich (http://ginsengpress.com), who continues to be my knight in shining armor, without whom I'd be totally lost. Sending you love and kudos and hoping you hang in there with me through the many stories I have yet to write.

Long Live Darque and the Dragon Clan

Twins of Power, Twins of Fate

MIDSUMMER

O'ER NINE WINTERS AFORE THE BATTLE FOR THE DRAGON CLAN

~~~~~ THE DRAGON'S DEN OF DREKINN VILLAGE ~~~~~

In the darkness of their tiny bedroom in the castle of the Warrior Brotherhood, Darque lay back, one arm under her head, the other reaching up, fingers outstretched to stir the churning colors of the Vision o'er head. At the Summer Solstice she'd gathered nine winters, Storrm eight, and she oft times dreamed of the day they'd take the Oath together, becoming members of the most elite fighting force on all Kadoor. If Visions spoke prophesy, she was confident that dream would be realized.

Her father was Battle Commander of the Dragon Clan, and Darque was destined to follow in Grifynn's footsteps if she proved herself in the field. 'Twas a goal to which she justly aspired. Already a dynamic fighter, she didn't allow the knowledge she obtained through her Visions to sway her from their daily training regimen. She and Storrm worked hard to realize their full potential, and their mutual dreams. There was no time to be lazy. Being the daughters of the Battle Commander meant they had to be better than, and work harder than, anyone else. No quarter was ever asked for, granted, expected, or desired. To be a Warrior, you had to pass Trials and if unprepared, you could Pass the Veil. Not a'purpose, for 'twas not a fight to the death, but practice weapons were only used by children and early Trainees, and accidents could occur. Besides, you had to fight well so that once deployed you could live long enough to retire. 'Twas not a career for the faint of heart, nor for the deceitful. You could not fake being a good fighter, and the Dragon Clan was home to the Brotherhood, the best of the best.

Once again, Darque Saw something of her future and this time 'twas the voice of her little sister Storrm, currently sleeping at her side, who spoke the words coming as from a great distance through the misty swirl of colors that filled the room. From Visions of the past she'd learned that many changes approached them and she didn't question much anymore, merely filing the knowledge away in her mind for future reference. She pushed back the lightweight cotton blanket and sat up, immediately shivering as freezing winds near knocked her out of bed, the swirling colors coalescing into a dawning sky with angry clouds, the Great Plains of Drekinn showing through the gaps below while she sat astride a big blue Dragon flying swiftly away from the Den. This Dragon was one she'd Seen herself riding afore, and at their wingtip was another familiar pair. Surely 'twas one of her Warrior friends, Rakkah or Mikkal, the 'bad boys' of the Brotherhood. 'Twas late winter following a hard blizzard, and all was covered with snow and ice, their flight fraught with many dangers. Not only were they threatened by the weather conditions, they were being chased by those who sought to kill them. But why run? She frowned with the certainty that 'twasn't her at all, for somehow she knew she was elsewhere, engaged in another battle.

She and Storrm had excellent night vision and hearing, and even though 'twas still dark, as the Vision faded she found herself staring at the rock walls and plaster ceiling once more. The chilling winds became mere breathes of warm summer air ruffling the hemp curtains o'er the window 'cross the room. She concentrated and tried to recall what she'd just heard. Whispering to herself, she repeated, "A chess move shall lead the feint. To win the battle, you must use your twins of power, twins of fate." She analyzed the words as she braided her long red hair, brows furrowed and blue eyes flashing with awareness that she had no twin, and chess was a game of war strategy, a game at which she already excelled. How did the two fit together?

Dangling her short, bare, muscular legs o'er the edge of the heavily stuffed down mattress, she finished the thick braids, eight in all, afore looking back at Storrm. She bit her full bottom lip in her family's characteristic idiosyncrasy while pondering. They were clearly sisters, but no one would ever mistake one for the other. Of the many Visions o'er the past few winters, few of them made much sense, and sometimes she felt they all ran together. Would she ever understand? Although most would consider them to be frightening, she was not 'most', and merely hoped by the One, she'd be able to utilize the information thus garnered, to win the battles she was certain were coming. She sat in the darkness, staring out the small window for near a mark, wondering just who was this imposter pretending to be her, and what were they doing?

CHAPTER ONE
Escape by Pearls

LATE FALL/EARLY WINTER

NEAR 17 WINTERS AFORE THE BATTLE FOR THE DRAGON CLAN

~~~~~ ALONG THE SOUTHERN SLIPPES
OF THE OCEAN OF FEARS ~~~~~

</div>

Ardyth missed her father and uncle, who, along with her grand-mother, were all the family she had left. Her mother and elder brothers and sisters, had died in the past few winters since Shytin took the throne. 'Twas the same story throughout the village. The two men left o'er three moons past, hoping the huge deadly look-ing insect they'd found tangled and near drowned in their fish-ing net, would please the High King and mayhap they'd be re-warded, or the village might be given more time to produce their taxes. Their return was long o'erdue and Ardyth didn't want to think about what might have happened.

Treading water in her strong eggbeater style providing her with consistent buoyancy, she noted 'twas near dusk. She was fully aware she'd traveled many leagues, for she could see not their fishing fleet from atop the cliffs. But after discovering the rich new oyster bed as if lured here in her solitary explorations, no one would believe her unless she returned with some evi-dence. The closer beds were played out, poachers raided them all, taking even some of the smallest oysters for food, and 'twould be generations to fully restore. She couldn't blame them, everyone was hungry these days, but it left them in debt. The waters were deep at the mouth of the cave, but she was a good diver, and at just eight winters, could hold her breath longer than any of her siblings or friends. She wasn't supposed to be so far away from home, and she should never dive without a partner, but she justi-fied breaking the rules and taking such a dangerous risk because
~~~~~

they needed these treasures. She'd heard the elders discussing such, as well as the danger they might be facing if the men failed, the night afore they'd left for Evanntyr.

Something had to give. She wanted to help, and the multi-colored pearls as big as marbles would certainly do that. The real problem was the cold. She knew what creatures and terrain to avoid, understood the currents, and the Fears didn't frighten her. But hypothermia? 'Twas early winter and the sun would set quickly. She'd make one last dive and then beach inside the cave, start a small fire, and spend the night. At dawn, she'd begin again, make as many dives as she could by midday, then return. Home by tomorrow's dusk, she'd also be home afore anyone even knew she'd been absent, and she'd have a kayak full of treasure.

Ardyth may have been young, but she was blessed with a nat-ural athletic build and aptitude. The baby of the family and small for her age, she was near as strong as the others and took to the water like an eel, learning to swim afore she could walk. Fishing had been hard o'er the last few winters, but Ardyth blamed the High King for taking food off their tables to fill his treasury and pay for his increasing military presence. Weakened by malnutri-tion, each of her family had Passed with pneumonia or infections they couldn't fight off through the hard winters. Her mother was the last to die, and 'twas then she began to experience true hun-ger. That was when she learned they'd been sharing their food with her, to their own end. Her father could hardly look at her, let alone continue to share. Her empty stomach grumbled. Guilt and shame threatened to choke her and she took several deep breaths afore she dove. She couldn't bring them back to life, but she could try to make up for their loss by presenting him with a bounty. These pearls would pay the tribute for the entire village for o'er a dozen winters! He'd be proud of his little girl. Mayhap he'd even find time to spend with her again. If he ever came home.

<div align="center">~~~~~~~~~~</div>

With just one more dive, her pearl bags were stuffed. She'd not been willing to leave any behind, putting the last ones she'd harvested in her mouth, but she was shivering and the sun would set in less than a mark. Her shoulder strap secure, she towed the kayak into the cave, beached under cover, stripped quickly out of her wet suit, and changed into dry clothes. Finger-combing her long red hair, she braided it back tightly and then climbed up the rock face outside of the entrance in search of wood for her fire. Bringing back an armload, she went into the forest again and again, 'til 'twas near too dark to see where she was stepping, and 'twould be too dangerous. She made quick work of the fire using her kit, and soon had her suit drying on a nearby rack she'd built. Sitting by the warmth of the crackling fire and letting it soak into her skin, she ate a small portion from what meager provisions she'd brought along, adding a handful of late berries picked while wood scavenging. As exciting as the day had been, she was young and had worked very hard, and soon sleep found her.

<div align="center">~~~~~ THE FOLLOWING DAWN ~~~~~</div>

For one brief instant, she thought she heard the voice of her grandmother telling her to wake up, and then felt the woman's hand upon her cheek. But her grandmother was at home where she'd soon be, and she shrugged it off as simply the sun's rays reaching into the cave, gently caressing her face. Still, 'twas so real, she had to look all around to believe that no one was there. The smell of smoke was faint, but although her small fire was cold since she'd been too tired to keep it fed through the night, 'twas close to where she was lying and 'twas easily dismissed. Donning her suit, she pulled on her shoulder strap, waded into the chilly waters, and began swimming out toward the oyster bed to make a few more dives. She didn't have long afore she'd need to leave to get home by dusk, and her grandmother would be looking for her. She was excited. However, the scent increased as she left the cave and she could just make out the billowing black clouds above the horizon to the southeast.

Discarding the plan to dive again, she swam back inside and beached the kayak, afore she climbed up to the highest peak o'er the cave to get a better look. She couldn't believe her eyes. 'Twas coming from the general direction of her village, and the tiniest dot in the sky was flying northward. The black smoke transformed to white even as she watched, indicating the burn was dying out. Quickly breaking down her camp, she changed clothes once again, climbed into the kayak, and pushed off from the shallows of the shoreline, paddling smoothly into open waters. She had to get home to warn her grandmother and the village. Hot spots were a danger to the entire forest, and even if they already knew, which was highly likely, they'd need all hands to assist. Even little ones.

As she traveled, the dot became two or three, but since they turned and moved further inland, she couldn't be certain. Massive, they were too big to be the giant birds of prey that lived in the higher peaks of the area known as Abysmal Gorge. For several leagues, she paddled and wondered how the fire started and why it appeared to die out so quickly. She hadn't heard any thunder last night, but the smoke seemed to cover a larger area than what lightning would have caused. Unless it got out of hand, that is. But again, there'd been no thunder. She'd heard stories of lightning strikes without rain, but never without sound. Mayhap she'd slept through it. Paddling and pondering, she continued steadily homeward, her treasure wrapped around her waist in a special pouch under her shirt.

'Twas near midday when Ardyth turned the final bend of the rugged cliffs that blocked her view of the inlet she'd called home. Even from the distance, the closer she'd paddled, the more concerned she'd become, and having confirmation of the fire's true location didn't help calm her fears. Still, her little arms could only paddle so fast, and she'd been pushing herself as hard as she could. Beginning to cramp, she realized 'twould take at least another mark to reach her destination. She bit her tongue to prevent the tears as she continued toward home, but hope that she still had a home, disappeared the closer she came. Was anything left? Had anyone survived? What could have happened? In her heart, she knew. The dots she'd seen earlier were Dragons. And they were flying toward Evanntyr after completing their mission of destruction. But why? Would Shytin destroy an entire village because they were late with their taxes? Her father and uncle should've been home long ago. She swallowed hard, accepting they were most likely dead. The strange scorpion/spider as big as she was, had something to do with this. Seething, she paddled onward. Her grandmother would need her now, more than ever.

When she finally beached, leaping out and dragging the kayak under some brush out of sight, she stealthily approached the village in case whomever made this horrible thing happen, was still around. She couldn't be certain 'twas all Dragon-deed. Breaking through the underbrush, the view was shocking, and she knew there were no survivors. The color drained from her face as the acrid stench invaded her nostrils, making her eyes burn and her heart ache. Gone was the row upon row of racks of drying fish that should have been hanging by the boats that weren't there, that should have been tied to the now missing docks, and the lines of canoes that used to be upturned upon their frames along the beach were now permanently encased cinders in the newly created sea glass upon the scorched sands. She could smell the burned thatch and wood, the pitch they used on the docks and in their watercrafts, even the smoldering flesh of her people mixed with all their animals. Nothing was left but rubble. Everyone she'd grown up with, everyone she knew, was dead. 'Twas Flame for certain, as normal fire wouldn't have burned this hot or this thoroughly. As if the new sea glass wasn't enough evidence, even metal was melted.

For multiple marks, she sat in shock upon the wreckage of who knew what, staring into space. Her mind blank, her heart awash with anguish, tears flowed down her cheeks 'til there were no more to shed, and her chest hurt from taking ragged breaths. Several times during this period, Ardyth felt her grandmother's arms around her, heard her soothing voice encouraging her to live on for them, to survive. Her emotions played out, a calm numbness took hold and Ardyth looked up to focus upon her grandmother's face. She'd never seen a spirit afore, but surely this was one. Sitting upon the wreckage beside her, the woman who appeared as she had in life, slowly faded as soon as Ardyth acknowledged her presence and began to recover her senses.

O'er the course of the next several days (Ardyth never remembered how many), she picked methodically through the remains, looking for salvage and answers. Since 'twas Flame, and was acidic to human skin 'til the first rains, she had to wash in the ocean multiple times throughout the days, slowing her progress. Sleep came easily, for she was exhausted, and crawling under her kayak for warmth during the increasingly cold nights, she rose afore the sun and started again. The remains of the bodies she first encountered, were unrecognizable. But along the paths into the forest she discovered many more, as if fleeing the attack, the Dragons avoiding Flaming the trees. As she worked from the beach toward the forest, she found evidence of fighting, and even found remnants of uniforms on some of the bodies. The story of her village's demise was pieced together day by day 'til she deduced what happened. Their cleanup effort was careless, and 'twas clear they were attacked by King's Agents afore the Dragons Flamed much of the village, the humans making a sloppy effort to burn what was hidden under the canopy. At least the peaceful villagers, armed with little more than bamboo fishing spears and knives, had put up a good fight, taking a handful of their attackers with them Past the Veil.

Ardyth was a very intelligent little girl, and she knew there was only one thing that would link her entire village together, dooming them to such a fate. That insect. Shytin must have killed her father and uncle and then destroyed her village, either due to anger at being asked to substitute it for their taxes, or to keep it a secret. She'd seen that insect. She knew how greedy was the High King. Her sharp mind told her 'twas the latter of those options. Besides, 'twas the only explanation that made any sense.

<center>~~~~~ SEVERAL DAYS LATER ~~~~~</center>

Ardyth stood at the edge of the inlet and gazed o'er her shoulder at the ruins. Her hands assured her the leather pouch was wrapped securely around her waist, disguised under her blouse. Inside was not only the abundance of riches she'd collected earlier, but a jewel she'd uncovered beneath her own hut at the edge of the village. As the village was totally razed with no remaining landmarks, 'twas only the fact that she saw and felt her grandmother's presence, holding her hand, guiding her, that she was able to locate the burned-out hut. As she'd moved the debris piece by piece, she'd found that for which she sought. The gold chain was melted, but the blood red gem from the pendant remained untouched. 'Twas about the size of a walnut, gloriously beautiful, and once sat within an intricately entwined golden cage. Her grandmother kept the necklace in her dresser, telling Ardyth 'twould one day be hers, as well as telling her the most fantastic story about how 'twas given to her as a child by a Dragon. The gem was supposedly indestructible, and not only would help her See the future (amongst other things), but was the color of her destiny. She'd called it a Dragon's Eye and it certainly looked like one, never revealing its existence to anyone else, and securing Ardyth's pledge of secrecy. When she'd tried to question her grandmother about the meaning of all this, she'd merely wink and say, "You'll see," afore laughing merrily as she went about her chores. Ardyth believed her grandmother had the blood of the witch women coursing through her veins, and she'd fallen to her knees in tears of gratitude when she'd discovered the gem in the ruins. 'Twas all she could find worth salvaging. Amazingly, instead of causing harm, the heat of the fire made the gem even more dazzling.

As she mouthed a silent farewell to everything and everyone she'd ever known, she turned for the last time and made her way back to the brush under which she'd kept her kayak. Uncertainty took its toll, and she sat on the ground to consider. She had to make some tough decisions. O'er the last few days she'd saved her provisions by supplementing with clams and mussels she dug in the shallows, as well as harvesting most of what was left of the oyster beds, adding roots and berries from the forest, leaving her with a four-day ration of jerky that she could stretch to last twice that long, more if she hunted or fished successfully. She had her diving blade and her camping kit, including a small pair of pliers, an extra blade, a snare, three fish hooks and line, a piece of flint, some healing herbs, a roll of cloth for binding minor wounds, leather strips, and some fish bone needles and thread. She had her diving suit, her kayak and paddle, and one set of dry clothes which she was currently wearing. No change, and no winter clothes. She'd not had room to put them in the kayak when she left, hadn't figured to be out that long anyway, and now everything was gone. 'Twas getting colder, especially at night, and the snows would soon fall. She had a lightweight pair of sandals designed for diving or walking in the shallows upon the sands, not for rugged rock climbing or hiking, and would probably break down quickly if she tried to walk very far. She frowned. She had no relatives, and knew not any other fishing village that would take in another mouth to feed, anyway. She was smart, learned quickly, was good at basic survival, but she'd never been on her own afore, and the furthest she'd ever traveled was the cave where she'd found the pearls. She squinted, thinking about how she'd felt drawn to that cave, and hugged the pouch tightly to her belly.

Truth be known, she was rich beyond her wildest dreams, but such riches for one with only eight winters made her a target for thieves and cutthroats, and she could think of no way to safely sell or trade even one of the precious beauties responsible for saving her life. The sole survivor of the fishing village pondered her situation. She needed shelter, water, food, and clothing, in that order. She'd return to the cave. Fresh mineral springs were inside most cave systems along the Southern Slippes, and 'twould afford protection from the elements, thus providing her with the first two necessities. From there, she could work on the others.

CHAPTER TWO

Seer of the Dead

~~~~~ O'ER ONE MOON LATER ~~~~~

Her days became a mindless blur of trapping and tanning for food and creating warm clothing, including rugged fur-lined footwear, and bedding to insulate her from the cold sand-covered rock. She'd done so well she even made a blanket with an additional smaller piece sewn along the top edge, which could be rolled into a pillow and served double duty as a cloak, the 'pillow' becoming the hood. She made it from the hide of an ellka, a huge, split-hoofed descendant of ancient elks, with enormous, one-piece antlers that were relatively circular, appearing as a Giant's ribcage, and whose fur grew quite long around their necks and down their backs in preparation for winter, which she left intact. She covered the rack in skins and set it upside down to create her own sleeping tent into which she could crawl for increased warmth. Her Grandmother had taught her how to sew near four winters past, and told Ardyth her work was as good as any adult tailor. She imagined when wearing the cloak she might appear from a distance as a young ellka. Although she would have liked to take credit for the hunt, 'twas quite by accident that the beast fell into a crevasse not far from the entrance, breaking its forelegs and leaving it to a slow agonizing death. She'd merely taken advantage, and done the beast a mercy at the same time. 'Twas a gift from the One True Liege.

During the initial fortnight, she ate very well for the first time in ages, and stocked plenty of provisions to get through the coldest part of the season, but she couldn't rest, for she knew not what would happen during the Spring Melts. The forest here was pristine, she'd found no nearby villages or evidence of others, and fishing and hunting were good. There was plenty of fresh spring
~~~~~

water inside the cave, and if she ventured out, there were nearby creeks and a larger river further away. Already adept at the use of her village's bamboo spears, she used one of her leather strips to attach the extra blade to a straight, sturdy branch, creating a much more effective weapon for stabbing as well as throwing, with which she was becoming quite accomplished. Gathering the long stringy fibers from local plants and vines, she knotted a cast net for fishing, like the ones she'd made at home with her uncle and brothers. As far as she knew, she was alone for many leagues in all directions. She'd been working hard all her young life and 'twas no different, except that everything she did now was for her own benefit. What she couldn't do by herself, she modified, and if she couldn't modify, she did without.

Then o'er night the first hard storm struck. 'Twas not only late for such a storm, 'twas so cold the sands along the shoreline inside the relatively small entrance glistened with ice crystals, and Ardyth was concerned. If the snow drifted enough she might be blocked in, and she'd have a difficult time getting out to check her traps. The fish had all moved to deeper water and her cast net was small and designed for the shallows. She'd considered moving further into the cave for warmth, but convinced herself that 'twas safer to keep her fire close to the inlet. Yet the truth was the sensation she had whenever she'd tried to move in further, as if her grandmother was warning her that there was something sinister about this cavern. Still... she was stuck here, at least through the coming Spring Melts, and she might as well find out what caused that feeling of apprehension, as well as needing to find another entrance, if one existed. 'Twas time to do some serious exploring.

<p style="text-align:center">~~~~~ <b>A FEW DAWNS LATER</b> ~~~~~</p>

Ardyth learned that the system held few larger chambers, but plenty of distance end-to-end, and a multitude of side chambers. The entire thing reminded her of the shape of a lightning bolt crackling through the night skies. After exploring at length she'd located not one, but two other entrances. Apparently, the ocean entrance she'd found originally, constituted the southeastern end of the system. The far northwestern end was larger, opened close to the cliffs, and was much higher in elevation. There was one more opening about midway 'tween the other two, which was very small and well hidden, leading directly into the deep forest to the north. She doubted anyone had, or would ever, find that entrance as 'twas completely invisible from the outside, one would have to navigate through giant tree roots, and wasn't even used by animals.

The northwestern entrance couldn't be seen from the ocean, as from a distance the craggy face of the Southern Slippes created an optical illusion, and was concealed from above by the forest. Anyone not actively seeking its presence would miss it entirely, even though 'twas wide open, level with the ground, and large enough for a team of horses to walk through and shelter. 'Twas peculiar, when she'd found it and explored outside for about half a league she'd had difficulty locating it again, almost as if it hadn't wanted to be found. And she'd become leery, for she'd seen evidence of a traveler in the area. After careful examination, she concluded that someone did visit here, using a horse drawn wagon and making an effort to cover their tracks. She'd not have noticed except that the visitor was apparently in the area within the last two or three moons. The forest would have erased all evidence soon.

Snooping around, she discovered a leather bag tossed behind a rock close to the entrance, containing an odd assortment of colorful scarves and beaded necklaces, bangles, and other jewelry. She carefully replaced the contents and the bag, then just as carefully covered her tracks. Backing away, she near fell into a chasm in the shadows. Grabbing for anything as she lost her balance, her small hands latched onto a chain and she held on tightly, wrapping both arms and legs around it. Breathing hard, her heart rate slowed as the chain eventually stopped swaying with her unexpected arrival. When she could think again, she noted 'twas attached at the edge like a well-arm, and she wondered what was at the bottom of it, as she could feel something heavy, weighting the chain. Looking down into the darkness she felt ill and then she felt a sensation as if something was rising from the depths. Staring with alarm, she could see nothing in the blackness, and after a few breaths she decided 'twas too dangerous and not worth the effort 'twould take to go down into the unknown without a torch. Scrambling out of the chasm, she returned to her own camp.

The following dawn, while shivering in the cold despite her gear, she determined she'd have to move inward to avoid the blustery winds, but with the knowledge that someone else was using the system, and the strange sensation that something wanted to grab her from inside that chasm, she kept her fire at the seaside entrance. Staying ever alert, she watched and waited for the next few dawns for the visitor to return, wondering why they did. It had to have something to do with whatever was on that chain. Just thinking about it made her shudder.

<div align="center">~~~~~ LESS THAN A SENNIGHT LATER ~~~~~</div>

Ardyth's heart pounded so loudly in her ears she was afraid 'twould be heard as she huddled behind the rocks in the shadows, her hand clamped o'er her mouth to prevent involuntary gasps. She watched, as hand-o'er-hand, the beautiful woman with the long brown hair laboriously pulled up an enormous package dangling from the end of the chain. She laid it lovingly upon the rocks and unwrapped a large book from its bondage of cloth and leather, speaking to it as if 'twas a beloved mentor, but nothing happened. Ardyth was confused and frightened as the woman tried first petting and cajoling, then screaming at the book as if 'twas a living thing. Her voice shrill, she'd yelled, "You are the Book of the Conqueror, but I am Koryl, and you will open to me!" After near a mark, unable to force it to open, she cursed loudly afore wrapping it up again and lowering it back down into the chasm. Even though she appeared quite angry, 'twas clear the book meant a great deal to the woman by the reverence with which 'twas handled.

Grabbing the bag, thankfully without noticing the prior search, she donned the scarves like a dancer's wrap skirt and bodice, added the jewelry, and left. Her horses were agitated and so was Ardyth. Senses a'Flame, she could feel that woman, and that book, were evil incarnate. When 'twas certain the woman was gone, Ardyth made her way back to her campsite and decided she had to leave, too. Although this cave had been home to her for several moons, 'twas not safe anymore. Besides, she couldn't realistically live here alone for her entire span of days. As soon as summer arrived, the dangerous Spring Melts would be o'er, and she'd go out and find a new home. But where to go, and how would she get there?

~~~~~ EARLY SPRING ~~~~~~

Ardyth spent the next two moons thinking of multiple scenarios of escape to anywhere and everywhere, but nothing that would work. Although proud of her creations, she had to admit that her boots were not rugged enough for distance travel a'foot and would require replacement in the field. She was still small for her age, so she couldn't carry enough supplies to avoid such necessity, and 'twould take an inordinate length of time alone in the wilds to resupply on the way. Along with the need to defend herself against the various predators of the Edge, she'd never make it out alive. 'Twas simple logic. Eventually, she struck upon the only plan that had any chance of succeeding. She'd hitch a ride with the beautiful lady, whom she now realized was a witch, the next time she came to visit the book.

Although the very notion made her grimace, 'twas the only way out. The lady had a team of horses, 'twas obvious she traveled frequently and alone, therefore, she knew how to get somewhere
~~~~~

safely. Ardyth just had to make herself appear to be more vulnerable than she was, and not end up becoming more vulnerable than she appeared, for no doubt the lady was wicked and would not bother with her unless she thought there might be gain. The elders had taught her that children were bought and sold in evil places to evil people. If she thought that Ardyth had no protection, she might take her all the way to Port O'Kings, or even Tupry, where she could then escape (never doubting her ability to do so). This plan would lose her most of her belongings, for she couldn't carry them, but she'd lost all and survived afore. Mayhap she'd return one day and reclaim them.

Making up her mind, she began to sort through her meager possessions, deciding which to take and which to leave. Ultimately, she chose to leave most everything, taking only what jerky she could carry under her clothing, with the idea that the lady might feed her if she handled things well, but she'd have to keep her eye on it or she might be drugged. She'd also take her blades, a few essentials from her kit that she could pack in with the pearls and the Dragon's Eye, and although she'd have to leave her extra sandals and boots, wearing all her clothing layered under the ellka cloak would give the appearance she'd recently been lost in the forest, wandering about. Fully dressed, with everything wrapped around her small body, she didn't look so small, and this would help her disguise. The appearance of a healthy weight would reinforce the lie of being from good family. She might be able to keep the lady from attempting to harm her afore they reached their destination, if she thought the possibility of ransom existed.

With a solid plan and all decisions made, Ardyth was confident she could drop everything at any moment, race out via the hidden entrance to the north, then further on another league to where the lady would be driving her team of horses after she left the cave, crossing paths as if by coincidence. All she had to do now, was wait for her return.

LATE SUMMER/EARLY FALL
~~~~~ NEAR FIVE MOONS LATER ~~~~~

Koryl used another name when traveling in disguise 'tween Tupry, King's Gate, and the cave where she hid her greatest treasure. 'Twas most fortunate that she'd chosen to make another visit so soon after the last, or this little one would have perished in the forest. The Book was priceless, but the girl was almost as valuable. It took her a few days to make the discovery, for one of her family, mayhap a grandmother who'd died in the accident, enveloped the girl and tried to hide the Gift. But her influence faded with distance from where the child had been found, and once her unique ability was exposed, 'twas most difficult keeping the knowledge to herself, for the child apparently knew not. Those who could clearly see and speak to the dead were rare on Kadoor, and all had direct lineage back to her own people, the Rashei, known as the witch women. If Koryl had the Gift 'twould have given her much power, mayhap 'twould even help open the Book, but selling such a child would give her much coin. She'd contemplated keeping her for her own purposes, but 'twas near certain the Sorcerer would discover her talents and take her as his own. But even more of a problem was how to explain why she'd been in her oracle costume, and in that part of the Talons in the first place. No, the child must never meet anyone who knew her in her other identity. Selling her was the only viable option.

~~~~~~~~~~

Ardyth didn't make a sound, as in the darkness she gathered what few things she didn't keep always on her person, along with as much as she could tuck away of value that didn't necessarily belong to her, and slipped out of the third-floor window of the boarding house. Climbing down the vined stone wall wasn't that difficult, a fact unbeknownst to the witch who thought 'twould keep her there. Tupry was a vile community of the worst of Kadoor's inhabitants, and if she'd not been prepared for this all along, 'twould have ended up being her final resting place, for the witch was even now negotiating her sale, thinking she'd locked up the little girl and left her helpless in her room. Although she'd had to do some very good acting, she was a tad embarrassed that it hadn't been more difficult to fool the witch with her story of losing her family in a carriage accident on the road, being the only survivor (which truth did bring real tears to her eyes), wandering for days not knowing how to get home again, and that she was so stupid as to believe every promise and lie the witch told her, playing the role of spoiled helpless child to the hilt. She'd never been spoiled or helpless, so it took a bit of imagination, which grew as the journey lengthened. Originally thinking they were heading to King's Gate, she began to suspect Tupry when she observed the position of the sun, but never let on to her benefactor.

Ardyth made her way swiftly through the alleys, hiding in doorways, under rubbish and woodbins, to avoid being seen by any passersby, for everyone here was her enemy. Working her way toward the surrounding forest, and freedom, her eyes well-adjusted to the darkness, she wondered what the witch would think when she discovered her escape, and near laughed out loud. Clapping her hand o'er her mouth to prevent such, she scanned all around the buildings at the edge of town, and when she saw her chance, she broke cover and ran for the trees, melting into the inky night just as she heard the witch's furious scream rising above the raucous nightlife of Tupry.

CHAPTER THREE

The Veil of Deceit

16 WINTERS LATER

THREE MOONS AFORE THE FIRST LIFEBOND

~~~~~ THE ISLAND OF DREAMS ~~~~~

'Twas most unfortunate they'd been so easy to force Past the Veil. Killed in their youthful exuberance during simple hand-to-hand in an ambush, they would have been more useful if taken alive, but the Hoardsmen sent after them had botched the job, through no real fault of their own, and were also sent Beyond for their failure. However, the opportunity to continue to use their mother still existed, if the situation was handled correctly. 'Twould take a delicate touch. 'Twas entirely possible she'd see through his deceit this time, and realize that not only was it his fault they'd left home in the first place, but 'twas his fault they'd died. He near drooled at the challenge to extend her misery.

Deciding to chance the meeting after all, he found that nothing had changed. Her love for him smoldered evermore in her heart, and she was willing to believe anything, even after all these winters. With great pretense, the Sorcerer held the woman tightly, her head tucked under his chin to avoid her seeing his facial expression afore he gained full control. He so enjoyed the game. 'Twas stimulating. His deep voice purred, "I'm so pleased you were able to get away and meet me here."

The Sprite female would do anything to touch her former lover again. She'd dreamed of this moment. She'd been so hurt when he'd left, forcing her to mate another. She'd tried to forget him, tried to say no, even as far as to deny him the information he sought so many winters past. And then her children disappeared and she was devastated. So long, it had been so long since he'd come to her. "'Twas difficult, but when I received your message, my heart leaped for joy."

Peeling her away from his body, he held her at arm's length. "I have news. With total disregard for my personal safety, I've discovered that your children live. They're being held in torturous circumstances in the dungeons of the Black's Lair and have been used as entertainment since they disappeared. But 'twill be your stubborn mate's refusal to provide ransom, that may be their final doom."

"What? They're still alive? I don't understand. The Black demanded ransom? I was never told, only that they were forced Beyond."

"Yes, my dear one, many demands were made, and no response was ever forthcoming."

In the depths of her eyes bloomed hope o'er anguish, an expression he'd noted often through the ages in many a mother's eyes, when offered the slightest chance their loved ones survived a battle. But the Hoard kept few prisoners. She hated the man whom she believed to have taken her children away from her, but 'twas not the one standing in front of her now, whom she blamed. In her madness, innocence and guilt were reversed. "You've seen my children? You're certain they're alive?"

"With my own eyes. I didn't come here seeking information this time. You've served me well in the past, and as reward I came here to help you get them back. But 'twill not be easy, and 'twill take time. The lack of response to his demands made the Black quite angry. He has taken out his anger on their youthful bodies, but I've been able thus far, to keep them from succumbing." He relished her look of horror, as she cringed at the mention of the torture they must be enduring. Trying not to smile openly, he continued as if in deep thought, "I need something to appease him, something of great value."

"I'll do anything you ask, give you anything you want. Please! We were once lovers, surely you can help me now."

He could not pass up the chance to punish her for her past denial of his requests, to make her feel totally inadequate. Ahhh, the taste of sadistic dominance made his mouth water. "Mayhap you can provide the ransom riches?"

Hitting the mark perfectly, her despair was priceless. "I cannot, for I do not have access to such, and my mate keeps tight reign o'er the family wealth. He could not be persuaded anyway, for he perpetrates the lie that our children are already Passed. I have only my personal possessions, but I would give you all gladly, to save them."

Sensing she was close to losing faith in their relationship, he softened his tone. "I would never have left, you know that. I need you more than my own beating heart," he lied with flair.

Instantly, her misguided faith returned. "I know, I know. Our paths crossed for but a moment in time. We were ever at the mercy of the Fates. You must remain where you are, and I must stay here," she replied miserably.

Truly, he cared not for any riches she might have. "My dear one, I need no information now, and your personal possessions are a mere pittance. They could not be handed o'er without your mate's knowledge, at any rate."

"But, there must be something more I can do, something I can give you! Please, I've given you so much in the past, what more could you require? Through the Assembly, I can give you anything. I'll do anything you ask, anything you want of me!"

He feigned pondering the issue, afore replying almost hesitantly, "Mayhap there is something you can give me."

The woman leaped upon the opportunity, whatever it might cost. "Anything, just name it, and 'twill be yours!"

"The 7th Egg."

Aghast, she replied, "But, I can't. Royal blood is required to break down the Protection Spell. My lineage is not of such. How can I steal the Egg?"

"All you need do, is deliver this mirror. A simple task, but 'twould be most helpful. I will refresh your Spell of glamour, so you'll not be recognized." He stooped o'er and whispered a name in her ear. She trembled with excitement mixed with terror. This was more than he'd ever requested, and without him present, she'd not be able to escape if she were caught, adding an extra degree of daring. Although, she was also confused. Of what value was this task? How would a mirror help procure the 7th Egg? Providing occasional information had never seemed so bad. In fact, her secret scandalous life made her quiet reality near tolerable. But this request seemed destined to escalate, and could she trust the one to whom she was to deliver the mirror? With her hesitation, the Sorcerer felt he needed to remind her of the circumstances. "Given this assistance, I might be able to prevent the continuing gruesome torture and probable death of your children for a few moons, or mayhap winters, 'til I can gain their release."

Peeling back his shirt at the neckline, he bent o'er and pulled her to him, his hand against the back of her head, guiding her lips to his skin, his head thrown back and eyes closed in ecstasy. As he Drew from her with her touch, he felt the Draw of energy that he offered her, but would not allow much, quickly breaking contact.

The Sorcerer felt her total submission to his request and was amazed at the ease with which she was manipulated. Even after all he'd done to her in the past, she should be able to sense the lie. Of course, he'd captured the twit's heart at a tender age, using very little Magical influence, and she'd believed everything she was told. Apparently, she still did. Such a weak mind, such naiveite, he thought. Her groveling was near nauseating, and yet, 'twas powerful and he was aroused. The past played forth in his mind. She'd been quite useful for when he'd desired relief, yet once he'd groomed her, he'd had to be very devious to get her to agree to go through with the arranged mating to another, for he didn't want a mate of his own. He wanted someone on the island, someone he could use to fulfil his ultimate desires. That he could hide her physical and emotional past, as well as her deceptions without anyone detecting, was a feat of remarkable Magic for which he took full credit. 'Tween the mating and the birth of her children, she'd continued to be quite forthcoming with any information he'd requested. 'Twas after her children reached maturity that the Sorcerer made contact again, to set his original plan in motion, but she'd surprised him by resisting. She'd apparently been peeved with the length of time he'd been silent. He'd actually been quite busy elsewhere, but 'twas no problem. 'Twas too easy luring her children away without her knowledge. Females. Mattered not their Race. Holding the lives of their children o'er their heads, did seem to motivate them.

CHAPTER FOUR

A Royal Sleuth

A SENNIGHT AFORE THE FIRST LIFEBOND

IN THE DEPTHS OF DARKLING FOREST

~~~~~ THE WYRDRITCH ~~~~~

</div>

Anastasia stood in front of the majestic oak and waved her small hands in a sweeping motion, as if painting the air in front of her eyes with her fingertips. The tree now appeared robust, with healthy brown bark and deep green leaves. Pushing her long brown hair behind one pointed ear, she gazed with almond eyes at the various shades of greens and browns fading slowly 'til all was purple once again. She furrowed her brows. Looking up at the green sky and yellow clouds peeking through the multi-colored canopy of the forest, she tilted her head and wondered. The grass under her feet was blue. Did that make any sense? Yet although she'd never been outside the Wyrdritch, having been born less than a dozen winters prior, next to the youngest Elf in all of Haven (her little brother Coltyn was the youngest), the artwork in the library from afore the Last Holocaust showed the trees were once shades of browns with green leaves, the sky was blue, clouds were white or shades of gray, and the grass green, not this odd mix of rainbow colors that continuously changed. Was something wrong with their eyes? The air? No. 'Twas something else. She could Hear the melodies surrounding her and 'twas conflicting. Ana reached for the closest shadow to Dance back to Haven, where she planned to try once again to discuss her theories with her sister, Persephone.

<div align="center">

MID-MORNING

IN THE HEART OF THE WYRDRITCH

~~~~~ HAVEN, THE CASTLE OF THE ELVES ~~~~~

</div>

<div align="center">

</div>
~~~~~

Anastasia had been waiting impatiently all morning, and catching Persephone at last, just finishing her shower, she began, "I'm telling you, 'tis wrong."

Persephone was used to her little sister's inquisitive nature, and especially this latest passion of which she was so absorbed. Indulgently, she asked, "What exactly is wrong? How is it wrong?"

Ana's shoulders dropped, her face taking on a puzzled expression. "I don't know, everything, the air, the water, the trees, the sky, the very shadows themselves. 'Tis just wrong."

Within her chambers they were surrounded by the sweet scents of flowers of all varieties along with the voices of multiple species of birds. Most had not been seen since long afore Ana's birth. Persephone dissipated the raincloud she'd formed o'er her head, dried herself and the marble flooring with a flick of her wrist, and Reached for a gown to don. Nothing elaborate, just a simple design with plunging V-neck, high imperial collar, and matching sash. As it materialized in her outstretched hand, she added a sprinkling of emeralds and pearls to the flowing skirt and the tails of the sash, and as an afterthought she lined the neck with crystals, setting off the sheer glimmering green to perfection. A mother-of-pearl comb appeared in her other hand as she swept up her long brown hair, securing it in twisted loops atop her head. The eldest of the Elven Princesses, Persephone was the epitome of perfection in everything she did, even the simple things, and she preferred to practice the old ways. The dress donned, she cinched the feather light fabric around her slight waist and stated, "Ana, you've been acting very strange lately. I'm worried about you, but my hands are tied helping father. If you can't give me more information than that, I don't know what to say."

The younger Elf could sense her sister was greatly fatigued as well as irritated, but she was headstrong and desperate to get someone, anyone, to listen to her theories. "But you're the one who can Heal the wrongness in things. Can't you see it? Can't you hear?"

"Strictly speaking, I don't Heal anything. Unless I am sadly mistaken, I'm not a Highland Dragon, nor am I trained as a Skald. And no, I can't Hear anything, either. You're the one who hears things," she laughed.

Ana suspected Persephone's Healing power was untouchable, she just wasn't certain how 'twas to be used, and she could never get her sister to cooperate long enough to make that discovery. Ana's ability to Hear and decipher the musical heartbeat of everything around her, was not discussed nor trained, as 'twas denied by the King. There seemed no other with such a Magic, and so 'twas considered a weakness, for they knew not what to do, nor for what 'twas to be used. But she felt 'twas a power to someday be reckoned with, as was her sister's, so she practiced on her own, perfecting her talent day by day. Still, much of her 'practice' was basic trial and error. She truly believed that if Persephone worked with her, they could lead her to her Magical power by organizing the song, like following a trail on the hunt. She'd even approached her brothers to allow her to try to discover what was wrong with their father, but she'd been all but ridiculed and never mentioned it again. If her mother was less busy trying to rule without father, she'd have pursued it with her. The rest of the brood were half siblings, for Bryanna was Queen to Jeeryd afore Alyssa. She'd been one of the first to disappear after the Last Holocaust. Queen Alyssa was walking a fine line trying to rule what was left of the Elven Nation without true consent of the mad King, and she didn't want to burden her when 'twas merely a hunch.

Persephone was the eldest of her siblings, since her brother Myrrdin missed the Retreat. Everyone told her he'd Passed the Veil, but she didn't believe that. Somehow, she could still Hear his life's song. However, her sister's laughter gave Ana all the encouragement she required to press her point. Following like a lost puppy, she threw out her questions. "Then why are the paintings in the library different? The ones from afore and after? The colors are all wrong, things don't fit right, and the forest moves."

Persephone kept walking away as she stated firmly, "There's nothing different, nothing changes. 'Tis all normal."

"But..."

"Not now!" Exasperated, Persephone stopped and turned, catching the wounded expression on her sister's face. She hadn't intended to cause that pain by her words. Something had happened that would cause much more, and trying not to tell her, was making it worse. She clasped her hands together and bit her lip. 'Twould certainly not be the first time she'd defied her father. "Anastasia, you should know. We lost two more last night."

Startled, the little Princess asked, "Who?"

Persephone hesitated. She still couldn't believe such a tragedy could hit her family again. A lump formed in her throat and she had to swallow hard afore she stated reluctantly, "Leisalarr and Dyraserrah."

Her brother and his girlfriend. Incredulously, she asked, "What happened?"

"I don't know, Ana, I'm sorry. They just disappeared like the others, and we can't find them anywhere. And not a trace of their Dance signatures. This hasn't happened in so long." Words failed her as her thoughts strayed to her mother. "I have to help father. He's getting worse, this has devastated him. And Alyssa is doing her best to keep his status under wraps." Biting her lip again, she shook her head, then continued. "I can't believe everyone is gone. I just can't believe. We can't be the only Elves left. But the King still thinks... I don't know. I'm so tired, Ana. Go practice your music lessons, I can't discuss this now."

Ana watched her sister retreat down the hallway as she thought to herself. Her friend Dyra had encouraged Leis to talk with her just the other day about her theory that the Wyrdritch was encased in an altered Spell, that what they saw was only within, and that those Elves who'd left at the Retreat, may still be alive somewhere on the outside. Mayhap they thought the Wyrdritch destroyed, and 'twas why they didn't return. But how to determine the truth? They had to get outside. And if 'twas now invisible even to Elven eyes, surely if they could find a way out, they could come back in by reversing their steps. Had they left the Wyrdritch because of her? But if they had, why hadn't they returned to tell everyone? Was Jeeryd telling the truth? Was the Wyrdritch all that was left of Kadoor?

LATE AFTERNOON

~~~~~ ANA'S CHAMBERS ~~~~~</div>

Ana gathered a few things together. Elves were creatures of the night, but she'd stayed awake all day, thinking. The trees moved, of this she was certain. Although the others seemed not to notice, she had a very good memory and paid close attention to detail. Not only were the color schemes changing, so were the physical locations of the trees and boulders from night to night. The forest appeared differently almost every time she looked, yet 'twas 'normal' to everyone else. Was it because she was still a child that she questioned such? Being the last born in the Wyrdritch, she and Coltyn had not lived through the Retreat or the Holocaust. And they hadn't been under the Protection Spell for centuries. If her theories were correct, one might not end up in the same place one expected, if one Danced to a shadow that had moved. Mayhap 'twas why none of the Elves who'd disappeared, had returned. Wait! Mayhap 'twas why they'd disappeared in the first place.

She twirled a thick strand of hair around one finger as she considered. Mayhap this, mayhap that. They couldn't Dance inside close to the Spell, they might end up outside. They couldn't Dance back inside because the shadows moved. Carefully, she packed her art supplies into the bag. There was something wrong with their world and she needed to find her brother, Myrrdin. He could fix whatever 'twas, for he was the Heir Apparent and a great
~~~~~

leader. And they were sorely in need of both, for although the King had insisted his first born was dead, he would not declare it so, leaving Persephone hanging. And he would not allow Queen Alyssa to take o'er the rule, even though he was ill. Their family dynamics issues led her to another thought. Mayhap those who'd disappeared in the past, liked it better outside and didn't want to return.

She huffed and crossed her arms o'er her chest. She'd never know if she could leave or return, or even if the Wyrdritch was all that was left, 'til she went out herself. If Kadoor was gone then so be it. Youthful curiosity prevailed o'er fear, and with her Hearing, although 'twas chaotic at the edge, she believed 'twas more on the other side of the barrier. The King might have put a restriction on attempting to leave many winters past, and with harsh results if one was caught, but Ana wouldn't be punished, for she was a disappointment and he barely acknowledged her existence amongst the royal brood of seventeen. There was a certain advantage to being one of the youngest of such a large family. No one knew where you were, let alone what you were doing.

Grinning, she grabbed her pack, tossed it o'er her shoulder, and went into her private dressing room where she kept a huge potted ivy to practice, unbeknownst to others, for the King had decreed that Dancing was not allowed within Haven. That was because of his growing paranoia since Myrrdin's escape. She snickered. 'Twould be good to meet her big brother. Closing the door behind her, she touched the leaves, drew her energy, and Danced out of the castle all the way to the very edge of the Wyrdritch. The edge of the world as they knew it. Sitting on a flat rock, she stared at the trees, waiting for darkness to fall for her Magic to peak, when she saw it happen. Just as dusk fell, in the blink of an eye, the tree in front of her switched places with the big boulder at its roots right after she'd Heard something akin to a fluttering heartbeat. Then she felt the 'normalization' phenomenon. 'Twas almost as if she'd been told that she'd not seen what she'd seen, as if the tree and the boulder had never been in their prior places and had always stood where they stood now.

She sat up straighter, and with determination, pulled her sketch book, graphite sticks, and pastels from her pack. Although she could draw by Magic, she didn't trust the results. She'd tried this in the past and swore her pictures had all changed, as well. For marks, she sketched and colored 'til she had multiple pages of detailed images of the forest surrounding her. She was tired of everyone believing, what she believed were lies. Committed to discovering the truth, she made careful note of the timing of the switches, the changing colors, the movements, and as she studied them, she saw a pattern. 'Twas a forlorn melody, as an ailing heartbeat she Heard, one that told a story of struggling to survive great turmoil, weak, erratic, but still beating to a definite rhythm. 'Twas a rhythm to which she believed she could Dance.

CHAPTER FIVE

Invasion

JUST PAST MIDNIGHT

THE ROYAL HOUSE OF THE SPRITES

~~~~~ **THE ISLAND OF DREAMS** ~~~~~

'Vampyre.' The crude slur was a common name-turned-insult to the cousin Races of Sprite and Elf, dating all the way back to the War of Chaos, when, through the High Races Counsel, they stood shoulder to shoulder with Man against the Evil One and his Hoard. Referring to the manner in which all Magic bearers drew energy by touching skin to skin, the cousin Races had refined the technique, and although 'twas used quite effectively as a weapon throughout the long war, o'er the many ages since, Humans embellished such encounters, altering the tales of heroes and legends to the stuff of nightmares used to scare their children into blind obedience. However, such fear was not entirely unwarranted. Energy could be Drawn from any organic, but the Life Force of Humans was more stimulating and quite potent, most easily taken from the large femoral or carotid arteries during intimate moments, although that was the exception, not the rule. But, with their relatively short span of days, 'twas what the Humans remembered and held against their one-time allies.

'Twas interesting to note that Humans and animals were not the only organics from which they could Draw. Old growth oak and a multitude of evergreens were at the top of their preferred 'feeding' list, as 'twas the most compatible with their energies. Such was needed to fuel their Magics, greatest of which was their distinctive method of travel known as Dancing the Shadows. Folding time and space, they'd move from shadow to shadow in the blink of an eye, but 'twas always the chance of never returning to reality, becoming stuck as in the Hades of the
~~~~~

Fade. 'Twas necessary to Draw enough from the host prior to the Dance to prevent such from happening. Since the Separation, when the Sprites left their cousins to the Wyrdritch long afore the Last Holocaust, no one had misused their powers, seeking only enough energy for their health or for the Dance, a barely noticeable whisper of a touch. But in the skilled hands of a master, 'twould leave a gentle sense of anticipation, and was easily translated into sexual pleasure. Sprites avoided the mainland, and no Human had ever lived upon the island, therefore such was now considered foreplay 'tween consenting Sprite adults.

She'd heard of no one forced Past the Veil by total draining since the Last Holocaust. So, what happened? And why would any Sprite assist in the slaughter of their own, in such a manner? Of course, she was the only one who thought the family of six, two elderly adults and four children, were fed from afore being butchered, already close to the Veil by the draining of their Life Force, too weakened to put up a fight. There'd been so many unanswered questions, and the clues were vague. No witnesses ever came forth and no sound of a skirmish was noted, even by the nearest neighbors. But regardless of her attempts to persuade the Lord, he was irrationally closed minded to her theories. Tialani convinced Rohar that 'twould cause panic throughout the island and he'd ordered the entire investigation classified. No one knew of what occurred in the tiny house upon the cliff of the western shore less than three winters past. No one except Caleichante and her team of Elite Guard. The case was considered closed, but the Captain still thought of it as merely 'cold' as she felt a certain obligation to her best friend and First Mate, Natanamia, the eldest daughter of the family, who'd already been a Guardsman at the time of the murders. The only other survivor of the butchery was the second daughter of the brood, Niamia, who was fortunate enough to be away during the incident, or she likely would have been killed as well. Niamia had since entered the Guard, her goal to join the Elite, and under her elder sister's tutelage, was rising rapidly through the ranks.

'Vampyre'. 'Twas revolting. Her lip curled in disgust yet again, her senses on high alert. Humans in ancient times became afraid of them and after the Last Holocaust some began to hunt them. That was the problem with allying oneself with a Race so short-lived. They relied on written memory, were easily swayed to political pressures, even rewrote their own history. She wasn't trying to excuse their betrayal, simply listing the fact that Humans forgot who'd helped save their ungrateful butts and how 'twas done. Once hailing them as champions, they now hailed them as murderers in the darkness, stealing their babies and performing ghastly rituals involving the drinking of blood. She almost laughed out loud. For one thing, blood was the Life Source not the Life Force, and although Elves were creatures of the night shadows, the Sprites were of the sun, but still... she shook her head at the absurdity. No wonder using Human hosts was so discouraged now.

Calei's Dancing skills were unsurpassed, the shadow required, miniscule. She could even Dance through the walls of her quarters, using only that from the ivy growing o'er the window ledge and up the walls. Thinking about the few Humans she'd met in her span of days, her fingers absently traced the thin scar 'cross her left hip, as the memory of a long-ago fight filled her mind. Of all the Humans upon Kadoor, a few could be trusted, like the Dragon Clan who kept the old ways. And yet Lord Rohar still refused to rejoin the war effort, holding a bitterness fueled by the relatively recent deaths of his eldest sons, even though 'twas not the fault of the Humans. Nevertheless, it seemed that history was repeating itself. The Black had returned, the Highlands were preparing to recreate the LifeBond, while the Sprites sat firmly on the sidelines. Even so, their return was inevitable, however, 'twas her belief that if they waited too long this time, the Black might win the war. Or at best 'twould be another 'Last Holocaust tie'.

The winter solstice would be upon them soon, she thought, as she lay naked on her rack in the shadows, staring at the thick ivy covering the stone ceiling far o'er head. A cool breeze played o'er her bare skin and she wondered when the snows would arrive. With her delicate oval face, high cheekbones, almond eyes, and sharp tipped ears, she was unable to pass as Human without Allure, as could some. The cousin Races shared physical attributes such as tall lean frames, pale skin, the shape of their eyes and ears, and given that all Sprites were fair haired and pale eyed, all Elves dark haired and dark eyed, even her coloring was extreme, her eyes and skin a golden shimmer, her hair snow white. Although ever youthful, pale and beautiful, one would be a fool to disregard the fact that she was also chillingly lethal, which had nothing at all to do with the power of her Magic.

Inhaling slowly and deeply, she savored the rich scents drifting from the Royal Gardens just outside the tall narrow window of her private room in the Guard quarters. As one of the few 'real' windows in the Hold, she treasured the fresh air, the sounds of the night, the view of the moon and stars. Spells could recreate much, but reality was always more pungent, more striking, more treasured. At least, 'twas to her. If she had her way, she'd never sleep indoors. Not that she'd been sleeping much lately.

The royal house, known as Dream Hold, was built around the time of the Last Holocaust when there was need for heightened security, and what windows existed were heavily barred. But 'twas her duty to keep them safe and she was vexed, as the openings were difficult to secure properly and these bars wouldn't keep out a determined enemy. Given their love of nature, powerful Spells of Illusion had transformed the appearance of the once impenetrable fortress into a stunning palace fit for the royal family. But for those who took the time to look past the illusions, the decay brought on through ages of neglect was glaringly obvious. If they didn't do something soon, the entire Hold might begin to crumble. With the support and encouragement of Myrrdin, her Elven cousin, longtime friend, and past trainer, she recently pushed for reconstruction to improve security, but her campaign hit unexpected opposition from someone high in the Assembly. She frowned. The fools couldn't see past their aristocratic noses. 'Twas like swimming against a rip tide with them, and she only hoped 'twould not be their undoing.

Mayhap three generations of Elite Guard had fulfilled their duties a tad too well, for there'd not been a major invasion on the Island of Dreams since they'd taken it as their adopted homeland. Their very success seemed to cause a false sense of security, and Calei couldn't raise a sufficient level of awareness about the coming danger for their citizens. Meanwhile, skirmishes, near misses, and security breaches were increasing, and the need for change was on the horizon. While most Sprites lived in relative denial isolated upon the island, the truth was manifesting upon the mainland and would not be restricted by the water's edge. This time the Evil One's influence would cross the Sea of Dreams like a tsunami, and the Sprites would no longer be able to hide. The Last Holocaust merely afforded them a respite from the war, and the Hoard was once again gaining momentum. The Highland Dragons were planning on coming out of seclusion to openly recruit the Dragon Clan, and together they'd invoke the most ancient, and arguably the most powerful of all Magics, the LifeBond.

She tried to close her eyes again, but thoughts of the murders were eclipsed with something else nagging at her conscience, and 'twouldn't allow her peace. 'Twas maddening but she'd learned long ago to trust her gut instincts. Pushing aside the cold case for the moment, she pondered the latest events. No one else noted anything amiss, but she knew trouble was looming. Her golden eyes glittered with agitation and she squinted in her effort to determine its cause. She'd first felt something was wrong at evening meal in the Royal House. But no, she had to admit something had been wrong for a while now, and not just because of the recent mishap. Pondering, her focus kept returning to the 7th Egg.

For the last sennight since her 'rash decision', when making her nightly rounds she'd felt an urgency, a remnant of anxiety, reach out to her through the surrounding Protection Spell as she'd approached the carved marble pedestal upon which the Egg rested in the middle of the circular, triple storied library of Dream Hold. 'Twas not the only library upon the island, nor the largest, but this one held the most ancient and valuable collections of their Race. With a stepping pattern of tall narrow windows beginning at floor level and ending at the dome above, following each landing along the wall, it created the illusion of a stairway to the heavens. These windows had been added long after the original structure was built, and Caleichante was one of only a handful of her people who knew they were real. She pursed her lips. She liked it not. Even though upon the outside they could not be seen, they afforded no real protection from forced entrance.

The library was off to the side of the banquet hall, another large room which was used for gatherings and socializing on special occasions by invitation only, and a good third of the wall 'tween the two areas was open, except for a row of five wooden columns separating them and creating the entrance. One approached via a long hallway which led to a split. In one direction lay the private chambers of the royals, in the other, the common areas for meeting, eventually leading to the library. The two outmost columns were embedded into the walls on either side, and were connected to the next two via a long, low, counter height wall of glittering solid quartz with an ornately carved top rail. The last column stood alone as a silent sentinel in the middle of the entry. Highly polished and richly carved with fine detail of bark, leaves, and flowering vines creating a woodland feel, 'twas as if they were still the giant living trees they'd once been, now standing vigil o'er their private garden. The library was otherwise built of native stone covered with intricate and colorful tapestries. In the center was a huge tower with a gold plated domed ceiling. The stairs continued around the outer wall, but one could step off onto several balcony landings with reading lofts and more bookshelves. Luxurious, shimmering, translucent pastel fabrics, seeded and embroidered with gold, silver, and copper threads, decorated the entire room. There were hand carved chairs, desks, and bookshelves from floor to ceiling following the stairs up and around the outer wall, as well as along the balconies, and in various sitting areas throughout the massive space. There were statues and busts of their ancestors and important Assembly members, and books by the thousands. The Sprite Royal Library held more ancient manuscripts and had a larger collection of books than Evanntyr, and might rival that of the Dragon Clan. The 7th Egg, which appeared to be a large oval chunk of blood red quartz, sat off-center, backed by an enormous open geode which was taller than three of the tallest Sprites, and nearly as wide, with huge exposed pink-tinged white crystals. The pedestal upon which the Egg rested sat under an enormous crystal chandelier. The light from both sun and moon entering through the dome above would set off its glittering surface, washing all in a pale red radiance. Ivy gracefully hung from the dome, appearing as if 'twas spilling o'er from the outside, and grew around the chains of the lighting, clinging to the walls and around the windows. Flowers of infinite variety bloomed from near every surface, inundating one's senses with their sweet, heady fragrances. Their guest had been given a place of honor and security there, and they'd kept their promise to the Water Dragons and the Last Dragon Matriarch without difficulty, for eons. Initially, she'd shrugged off the feelings seemingly emanating from the Egg. Mayhap 'twas her own growing unease. However, in the silence of the night she wasn't so sure. Had something disturbed their guest?

After spending the last half mark tossing and turning, she sat bolt upright in frustration. Blast the Fates! Grabbing the thin strip of leather from the foot stool upon which she'd tossed it haphazardly just a short time ago, she gathered her long white hair into a single tail, expertly weaving the laces in a criss cross pattern around her silky mane, tossing it o'er her shoulder to flow down her back, glistening in the dim light of the moon streaming 'cross the stone floor. Then she donned her leather halter top and britches, stepped back into her boots, armed up and took one last look out the window. What in Hades? She stared intently toward the distant shoreline, past the terraced slopes of the fortress yards, lying beyond the surrounding woods. What was that? A glint of light? No! 'Twas a mirror, another signal! Spinning around, her long slim finger slid 'cross one heart shaped ivy leaf, and she Danced through the walls and was outside racing to the shore in a heartbeat.

Traveling swiftly a'foot, she Alerted Schlynn, her Water Dragon, to meet her where she'd seen the flashing lights. She had to make certain this time, afore notifying her troops. Right or wrong, another disaster would see her demoted in disgrace. There was a spy amongst the citizens of the island nation, and something sinister was happening. She could trust no one. Afore Myrrdin last sailed, he warned her to be vigilant against the growing Hoard and their spies. She couldn't fail him or the royal family now.

She thought back to the last time she saw the lights. Suspecting an enemy invasion, she'd alerted the entire Guard and locked down the island in a futile search which uncovered nothing. She finally had to admit defeat without any evidence, or anyone who could back up her original sighting. Worse yet, her honor was questioned by the Assembly, the lock down was inconvenient for them, had cost them a full day of playtime (they'd called it 'work time'), and they'd not believed her explanation of why Magic hadn't been used for signaling, IF there'd been a landing upon their shore. She rationally explained that Magic would leave a trail as evidence of its use, whereas mirrors would not, unless the physical evidence was discovered. Unfortunately, none had surfaced, and nothing was found amiss. Except the feeling of unease which began immediately after, whenever she passed the Egg. In her heart, she knew they were related. She merely had to wait for it to happen again. And it did!

Racing to the shore, she arrived at the landing site of a skiff, the sands still indented by the keel as 'twas dragged in for the occupants to disembark. They hadn't needed to try to hide the ruts, the lapping waves and incoming tides would erase them afore she'd be able to gather the others to make witness. She'd barely made it herself. But she didn't have time for that, nor did she stop to consider her reputation, as she learned their trail was divided. One led her roundly back to the shore, and the other was leading her circuitously into the forested hills. She grimaced as she realized 'twas a diversionary tactic and she must be further behind than she thought, the shore group having already taken off with the skiff. This group must have done the signaling, a ploy to get her out of the fortress. But why had they signaled so late in their invasion, whom were they signaling, and why not simply wait for her? 'Twould have been an easy ambush. Mayhap they'd planned to use her failure to divert attention from their missions, mayhap even frame her for whatever they were doing here tonight? Removing her from the Guard would strengthen their hold on the Assembly. The skiff had to be just offshore, waiting for the rest of the team.

All this and more did the Captain infer, as she swiftly tracked the group heading inland. With no Magic used by the offlanders, not many could track them o'er the rough terrain, but her skills were near legendary, which was probably why she'd been able to keep her rank after that last fiasco, despite rumors of opposition from some unnamed source. The Lord himself ultimately prevailed o'er the negative voices in the Assembly. His support made her swell with pride as her resolve increased a hundred-fold.

Heart hammering as the plot thickened, she came to the only logical conclusion. Deserting the winding trail, she ran swiftly through the remaining terrain in a direct line to the Hold, hoping against hope that she'd not miscalculated and lost the prey she so desperately needed to apprehend. If she were correct, she must be swift. Their guest had tried to warn her, and now as she approached the eastern edge of the wall, she slowed her pace and stealthily made her way around the Hold 'til she located the trail of the intruders once again. 'Twas clear they'd not had to break in, and that at least one of their party had very strong Magic. Close, but still not knowing who was involved, she soundlessly made her way through the long halls toward the Royal Library. Why not just use the windows? The Magic bearer could get them through. And why was the Hold so hushed? Suddenly, she realized this route took them past the hallway to Kevon's chambers, and fearing for his safety, she ran quietly down the lengthy passage and up the flight of steps leading to the child's room, opened the great door, and stared at the moonlight streaming 'cross his very high, very large, and very empty, bed.

<center>~~~~~ EARLIER THAT EVENING ~~~~~</center>

Kevon had barely finished cleaning up after weapons training prior to evening meal, and whipped his youthful body gracefully into his chair to the right hand of his father, the Lord of the Sprites, thinking he'd dodged that stone well. Caleichante had distracted his royal parents while the tow headed, blue eyed boy snuck in and under the elongated table, crawling 'tween multiple sets of knees and leather boots, making his way to his rightful place, then popping up quickly and pretending he'd been there all along. Little did he know, and he couldn't have seen, as Lord Rohar winked at the Captain. Tucking her chin and lowering her eyes in a subtle nod of salute, both knew the boy was in place as he should be, both unwilling to chastise him for being late. Again. Ah well, he was young, and youth had its privileges.

Kevon was a good student and the only living child of the royals. He'd been birthed close to eleven winters past and was a welcome addition, bringing love, light and laughter to the royal house once again. His two elder brothers died in battle on the mainland after having defied their parents, attempting to join in the war effort against the Black. Unfortunately, the Lady confided in her that the Lord had chosen to neglect his sons' fighting education, depending on the Guard to protect them all, and had fully expected his children to obey him and live happily ever after upon the island. They'd been born and raised here, and not having any experience on the mainland, with their ignorance of the reality of the war, they hadn't stood a chance. Royal or peasant, their blood made no difference, and they died along with so many others, without making their mark in Legend Song. The Lord and Lady were childless for many winters 'til finally she'd been able to convince her mate to bring forth life once more. Of course, the Lady didn't want her to discuss any of this with the Lord, and Kevon wasn't supposed to know, but Calei felt 'twas disrespectful for his brothers to go unnamed and forgotten, as they'd been righteous in their efforts. Warriors stuck together, from any Race. So, the boy's education on his brothers, and his history, and the Sprites, and the war, mostly came from the Captain without the permission of either of his parents. The Lady made it clear that the Lord knew not about their arrangement, asking only that Caleichante ensure Kevon knew how to wield a weapon to defend himself, his family, and his people, should the need arise. She'd agreed, and they'd spent many marks o'er the past five winters, learning how to do just that, in secret. 'Twas a complicated ballet in which she participated, but 'twas necessary. The royals were good people; they were just disillusioned. They still felt the betrayal of the Elven Nation from the time of the Separation, and then again during the Retreat, although the Sprites fared better than did the Elves through those dark days.

JUST PAST MIDNIGHT

~~~~~ THE PRINCE'S BEDCHAMBERS ~~~~~

</div>

Kevon was restless, he'd been trying to get back to the Library all day. Afore dawn broke he'd sat on the marble floor staring at the Egg o'er half a mark, wondering if he'd ever Hear their guest's
~~~~~

voice again, and wondering even more if he'd Heard it when he thought he had. *"Evil comes... "* he'd thought Bryynn said. But there were chores to do and classes to attend, and he had to leave without his desired confirmation, fully aware that he wouldn't be able to return afore tomorrow's dawning.

Being the only living son, he was the Heir Apparent to the Sprites and held the title of Prince, even though his father and mother were called the Lord and Lady. He knew they were cousins to the Elves, and the King and Queen of the Elven Nation and the Lord and Lady of the Sprite Nation had a rather volatile disagreement at one time. The Elves and Sprites had gone their separate ways, but such had occurred ages prior to the Retreat. The Sprites had not set foot in their mutual homeland since that ominous day, however, they discovered other ways to survive outside the nourishing Wyrdritch, and their Magic finally began to flourish again, once they aligned themselves with the Water Dragons and the Island of Dreams, providing them a new Link to Kadoor. Life for a while was truly idyllic, but they fooled themselves into believing they could remain totally secluded from the rest of the world, for the world came to them.

Kevon understood he must leave the island one day, he must join the war as had his brothers, but he would not be naive. He fully intended to seek out the Dragon Clan when he was of age, and make an alliance. The Sprites had much to offer, were excellent fighters and bowmen besides being Magic bearing, and their Water Dragon Ties could be most helpful. 'Twas wrong of them to hide here, they needed to unite once again, for the Hoard would not leave them alone in peace. 'Twas everyone's duty to fight the Evil One. The Sprites' assistance could help turn the tide. The Elite Guard was the best of the best the Sprite Nation had to offer, rivaling even the legendary Warriors of the Dragon Clan, and Kevon felt his Guard could take on the Clan anywhere, anytime, any day. But they were unknown to the others, and despite the recent happenings, the royal house still withheld permission to divulge their existence. He had to make his parents see the truth. He had to convince them. But first he had to become a better swordsman and archer than he was already. The Captain assured him he was making good progress. He could throw a decent dagger. He smiled. She was a relentless task master and never lied to him. Nor did she coddle him or treat him like he'd break in a stiff breeze. No, she made him work harder than she did her Guard, for she knew his destiny and for that, he was grateful. He trusted her as he could trust no other. She saw him for who he was, not for his succession or for what he could do for her career, and she asked nothing from him except that he give his all to learn and progress. Failing his bloodline wasn't an option. Neither was failing the Captain.

He'd not been able to separate himself from his duties after evening meal, and now he lay very still, staring at the tall posters that near reached the high ceiling o'er head, thinking about their guest once again. He should have been sleeping, 'twas the middle of the night, but he could hardly close his eyes. Unexpectedly, his acute hearing caught the low sound of shuffling steps down the hallway outside his room. Knowing 'twas not his imagination, and as 'twas most indicative of someone being where they shouldn't be, he got up, cracked open the door, and then stepped out. Peeking o'er the banister, he just caught sight of the edge of a long dark cloak as it whipped around the corner downstairs, heading in the general direction of the library. Returning, he quickly donned his tunic and britches o'er his bedclothes, pulled on his boots, and snuck back out of his room in silent pursuit.

<div align="center">~~~~~ A FEW MOMENTS PRIOR ~~~~~</div>

The Sorcerer sneered and gathered his cloak after ensuring the boy would follow. He gestured impatiently for the others to move aside so he could take the lead, and proceeded swiftly up the hallway straight for the library. His spy didn't have what it took to break down the Protection Spell, but he didn't need anyone else's help. Although they knew not, the team who accompanied him were handpicked to be expendable, for he'd be leaving alone this night. Their continued existence would only hinder his desired outcome, an outcome of which he did not want the Black to know. If one could see his expression under the hood, one would tremble with the stark realization of his madness.

<center>~~~~~ MEANWHILE ~~~~~</center>

Caleichante trailed the intruders through Dream Hold. 'Twas obvious they were on a single-minded mission, and her anger grew with the increasing certainty of what that was. Had they taken the boy hostage to serve in their heinous plan? Leaving his empty chambers, she continued to the library, fearing the worst. When they discovered they couldn't take the Egg out of the Protection Spell, what would they do in retaliation? The Spell could only be unlocked by one of royal blood. If they already knew that, 'twould be the reason they'd taken Kevon, if they had him. She shivered with revulsion at the prospect of the handsome young boy in the hands of the Hoard, for the fact they were Hoard, was certain.

She Heard Schlynn moan in anxiety and Ordered him to hunt, then come to her via the north well of the dungeons. He'd soon need the energy that feeding would provide. Her voice soothed him and he Reported that he'd just fulfilled that order, as after a brief search he'd found the skiff with two Human rowers aboard. They'd been truly surprised by his appearance, which bewildered him somewhat, as all Water Dragons held a self-image of being terrifying beasts of the Sea of Dreams, surely known to all throughout Kadoor, and that no one could cross their waters undetected. Calei tried not to laugh at his childlike arrogance. 'Twas true enough, no one could cross if the Dragons were aware, but the scaly beasts were not known for their concentration and required the assistance of their Sprite Ties to focus their efforts. Schlynn continued his narrative, Speaking to her in his typical grandiose manner, using few words (for thinking in Human languages was as difficult as was speaking them aloud) and weaving the tale as for an audience of his peers. He dispatched them forthwith, although he didn't find them particularly tasty, then searched for the ship in which they must have sailed. But he decided 'twas more important to return to his Tie and was now back on the shore. He sent another to search for the ship. If that one wasn't Tied to a Sprite partner, 'twas entirely possible the search would not occur, the good intentions of the Water Dragon falling to the wayside with the first opportunity to play with a jellyfish. Calei preferred that no other Sprite be alerted to this situation 'til she could ascertain the details, so she wasn't concerned. But Schlynn's intent was well thought out, in that, if the other's search was fruitful, the intruders would have no known escape route. Calei was proud, and thanked him. She'd have preferred to question the rowers, but suspected they'd not known anything important, and having Schlynn well fed, was vital. No matter what else happened this night, she wanted his Magic at its peak.

Approaching the library, she spotted Kevon crouching at the railing. Breathing a sigh of relief, she slid in behind the boy who near jumped out of his skin when she covered his mouth with her hand. How does she do that, he thought, as he gathered his wits about him. Nodding his head, Kevon let her know he wouldn't give away their presence. Turning him to face her, she pointed toward the entrance, and then wiggled her fingers asking how many he'd seen. Kevon immediately raised one hand with all fingers extended. She squinted and scowled. Five enemy weren't too many for her alone, but she needed to keep the Prince safe. He seemed to know what she was thinking and pointed toward her dagger, indicating he wanted to help and needed a weapon. She was pleased he didn't seem to question that she was alone, and made no move to leave her. He trusted her, and his trust was humbling.

She slowly drew her side weapon, a falchion, from its sheath at her hip, and handed it to the boy. After expecting to be given the dagger for throwing, he was more than amazed. The machete-like blade had the power of an axe and the maneuverability of a short sword. He'd shown great promise with it in training and she felt 'twould meet the current need. As he locked gazes and held steady, he took the hilt with a solid grip, ready to fight. Then she pulled her slightly longer, double edged curved blade from the scabbard on her back and crawled past the Prince 'til she could peek around the corner. What she saw made her blood boil. A five-member Hoard patrol presented themselves surrounding the pedestal. 'Twas apparent the one standing closest to the Egg was a Magic bearer of some power, the rest merely Human. With one man at his back and the last three fanned out behind them, he should have been well protected, yet apart from the cloaked Magic bearer, all had their weapons drawn but not at ready and never even glanced to the entrance, demonstrating either poor training, or the false confidence that comes with thinking they'd already ensured their safety and had nothing to worry about. That, in and of itself, made it quite clear she and the boy were on their own this night.

The Magic bearer had his hands raised, the volume of his voice becoming erratic as he chanted. His men began to show some discomfort, but all eyes remained upon him as if they couldn't help themselves. Then she, too, felt the mesmerizing power emanating with the building tension in the library, the result of the Brew of very potent Magic. As the moments slipped past, her eyes riveted to the Egg 'til she noted tiny ripples in the air surrounding their guest. Truly alarmed as she realized the impossible appeared to be happening, she caught Kevon's eyes and nodded her head. She didn't know how these men had entered, she didn't understand how they'd managed to navigate to the island, but the Assembly itself was infiltrated at the very least, and that meant the Evil One's influence might have seeped all the way through to the Lord and Lady. Only this one boy could be trusted and her entire career was spent to protect him and the 7th Egg. How could she choose 'tween them? He nodded his agreement with her plan, he knew the turmoil she faced. His life was also dedicated to keeping their promise to the Water Dragons, ultimately to the Highlands themselves, to protect their guest at all costs, and the one person upon the entire island he was sure he could trust, crouched in front of him now. He would fight Past the Veil with Calei at his back.

She mouthed her words to the boy, his lip reading extraordinary. "Stay here, do not attempt to protect me." When he didn't immediately agree, she frowned her disapproval 'til he relented. He'd not enter the fray to protect the Captain, but capitulation didn't matter, for she'd not be the one who'd need help. He'd also seen the Spell waver. Turning away, she slipped around the column. Attacking the three men standing as the first barrier 'tween her and the Egg, she skillfully dispatched two, who seemed to have difficulty getting their thoughts together, leaving her in a clash with the third, who'd turned awkwardly at the noise, surprised to see anyone there. Although he'd been slow initially, this one turned out to be a decent opponent, and his demise would not be as quick or as clean.

While Calei was busy with the Hoardsmen, Kevon watched the Magic bearer, and was shocked to see the Spell continue to falter. Yet, there was still no retaliation from their guest. Without hesitation, he ran forward, leaped o'er the two dead men and slipped past the Captain with her current opponent, toward the cloaked intruder. There was only one man left 'tween him and his target. Swinging his blade wide and high, right to left, he met the other's block squarely as the man just turned in time to face him. Immediately he dipped and spun, swinging his blade gracefully, bringing the weapon down and around as he twisted back to his right, staying close under his enemy's arm to prevent him from effectively using his longer weapon. Completing the spin, he struck true, hamstringing the other's right leg. With his aggressor now on one knee they were of more equal stature, but the youth didn't slow down to think about it as he continued his lethal dance. Ripping the blade back, he lifted it up o'er his head, circled and swung down and back to his left to block his opponent's incoming strike once more. 'Twas weakened by the injury, giving Kevon his chance. With grace beyond his winters he faced the hapless swordsman, gripped firmly along the top of the blade, and forced the sharp edge into the man's throat, putting his weight behind the thrust, cutting through his windpipe. The Hoardsman fell o'er drowning in his own blood, but the Prince didn't stop there. His eyes upon the now turning cloak shrouding the Magic bearer, he rushed him, his blade poised to stab. Then something happened. There came a blinding flash from the Egg, a warning scream inside his mind, and instantly he felt as if he'd been hit in the chest with an invisible ramrod, stopping his forward momentum so forcefully, his blade was jarred from his grasp to clatter 'cross the cold marble.

JUST MOMENTS PRIOR
~~~~~ 'CROSS THE ROOM ~~~~~

</div>

Calei was stunned at the ease with which she'd forced the first two swordsmen Past the Veil, but the third was somewhat prepared, having been alerted by his ill-fated brethren. He lasted a little longer. But not much. At least he gave her a worthwhile effort. Surely the Hoard would not have sent such ill-trained swordsmen to protect someone so powerful on such a mission? Nevertheless, afore she pushed him to join his ancestors, the boy rushed past her toward the Magic bearer, and she could not afford to ponder further. Engaging the last of the swordsmen blocking their path, Kevon showed remarkable skill for his first real battle. She couldn't help but be proud, and for the briefest instant she hesitated afore finishing her task and coming to his aid. She would question that hesitation for many moons to come.

Watching him, she finished her own fight and then started toward the pair, just after he'd forced his opponent Past the Veil
~~~~~

in a brilliant close combat maneuver. Staying near to the other, not allowing him room to swing or stab, he'd taken good advantage of the wound inflicted, and with their height differences thus equalized, he'd slashed the man's windpipe with the edge of his blade. In fact, he'd not only slashed it, he'd hit him with such force fueled by Battle Lust, that he'd near cut his head off his shoulders.

Then several things happened at once. She felt a strange sensation fill the room, which she likened to wading chest deep against the incoming tides. Appalled, she struggled to step forward. Afore she could do so, Kevon rushed the hooded one. At that point, a sudden burst of energy, like a dazzling flash of light, emitted from the Egg, enveloping the boy. A fraction of a candle drip afterwards, Kevon appeared to slam into an invisible wall, dropping to his knees in excruciating pain. She rushed past him and when he attempted to rise, both hands holding his chest, she shoved him back down behind her as she confronted the last, and undoubtedly the most powerful, Hoardsman.

His face was hidden in the depths of his hood, and she squinted in disbelief as she recognized the 'tell' of the Fay, the tiny sparks of lighting flashing in his dark eyes, from under the folds. Hesitating not, she stabbed forward with her sword, but her blade was met in thin air and diverted. Somewhat taken aback, as the other hadn't moved a muscle since facing her, she swung again, and although rather awkwardly, her blade struck something solid for the second time. 'Twas a weak resistance, but 'twas just enough to throw off her aim, and she spun around to keep her balance, striking again with an outside swing. When her blade glanced off afore hitting the Magic bearer once more, the sun dawned upon her and she was repulsed by the knowledge of what she now faced. 'Twas a Spell Sword, a thing of evil Magic that wielded itself to defend its creator. Its slightest wounds were always fatal, usually death occurred within moments if not instantly, and nothing could prevent the inevitable. Fighting off the numbness of shock, she realized Kevon had run into it full force. 'Twas unnerving to think the Fay were involved, for if 'twas true, her odds just lowered by a good half. But she'd never been one to believe in odds, only her own determination or lack thereof.

The Prince was in dire straits and this pushed her well beyond her need. Attacking with a vengeance, she allowed Battle Lust to fuel her actions, raining strike after strike, meeting and deflecting each invisible swing of the Spell Sword. Her intuition dictated her moves without conscious thought, while she participated in a lethal game she knew not if she could win. But she'd never quit, never stop, 'til she'd Passed the Veil. And by the 7th Egg, she'd surely take this one with her, and damn whatever Race to which he laid claim.

As the fight wore on, she noticed the other's response was slowing and weakening, and hope blossomed of getting past the Spell to meet the architect. 'Twas more and more obvious he was no fighter, and although his Spell was powerful, his lack of fighting knowledge was apparent. Suddenly, her sword sliced through her opponent's strike and the Spell fell apart. The Hoardsman stumbled backwards as if shoved, and crossing his arms o'er head, he disappeared in a scattering of dust. She knew he must still be in the area, as no Magic bearer was capable of true teleportation. Dancing the Shadows was similar, but 'twas a Sprite and Elven Magic and required the use of actual organic shadows through which to travel. After determining he'd truly left the vicinity under his guise of distraction, she abandoned the search, for there were other matters to which she must immediately attend. After all, the Fay were Shifters, he could be anything and anywhere by now. Turning rapidly, she was surprised Kevon wasn't still where she'd left him.

<div style="text-align:center">~~~~~ MEANWHILE ~~~~~</div>

The Prince understood what was happening, and as the only person in the room who should be able to dissolve the Spell of

Protection, seeing it waver was a jolt to his senses. He couldn't allow the Hoardsman to take the Egg and no matter the outcome of
the battle, he accepted his duty and his destiny. While his Captain
and her foe battled, he began to make his connection. He didn't
know why he'd been repulsed afore, but he could not fail now.
Turning his back to the fight, he stepped closer to the pedestal,
cleared his mind, and settled himself into a semi-trance. Seeking
entrance to the Egg's private domain, he requested permission to
approach and release the Spell. Kevon was initially disturbed at
not receiving a positive response, but neither did he sense a negative one, and so he determined their guest was back in stasis to
prevent his own hatching, a result that would be exceptionally ill-
fated timing. Since he'd never attempted this, 'twould be his own
audacity that might get him killed if he were mistaken. But the
urgency of the situation must be clear to their guest, even within his confines. Mayhap his injury was an accident? Their guest
merely attempting to protect himself? A delayed reaction? Kevon
made his choice. He'd take that risk for the greater good. He tried
to raise his arms, but the stabbing pain in his chest brought tears
to his eyes. Thinking every rib must be fractured, he fell to his
knees, breath stuttering. Stooped o'er, he groaned, hugging himself tightly to ease the pain.

CHAPTER SIX

No Allure!

~~~~~~~~~~

Calei returned rapidly to the center of the library and found Kevon crouched near the pedestal. His face was drained of all color and his agony was evident. Lightly stroking his forehead, she calmed his thoughts and slowed his breathing, pulling him back from the edge of shock. Speaking in a very low voice, she urged, "We must hurry, m'Lord. We can trust no one. These men were with the Hoard, of that I am certain, and we know not who is in league with them. I fear the worst, my Prince. Infiltration of Dream Hold through the Assembly."

Kevon nodded his head in agreement, gasping out, "You must leave 'til we can uncover the truth and this evil can be routed. You're not safe here. The Assembly may not even believe me, for I have only recently taken my Acceptance Oath, and I've heard many rumors that now make more sense. We have no time to discuss this, you must go without anyone knowing. I will cover for you."

Smiling with confidence, she replied, "Fear not, m'Lord, I am the whisper of butterfly wings and can disappear in a flash, but I have no intention of deserting you. The Magic bearer has not left; he is merely waiting for us to vacate so he can return to complete his mission. They came to take the Egg, but in so doing they've managed to silence the entire Hold, and I fear more evil Magic in the Brew. We must go together, as you will certainly be their next target, and the Egg must go with us."

Kevon understood what she wanted from him and fearing to disappoint her, in great distress he replied, "I cannot penetrate the Spell to approach, when I tried, I was repelled. It caused me great pain."
~~~~~~~~~~

Her hesitance brought a frown to Kevon's face. "No, m'Lord, 'twas not Bryynn."

Eyebrows furrowed in confusion, he replied, "This makes no sense. We've beaten the enemy, prevented Bryynn's abduction, yet your face tells me the worst is yet to come. You've never lied to me, you're the only Sprite upon the whole of the island whom I can trust to tell me the truth no matter the impact. If not Bryynn who caused this pain, then what?"

Unusually reluctant to speak her mind, she replied softly, "The Hoardsman used a Spell Sword for his own protection. You've been run through. I know not how Bryynn managed, but if not for his interference, 'twould have taken you Past already."

Kevon's eyes widened as he took in this startling revelation, for he knew well the prognosis of such a devastating Spell. Clenching his jaw, he resolutely stood up as straight as he could and raised his arms again. Calei could see the effort it took, the amount of pain the boy withstood to finish breaking down the Spell of Protection. As she saw it collapse in a sparkling dust upon the marble, Kevon crumpled in her arms. "Take Bryynn and go," he wheezed, but she'd have none of that. Picking up his slight body, she lifted him and stepped forward close enough that he could pluck the Egg from the pedestal, then cradled him in her arms. He broke out in a sweat as the pain escalated with his exertion. Locking her eyes to his, she stated emphatically, "You've done well, m'Lord, be still and hold on. The next few marks may be the worst of your life, but I swear upon my own, I will see you through this or I will journey with you Past the Veil. Wherever you are, wherever you go, I will not leave you. You shall not be alone."

Kevon was voiceless, and with facial expression his only means of communication, he placed his faith in her, no matter the outcome. This night would beyond doubt be the worst he'd ever experienced, as 'twould be for any newly injured warrior, however, he was just a boy and awareness abruptly left him. Still clutching the Egg to his chest in a death grip, with a slight intake of breath, he fell mercifully unconscious.

Carrying the Prince, she crawled through a small, secret trap door behind the geode, leading to an underground passageway. Once she reached the bottom of the short ladder, she had to stoop low and push the Prince ahead of her, the Egg still held tightly. They'd barely vacated the library afore she heard someone enter behind them. 'Twas quiet for several moments as she listened intently, hearing only a slight shuffling, afore she heard another enter. Moments later, the rest of the Guard presented. 'Twas evident they misunderstood the scene, and she'd just been framed for the abduction of both the Prince and the Egg. How could they not understand what happened, when they'd left behind four dead Hoardsmen? With Battle Lust flaring, she heard them vow to take her, if not kill her, and then the boy would have no chance. This became a race, and in her battle-hardened opinion, with more than one life to lose. She Called for Schlynn to meet her at the well within the lower levels of the Hold. Circling around and leaving the others in their wake, she and the boy had very little time to act, afore the area would be secured and unapproachable.

'Twas difficult with her charges, but very soon they made it to the well. Schlynn rose high out of the water, prepared to take them by covering them in Allure, but Calei prevented him from touching the Prince. *"We cannot use Magic, my friend, for they can track us that way. This must be done without."*

Curiously, Schlynn cocked his wide, short-muzzled head as he gazed at her, his muscular forelegs hanging limply o'er the edge of the well by his armpits, his silver-flecked, dark brown scales and matching eyes a'glow. Speaking aloud for a Water Dragon was quite a project, having to pull their lips back o'er their rather impressive fangs, their great tongues slipping 'tween to splatter saliva everywhere, and their child-like, heavily accented lisp making it even more difficult for anyone who wasn't used to hearing them, to decipher. Using telepathy, their preferred method of communication through their Link, he Spoke, *"No Allure, I no help?"* Resting his elbows on the edge of the well, his great paws now cupping his chin, his thick body still dangling down into the water, Schlynn's long tongue drooped out of his mouth as he considered the logistics of the journey. *"Closest air Grotto. Long way. You hold breath, hold tight, twist, turn, swim fast, might lose you. Prince sick? He hold breath to Grotto?"* Schlynn shook his head sadly, sucked his tongue back into his mouth, and then gave his honest assessment of the outcome of such a daring stunt. *"If hold tight, Calei just make it. Prince, too far."*

The Captain quickly detailed her plan while he trembled with excitement. After all, 'twas an adventure, and Water Dragons were always looking for an adventure. *"I believe our guest is helping the Prince in a way that cannot be detected, or duplicated. If true, then he'll be fine, 'twill be up to me to hang on and hold my breath long enough to make it to the Grotto. And even so, 'twill be merely a stepping stone for our journey. From there we go to the stables. I think the distance underwater from here to the Grotto is slightly further than from there to the stables. At least I hope so. Now hurry, and remember, NO ALLURE!"*

Schlynn turned around to make ready for a quick descent and Calei wasted no time in mounting the beast from inside the edge of the well, lying head down along his back with the boy 'tween them, holding him fast to the Dragon. She'd never actually attempted this afore, and 'twas as if she were trying to climb down a large pine head first, carrying the boy and the Egg at the same time. Getting a grip, her legs squeezing tightly to the beast's sides, she took several deep breaths, then one last long one, and squeezing her knees tighter, Schlynn immediately dove.

Down through the well they swam, speeding out and around the curves, following the underground system 'til she felt the change from fresh water to salt and still they swam, 'til her lungs ached and burned for air. She hung on tighter and willed Schlynn to go faster, but still they swam. She thought not about the Prince, 'twas the only option they had. Using Magic would have them caught immediately, their trail clearly visible to her Guard who'd be searching for just that. Hopefully, Kevon was being helped as she'd said. If not, then she'd have to manually resuscitate him when they got to the Grotto. Of course, 'twould depend upon whether she made it herself. 'Twould be no one to resuscitate her, if necessary.

Lungs on fire and vision darkening, she was about to scream out in defiance, gulping in the salt water with which she was surrounded, when they abruptly reached their destination in an explosion of sea spray, as the Dragon broke the surface and soared within the confines of the cave to belly flop upon the nearest ledge. Calei gasped, choking and coughing, still trying not to lose her hold upon the boy and Bryynn, as she wretched. Her eyes streamed tears from the salt water, her lungs ached with the need to fill them again and again with the cool air. Appreciative of both the lighting and the air, supported by luminescent algae and a few good Spells, Calei continued to gasp as Schlynn slid along on his belly further up onto the smooth rock shelf while his passengers rolled off. But the Prince was silent and moved not. Still coughing, she quickly checked and found him to be in the same condition as he'd been upon the start of this 'adventure', so she rolled onto her back to catch her breath. She was correct. Their guest was doing something to assist the boy, but only him. She was on her own. That was fine with her, she'd been on her own her entire life, 'twas no real hardship, but she was truly grateful for help with the boy. Schlynn had also been correct. She'd barely made it to the Grotto alive. Another heartbeat would have seen her Past the Veil.

As soon as she could manage to stand up, she checked the area. No one here. 'Twas as she figured. At this time and date, few visited the Grotto. 'Twas deep under the island, where the eggs of the Water Dragons were incubated, and that was a long, slow, lonely process needing little assistance now, or even in the next few moons. Not like during the Last Holocaust when the entire Sprite Nation stood guard o'er the eggs as they were brought in from all o'er the Sea of Dreams to this one place. But that was a long time ago and she couldn't think on it now. They weren't safe yet. Once 'twas discovered they weren't in the library, they'd look to the well. Finding no Allure, they'd continue for at least a mark searching the Hold. Once the Hold was secured, they'd know she'd slipped past them, and they'd look to secure the Port District and the stables. The port wasn't an option for them, since most of the coastline along this end of the island was well populated and guarded. To avoid capture they'd need to avoid the shores. But the stables? She had to get there first, which meant leaving immediately.

Water Dragons had an odd characteristic (a part of their Magic) that made them near invisible when wet, and without using her own Magic, she'd experienced that phenomenon first hand for the first time. 'Twas all she could do to try to hang on during the journey, barely able to see his sleek body even with her Sprite vision, as they made their way through the system. Looking about for him now, the glittering object just under the surface of the water in the distant corner, gave her pause. She waded o'er to the pile of 'treasures' that she knew belonged to Islyth, Myrrdin's Tie. He allowed his Dragon to store her treasures here, and no one had ever said a word. Of course, as he was the Heir Apparent to the Elven Nation, no one would speak against him. 'Twas fortunate he was an honorable Elf.

She had to leave, and yet... an idea sparked, and she reached out for the object that caught the constant light shining throughout the Grotto. 'Twas a sunstone. Islyth must have found this in the wrecks along the coastlines where she often played. The sunstone was a tool of the ancient mariners, and reminded Calei of an old conversation she'd had with her cousin. Would Islyth notice 'twas missing? No doubt. But would she understand to tell her Tie? Mayhap. The Elven Prince was good friends with Corbyn the Fay, and she needed Myrrdin's help to locate Corbyn. Even though she was not sure if the Fay could now be trusted, 'twas certain the strongest of the Magic bearers was her only chance to Heal the Prince. 'Twas all she had. Locating the Dragon, she returned quickly to Kevon. Holding the sunstone in one hand, the Egg firmly tucked 'tween their bodies, she told Schlynn, "I'm ready. Take us to the Stables."

The distance to the next well was less, but the journey was the same. These were not the Royal Stables, nor were they the ones used by the Elite, for those would be well guarded. If they suspected her of using a horse, 'twould be her current mount, however, she kept her retired horse in the most isolated stables, the one used for practice and surplus tack. Few horses were kept here, and the well was rarely used. This time she didn't take a rest break. Jumping down from the edge into the soft sand, she left the Prince and ran to the tack room, grabbed a blanket and a saddle bag and stuffed the Egg inside along with the sunstone, while racing to the farthest stall. Schlynn dove back into the well and disappeared, awaiting further instructions. He needed to hunt, for all this adventuring was making him hungry. Swinging the blanket o'er Prea's short back, she ground her teeth against what she was asking of the mare. Taking just a moment, she faced the horse, held her head in her hands, and stared deeply into Prea's soulful brown eyes, pleading for forgiveness for her choice. This little mare was older but sure footed, and although not the fastest, she'd been swift and solid in endurance runs. As she pawed the ground, Calei breathed into her nostrils and calmed her with her hands.

She not only needed to evade the Guard, but soon even the citizens of the island. Their only chance was on the mainland. No doubt Lord Rohar would send a chase team to track them, so she'd have to leave the island without a trail. That meant continuing her policy of no Magic. Not even taking time for reins or saddle, she scooped up Kevon and threw him o'er Prea's back, then vaulted aboard while she Told Schlynn what she had in mind, so he'd come prepared. No one had ever attempted what she was doing, but then, no one had ever had such need. Calei held tightly onto the boy, the saddlebag slung o'er her shoulder and his, linking them together as Prea raced like the wind out of the stables, through the empty courtyard, past the gates, 'cross the fields, and dashed into the shelter of the surrounding heavy woods. Sprites were creatures of nature, and nature for them, unlike their cousins the Elves, was at its best in the light of day. But Sprite vision was still sharper than Human, and 'twas assisted by the waxing moon.

Allowing Prea her head, they managed to clear the woodlands, the valleys, the hills, 'cross the rivers and around the lakes, ever heading toward the Northern Cliffs on the far end of the Island of Dreams. She knew this island better than anyone, had the best survival skills of the entire Guard, but even she knew they had slim chance to make it 'cross the entire island by the next nightfall, and even less chance of avoiding being seen. At full gallop 'twould take dusk to dawn for the journey, but that would be non-stop and without the detours forced upon her. She'd lost several marks of night from dusk to escape, leaving less than half that time afore dawn broke, therefore she had to face the fact that much of this journey would be in broad daylight.

During the ride, the Prince slept cradled in front of her, clutching the bag holding the Egg close to his chest as if it gave him some comfort, even in unconsciousness. That he yet lived kept her energized. She'd never used her skills with such fervor, 'twas the ultimate test. Always, she acted as if her Guard were one step behind, hounding her trail, for surely, they would soon be.

By dawn she was out of the most populated area surrounding the castle, and into the back country. 'Twas more difficult as the day wore on, and several times she had to stop and change directions or back track to avoid exposure, but thus far she saw no evidence that her trail had been found. Apparently, her plan was working and they were stumbling to find her. Despite the changes of pace required, the little mare was beginning to lather. Calei's eyes watered. Sadly, she knew not if 'twas from the wind, knowing Prea's fate, or the realization that she was now a hunted criminal, facing death at the hands of her friends and family. For what she was doing, they need not even give her fair hearing. She'd be killed on sight. She had but one goal, get off the island. If she accomplished that, 'twould be a miracle, but then she'd have to find some safe place to think.

Calling Schlynn once more, she Reminded him, *"Meet us at the well of the Northern Cliffs at dusk. From there we repeat our performance to get as far out to sea as my lungs can handle. We then skip, swimming underwater for a distance then surfacing for air, the rest of the journey. But we must be to the mainland afore dawn tomorrow. We must make landfall in the dark so we can travel to a safe place to rest for the day."*

Schlynn was excited to be a part of this ongoing adventure and Replied, *"Mainland wells? Schlynn take you any well!"*

"No, my friend, not after this one, at least not for a while. We'll need food and water since this well is so close to the sea, 'tis not fresh. But don't let yourself be seen, they know I'm your Tie. You'll compromise our location, and that is very bad."

"How bad?"

"They want to kill me. They think I hurt the Prince and stole the Egg. Well, we did sort of steal the Egg, but if we hadn't, the Hoard would've."

"Calei protect Egg, protect Prince!"

"They know not this truth, and there's nothing to be done 'til I can find a way to save them both. In the meantime, your life is now in as much danger as is mine."

"Schlynn care not. No one see."

Calei continued to guide her horse through the thickest stretch of forest 'cross the middle of the island, heading ever northward. Although she had faith in her Tie, she had to hope he didn't lose focus and forget about their rendezvous.

A FEW MARKS PRIOR

~~~~~ SOMEWHERE IN DARKLING FOREST ~~~~~

"Oh dear," Anastasia mumbled as she crawled out from under some scrub brush where she'd found herself half covered in dirt and pine needles, pushing her disheveled hair away from her face. Her first attempt to Dance through the barrier appeared to have landed her in something of a mess. Still on all fours, she looked in every direction, but recognized nothing. 'Twas exciting, for there could be no doubt that she was outside. The colors of the surrounding forest were just as pictured in the library from afore the Last Holocaust, and the sky peeking through the canopy was a most stunning shade of blue. Taking a deep breath, she closed her brown eyes and inhaled slowly. Even the air was sweeter. Delighted, she stood up, brushed off the dirt and then yanked and tugged and untangled all the twigs from her rich brown hair afore holding very still to just listen for several moments. She had to give her sister credit. Persephone was good. All the birds sounded just as did those she created by Magic. But then, Persephone had been outside afore.

Ana had to sit down and rest, but didn't want to wait too long to return, for she'd been apprehensive about finding the same rhythm from outside the barrier. Nothing was certain about the Spell, and she didn't want to become one of the lost. 'Twas more difficult to traverse the portal than she'd originally thought, for she hadn't truly Danced at all. Adjusting midstream, 'twasn't a shadow that she used, and 'twasn't powered by energy from an organic, although 'twas apparently, the same concept. She'd been mistaken about that, but she was certain Dancing inside the Wyrdritch was adversely affected, the closer to the edge one was.
~~~~~

CHAPTER SEVEN

A Selfless Sacrifice

THE FOLLOWING EVENING, GATHERING DUSK
~~~~~ THE NORTHERN CLIFFS ~~~~~

"Come on, Prea, just a little further, please don't fold on me now, girl." The horse couldn't keep going much longer, although 'twas not far to the well. Atop one of the highest points upon the edge of the sea via a steep, narrow, hazardous pathway, 'twas hidden from the rest of the island. If her horse collapsed now, she'd have a hard time getting her charges up there by herself, and when the other Water Dragons found the carcass, they'd have a trail to follow. She couldn't see Schlynn yet, but even if he arrived soon, he couldn't take them in prime Slyder style upon his belly up the rough passage. "Please Prea, please hold on, we're almost there." She could hear the wheezing breath of the horse in response, and the coughing increased. Pushed past pure exhaustion marks prior, the tough little mare refused to quit. She'd brought them 'cross the whole island, often at break neck speeds, avoiding every danger, every exposure, never faltering, as if she knew the importance of her task. Even when Calei stopped to take a break to allow the mare to eat or drink while she checked on the Prince, Prea had been reluctant, almost resistant. 'Twas as if her entire focus was on getting them to the well. Although Sprites could only Hear their Dragons, Calei knew the little mare was aware of the need. Somehow, she'd sensed it, and was responding in the only way she could, to help complete the mission.

Prea slowed down considerably as she tried to scramble up the rough path with her passengers. Slipping on the loose rocks, she huffed and snorted and tossed her head, but kept on climbing. Her breath now coming in ragged gasps, her coat lathered, Calei could see the bright red blood splatter o'er the rocks, and her eyes began to tear once more. 'Twas obvious the little mare was failing, and she hadn't wanted to think about what to do with her once they got to their destination. She could have let her go, hoping she'd return to the stables without being caught, however, once caught, depending on where she was at the time, her trail was compromised and they'd be hard pressed to swim far enough away to avoid the searchers, their Ties finding them fast. Without care, the little horse would probably not make it down the rough path, let alone back to the stables, and she had no care to provide. She had to get the best head start she could and letting the mare go, was not the way to do that. She knew better than to depend on luck, but she needed it desperately. 'Twould take more than her skills to get them through this.

Prea stumbled again and caught her footing with much effort. Calei would have led her, but there was no way to hold the Prince on her back along this narrow path. Prea stumbled and fell to her knees, taking more time to get up. They were almost there. Abruptly, the path widened, allowing Calei to dismount and walk beside her while holding the boy steady, the saddle bag 'cross her left shoulder. Slipping and scraping her palms and legs, they struggled up the remainder of the jagged trail together, near to the top. Not many could find this well, few Sprites or Dragons used it now, and 'twas too far out of the way to be regularly trafficked. The Captain was counting on that out-of-sight-out-of-mind mentality for both her Guard and their Ties. 'Twould be some of that luck she'd hoped for earlier.

Finally, they reached the top, where the well sat in the middle of a relatively flat expanse of rocky ledge dug back into the cliffs. With her hooves now on level terrain, Prea panted and dropped to her knees one last time. Waiting for Calei to drag the Prince off her back afore she rolled o'er, Prea took her last breath and collapsed as her heart stopped beating. Calei could almost hear it as she held the little mare's head in her hands, thanking her for her bravery and for her help. After but a moment, she returned to the Prince's side, trying to forget the pain of her loss. Prea had been with her for many winters, and she felt her death as of a good friend.

Suddenly, Schlynn appeared o'er the edge of the well with a splash. He managed to secure enough food for one meal as per her instructions, bringing a bag of fresh water, too. 'Twas not much, but they couldn't carry anything extra with them on the next leg of their journey and 'twas easier for him, being careful not to be seen. As Calei kneeled beside Kevon, Schlynn turned his nose toward the carcass and sniffed in puzzlement. Water Dragons had learned that such creatures were treasured by their Ties, and often caused much distress when they Passed. Still, he didn't understand what happened. The little mare was in good health, although old for her species.

Knowing his thoughts, Calei didn't even look up from her efforts. "Her heart and lungs gave out. The trail was too hard."

The Water Dragon sat upright, rubbing his eyes with the backs of his huge round paws, mimicking distress as he looked from the dead mare to the Captain. *"Tears?"*

She bowed her head. "Yes, Schlynn, tears."

He nodded. His Tie was upset and 'twas more than the adventure. He wanted to ease her pain, but he still didn't quite understand. Spitting saliva everywhere with his efforts, he stated aloud, "She brave. Help much."

"Yes, she helped us much. But in so doing, she died," Calei stated softly.

"Died?" His tongue lolled out of his mouth as he cocked his head to the side and wrinkled his upper lip and nostrils. He was still puzzled.

Completely aware nothing should be amusing in the current situation, she couldn't help but be amused by the look on his face at that moment. The weight of the sadness now relieved somewhat, she could again focus. "She went Beyond. Now I need your help. We can't leave her body here, and we can't bury or move her."

"Schlynn hungry," he stated without emotion. He sat on his haunches, his front paws pushed together back to back, tucked up against his chest, while his long tongue pushed against the inside of his muzzle as he licked his fangs.

She shook her head and rolled her eyes. "I know, my dear, you're always hungry."

Enthusiastically he responded, stretching his short front legs out to the sides, his thick body weaving back and forth, "Want Schlynn eat?"

Even knowing what was coming, the question was so blunt it caught her momentarily off guard. Calei hesitated, and covering her face with her hand, took a deep breath afore responding. "Yes. Please."

Schlynn dropped to all fours and slid toward the carcass, then looked o'er his shoulder at the Captain. "Prea work hard. Prea help more."

Calei frowned. "Help? You mean to feed you? Fuel your Magic?"

"No. Prea still help."

"Well, if her death can be made into something positive, 'twould certainly help the tears."

He solemnly reprimanded her. "No tears. Prea make good sacrifice. No want you cry."

As the Water Dragon ate, Calei attempted to wake the Prince to eat or drink, but was unsuccessful. 'Twas as if Bryynn had enclosed the boy in a cocoon of protection, oblivious to their plight. She heard, rather than saw, when Schlynn's dining was complete, and turned around with unease. 'Twas amazing. No trace of the little mare could be seen, not even blood. Except for one internal organ. Her stomach. 'Twas intact and licked perfectly clean. Knowing the internal organs of any creature were considered a delicacy to all Dragons, Calei looked questioningly at her Tie, who proceeded to crawl up and o'er the edge of the well, and hanging by his back legs, he washed the stomach. Sliding back out, he rinsed the stretchy organ with the last of their fresh water, shaking out the excess and tying off one end, leaving a short length of esophagus open. He sat on his haunches and wrinkled his muzzle into a toothy grin, holding the stomach out to her. "Calei not hold breath long enough. Calei need help. Prea still help."

Tears shone anew, but this time with gratitude. Nodding her head in approval, she said, "You are a genius, my friend."

"Only if works," he spit forth dubiously. Full of concern, he truly feared for her ability to succeed in this adventure.

<div style="text-align:center">~~~~~ THE ROYAL LIBRARY OF THE SPRITES ~~~~~</div>

The Sorcerer was terrified, yet energized. The Suggestion Spell o'er Dream Hold, keeping all ignorant of their danger 'til he released them, had taken much planning, and he'd had to rely on another to perform their part of the task in order to succeed, something he detested, especially when his own safety was involved. Now, hiding in plain sight within the Library, no one was aware of his presence as he watched and listened from under a bookshelf, with his beady black eyes and large pink ears. Velvety smooth, soft gray fur covered his body, and as he sat up on his hind feet, his long hairless tail swept the floor while he absently cleaned his whiskers with his front paws. The chaos was delightful, their fruitless search charming. He gloated as he breathed in the multitude of high emotions, savoring the richness of the miasma. His spy had followed orders perfectly, covering their invasion and framing the Captain. Soon however, his thoughts turned to his next task. Facing the Black. His plan was working well indeed, but 'twas not the plan he'd been sent here to execute, and if he didn't handle this correctly, he'd be the one executed.

CHAPTER EIGHT

Wind Chimes in the Breeze

PRIOR TO THE INVASION OF THE ISLAND OF DREAMS

THE MAINLAND

~~~~~ KADDART VILLAGE ~~~~~

Diadranei's heart hammered in her chest, her breath stuttered through her lungs, and her silver-gray eyes flashed near black as coal with the strength of her emotions. The firelight from the hearth flickered off her ivory pale skin as she struggled to regain her composure in the face of the handsome man's bold assertion. She was tall for a female, but had to tilt her chin upwards to see his dark eyes. She wiped her sweaty palms nervously down her thin, ankle-length woolen skirt, and tried to understand what was happening, even as she began calculating her escape. How did he know, she wondered? How did he see through her glamour? Flame it all, she should have Masked, but the effort she'd expended to indoctrinate herself into this village took its toll on what little energy she could gather after her arrival. There'd been nothing left with which to power a Mask, and the Fay were the best at that Magic anyway. If one didn't perform a Spell successfully, tragic backlash could result. Magic was not to be taken lightly. Besides, she'd not even felt another Magic bearer in how long? She'd grown lax 'twas true, but chastising herself now meant nothing.

The willowy young Elven female was indeed arresting in her beauty, although she'd always thought of herself as plain. In truth, she bore no resemblance to the man and woman even now sleeping in the tiny room o'er the kitchen of the Clear Water Inn, for she was not their blood daughter. She'd stumbled upon the farming community just a few moons past, discovering the young girl partially concealed in the mud and brush at the side of the trail, as she was attempting to skirt around the village. The innkeeper's daughter had been brutally gang raped, beaten and left for dead. Bleeding profusely from near every orifice of her adolescent body, she'd still managed to crawl away from the barracks of the King's Forces, but couldn't go any further, and simply collapsed at the edge of town. 'Twas a sad scenario, a senseless act of violence that sickened the Elf. The injured girl was barely able to speak, and the story she imparted was horrific. Walking back home to the Inn after delivering food to the Barracks, she realized she was being followed. The rest didn't matter now.

Diadranei could only shake her head at the insanity. Mankind was the only non-Magic bearer and yet there were so many Humans who knew not how to fight, how to defend themselves, nor even seemed to understand when self-defense was appropriate. There appeared to be no other Race so poorly educated in their own survival. All Elves were trained practically from birth in fighting and self-defense techniques that didn't include the use of their Magic, and in fact, all Magic bearing Races could say the same. Pondering this notion for a moment, she knew the Warriors of the Dragon Clan were of a handful of Humans who still held to the old traditions and values. But then, she was not so worldly as to consider herself an expert in the Human tribes. At a mere few centuries, she was still young and had much to learn.

Touching the girl again, she'd been rewarded with a whimper of pain, and then nothing. If she'd been stronger, her Magic at full force, she could've attempted to save the girl, but when Diadranei had stumbled upon her, she'd been too close to the Veil. 'Twould have been wise to move on quickly, for staying meant to risk becoming enmeshed in the foul happenings here, but she'd also recognized her own need for respite. In her travels of late, she was finding more and more frequent evidence of the return of the Evil One, but to discover the new King was involved had been a bitter pill to swallow. Not that she cared much for that disgrace of a Man, but she did care about Mankind in general, and these events spoke volumes. She'd always felt in her heart that the

Retreat was wrong, and they should not have left Mankind to face the Black alone. She'd pushed to stay and join the fight with Man and the Highlands to avoid the collapse, but her opinion had been ignored and she'd left the Gathering in a huff, missing out on the Retreat and becoming stranded through the ensuing ages. However, she believed now that the Last Holocaust was inevitable. 'Twas all in the prophesies that ran so deeply through the Dragon Clan, and if they continued to prove true, as they appeared to be so doing, then the time for the Return was nigh. That is, if any of her people still existed to make such a return. She'd seen no others here, had felt no trace of the familiar Magic of her own Kind since that fateful night.

She had, of course, done the compassionate thing and assisted the girl to Pass the Veil quickly and painlessly, while at the same time boosting her own strength by absorbing the last dregs of waning Life Force. Laying her palm against the chilled bare skin of the girl's mid-thigh, she closed her eyes and could almost taste the energy within. Shivering with an unfamiliar excitement, Diadranei slid her hand gently up to the girl's groin and located the slow thump in the large femoral vein, indicating how her heart struggled in its doomed effort to keep her Life Source flowing through her body. Closing her eyes, she knew the failing heart would try to maintain life for countless marks, but the damage would never be reversed. The end was foreseeable, and the girl moaned out in her suffering.

Empathic senses assaulted with the ragged emotions, she'd made her decision. Taking a firmer hold, she licked her dry lips and Pulled. She'd never sent another Past the Veil afore, and the sudden surge of power obtained as the girl was drained to emptiness, shocked her with its potency. She wondered if this was how 'twas with every feeding that led to the Veil. Still, as weary as she'd been herself, she knew 'twould not last long, and she'd had to quickly determine how best to use such energy. She'd decided to stay put, reconnoiter the area, and mayhap be at peace for a time instead of constantly moving and hiding. How long had it been? She could scarcely recall.

Casting a glamour o'er herself so that others would see her as the girl, she'd taken the girl's memories obtained through her Life Force, and gone 'home'. Her 'parents' were jubilant, had never expected to see her again as she'd been so late to return, and through the subsequent dialogue Diadranei learned that other young men and women of the village had simply gone missing recently under similar and increasing circumstances. This situation was helpful to her disguise, as the man and woman took great pains to hide her from the King's Forces, keeping her at the Inn, providing her with the perfect excuse to be reclusive. With fewer eyes upon her, she was able to ration her energies much longer than in the past. She wondered if it had anything to do with the type of strength she'd Drawn from the Human. 'Twas an interesting notion that she'd pondered o'er many sleepless nights.

Meanwhile, she'd spent the rest of her time cooking and cleaning and watching every new traveler being taken for the arena. At first, she'd justified her silence as self-preservation, but then Tonn, the boy Runner, discovered the bloodings. They'd become acquainted at the Inn and quickly grown to be good friends. Musing, she felt remorse that he'd thought she was the Human girl, for 'twas apparent he'd been infatuated with her, prior to her Passing. She'd almost told him once, and mayhap she should have, but the past could not be changed. Instead, she'd told him about the arena, warning him to stay away from there, but he'd not listened. Young and headstrong, his Life Force had been a heady scent to her whenever he'd been near, and when he'd gone to see for himself what she'd described, he'd been captured, beaten, tortured, and imprisoned. Despite the boy's popularity, and the fact that both his older brothers were Warriors, she found she was the only one to try to help him; all others had become too fearful of retribution. She'd managed to sneak in food and water, and they'd orchestrated a daring escape plan. She'd even shared a bit of her Magic with him to prevent serious injury, but things had not gone entirely as intended. He'd almost been recaptured and was badly burned during his ill-fated departure, though her Magic likely kept him alive long past what would have been. She'd wondered for a time if he'd made it to Drekinn, but when the Warrior Team arrived soon afterward, her senses told her what had happened, and she was saddened by his loss.

The tall, dark haired stranger spoke with an odd accent she couldn't quite place, as he continued to stare. "You are not Fay, not a Shifter, yet the villagers see someone else when they gaze upon you, do they not?" His voice brought her back from her reverie. 'Twas a bit unnerving, but she'd been in worse situations and had no doubt she could hold her own with this one. Or at the very least, she had to make him think so. But as she opened her mouth to speak, she felt the Compulsion. Trying hard not to spew forth that which was on the tip of her tongue, she exploded, "ELVEN!" After which, she clapped both her hands o'er her mouth in absolute surprise, since no one had ever managed to Compel her to do anything she did not wish. And just how did he know she was an Elf? The stranger's satisfied smile didn't quite reach his eyes. He nodded his head as if he'd already known the answer to his unasked question.

Flatly, he stated, "Nothing is as 'twould seem, but do not fret o'er your indiscretion, 'twas not your fault. I merely required the truth, and have no time to delay for negotiation."

Somehow his words had not the desired result, and Diadranei became angry. Clenching her hands into fists at her sides, she stepped up to the stranger aggressively in total disregard for her own safety, as his demonstration should've proven that he was the stronger. Caring not, she stood up on her tiptoes, and with her sweet breath upon his face, and her own countenance a study in burning rage, she opened her mouth to chastise him. But afore she could produce a single sound, her throat began to constrict as surely as if the stranger was physically choking her. Dark eyes widening, her delicate hands gripping her neck, she crumpled to the floor, struggling to bring air into her lungs. As soon as her body touched the cold hearthstone, he Released her and she gasped for several heartbeats, her huge eyes watering with the strain.

"I admire your spirit; however, such will get you forced Past the Veil upon the next display. I have not the time to play these games with you, Elf. I desire your assistance but I can obtain another's, and will permit you to choose your own fate." His black eyes burned into hers as he continued. "After performing this task, I would advise you to vacate this village as soon as possible. And I do not think I need to tell you, nor Compel you, to remain silent," the stranger grimly informed her. Despite his outward indifference, Diadranei was more than aware of his inner turmoil. She was an Elf of some power among her Kind, and her specialty was Empathy. She could feel the other's broiling emotions, taste his need, his anger, his sadness. 'Twas an odd combination. Sitting up, she dropped her hands to her lap and stared momentarily at them while she settled the emotional barrage with which she was surrounded. The stranger sat on his booted heels in front of her, and when she looked up into his eyes she saw flashes of lightning in their depths.

In a quiet voice, she asked him, "What would you have me do?"

Hesitating not, he replied, "The new travelers staying here at this Inn, are to be taken tonight to the arena. You will give them a note, written in your own hand, telling them to beware the King's Agents. I care not which one of them receives it, but they must have this warning afore dusk, or 'twill be too late."

Dusk? Tonight? She didn't even care how he knew this, she was horrified. There was no doubt that she'd try to help them! She'd thought the younger one was quite good-looking and had fantasized about... well, it mattered not now. She made the agreement by nodding her head, and grasped the hand he offered to help her up. He easily lifted her tall frame and set her lightly back down on her feet. Keeping a firm grip upon her hand, he drew a blade from his boot and nicked one fingertip. As the blood droplet formed, he brought her long slender finger to his mouth and suckled gently, thus securing the deal. All the while he stared into her dark eyes, not wavering in his gaze, when mesmerized she Heard, *"And remember girl, next time Alter your voice. You Elves sound like wind chimes in the breeze. 'Tis not natural to Human ears. 'Tis certain to bring unwanted notice."*

That was peculiar. Shaking her head, she was alone. The stranger had disappeared. Not as in, vanished, but as in, she had no idea how or where he'd gone. Hearing a fluttering noise o'er her head, she noted the blue-black gloss of a starling amid the rafters, immediately afore hearing the front door open. As the two travelers entered, the starling exited, and she knew 'twas the stranger. So, he was Fay. No wonder she'd not been able to best him. Then a tiny squeak came unbidden from her throat as she realized just how very close she'd been to the Veil when she'd dared to make challenge. Apparently, as she yet breathed, the Fates were still ignorant of her impudence.

Feeling an urgency that hadn't been forced upon her, she hurried to the kitchen to fetch ale, stew and fresh baked bread for the merchants. They'd need a good meal to get through the approaching trials. While they ate, she scribed the note and brought it to them with a refill of their mugs. A handful of villagers had wandered in for supper and talk near the hearth, but she wasn't listening tonight. Out of the corner of her eye she saw the two Warriors steal upstairs. They'd managed to vacate the Inn by the time the Agents burst into their room. Of course, so had she.

CHAPTER NINE

A Game of Riddles

~~~~~ THE ISLAND OF DREAMS ~~~~~

</div>

The insistent banging on the door startled the Lord and Lady awake from their peaceful slumber. Rohar leaped out of bed at the intrusion, shaking an unusual sense of grogginess from his mind, hoping his mate, Tialani, could go back to sleep. Fully expecting to see the Captain of the Guard standing there, to his surprise 'twas her First Mate, Natanamia. And if that wasn't strange enough, four others of his Elite Guard were flanking her, all with their swords drawn down. Rohar was understandably apprehensive but said nothing, waiting for the ranking female to report. The Lord was not apt to panic, even with cause. But afore she spoke he knew in his heart 'twould be bad, mayhap even worse than that fateful night he was awakened with news of the Passing of his sons upon the mainland. In the war. A war he'd attempted to avoid his entire span of days. A war his people had tried to disregard.

"There's been a breach, m'Lord Rohar. Dream Hold is secured, but the sweep continues upon the island. 'Twould be wise for Lady Tialani to remain in her chambers," she began with some reluctance, as one who wasn't quite sure of her station. Leaning forward and peering around his imposing form to ascertain they'd not been heard, she returned her attention to him, speaking softly, and urgently, "M'Lord's presence is required in the library, without delay." Natanamia wasn't familiar with reporting directly to the Lord of the Sprites and she felt awkward. 'Twas Caleichante's duty, and she'd always sheltered her Guard from such diplomatic responsibility, as she believed their skills were best utilized elsewhere. And to make matters worse, she'd had to disturb them in the middle of the night, and the news she came to impart was nothing less than dreadful.
~~~~~

Rohar spun around, silencing his mate's unasked question with a glance, then quickly pulled on his britches and boots, and grabbed a shirt on his way out the door telling her o'er his shoulder to remain in their chambers. Donning his shirt on the run without bothering to lace up the front, he raced down the hall following his Guard toward the library. He reached out his hand and easily caught the curved sword Aiisabeau tossed to him, and rounding the corner his heart pounded in his ears, for he was aware their guest was quartered there. As the first Guardsman on the scene, Niamia stood firm, her eyes roving anxiously 'tween Natan and the Lord. Prepared for the worst, he was still shocked to see the empty pedestal. Everything appeared differently from what he'd remembered. For ages, the light streaming through the skylights above, regardless of day or night, had reflected off the blood red Egg onto the huge pink and white geode behind it, and washed the entire library with a warmth of color. Now, without the deep glittering blush, the illumination of the room was cold and eerily sterile. His eyes took in the scene in the span of a breath, the books strewn about, the broken shelves, the blood. The Spell had been dissolved and the Egg removed, but the pedestal was intact. Rohar knew their guest had some ability to protect himself and if he'd been taken without consent, much more damage should have resulted. He also knew that only one of royal blood could dissolve the Spell. Squinting, the sun began to dawn upon him. His head jerked around to see his Guard flanking him nervously. None could meet his gaze, save the First Mate and Aiisabeau, the most outspoken of the Guard, who stood at her shoulder. His heart burned with trepidation and his throat tightened. He pursed his lips and grit his teeth to avoid any outward show of weakness. Opening his mouth to speak, the First Mate spoke first. He had to give her credit. She didn't back down from his obviously growing fury, despite her discomfort.

"The Captain is also missing, m'Lord." Then with dismay she stated as clearly as she could, "As is the Prince."

Thinking back, 'twas his greatest fear realized. But even though he'd made every effort to avoid the war, he now faced the reality that the war had not avoided him, and all was for naught. 'Twas time to make some hard decisions. But 'twas uncertain what took place here. And how was a battle waged without anyone the wiser? His quick mind already considering the possibility of foul Magic in play, he spoke first with Tialani, then gathered his forces. Despite her urgings to go directly to the Assembly to immediately declare the Captain a traitor, placing a death sentence upon her head, with Calei's recent upheaval of their system he believed there was a spy amongst them, so he avoided the Assembly altogether. Even if they weren't intimately involved, they'd know soon enough. He asked for volunteers. He'd need the best the Guard had to offer to track down the Captain. The only way to find his son and unravel this mystery, was to interrogate Caleichante, but one could get little information from those already Passed. He refused to believe she was a spy or that she'd taken the Prince (let alone their guest) by force, but Tialani's dire words tormented his spirit. What else were they to believe? Initial cursory investigation disclosed 'twas his son's blood upon the floor, the only indication aside from the mess and the missing Egg, that anything was wrong. He didn't even try to squelch the rumors he knew would be all o'er the island within marks, as the sun spread its light upon them from shore to shore. That would have to wait. Besides, everyone's righteous anger might bring in more information, and mayhap something that would prove helpful in the search. Still, he would prefer to see her brought in alive, but the Sprite Nation owed their lives to the Water Dragons, and the Water Dragons had entrusted them as the caretakers of the 7th Egg. Both his son and the Egg must be found and returned unharmed at all costs.

~~~~~ THE WELL OF THE NORTHERN CLIFFS ~~~~~

Calei held the stomach with one arm and Kevon with the other, the saddlebag clasped to his chest even in unconsciousness, sand-
~~~~~

wiched 'tween her and Schlynn's scaled back, her legs squeezing his sides tightly. The Dragon was once again perched upon the edge of the well, ready to dive at her command. His scales glistened with excitement, his long nostrils flaring, his tongue licking in and out of his muzzle as he tensed his muscular body in preparation. Calei blew up the stomach and tucked it tightly under her arm as she took several deep breaths, exhaling each fully afore taking the next. With one final long breath, she signaled she was ready. Immediately the Water Dragon dropped into the well and swam. 'Twasn't that far from the well to the sea, but they had to get as far away from the island as possible afore surfacing for air, all the while praying no other Dragons happened to be around. Calei was counting on those who might report their escape, to be currently busy helping their Ties in their search at the other end of the island. This well, high in the cliff, was deeper than the Grotto afore it opened to the sea, and Calei would have to hold her breath much longer than she had either of the other times. She was hoping the stomach balloon would make the difference, giving her the advantage she needed. Every time she thought her lungs would burst, she exhaled into the sea afore gulping in the air from the stomach, allowing them to travel near three times as far underwater as she could have withstood on her own, surfacing less frequently during the long journey. Schlynn swam on, his short thick wings, powerful legs, and long tail propelling them through open waters, taking them further and further away from home.

~~~~~ **NEAR TWO DAWNS AFTER THE INVASION** ~~~~~

Corbyn the Fay, AKA Corbyn the Raven, AKA Corbyn the Shade, AKA Heir Apparent to the Fay Nation (although, inconveniently, at present cursed and in exile) could not believe what was happening. Perched upon the highest branches of the old cypress outside the Royal Library of the Sprites in his preferred Shift as the Raven, he had to flutter his wings slightly to adjust for the sway from the steady sea breeze, his iridescent feathers glis-
~~~~~

tening, his beady black eyes flashing with annoyance. Had the entire Sprite Nation gone insane?

The Raven had just arrived from the Dragon's Den in Drekinn, drawn by the feeling that some horrible event was taking place here, and now he feared he was too late. Watching and listening with growing irritation, he pieced together the recent events. His longtime friend and onetime student, Captain of the Elite Guard, protector of the 7th Egg and the Sprite Heir Apparent, was missing, as were both of her charges. She was being accused of violent abduction, and the Prince was injured in the process. But his senses told him there was more to this mystery than what seemed apparent.

Suddenly, he spotted a familiar head breaking the surface of the waters just off shore, and he flew swiftly to make contact. Islyth was Myrrdin's Tie, an attractive specimen for a Water Dragon. Her deep green scales and eyes a'glow with golden flecks, 'beautiful' wasn't quite appropriate for her species, although she near qualified. He'd heard other terminology used, such as, 'cute', 'adorable', 'sweet', 'childlike', 'precious', and even 'loveable'. But the most accurate were, 'lethal', 'vicious', 'swift', 'remorseless', 'deadly', and 'immoral'. Corbyn laughed at the last one, for 'twas an adjective earned simply because they thought nothing of consuming their enemy, which at times, included Man. 'Twas a practical solution for which he had respect, rather than condemnation. After all, they could and did distinguish 'tween friend and foe, unlike so many others he knew.

Water Dragons were the fastest creatures in the seas, and swam so fast they essentially flew through the water. With scaled hide, a saw-like ridge they could lay flat along their backs, a vicious row of serrated teeth with front fangs, and a bite that had no rival on Kadoor, they were feared by anyone who knew of their existence. But their unique Magic of invisibility when wet, along with their habit of eating those they caught, left few to report them, therefore, they existed mostly in Legend Song. They'd created the wells throughout the world as their gates inland, for they were awkward on land. Within close range, they could spit a steady stream of water with such velocity and power, 'twould cut an animal in half, or slice through a tree trunk, or break down solid rock, and mixed with special enzymes from glands near their fangs, their saliva became multiple times stronger than any mortar. 'Twas used to solidify the well structures, some of which had stood since long afore the Last Holocaust.

Corbyn and Islyth became friends after her hatching, when she'd Tied to Myrrdin, and she was happy to see him. She'd just been swimming by to check her treasures when she discovered the hostility and fear surrounding the island. Now she was worried, and diving back down to enter the Grotto from beneath the island, Corbyn Shifted to his Fay form, latched onto her thick neck and joined her.

Soon, they arrived upon the ledges of the Grotto, and Islyth slid her way to her pile of treasures. It had grown abundantly since his last visit, but Islyth knew every piece, and nosing her way through the pile, she searched in vain for her most valued treasure, a sunstone she'd discovered o'er a century past, in the wreckage off the barrier reef of Port O'Drekinn.

Both could sense who'd been here recently, and 'twas obvious the piece had been taken by the Captain. Corbyn walked o'er to the distressed Dragon and sat on his heels beside her. Although to most the pile would seem quite disorderly, to Islyth 'twas perfect, and she carefully replaced every treasure the way she'd originally had them arranged, huffing and puffing her irritation all the while.

"Calm down, my friend, 'tis not stolen. 'Tis simply borrowed. You know Calei would never steal from you."

Islyth didn't slow down in her efforts, merely stating, "Calei friend. Calei take. Why?"

"She must have great need to do such."

Islyth suddenly appeared dazed and muttered, "Calei keep. Protect Calei."

Had she spouted prophesy once again? Corbyn furrowed his brows and asked, "What do you know, Islyth? How would it protect her?"

But the Water Dragon was not forthcoming with her knowledge, if knowledge 'twas.

After a few moments, assuming 'twas a simple reference to the Captain's obvious cry for help, Corbyn went on with urgency. "I think I know why she took it, but 'tis very important to find Myrrdin as soon as possible. Things are getting out of hand, and our friend is in serious trouble. Islyth, you must go swiftly to tell Myrrdin what is happening here, and tell him about your missing treasure." Corbyn knew, as well as anyone, that Water Dragons did not take commands kindly, needing the sense that 'twas their idea to perform whatever duty was required, and so he added, "We need to find her afore 'tis too late."

That got her attention. The Dragon turned from her task and sat up on her haunches, her front paws pushed together back to back at the wrists and tucked in o'er her chest as she reflected. "When too late?"

"When they find her."

Now she squinted as the sun began to dawn upon her. "What they do?"

"They will kill her," he stated frankly, knowing full well what her reaction would be.

Islyth reared up high upon her back legs, her thick tail twitching, the saw-like crest along her low back and down the length of her tail, extended rigidly in defensive rage, her short front legs stretched wide, her fangs bared and talons poised to slash. Even her thick wings were fully stretched. "NO! Islyth tell Myrrdin!" High emotion had her spitting like the ocean waves crashing against the cliffs, and Corbyn stepped back a pace to avoid being splattered. As the mighty Dragon turned to dive into the sea, Corbyn had to be quick so as not to lose her, for she'd locate Myrrdin afore he could, and 'twould save him time to allow her to take him there. But finding the Krakken wasn't his foremost concern. Finding Caleichante would be a lot harder.

JUST AFTER THE INVASION OF THE ISLAND OF DREAMS
~~~~~ SOMEWHERE IN THE FAR NORTHLANDS ~~~~~

Finally, they'd reached the mainland. After skipping 'cross the Sea of Dreams, surfacing only for air and to fill the 'balloon' as needed, Calei was exhausted but satisfied that her plan was working. Schlynn traveled faster than any sailing vessel upon the seas, the Krakken coming in a close second, and they arrived afore dawn broke the following day, giving them time to disappear while still dark, mounting the Slyder and riding further inland. This region was not heavily populated and already experiencing hard winter conditions. Without Magic 'twas impossible to sleep, as she was forced to physically hang onto both her charges as well as Schlynn, while he belly-surfed o'er the terrain, propelled by both front legs then both back legs together, creating a straight path upon a slippery surface of a special oil exuded from glands along his sides (which was how they'd become known as 'Slyders'). Since the oil dried and vanished within moments, 'twould be a most difficult trail to follow. 'Twas not the easiest method of travel, for Water Dragons were quite cumbersome on land, but she hoped her chase team would not think to look for such evidence, and by the time they did, 'twould have completely disappeared. Furthermore, she was freezing, and the forward/backward thrusting motion gave her a headache, but at least she hadn't been required to hold her breath for leagues at a time.

Once the sun's rays broke o'er the horizon, they'd found a copse of trees in the thick of the forest and hid underneath the branches 'til dusk, when they mounted the Water Dragon once again, and moved further south. Several marks later, they'd closed in on a small village where Calei stole a horse and blankets. Her Kind never worried about theft on the mainland, for once she had no further need for the horse she'd simply send it back
~~~~~

from whence it came. Kevon had wanted to assist, but his condition was too fragile and he needed rest to keep up his strength to battle the evil Magic within him. He could sit up, feed himself, and converse for short periods, but 'twas an enormous effort to fight the pain, and therefore he slept most of the time. Schlynn returned to the sea to reconnoiter and to find his friend, Islyth. Working their way ever southward, they stayed out of sight, stealing what was needed, staying attuned to any rumors that might pertain to them, hunting and camping to survive. All the while, she hoped beyond hope that Myrrdin would get her message and help would arrive soon, for she knew not where else to turn, out of ideas and running out of time. Surely, he could contact Corbyn, and the Fay would know what to do.

THE KRAKKEN

THREE DAWNS AFTER THE INVASION

~~~~~ SOMEWHERE IN THE SEA OF DREAMS ~~~~~

</div>

With a scowl of frustration 'cross his handsome face, Myrrdin stood upon the quarterdeck, his feet apart, long dark hair pulled back in a single tail with a thin leather strip, hands clasped behind his slim hips, and dark eyes scanning the waters. His white shirt was half laced up the front, revealing smooth, bare muscle, and was tucked into skin-tight leather pants which were tucked into black knee-high boots. He'd been shocked when Islyth suddenly appeared with Corbyn in tow. Stranger still, she was upset but not angry, to report one of her favorite treasures missing. She also reported the island was under a Spell, and she could not travel above the Grotto. They knew that Calei had taken the sunstone, and Islyth offered to give it to her, saying something about it being quite useful in the future. 'Twas baffling. But more baffling, was the whereabouts of the Captain.

He set his jaw, as his mind drifted back to a conversation they'd had long past, which he'd shared with Corbyn while they made their plans. Calei teased him about letting Islyth keep her
~~~~~

treasures in the Grotto. "I merely allow her a place to store them, they cause no harm. Besides, she worries they'd be lost to her, if kept elsewhere." His lovely cousin had retorted with a twinkle in her eye, "And now that I know her hiding place, I suppose if Islyth ever lost one of her treasures, 'twould be I, who'd be blamed for the affront?" His grin had accentuated his good looks. "I'd never suspect you of stealing, just for gain of the item. No, I'd suspect you of being in need, sending a message. Such would be your line of reasoning." Calei had nodded her head and smiled, her golden eyes lighting up with the challenge potential. Myrrdin knew her well. "So, I'd have to ensure my choice was obvious, but not too obvious. A game of riddles. A cup, say, might indicate a need for water, or a platter, food. But those choices are easy to deduce. I suppose I should take something to indicate if I required assistance, or where I'd be found? Indeed, 'twould prove a fascinating game of hide and seek, my cousin. Mayhap we shall play one day."

Corbyn clarified that the island was under a Spell of Silence, with an enhancement to lock down all travel. This, they agreed, meant Calei and the Prince were still on the run. From the old conversation, 'twas determined her choice of the sunstone was not by happenstance, but was to initiate clandestine contact. 'Twould mean she was headed out to sea, and he felt certain she'd been successful. Again, if the choice was not too quickly made, 'twould also indicate where she planned to go. But such had two distinct possibilities. Islyth found the treasure off the barrier reef of Port O'Drekinn, mayhap she sought rescue there? But they originated in the Far Northlands, mayhap she planned to make landfall there? Reasoning further, Port O'Drekinn was near twice as far down the coast from the island, therefore, 'twas near certainly telling him she intended landfall in the Far Northlands. However, if he was correct in how she managed to do this, she'd be long gone by now, and he was a Mariner, not a landlubber. How could he help her if he couldn't find her?

His voice resonating 'cross the deafening waves, he yelled forth his orders, and the crew of the Krakken leaped forth to obey. The Raven flew off 'cross the Sea of Dreams toward the Far Northlands, while the Krakken turned to set sail toward Port O'Drekinn, situated roughly midway along the coast. From there, they'd begin to make their way slowly northward toward Port O'Teliv, watching the coast for any sign of Calei and the Prince, on their journey. Once they arrived, they'd lay anchor and wait for three dawns afore going out to sea. There they'd wait for another three dawns, for Schlynn. If nothing was heard, they'd reverse their course and travel back along the coast, the plan upon which he and Corbyn had agreed. 'Twould give Calei no more window than a sennight, but if she were in need elsewhere, a sennight would be a long wait. Starting at Port O'Drekinn allowed him to sail at a moment's notice to wherever she may be, if Corbyn found her first and sent her to him, and 'twas certain to be the furthest possible site of landfall. Islyth would shadow the Krakken searching for Schlynn. They were doing all they could, but he still felt helpless. Nevertheless, 'twas nothing more he could do while he awaited further revelation. The Highlands were recreating the LifeBond Magic in a mere few dawns, and he knew not how 'twould affect them. "Corbyn, my old friend, be swift," he murmured into the salty air.

CHAPTER TEN

What Magic Was This?

LATER THAT NIGHT

~~~~~ **NORTH BYNDYNN FOREST** ~~~~~

'Twas dark as Calei led the horse o'er to the Prince, and after getting the beast to lie upon the pile of evergreen branches she'd woven to insulate them from the cold ground, she curled up on the opposite side of the boy, sandwiching him 'tween their warmth. Absently, she tucked the blankets around him as he slept. She was exhausted, yet energized with renewed hope. Corbyn had just left, after giving her both good and bad news. The Krakken would soon set sail to Port O'Teliv and she had to hurry to get there afore they weighed anchor and reversed their search along the coasts again, sailing further away for who knew how long. Her best chance lay in reaching them afore they left port. She'd have no more than two or three moons at best, to make that happen. Travel was slow, but she felt confident in her ability to get there in time.

'Twas a great relief to learn that Corbyn was still her ally, but she was too fatigued to be concerned with how quickly he'd located them. After all that had happened thus far, 'twas not hard to accept that Bryynn Reached forth in their need, drawing Corbyn to their camp. The Fay was shocked to learn of the battle in the library, and after confirming neither she or the boy had any outward wounds, 'twas agreed the spy framed her. 'Twas also apparent, although not stated aloud, that the leader of the invasion force had tried to frame Corbyn himself, or at least cast doubt upon the Fay Nation. Staring at the stars twinkling through the branches, she pondered her next move. What she was concerned about, was his near demand that the boy and the Egg be separated. She pointed out that Bryynn was helping him survive,
~~~~~

and in response, Corbyn set a Spell to help relieve Kevon's pain. 'Twould last but a few moons at best, and watching his youthful face as he slept, 'twas effective. And, she had to admit the Egg would draw the Hoard to them now that 'twas off the island. Dare she do as he'd suggested and bury Bryynn in the Bog of St Swiftyn's? Without the Egg, they could travel faster, but to where? And would Bryynn be safe? She had to find the Krakken first, 'twould give her a reprieve from the Guardsmen chasing them, and 'twould provide temporary safe harbor. She'd been so hopeful that Corbyn could Heal the Prince, after all, the Fay were the strongest. Nevertheless, when he'd dashed that hope, he'd provided another. Myrrdin. Closing her eyes for a few well-deserved and very much needed marks of relief, she wondered. What could the Elven Prince do, that the Fay could not?

<div align="center">~~~~~ IN THE SKIES O'ER BYNDYNN ~~~~~</div>

Having seen Calei and the Prince upon their path, Corbyn set wing back to Drekinn. Nothing made sense. Mayhap someone had attempted to frame him for the abductions, and then took advantage of the failed situation to frame Calei. But she'd been certain. The Spell wavered afore the Prince brought it down, and she'd seen the lighting flashes in the Magic bearer's eyes. 'Twas a necromancer of the highest order, one who's identity had eluded Corbyn for eons. The Sorcerer. Who, and of what Race, could he be? For the Spell protecting Bryynn to falter as described, he must have royal blood. But there were only four in the royal family of the Fay. His father, Bardyn the Bear, his mother, Alyphia the Fox, his brother, Brannyn the Falcon, and himself. He'd recently confirmed Brannyn still lived and that the Fay Nation had survived the Last Holocaust, but although he'd made several attempts to contact his brother, his Life Force was shrouded and he knew not what was happening with him. Had he cast his allegiance to the Hoard? His mother was a gentle woman, his father steadfastly refused to acknowledge him or his succession due to the curse, but never left the realm and refused to get involved in the affairs of Man or the outside world. He couldn't believe 'twas his brother, and it couldn't have been his parents, so, how had the Sorcerer made the Spell waver? How had he managed to alter his eyes to appear Fay? What Magic was this?

Corbyn flew ever southward after taking his leave. If a bird could scowl, 'twould be fearsome indeed. Her report was confusing, but even worse was the use of the Spell Sword to try to kill the boy. 'Twas apparent he was only alive because of Bryynn's interference, but now that he was back on the mainland, Bryynn was in as much danger as were Calei and the Prince, and with the attempted abduction 'twas also clear he wasn't safe on the island, either. For the time being, burial in the Bog was the safest option, as Calei would soon find she had an arduous and lengthy journey ahead, and if she didn't succeed, the Prince would die. Calei must not fail, and the Sprite Nation must realize they had to return to the war, for the war had returned to them. The old conflicts 'tween Sprite and Elf must be resolved so they could join again in their strengths. However, the Fay and the Elves had once been close allies, and if the Prince did die, both nations would be blamed, and 'twould be chaos once more. Myrrdin would know what to tell Calei, for Persephone was now their only hope. That is, if his sister yet lived, and if they could locate the Wyrdritch, for the Elven Nation's homeland had been missing and presumed destroyed since the time of the Last Holocaust. But Corbyn never believed that. By the Ancients, let me be right, he thought, as he flew onward to Drekinn.

CHAPTER ELEVEN

The Needle in the Haystack

NEAR DAWN

A SENNIGHT AFTER THE INVASION

~~~~~ THE DAY OF THE FIRST LIFEBOND ~~~~~

Within marks after securing the island and convinced the fugitive had successfully escaped, a volunteer squad of the best of the Elite stepped forth to give chase. First Mate, and now acting Captain Natanamia, left another to stand beside the Lord and Lady as she took command of the chase team. After they sailed, a powerful Spell was Brewed o'er the entire island, to repel anyone from landing or leaving, to maintain security. She was joined by her little sister Niamia, along with fellow Elite, Naftaleah, Aiisabeau, Lyrianei, and Kalisadei. They all agreed that six to one would be at best, even odds, considering whom they were after. With no sign of their quarry, they headed straight for the mainland. Sailing forth, they made landfall near three dawns later, their Dragons returning to the sea. 'Twas the winter solstice, and they huddled together to plan, afore the Magic to be Brewed in Drekinn at dusk, caused issue throughout Kadoor. 'Twould be so strong, 'twas feared her trail might vanish, and they hoped not to lose any more time.

Caleichante was in hiding and covering her path, which in their minds near proved her guilt. They didn't want to believe that, but the evidence against her was mounting. The most obvious questions led to still more. Why did she run instead of reaching forth to her Guard for assistance, and where was she going? How had she escaped? How severe were the Prince's injuries, and why had she not taken him to the Skald? They'd found no indication of her making use of the waterways into the Mainland, their initial efforts to trace her left them bewildered. She appeared to have simply vanished. If she'd abandoned the wells and their Dragons, then the next best method of travel was to Dance the Shadows. But each Dancer left an individual signature which the Guard could identify when set in motion, and not only was there no trace of the Captain or the Prince initiating such upon the island, they'd had no luck finding one along the coastlines they'd checked thus far. Was Kevon still this side of the Veil? And what had she done with Bryynn?

Huddled about a small fire awaiting the dawn, the Guardsmen tried to determine their next move. Aiisabeau's voice broke the silence, saying that which they were all thinking. "We cannot Dance without a known destination, for if she's gone o'er land we might miss her trail. We have no alternative but to trace her a'foot or a'horseback, and to do that we must first locate where she made landfall. If by Schlynn, could be anywhere on Kadoor, if not, anywhere along the entire coast from the Far Northlands to the Southern Slippes of the Razor's Edge. 'Twill be a needle in a haystack hunt, but this needle is invisible, for we seek the best of the best, with a sennight lead. 'Twill take more than skill to find the Captain. 'Twill take the help of the Fates themselves."

Lyrianei nodded her head. "I say Schlynn is the weak link. Send our Dragons to locate him. Surely, he had a part in this. If they can find him, and if they can get him to talk, we might have that help."

Natanamia's eyes narrowed in consideration of the suggestion. "I may add, send our Dragons to speak to all others, tell them to be on the lookout. If seen, or have been seen, they can bring us word of such."

Niamia was restless and irritated. She grimaced. "All good suggestions but hardly useful, as you know as well as I, that Slyders are temperamental at best and forgetful liars at worst." Nia had never Tied, avoiding Water Dragons whenever possible, using the excuse that she didn't want their Magical influence to open her mind to recall that night. She'd rather not remember.

Besides, 'twas clear she had little faith in the creatures. "They gave up their greatest charge upon the first opportunity," she'd retort when others regaled her with stories of their integrity, referring to the transfer of the 7th Egg into Sprite hands after the Last Holocaust. Eventually, all stopped their efforts to get her to Tie.

Defensively, Naftaleah chastised her. "They do not forget. They choose not to recall. Priorities are on a different scale for them. We must always be aware to ask suitable questions to ensure they provide the answers we seek. One can never assume a Slyder will offer up the information on their own, even after we've made it clear 'tis imperative. But they will not lie."

Natanamia was vexed. Her immediate reaction was to defend her sister, but this mission was bigger than their relationship. She squinted and bit her tongue as she allowed her Guard to continue their thoughts. Such was needed to devise a plan.

Lyrianei and Niamia were close friends outside the Guard, but she reluctantly agreed with Naftaleah. "Truth, Slyders are fickle creatures, but they're loyal to their own Ties. If we impress upon them the seriousness of this mission..."

Naftaleah interjected, "If the other Dragons get any notion that Schlynn might be in trouble from us, they'll never tell us anything about him. Only if that trouble comes back to us...for they will protect their Ties against all threats, even from each other."

Kalisadei had been listening to everything said, afore summing up the conversation. "What it comes down to is this. We know Schlynn is safe, if the others do not speak to us of his status. And if he is in no imminent danger, we know that both Caleichante and the Prince are also relatively safe. 'Tis thin comfort, but 'twill have to do."

Natan stood up, the first rays of the sun breaching o'er the distant horizon. "Break camp. We'll obtain horses at the next village. Then we lay low 'til the LifeBond is o'er. Once 'tis done, we ride. As foreign a notion as 'tis, she apparently used not her Magic to get off the island, and will probably continue that strategy, so 'tis not Allure we seek. 'Tis physical tracking we do from here on, to pick up her trail. We'll Dance in fan formation, move camp forward, spread out, and work our way back to each campsite 'til we've covered every square of this wretched land, leaving no gaps. I know you're all adept at such, for to be Elite, your skills are exemplary." Her unconscious glance to Niamia went unnoted, afore she watched as the others hurried to obey her orders. She hoped her sister was up to their current level of need, for this mission would seal her promotion to the Elite.

NIGHT OF THE FIRST LIFEBOND
~~~~~ KADDART ~~~~~

The War Horses of Drekinn were huge animals, quite capable of defending themselves from most predators, and very intelligent, taught to free graze and await their riders for up to a moon, afore returning unerringly to the Dragon's Den. Having located the two Horses a few leagues away from the village, Brannyn knew the Warriors had not left as they'd been advised. Why did Humans have to complicate everything so? He'd been very specific in telling the Elf what to say in her note, and he'd watched her give them the message in the Clear Water Inn, near a sennight past. Observing their escape through the window, he'd been satisfied he'd done what he could. Yet they stayed to continue their snooping, and witnessed the horrific butchery in the arena earlier this night. Now on the run from that stupid Dragon as well as several Agents, he had his hands full.

Known in the Hoard only as the Predator, Brannyn burned through his Magic swiftly, fiercely, replenishing often by borrowing the Magical forte of the Elves and Sprites, draining the Life Forces of the Agents he encountered during the chase. 'Twas ironic. To keep the filth away, he was using the end results of such. He knew he had to distance himself soon, to avoid falling into the same pit of depravity as the rest of the Hoard. He had to keep his wits about him. Melting into the village shadows and back alleys, he tracked the Dragon who was tracking the Team. But what to do with them if the opportunity for their rescue presented itself? He could not risk exposure. No one's life was worth that. Yet if he could, finding the Warriors still in Kaddart came at a most opportune time. The Magic being Brewed even now in Drekinn was of such power, it could mean only one thing. The recreation of the LifeBond. Not only were the Fay the strongest of the Magic bearers, but they knew more than most about the prophesies. Self-appointed care takers, he could sense an urgency, a need, soon to reach the Far Northlands, and these men could fulfill that need, as well as his own. How to get them there? 'Twould take substantial Magic, exhausting him, but any trace would be hidden by the happenings in Drekinn. He followed the Dragon for several marks, powering up his strength on those hapless Agents who fell behind in the chase, or who were just wandering about looking for trouble. Trouble. They'd need never look again.

After the ritualistic rape and blooding of more of Kaddart's youth in the arena, the Hoard Dragon was in a stupor, and although he managed to track the pair, he was always one step behind, allowing the Predator to save most of his increasing energy for the final Push. The Warriors were clever, swift, and daring, and had previously devised an escape route through the aqueducts from the edge of the village, which would take them all the way to Clear Water Creek. But they had to get into the aqueducts without being seen, and then through the tunnel quickly enough to avoid the Dragon's sense of smell. Even in a blood stupor (comparable to being very drunk), the Dragon was tenacious. Still, the elder of them was seriously wounded early in the chase and he'd had to disguise the trailing evidence as well as clean up from their multiple skirmishes (he had to admit they were very skilled), and gather their discarded weapons to keep the pursuing Agents at bay.

Finally, they'd entered their escape route, but the elder was dealing with much blood loss from the sword wound, and falling in the muck, he could go no further. Instead of abandoning his partner, the youth made his stand to defend him. 'Twas admirable, and made the Predator feel that he'd chosen well, for what they'd soon face was far more challenging than what they'd been through this night. Fatigued, weakened beyond belief, and surprised to see him, having expected to face the Dragon or more Agents, the father/son Team were easily subdued by Magic. Brannyn considered his plan. Healing the elder Human, the Push to the Far Northlands, providing for their needs, including their weapons, tack, Horses. 'Twas a huge undertaking, even for one of his talents. After this night, he'd require rest in a safe place for at least a moon, but with the upcoming events 'twould be well worth his efforts. Finding themselves unable to move a muscle, they could do naught but watch while what they perceived to be their final doom, approached.

<center>~~~~~ <strong>MEANWHILE</strong> ~~~~~</center>

The bitter winds hit Anastasia in the face so hard, she thought her eyes would freeze. This couldn't be right. This looked like the Icelands, not at all where she'd expected to be. Stepping forth from a rather elongated Dance, she was nowhere close to the Wyrdritch, and thinking about how she'd missed her mark, she thought she'd felt something while in the portal, as if a strong Magic was being Brewed elsewhere, dragging her further away. But then again, it might've just been this portal. Her long hair blowing in the frosty winds, she scanned the horizon and was certain of only one thing. She was not appropriately dressed. If any of the lost ones stumbled through this, there was little chance of their survival. Goosebumps covering her limbs, and fearing she'd be stranded, she turned quickly, near diving back into the fading portal. But not afore she noticed something very large, flying toward her in the distance. An Ice Dragon? And was that someone waving from astride the big female, or just an active imagination? She tried not to shiver as she focused on navigating back home.

MEANWHILE

~~~~~ IN THE LAIR OF THE HOARD ~~~~~

</div>

The Black sprawled 'cross his throne carved into the rock upon the ledge, giving him the advantage of looking down upon anyone who approached. He'd been conscious of the one who stood there now for some time, forcing him to wait while his anxiety and aggravation simmered. The Evil One was aware the other thought him old, weak, and slow-witted. Quite conscious of his hatred toward him, such knowledge made their confrontations most entertaining. Finally, he rolled o'er, stood up as with great effort, and stepped closer, glaring at his necromancer. His deep voice rumbled through the cavern. "You were to bring the 7th Egg to me. I see it not."

The Sorcerer had to lower his gaze or the Black would see the scorn upon his face. Maintaining this lowly demeanor to placate the demented Dragon, was getting more difficult by the moon. He near had to bite his tongue to spit forth the title by which he was required to address the one standing threateningly o'er him now. His plans were not the Black's, but he'd have to do some skillful mental maneuvering, or he'd soon be on the dinner menu. "Master... I control the actions of the entire Royal House with my contacts, without their even suspecting such. All except the Prince. His Captain appeared to be immune to my Spells, and was somehow able to blanket the boy."

Now this was interesting information, and not what the Dragon had expected to hear. "Immune?"

The ominous tone made him cringe, and 'twasn't an act. It reminded him of when he was a child. Of how the others would laugh at him, tease him. Very soon, he'd achieve the respect he sorely deserved. Still, his lies had to be convincing. "I, I tried, Master, I could not influence her actions."
~~~~~

The huge Dragon turned away and sneered. "What good to me, is a necromancer who cannot b'Spell others?"

Despite fear of retribution, the Sorcerer was smug. "Master, I am compelled to remind you of the enormity of my deeds thus far. The Sprites are not fools, and although it has taken much time, my spies have control of the Assembly, and have infiltrated into their very midst. Not to mention, but I shall, that they no longer have possession of the 7th Egg. The Highlands will soon discover this, and will attack. Their war will lighten our load. At the very least, I've planted significant doubt, and trust, one to the other, is now broken. Furthermore, the Captain will be elimi-nated by her own people, saving us time and resources to do it ourselves. She's still on the run, but her efforts are hobbled by the injured Prince. He will not survive, regardless. The chase team is gaining ground, and she'll not avoid them for long."

The Black turned around again and stepped aggressively closer. "I do not like this alteration of my plans. But it may amuse me, for a time." His massive head lowered 'til 'twas right in front of the other, his eyes blazing, his breath hot and foul, while the Sorcerer stood sweating profusely. "If this does not go as you say, 'twill be your head, which will also amuse me."

Hesitating not, the Sorcerer hurried out of the Lair as soon as he was released, and made his way deep into the forest, where his Dragon was waiting. He'd been expending much energy with his Magic, and without the ability to return to the Link of his own Race, his appetite grew. Even though travel was becoming more difficult, 'twas lessoned somewhat riding the Dragon instead of using his Magic, and he preferred to stay at Evanntyr, where he had more freedom and control. His Life Force was ever thinning with the Evil One's influence, causing him much fatigue and increasing pain, relieved only by feeding. Feeding had become increasingly difficult as well, as he was so involved now, that he could no longer eat food for sustenance. 'Twas only recently that he'd begun feeling ill when he'd tried to eat, and had become so hungry, he'd stuffed himself, only to throw it all up again, time after time. In desperation, he began doing what the others were doing. In the past, the thought of following in their footsteps was revolting and made him gag. But extreme hunger does something to you. Eventually, he'd been compelled to attempt to restore his Life Force with something other than food. He began to feed on blood, then upon depression, anxiety, pain, fear. He'd been successful. In fact, he enjoyed it far more than his memory of food. But he was still new to this, and the transition was taking its toll on his energy levels. Erratic strength was what he told himself had caused the failure of his Spell to take hold of the Prince and the Captain, causing him to alter his original plan. His delusions pleased him.

CHAPTER TWELVE

A Special Remembrance

O'ER A MOON AFTER THE INVASION

~~~~~ APPROACHING NORTH BYNDYNN FOREST ~~~~~

Calei sat up, staring at the rafters of the barn's loft, listening for any intruders to their chosen rest stop. Wide awake and thinking about the past few sennights, she sighed and returned her gaze to the Prince, asleep and covered with straw for warmth. He'd eaten better since Corbyn's Spell, and she felt she'd gotten enough fluids in him to prevent dehydration, but honestly, could she dump Bryynn? She knew in her heart that the little Dragon was helping them in many ways, but 'twas a rhetorical question, as she had to meet the Krakken and that would put off leaving Bryynn 'til later anyway.

Her route brought them south out of the Far Northlands, but 'twas convoluted by necessity, and 'twould be another moon or mayhap even two, afore she could safely reach Port O'Teliv, and then somehow approach to hang out and wait for the Krakken, trying not to draw notice. Her plan was to hide the Prince far outside the village and the port district, allowing Bryynn to care for him while she watched. Although all ships from the island surrounded themselves with the Mist of Forgetfulness whenever they were near the mainland, making them not invisible but simply ignored as if they were, if one knew for what to look and listen, 'twould be easily located. And to her eyes, clear to see. She just had to hope she didn't arrive too soon, or too late. Too soon, and she'd have difficulty keeping her existence a secret as well as avoiding the chase team, too late and they'd be left on their own once again.

She was drained. She'd already gone through several horses, sending each home after getting to their next rest stop, squelch-
~~~~~

ing any possible rumors that they'd been stolen, for mayhap 'twould not be noticed or thought that they'd just wandered off. And Schlynn was staying away. Corbyn told her that he'd pass along the message to meet them in the port, for he'd only draw the chase team to them on land. They'd narrowly missed them o'er the past sennight, and 'twas too close for comfort. 'Twas why she couldn't travel directly to the port, and why she was concerned about being late. At least she knew who was after them, and wasn't surprised at their identities. The best of the best. She smiled. Even being chased, she took pride in the fact that they knew they couldn't take her easily. They'd sent no less than five of her Elite, along with one candidate. This mission would surely push her o'er that line. Six. Six Sprite Guardsmen against one Elite Captain. Nevertheless, her pride quickly faded as the fatigue finally set in enough for her to close her eyes, but sleep came not.

O'ER A MOON AFTER THE FIRST LIFEBOND
~~~~~ KADDART ~~~~~

</div>

When he'd awakened in the abandoned barn, Brannyn had difficulty trying to recall where he was. Oh yes, that farm village. Starving, his efforts had drained him to the point of unconsciousness. Afterwards, he was barely able to climb up into the loft, placing a simple Spell of Avoidance upon the dilapidated door to keep anyone from attempting to enter, afore he'd fallen into a deep slumber. 'Twas evident near a moon had passed since his remarkable feat. No other could duplicate what he'd accomplished. Well, mayhap his elder brother. Thinking about his family never sat well with him, and he glared at his surroundings.

Brannyn stepped out into the dawn, to the view of Kaddart literally going up in flames, being attacked by the Hoard. He watched the demise of the small farming village from the distance, knowing they had no chance against the Black and his followers. 'Twasn't a single King's Agent present; those who'd been stationed here, were likely the first to perish. He felt no pity for
~~~~~

them, for they were expendable. While he listened to the distant screams of death, he wasn't certain what he felt for the hapless villagers. 'Twas not their fault, but war was war. They were in the wrong place at the wrong time, and 'twas nothing to be done about it, now or ever.

The smoke was irritating his eyes, but as he rubbed them he eventually realized 'twasn't the smoke. Still in Link with the Warriors, they Shared his vision, but how? The father/son Team seemed to share something more than just their stealth talents. He quickly broke the Link, and moved away from the village toward the forest. Hungry beyond belief, finding something to eat was his first need, which put him in the perfect place to observe an epic rescue by a LifeBond Team. So, the ancient Magic had prevailed once again. His senses told him that there were now 13 such Teams in existence.

The following dawn, after having spent several marks thoroughly quenching his appetite, he combed the fields, then the remains, salvaging the teeth of the Hoard Dragon killed by the two rescuers, in hopes of identifying the idiot. The Team who'd done the deed consisted of a big blue, swift, skilled, and vicious, his partner a Warrior of the Dragon Clan. She was a stunning specimen of Mankind, although rather short. But her buxom curves melded with her muscled body into a sensual package that would make any man's heart burn with desire. And, she was a dynamic swordsman, strong, fast, and tenacious. They were perfectly matched.

Now he stood at the edge of the forest, watching the pair who'd returned to the scene of their first successful kill, as they searched for something. 'Twas most likely the very blade he'd found earlier, after seeing it fall from her hand amid yesterday's aerial battle. He'd Masked as soon as they appeared in the western skies, abandoning the carcass and literally walked unnoted 'tween them in the field. But his strength was still somewhat diminished, leaving him unable to sense who they were 'til they left and he could drop the Mask. Amazed, 'twas Darque, the Human known as the Dragon, and Gunnarr the Mighty Blue, High Prince of the Highlands, of whom the Hoard so feared. The prophesies surrounding the pair ran deep, Darque destined to Command the Resistance. The Black would pay well for her demise. 'Twas her blade he held. Palming it, he smirked at his good fortune. 'Twas of greater value than he'd originally thought.

<center>~~~~~ THE FAR NORTHLANDS ~~~~~</center>

Near a moon after the two men were Pushed from the aqueducts, they awoke to the horror of the Battle of Kaddart as if 'twas a nightmare. However, they could not ignore the strength of the Magic that sent them to this place, healed the elder of the wound that should have forced him Past the Veil, and included their War Horses and tack, as well as all their discarded weapons now present and accounted for. 'Twas irrefutable, and they had to accept that what they'd seen was somehow reality. Kaddart was no more. Bastyen tried not to think about the girl to whom he'd been so attracted, for her fate might never be known. Instead, they immediately set to work on survival, for 'twas mid-winter with heavy snows, and they were in unfamiliar territory with limited resources. Finding their way back to Drekinn to make report to the Battle Commander could only be accomplished if they could positively identify their location, and lived to tell the tale. Working their way southward o'er the most challenging land either of them had ever experienced, Graasyn and Bastyen, the most highly skilled and respected Stealth Team operatives of the Warrior Brotherhood, traveled through the bitter cold, thick forested, mountain range, using the skipping stone method from one campsite to another, 'til they stumbled upon the Bog of St Swiftyn's. 'Twas initially disappointing, for this meant they'd not traveled true south, but almost as if pulled, they'd veered eastward. 'Twas proof of their location, which had been sorely lacking prior, nonetheless, such proof was merely a temporary victory, as the Spring Melts came directly after. Fast and furious, the rivers raged and swelled and surrounded them upon a triangular spit of land they could not escape 'til the dangerous floods ran their way to the seas beyond.

~~~~~ O'ER TWO MOONS AFTER THE INVASION ~~~~~

'Twas touch and go but Calei continued to avoid the chase team, using all her skills to keep from being found. The Prince was awake and able to assist about half the time now, and although he was weak, Corbyn's Spell helped. To save his energy, she gave him simple tasks to perform while she was away, such as making snares, or weaving branches for under their blankets as insulation. Usually, when she returned from her hunting or reconnoitering missions, he was fast asleep. 'Twas doubtful he'd even remember this time, or any of the events since he was wounded, and 'twas probably for the best.

Finally, they'd approached Teliv Village, and she found an abandoned storage barn about a league distant. 'Twas a suitable place to leave Kevon at night, while she hung out in the taverns of the port district, listening and watching for the Krakken to arrive. Upon the second night, she saw two Humans who were different from the normal clientele, and as she brushed past, was fascinated to note they were covered in the scent of Dragon. Watching them during the early marks, she determined they were not Hoardsmen, but were seeking information. Her acute hearing identified that which they sought upon the black market. 'Twas interesting, and she knew they had succeeded in making the 'Bond, so she followed them down to the docks when they left, and confronted them. The female was named Ariel, her Dragon, Zaydarr. She knew Zaydarr and Gunnarr the Mighty Blue, were cousins. This raised her confidence considerably. The male was Rygyl, his Dragon, Tegrynn. The Dragons knew what she was, but didn't break her confidence, and this gave her reason to assist them. After all, the LifeBond was recreated to fight the Black
~~~~~

and the Hoard, and this was a war they must win. Helping the Humans seemed the right thing to do. She couldn't tell them outright that Drekinn Village was situated upon the remains of the oldest mountain on all Kadoor, one that was once a Dragon's Lair, wherein was stashed much treasure and 'trophies' that included talons, fangs, and Dragon's Eyes. If she told them too much, too quickly, they'd suspect her of being a spy. Besides, she had her own mission, and wasn't certain of their loyalties. So, she simply set up a meeting for two nights hence, telling them to bring her something she wanted. A Clan sword. Rygyl had immediately offered his own, but 'twas too big for her hands, so 'twas agreed they'd return after getting that for which she'd asked. If her information was good, the sword was hers.

However, early the following evening, Calei watched with tears in her eyes as the Krakken tied up at the docks, Schlynn splashing in the water alongside. The Warriors and their Dragon partners were forgotten as Schlynn took her back to collect Kevon, and disposing of their stolen supplies, they returned in Slyder fashion all the way up the gangway.

ABOARD THE KRAKKEN

~~~~~ MYRRDIN'S QUARTERS ~~~~~

</div>

"The boy is in good hands, Calei. He's resting below deck. Let my Skald do what he can. Here, drink this, you look as if you could use it, and more." Myrrdin thumped a large glass in front of her on the table, which finally got her attention, and then filled it from a bottle with a cork he now held 'tween perfect white teeth. She watched in fascination as the amber stream poured forth from somewhere above her head, and quickly filled the glass.

Taking it in both hands, she lifted it to her nose. With interest rising, she asked, "And this is what?"

After filling his own glass, he re-corked the bottle, and replied, "Drekinn Whiskey. I have learned much from Humans, including appreciation for the finer brews. This particular bottle
~~~~~

has been aged several winters and hails from the Dragon Clan, known for some of the best brews in all Kadoor. I was saving it for a special occasion. I think 'tis appropriate for this night."

Myrrdin refilled her glass as they drank, encouraging her to talk. She told him about the invasion, the battle in the library, the Spell Sword, the harrowing escape, and subsequent chase. He listened for near three marks as she finally completed her tale with boarding the Krakken. He'd been leaning forward throughout the story, his elbows resting on the table so he could keep her glass full without her noticing his was not. He'd never seen her so battle-weary. She needed the rest she'd get tonight. However, her revelation that Corbyn couldn't Heal Kevon, and then sent her to him as if he could, was perplexing. He sat upright when 'twas clear she had no more to say, gazing into the remaining dregs in the bottom of her glass, which she continued to hold with both hands. Crossing his arms o'er his chest, he pushed back, balancing his chair on two legs, and sighed. "Calei, I cannot heal the boy," he began, sadly. She turned to him, an expression of defeat in her eyes. 'Twas a look he'd never seen there afore, and caused him great distress.

'Twas not what she'd wanted, or thought, to hear, and defeat was not in her vocabulary, yet for the first time in her span of days she felt it hit her square in the chest and she could do naught but stare in silence. What was she to do now? Was it o'er, then? Had she failed the Prince?

Myrrdin's heart went out to her as he rubbed his chin with one hand and desperately tried to think of some way he could help. As he sat, his mind retreated to the past. Suddenly, he understood why Corbyn sent her to him. 'Twas not just for the respite. Beginning with some hesitation, his voice grew stronger as did his confidence. "But, I know who can." Dropping his chair back to the floor, he continued, "'Tis a long story, and I need to give you some background afore I send you on your way, for I cannot make this journey with you. What I'm about to reveal is not common knowledge. I owe my life to Corbyn. Without him, only the Fates know where I'd be right now. I have much for which to thank him, but at this moment, I thank him for his long memory, for I'd not thought about my family in many winters. It all started shortly afore the Retreat, when I learned of a prophesy and tried to use it as incentive to get my father, King Jeeryd, to listen to a young Elf by the name of Diadranei, who was best friends with my sister, Persephone. Each of them had a rare and unique Magic, each unrecognized by the King. Diadranei argued with the Counsel that we could stand together and defeat the Evil One, something I very much wanted as well. Persephone was a Healer, but not any ordinary Healer, and I could tell 'twas much more to her Magic. But I was forbidden to speak of it, especially to her. Then I learned of the prophesy that said there would come an Elven maiden of extraordinary Gift, who would Heal the Nation. As a young man looking for a war, and a cause for which to stand, I believed that one was my sister, and I interpreted it to mean that she would Heal whatever happened to us as we fought in the war. However, immediately after mentioning this, Jeeryd informed me that he already knew of the prophesy. But he wouldn't let Persephone know, nor would he enlighten her to her strength, for he didn't want it to be realized. He couldn't kill her, for that would cause his own destruction, therefore, she was safe. I was taken by his guard and did not even have the chance to speak with my siblings afore I managed to escape, never to return. I later learned that Jeeryd had decreed I was to be killed on sight, and if ever I set foot in the Wyrdritch again, the same fate would befall my siblings. O'er the winters, I tried to think of a way to get back, to rescue my siblings, but then my mother would be in danger. I discovered evidence that Jeeryd was in league with the Black, and keeping my sister under his thumb to hide his past indiscretions, fearing the prophesy meant she'd disclose such. You see, he was responsible for the deaths of the past King, Lucien, and his sons, Typeth and Grygoth, who were all forced Past the Veil in an ambush. After which, Jeeryd, as Lucien's nephew and last living heir, stepped forth and took the crown, along with Typeth's promised mate, Bryanna. Calei, I am convinced my sister can Heal Kevon. That is, if she yet breathes, and if you can find her. For the Wyrdritch disappeared during the Last Holocaust. 'Tis both good news and bad, I know. But 'tis all I have to offer."

Calei was delighted. "'Tis much you offer, my cousin, and now I have a plan into which I can sink my dagger and hang on tight. You have given me new hope, as well as new energy!" Pushing her glass away, she attempted to stand up to emphasize her faith in the plan and in her ability to succeed, but somehow her legs wouldn't cooperate. The last thing she remembered was stretching out on the floor, while Myrrdin carefully tucked a blanket around her and placed a pillow under her head, for which she murmured her sincere gratitude.

~~~~~ NEAR THREE MOONS LATER ~~~~~

Niamia faced Natan, the others glaring at her from where they all stood around the fire, their frustrations with their own failure, building toward the 'lone wolf' newcomer. She didn't care. When she was the one who found Calei and returned the Princes safely to Lord Rohar, they'd really feel frustration. She clenched her fists and curled her lip in anger. The Captain had friends in high places, any of whom would assist her if needed. Calei had not been seen, and the few leads they'd found had led to dead ends, obviously planted trails to throw them off. The others were concerned as well. Surely, they'd not completely lost her. Once again, Nia defended herself to the Elite. She had to be the one who found the Captain. She'd do anything to satisfy that need. "I was trying to find her trail, of course. You know I work better alone. I can't concentrate when I'm surrounded, and I can focus out there in the quiet. Besides, we should have someone patrolling in a wider arc. The Captain could take advantage. And no, I found nothing." She crossed her arms o'er her chest and glared
~~~~~

back at the others. Mayhap 'twas time to unveil her theory. "Do you not think 'tis odd that there's been no real trace, no rumor, not a hint of her, for o'er three moons? She must be at sea, and not by Dragon. She's with Myrrdin, she has to be."

When the others gasped, taking to their feet in anger, Natan nodded and waved them down. She'd handle her sister. Although 'twas not wise of Nia to leave on her own, and technically violated orders, they were all frustrated. Nia was younger and more impatient than the rest of them, and she could forgive her. However, her accusation against Myrrdin was not only audacious, 'twas near treasonous. "We all know that Calei and Myrrdin are close, but he would not support anyone against the Nation. He would not cause harm to come to the Princes. We shall speak of this no more."

Nia opened her mouth to retort, but the look in her sister's eyes made her stop and rethink her brashness. 'Twas not wise to cause too much trouble. Still, she knew she was right and her sister had to be aware, as well. She pursed her lips together and vowed silently that she'd be the one to find them. If not, 'twould be Flame to pay.

<p style="text-align:center">~~~~~ PORT O'DREKINN ~~~~~</p>

The Ship's Master sat 'cross from Calei once again, at the table in his quarters. "Do you have everything packed? Is there anything else I can do, afore you take your leave?" He was concerned about his protégé, but there seemed nothing more he could offer. He'd taught her well; the mission was hers to complete. During the slow voyage to Port O'Drekinn, the destination and length of time chosen for several factors, including respite, rebuilding Calei's strength, putting her through special training for what was to come, and to throw off the chase team, they'd discussed plans and counter-plans, routes, dangers, timing, and more, at this very table, for days on end, which was why he was glad he'd finally gotten her to sleep that first night, after which she'd slept well throughout the voyage, with the Princes in the care of the Ship's Skald. For certain she'd not sleep so well again, for a long time.

Corbyn flew in once during the long voyage, reporting that he'd laid false trails to entertain the chase team, knowing Calei would require knowledge of their whereabouts upon departure. Calei had refused most supplies, for she could easily live off the land, only accepting that which Kevon would require, leaving them traveling light and fast. She and her cousin were very much alike. She could tell he was concerned, but his faith was empowering. Still, this mission was by far the most dangerous and important of her career, let alone her span of days, and whether she succeeded or failed, 'twould have long reaching consequences. She thought momentarily about what she could give him in return for all that he'd done for her as her past trainer and steadfast supporter through scandal and trial, good times and bad, as well as the special training that he'd provided for this mission. She was stronger, faster, and in better shape now, than she'd been o'er a century prior. How could she give him back the confidence that he inspired in her? She cocked her head. "This 'whiskey'. Do you have more?"

Laughing, Myrrdin reached into his cabinet and placed a new bottle 'tween them in the middle of the table, with a solid thunk.

Calei smiled, stood up ready to leave, then gently pushed the bottle closer to her cousin, keeping her eyes upon his. "Save this one for my return."

<center>~~~~~ SHORTLY AFTER ~~~~~</center>

She was gone. They'd left his cabin and finalized her plans upon the quarterdeck, while the Krakken tied up to the dock and lowered the gangway. No one heard or saw her daring departure within the Mist. They had few horses aboard, but all were fast and of good breeding and he'd offered her any of them, with full tack. But she'd not claimed one, choosing only a bedroll with her minimum of extra supplies wrapped within. Disappearing below deck, she returned to his astonishment, astride his personal horse, Demonseed, a thick muscled, pitch black, spirited stallion with long flowing mane and tail, his eyes blazing red like fiery coals. The strong-willed stallion was the fastest horse he'd ever bred and trained, and could be the most obstinate. Racing down the wooden planks, the boy was clutched tightly to her chest, the Egg in the bag 'cross her shoulder, her long white hair flying behind her in a single tail woven with a crisscrossed leather strip. 'Twas a breathtaking sight, as Demonseed near soared through the Port District, his hooves barely touching the cobblestones.

The Mist clung to them as they successfully navigated the early morning crowds oblivious to their existence, but would dissipate as they distanced themselves from the Krakken. He expected the stallion would give her trouble, as he'd never allowed another to ride, but then he chastised himself. Calei was an excellent rider, and her bold maneuver more than suggested she'd managed to establish sufficient rapport. Shaking his head, he hoped 'twould make the difference in their journey. Calei must travel halfway 'cross Kadoor, through Byndynn Forest, o'er the Raptor's Talons, then deep into Darkling Forest, and even if she made it that far, she had to find the Wyrdritch, something no one had done. Once again, he mused o'er the many fighters he'd helped train in the past, knowing their strengths and weaknesses intimately. All things considered, if anyone could complete this mission, 'twould be his cousin. The two Princes could not be in better hands.

For near a quarter mark he stood motionless. Observing the bustling port district, his dark eyes scanned everything, missing not a single detail. The sounds, the smells, the pace of life along the coasts, was that for which he lived. Finally, accepting 'twould be many moons afore he might have word of her fate and that of her charges, he turned away from the docks, whispering a plea into the winds for Corbyn's help. Barking his orders to the crew, they headed out to sea, where they set sail to meet their next client. 'Twas back to business as usual for the Krakken.

Lisa Dron

CHAPTER THIRTEEN

House of Cards

~~~~~~~~~~

The dash through the port district was exhilarating. With her heart racing, reflexes sharp, and her vision sharper, they'd left both the Krakken and the coast behind. She didn't look back 'til they were long away, positive they'd not been observed or followed.

Calei and Myrrdin had discussed the numerous dangers she faced. 'Twas a basic two step mission, but hounded by the chase team and the Hoard, along with who knew how many others, she had to eliminate as much as possible, allowing her relative freedom to complete the first step afore continuing on the main leg of the mission. Since 'twas impossible to eliminate the Hoard, she must eliminate the chase team. These Sprites were hers, the best of the best, her friends, comrades-in-arms. She'd chosen them, trained them, helped them through the many winters and trials of their careers, cried with them and laughed with them. She'd rather not shed their blood, but she'd do what was necessary. She'd been running and hiding since they'd left the island, accepting that she may never return home. Now that she had a plan, 'twas time to take the reins and do what she did best. She turned Demonseed northward once again, back to Byndynn Forest. Back toward the last place Corbyn told them he'd sent the chase team.

~~~~~ DAYS LATER ~~~~~

When she'd first arrived, 'twas with the notion that she'd have to do the unthinkable. Calei discovered them after some tracking, and was impressed with their skills. She skirted wide around and positioned herself 'tween them to the south and the Bog to the north, as she watched for her chance. Could she kill them? She had the expertise, but admitted to herself that she had not the heart, and 'twould be tragic. She considered. They had orders to kill her on sight, was turning the table any less honorable? 'Twas certain she should not take them all on in a frontal attack. 'Twould be too risky. She could take them out as they patrolled, one or two at a time. She sighed. Killing them without a fair fight was not something she could do, despite the situation. She had to at least give them a chance, but such meant she was taking her own.

Changing campsites every few marks, she'd just settled the Prince afore she briefed him on her plans, then covered him with the branches and left him hidden under the large pine. He'd barely heard her, but she was confident he knew enough to keep quiet. Truth be told, he was aware of less and less outside the world of pain in which he now lived. He'd sleep, while she went out again and followed the Sprites, hoping for another option to present itself. It did. Since finding the chase team she'd noted something peculiar. One of them would leave the others, usually for a period of a mark, mayhap half a day, returning at dawn or dusk in time for her watch. She was too far distant to lip read or hear their conversations. When she saw the one slip away again, she followed. Calei initially thought she was trying to track her, but was soon convinced by her behaviors that the Sprite was trying to contact someone.

Returning to the Prince after the third such observation in as many days, she laid awake for near a mark, trying to put the puzzle together. Why was Niamia going out on her own? 'Twas obvious by their reactions to her absences that she had no orders to do so and they were not happy about it, yet she seemed not to care. Who would she be trying to contact? Whomever 'twas, she'd not been successful and although she was not perturbed by her team members' reactions, she was distraught by the lack of response to her efforts away from their campsite. She shook her head. 'Twas as if she were seeking orders.

Suddenly, the past hit her and she gasped. Orders. Vampyr. Mouthing the word with distaste, enough clues came together to cast doubt upon one whom no one would have thought to blame.

The others could not sense her deceit for they were distracted, feeling only agitation with her for not following orders and slowing down the chase. But Calei's senses were a'Flame. Still, she must get on with her mission. Time was running out and she had but one option. Carefully crawling from under the branches, she covered the Prince once more, and then mounted Demonseed and turned back toward the Sprite camp.

<div align="center">~~~~~ <strong>NEAR A MARK LATER</strong> ~~~~~</div>

Natanamia sat upon the fallen log at the edge of the darkness, staring into the fire. The rest were on watch or patrol, and after careful observation, Calei knew they'd be out of the way long enough to complete her task. 'Twas her chance. Camouflaged with mud, twigs and leaves, the Captain of the Guard stepped quietly forth from the shadows to reach around her friend's neck, the blade held tightly against her throat, one arm locked behind her. She didn't want to cause injury, just prevent her from crying out or starting a fight. With a steady voice, despite the gravity of the situation and the energy expended in this maneuver, she spoke softly into the other's ear. "Truce, my friend."

Although startled by the move, showing her how inattentive she'd become due to her focus upon Niamia's behavior, the First Mate didn't flinch, but had to be just as soft in her reply, to avoid the razor-sharp edge of the blade. 'Twould be impossible to cry out for help afore her throat was slit. "Agreed."

Calei was proud of her protégé. Her reflexes were very good. But what she had to do was not something of which she was proud, and she'd wish it upon another. "Where's Niamia? Seems she's been absent much lately, has she not?"

Instantly, fear mixed with anger spewed forth as she hissed, "What do you mean? What have you done to her?"

Calei shook her head. This might be more difficult than she'd thought. Nia hadn't even been relieved of watch yet. Disappointed, she reminded her past student, "Oh Natan. Regardless of the truth, your first response should've been to make me believe Nia was upon my flank." She had to open Natan's mind to the truth. She sighed and then began again. "I've done nothing, for she's not found us. But as I'm sure you're aware, I have been watching. And as I'm also sure you're aware, if I'd wanted to kill anyone, 'twould have been done. You know of what I am capable."

Natan relaxed noticeably in her arms. With more control, she swallowed her pride. She knew she wasn't using her training, and she had to step up to become a better Captain. She chose to learn from her friend once more, and replied somewhat perplexed, "You know our every move and could easily avoid us, yet you walk into our very midst. We're actively seeking your capture, and you're outnumbered. Why place yourself in such danger? 'Twould not be to feed an inflated ego. Why are you really here?"

Hope bloomed as she realized her friend was listening. She might yet see. "I was framed, Natan. A Hoard contingent infiltrated Dream Hold and tried to abduct the Egg. During the battle, only the blood of the invaders was shed, nevertheless, the Prince did suffer severe injury. I knew the Hold had been compromised, and now Kevon and the Egg must be protected. I will do so to my last breath. Know this: there is but one in all Kadoor who can Heal him, and Kevon will die if my mission to reach that one, fails. The journey is long and extremely dangerous, and I can use all the help I can get, for not only do you give chase, so too, the Hoard, to ensure the capture of Bryynn and the death of his defenders. Thus far we fare well, but travel is slow, and time is running out. Make no mistake, I will do what needs doing, if the Fates bring us together again." She hesitated as she let Natanamia absorb all that she'd said.

Natan could sense something wasn't right. Not just the obvious, but something even more sinister. "'Tis more to tell?"

Calei took a slow breath. "I came to plead my cause to be allowed to continue my mission unimpeded, and to caution you that the island has been infiltrated. But worse yet, there is one amongst you now who no longer answers to the Sprite Nation, let alone the Guard. She will soon be ordered to eliminate you all, and then I would be obliged to hunt her down. But I have not the time, and I have few friends. I came to give you warning. Death sneaks up upon those who refuse to see the danger closest to them. If you want to return home alive, you must harden your heart, for you risk the worst type of betrayal: being forced Past the Veil by one you love, as have many in your life." Relaxing her lock on the other's arm, she slowly withdrew her blade as she spoke, her voice becoming a mere whisper. "You must open your eyes, or you shall be sent Beyond, still blind to the truth. As were we all, when your family was lost." She paused. "All but Nia."

When several heartbeats passed in silence, Natan reached slowly up to her neck, and then twisted around to confirm she was alone in the darkness. Even her Sprite vision couldn't penetrate the shadows. 'Twould do no good to seek Calei this night, and she'd be long away by dawn. She sat still on the log and pondered the cryptic messages imparted by her friend. Surely 'twas a powerful warning, or such an effort would not have been made. Given the situation as per their orders, not only should she be dead, she should still be in danger from the very one who should have already sent her Beyond. Yet she was not. 'Twas why she'd not resisted. 'Twas a palpable truce 'tween them that was not to be disregarded. She'd been in no danger from the Captain, yet Caleichante was supposedly a blood thirsty murderer and remorseless kidnapper. Had they been wrong about her and the Prince? What the Flame was going on? Was the Captain framed? 'Twould have taken much Magic... or... just enough mixed with the emotions of the night. Her eyes widened with the possibility. And who was there afore anyone else? Who 'stumbled' upon the scene, and then alerted the rest of the Guard? Seeking the answer, she glanced 'cross the fire to Nia's empty bedroll.

Her mind wandered back to a time she'd long since tried to forget. 'All but Nia,' Calei said. Had Nia known more than she'd revealed about the murders of their parents and siblings? There were yet unanswered questions about the winters-old cold case, but no one thought to ask Nia. She'd been in shock when they'd found her after she'd stumbled upon the gruesome scene, and her memory of that time was forever erased. Or so they'd been led to believe. Natan sheltered her little sister, harboring her own guilt for not being there for her and their family, for being unable to save them, and then for being unable to bring their killers to justice. Although Niamia was a very good bowman, long had Natan excused her sister's less than exemplary conduct in the Guard, protecting her on her rise to the Elite. Had she done the right thing by ignoring her brash behavior?

Natan was acting Captain now, yet she felt compelled to do as Calei said, open her eyes and be objective in her view of those for whom she was responsible. And that view kept getting uglier 'til dawn, while she remained staring at Nia's empty bedroll 'cross the fire. As the past replayed in her mind, every grisly detail, every word, every aspect of the timing and the investigation, all the unanswered questions, her jaw tightened and her anger grew. With eyes narrowed, she wondered, had Niamia truly not remembered that night? 'Twas convenient, as although she was not present, she could not recall why she'd left, when, or what she'd done afore returning to discover the carnage. Sprites could sense deception, but not if 'twasn't expected or focused upon. And why had she never Tied with a Water Dragon partner? Was her excuse of not trusting them, valid? Mayhap she didn't want their 'Magical influence' to see through her facade, for the deceitful could not make the Tie. If 'twas truth, she would have been rejected, her deception clear to all. There were too many questions, let alone the similarity in the situations 'tween the murders and the abductions. And then there was the type of Magic that might have been used to alter everyone's perception, Suggestion Magic, which fed on the emotions of the seer. Suggestion was a strength of Nia's.

Mixed with disbelief and shock, she knew in her heart that at least one spy in the Sprite Nation was her own blood. Nia had appeared to have an alibi, but now 'twas questionable at best. Regardless of her possible guilt, she couldn't have created the entire event alone. She would have needed assistance, but she could have orchestrated their deaths. If they'd been sedated by loss of Life Force, they'd not have moved, let alone screamed out, when they were so brutally slain. 'Twould make a lot of sense of the scenario they'd encountered. Vampyre. Her nostrils flared in disgust. But why had he or she not just sucked them dry? Why finish with a blade? Because there were six of them. Taking just enough to force a deep sleep upon the host would have been safer than taking all from one then another, and 'twould have caused problems with the consumer of so much energy, while one might have gotten away with taking small amounts throughout the afternoon. And, if one had awakened or noticed what was happening, who would be easily ignored for being less likely to cause them harm than someone they trusted? As well as the fact that the bloody scenario redirected everyone's attention from the true culprit. Yes. Nia could have been involved, even if not the wielder of the blade. She could have...

Lyrianei broke her concentration as she stepped up, seeking permission to speak. "Sir?"

The interruption brought Natan back to the present. She was in charge here. There were Guardsmen to protect, a duty to serve and to seek justice. Long had she known of the growing misgivings of the others for Nia. They merely showed respect for Natan's sake, but since leaving the island, confusing events and excuses were mounting, and there was but one truth. Without looking up, her eyes still fixed upon Nia's empty bedroll, she curtly stated, "Speak."

'Twas an account Lyri had made several times since the chase began, and had become somewhat routine. Every time Nia left, Lyri feared for her safety, knowing of what the Captain could do, but this time seemed different. Still, she wanted to believe the best and not think about what could be. "Aiisabeau reports that Niamia is missing again. We've not found her in the surrounding woods, but she and Kalisadei are still searching. No one has seen her since she was relieved of watch at second mark."

"And?" Natanamia could not bring herself to say more at this point. Not like in times past, when she'd leaped to Niamia's defense. After all, Nia had always appeared again, with some excuse or other. Mayhap 'twas the same.

Expecting a response that didn't come, Lyri noted the change and tried to answer appropriately, although she wasn't quite certain what more she was supposed to report. "Her water bag, horse, extra food, everything but the bedroll is gone." Again, she added cautiously, "No one heard or saw anything."

Natan's gaze wavered not from 'cross the fire, but she did sit up a bit straighter when she questioned again, "And?"

Lyrianei swallowed hard. 'Twas as if the Captain was asking her opinion about the situation. Caleichante always made such requests clear, but Natanamia wasn't giving her anything to go on. She decided to risk all and say what she thought. "'Twould be logical if she'd left of her own accord, that she'd take her belongings, and if not of her own accord, her belongings, especially her horse, would be left behind, Sir. Unless she Danced, of course… "

Finally looking up, Natanamia surprised her once more by simply asking again, "And?"

Lyrianei was becoming more perplexed with the line of questioning, but at this point, Kalisadei stepped into view of her superior and stated firmly, "I personally do not think she's on patrol, or whatever 'twas she was doing all those times she went off on her own, nor do I think this is the work of Caleichante."

'Twas what she'd wanted to hear, and not. Without leading them to this conclusion, 'twas in alignment with her own judgements. Still, she wanted the situation as they saw it, and she knew they'd been sidestepping that for some time. 'Twas her own fault.

Accepting the reality, Natanamia simply shifted her gaze from one to the other, and repeated, "And?"

Lyrianei hesitated to say that which they all felt, for Niamia was her best friend. Naftaleah had been listening to this exchange with great interest, for she was the one who had relieved Niamia at watch and she'd felt something wrong at that time. She had no such quandary and spoke first. "She seemed prepared to go, leaving her bedroll to avoid confrontation or early detection. I, too, believe she left on her own, Sir. And this time, I do not believe she intends to return."

Her summation was akin to what Natan used to hear given to the Captain. She stood up, her face hard, her tone even harder. "Call in Aiisabeau and break down camp. Our original orders are rescinded under my command 'til further notice. The Captain of the Guard is no longer our prime objective. For now, I believe the Princes are safer with her, than they would've been with us."

Lyrianei raised her brows in surprise. "Sir?"

With venom in her voice and fire in her soul, she looked at each of them and responded, "We've been used. 'Twas my sister all along. I don't know how she did it, but I shall learn the truth. She's to be considered unstable, wanted for treason, accessory to murder, attempted murder, and attempted kidnapping. Her disappearance tells me that she knows we've become aware of her deceptions, and that she's gone rogue. We must find her afore she finds Calei and the Princes, and adds to her list of crimes. And to mine, for I blindly believed, when as a Guardsman, I knew better. I want her brought in alive if possible, but I want her brought in!"

<p style="text-align:center">~~~~~ EARLIER ~~~~~</p>

At precisely second mark, Niamia's world collapsed. Even covered with mud and twigs, there was no mistaking Caleichante melting into the shadows after leaving her sister. The very thing she'd tried so hard to prevent, just happened right under her nose. With the meeting of the two leaders, the seed of doubt was planted and the truth would soon blossom. Nia's house of cards was tumbling down. Just relieved of duty, she'd already planned on making another short trip, coming back with some excuse or other in a few marks after she'd tried to get in touch with the Sorcerer... again. She was getting fed up with this arrangement. Seems she was on her own.

Gritting her teeth with the realization she'd been abandoned, she seethed in rage. All she'd done to try to best her sister, had become more than she'd expected. The unnamed Assemblyman only wanted information, and she'd been guaranteed boundless reward. She thought they'd told her the truth about what Natanamia said, how she lied to her, taking her place in the Guard and leaving her the caretaker of the rest of their family, when 'twas Niamia the Guard really wanted. But the more she participated, the worse things became, and eventually, even though she wanted to stop, they threatened her with exposure for what she'd already done. Then came the best offer yet. Give them a little more and they'd make her a Guardsman. She might even usurp Natan in a few winters. But she couldn't do that while having to care for her aging parents and siblings, and her parents would soon discover her treasonous past, for they were closing in on the lies and inconsistencies in her excuses.

She hadn't planned on the level of violence, the resulting loss of her family, but, 'twas what gained her sister's notice. The sympathy was sweet revenge, the leg up into training and then entry into the Guard itself, fulfilling her ultimate desire. Besides, she had to admit 'twas a thrill taking just enough, not crossing the line. She'd thought 'twas just so she could make her rendezvous without anyone noticing. No one met her, and after more than a mark, she'd suddenly realized why she'd been so ordered. Racing home, 'twas real emotion hit her when she saw the carnage. But although she'd been shocked and continued to be saddened by their loss, 'twasn't her hand that held the blade.

And yet, if the others knew of what part she HAD played, she'd be ostracized as Vampyre. 'Twas so unfair. Such was what she'd told herself o'er the winters, such was what helped her to sleep. Yet lately, nothing helped. More and more was expected. She'd had to participate in faking an invasion to discredit the Captain. And then she'd been required to help the Hoard invade Dream Hold. She'd been so scared, but more scared to face the others. She'd cleaned up afterwards. When they'd left the island her only burning need was to kill Calei to keep her from spreading the truth, and to become a hero by returning the Egg and the Prince. Her dreams could still come true. But things hadn't been so simple.

Skirting the fire in a wide arc through the trees, she grabbed her tack and gear from where she'd stashed it earlier and mounted her horse, quietly slipping into the very shadows she'd just seen her nemesis use. Knowing how successful was Calei's method of avoiding detection, she chose to do the same. There'd be no Dancing tonight. Not 'til she was away. Far away. Backtracking through the ravine, hoping the water would hide her reversed trail, she had to get somewhere she could think. 'Twas time to make some decisions.

<p align="center">~~~~~ SECOND MARK ~~~~~</p>

Calei watched Niamia as she made her hasty exit from camp. Trailing her for a short distance, she turned Demonseed back north when she was certain Nia had realized she'd soon become the hunted, and that they'd be traveling in opposite directions. 'Twould take o'er half a mark to return to the Prince, even at full gallop through the rough forest. But Demonseed had taken her through worse. She laid low o'er his neck and tensed, as the stallion's muscles bunched 'tween her thighs in preparation for the jump. Giving the horse his head, she clung to his mane as he leaped o'er the fallen tree and raced up the ravine, his glossy black coat smooth and sleek against her leather britches. She'd leave

Nia to the Guard. She cared not the outcome, only that 'twould get them off her trail long enough to drop her cargo. After that, all her concentration and skill would be called into play as she faced the search of an era, with Kevon's life at stake.

CHAPTER FOURTEEN
Making Amends

Nia rode hard 'til just after dawn, afore she realized the others could follow the physical trail she was leaving, near as easily as they could've followed her Dance signature. Once they stumbled upon either trail's origin, there'd be few places to hide. Out of breath and out of options, she slid off the horse and sat down to think. Calei left the island without the use of Magic and they had yet to figure out how, but how had she continued to avoid them so successfully upon the mainland? Envy of the Captain's skills and status began to envelope her, but then she stopped herself. She could no longer blame others for her situation. 'Twas her own decisions that led her to this place in time. Calei wasn't born with her present level of skill, nor was she born with any status. She'd earned all she had, through relentless effort.

Several times she'd attempted to contact the Sorcerer on her wild ride through the night, but 'twas no doubt he was ignoring her Call. Fine. She'd done horrible things, and even though she'd tried to stop, she never had what it took to say no to the temptations with which she was controlled. The mind games of the Hoard were like the strongest addiction, and ultimately led to an impasse. 'Twas but two in all Kadoor, who mattered to her. She wished she could have been a better daughter and sister, among all the other wishes and regrets, but mayhap she could make one last contribution, to help soften her memory in at least one mind. What she needed to accomplish would take another direct confrontation with that evil being, but the chase team would catch up with her too soon. She knew where to find the Sorcerer. He'd given her the mirror to signal others, surely it could be used to arrange a meeting, but 'twould take time for him to respond, and time was not in her favor at this moment. She had to devise a plan.

~~~~~ LESS THAN TWO MARK LATER ~~~~~

Circling back, Niamia searched for her former teammates. As she Cast her senses around their old one, she finally found their signatures, leading to the new site. And then she discovered, to her relief, they'd done exactly what she'd wanted them to do, fanning out to try to find her, leaving a single guard at camp. She wasn't the Captain and wouldn't have had a chance in Hades of winning against them all together, but one at a time? She liked those odds, especially adding the element of surprise, and Suggestion.

There by the stream, standing all alone, was the one Sprite she might have befriended, had her life been different. Knowing full well the other thought they were close, she rolled her eyes. But Lyrianei was a good Guardsman, and an orphan, as was she. They'd hit it off when she first entered training. Nonetheless, the tiny Sprite was easily deceived, too immature to advance beyond her present level, and happy to be nothing more. Her lack of ambition was something that Niamia held in disdain, although she didn't let the slight woman know, for 'twas easy to lie to her, making her easy to use. Nia unexpectedly felt a twinge of... what? Regret? Remorse? She didn't have time for this. If she was to survive long enough to complete her self-appointed mission, she must steel her resolve. The outcome was inevitable.

~~~~~ MOMENTS LATER ~~~~~

Lyri's mission was one of discovery. Natan's actual order was, "Don't get yourself killed." But she wanted the truth, or as much as anyone could uncover. Lyri was chosen to remain in the base camp as 'twas felt, since they were friends, she'd be the least intimidating and the one most likely to be approached if Nia sought audience. However, their encounter was o'er practically afore it began, and Lyrianei breathed a sigh of relief she was still this side of the Veil. She gasped as she caught her breath, then painfully picked herself up from the river's edge and wiped the mud off her cheek with her forearm. Niamia had Danced unexpectedly, and quite boldly, appearing right at her shoulder having used her own shadow, and being taller than she, as was most everyone, coupled with her faked lack of attention, lost her the hand fight. Ambushed from behind, she'd fought like a cave rat, seemingly to no avail, and found herself sprawled in the muck shortly after the fight started. 'Twas in the plan, although the plan hadn't included quite this scenario, yet, after the recent revelation, she was puzzled. "Why spare me?"

Niamia watched her warily from just out of reach. She wasn't the least bit ashamed of having used her forte Magic to ensure she won the fight. She understood Lyri was tougher than she thought, but Nia missed altogether, the fact that Lyri had not intended to hurt her, losing the fight a'purpose. "I require a messenger."

Her brows still furrowed in suspicion, Lyri replied, "What message would you have me impart? And to whom?"

Keeping her knife at ready and out of reach, Nia indicated the other's attempt to move closer, was noted. "Surely 'tis evident even to you, that I am guilty. If I must die, let it be by the hand of my sister, the last living member of my bloodline, to whom I've caused the most pain."

Something was wrong with what she'd just heard, but the admission caught Lyrianei by surprise. Since learning of Niamia's dishonesty and betrayal, she'd accepted her duty, pushing their friendship to the side. Such treasonous acts demanded the death of the perpetrator. Yet, she was confused, her genuine love for Niamia returning with renewed hope. "Pain? You have remorse for your deeds? But 'twill do no good to have only one pursuer. She will find you."

Softly, Nia replied, "No doubt, but 'twill take her some time, time that I need, for I have something to do first."

Lyrianei wanted to keep her talking, needed more information, and fearlessly stepped closer without making any attempt to hide her actions. "You wish to make Amends?"

Niamia suddenly recognized that she really had thought of Lyri as a friend. She was the only friend she had, but 'twas too late for such. She didn't want to cause any more pain, but her life would soon end and she had a task to complete afore that transpired. Wishing she could hug Lyri just once more, knowing 'twould never happen again, she responded, "What little I can, afore... Nonetheless, I've committed more wrongs than can be Amended in a single span of days. I cannot breathe life back into those who have Passed by my actions, though 'twas not by my hand."

Lyrianei felt strong regrets emanating from her friend, and shifted into full negotiation mode. "Return with me, Nia. Face your deeds, face the Assembly and your sister there. I'll vouch for your remorse. If truth, 'twas not by your hand, you'll be stripped of your rank, your rights, forbidden to return to the island, an outcast... but you'll be alive. You must come now, afore others are sent for you. We can escort you safely home."

Nia's eyes were filled with acceptance as she responded. "'Twill be time enough to face my deeds when Natan finds me. I deserve no better. And I seek the peace of Passing. This world holds nothing but heartache for me now. My execution will be seen as final, continued life would be a mark of shame upon my bloodline forever. I will not put more upon them than I have already."

Lyrianei was much saddened. "'Twill be a price upon your head. The honor of the Guard demands this. There will be many who will seek to end your days, and if Natan is not the first to find you..."

"Then go quickly. You must convince them to send Natan early, and to hold the others. I beg you. I ask only this one thing. They will agree, if you get there afore the others are notified. Natan holds first Right to Consequence. She's all the family I have left."

There 'twas again. Something was wrong. Lyrianei could sense her friend was not telling the whole truth. But she had nothing to go on, except the newly revealed fact that Nia lied to everyone. "This request will delay the inevitable but a few moons, at most."

'Twould not take a few moons, but she did not correct Lyri. Instead, she looked down and accepted her future. "I intend to make good use of them."

"Nia, when I heard of what you'd been accused, I was astonished. Then I was in denial. I could not believe. You're my best friend. You're not bad, you could never have done this. I know you."

Niamia's vision was blurring. She had to bring this conversation to an end. Irritated, she replied, "You don't know me, no one knows me. I used you, Lyrianei. I used everyone. I was angry. Bitter. Selfish. All I wanted was to get out of my responsibilities at home, and to be an Elite Guardsman like Natan. I was jealous. She was always the pretty one, the strong one, the talented one, the lucky one. She could do no wrong. When she was called to join the Guard, I was left behind, forever chained with duty. My whole life fell apart, I had nothing to look forward to, I had nothing."

Wisdom oozed forth as the smallest Guardsman responded. 'Twas an internal strength to Lyrianei that few understood. She sighed, and said quietly, "You had more than most of us, Niamia. Family, support, status."

Nia hesitated briefly, but her mind was not swayed. Standing up and brandishing her dagger for emphasis, she declared, "Never forget that I threw that all away, Lyri. For I shall not. Good or bad, 'tis one's choices that determine one's fate, and mine is sealed." With that, Niamia turned swiftly, and afore Lyri could prevent it, she Danced away.

~~~~~ MUCH LATER ~~~~~

Niamia tripped out of the shadow with a jolt and stumbled to the closest tree, where she grabbed onto the trunk and awkwardly disappeared again. After multiple Dances with little time to gather her senses 'tween, she could barely function. Just aware enough that if she tried again, she'd probably fail to complete the action and end up in the Fade, she crawled to the base of a broad fir and wondered if she'd ever find where she'd left her horse. When she made her hasty exit, she'd not given her direction much thought, Dancing fast to avoid being followed, and hopefully not step out in front of the others as they continued their search. Now she was afraid she'd lost everything, and she'd grown rather fond of that horse. Besides, he was fully tacked up and held all she'd brought with her on this mission, while she currently had only the weapons with which she'd stood guard, and the clothes on her back. How did Calei avoid them all for so long? 'Twas certainly not going to be as easy as she'd anticipated. Still holding the blade, she slumped against the base of the tree and slowly rolled o'er, asleep afore her shoulder hit the ground.

~~~~~ BACK AT THE ELITE CAMP ~~~~~

Natanamia listened to Lyrianei's report, but could not bring herself to say anything, for if she opened her mouth, she was afraid she'd heave. 'Twas true. Her little sister was a spy for the Hoard. Calei was right. Niamia would have gotten that order eventually, if she'd not received it by now. But, if she could believe what Nia told Lyri, then she was trying to make Amends. Should she follow Niamia, or was this yet another ruse to pull her into an ambush? She considered hard, then caught everyone's gaze one by one. "I have been blind. I know that now. I apologize to you all." She took a deep breath. "I wanted to be a Guardsman all my life. I was not pleased with this mission, for there were so many deeply emotional factors, but I was confident I could perform at a professional level. I did not. I now rescind my position as acting Captain, for I have failed not only you, but the Nation."

Stepping closer to Natanamia, they encircled her and together declared a resounding, "No!" Then one by one they reaffirmed her position, encouraging her to continue. No one criticized her for loving her sister, no one felt she'd failed them. Natanamia was a strong leader, and if she survived her next task, she'd be as good a Captain as was Caleichante. Not one of them envied her duty. 'Twas agreed they'd work their way o'er land, slowly but steadily, back to Port O'Drekinn. There they'd await the Krakken to take them home again, where they'd make report to the Lord and Lady. They knew not how long they could give Natanamia afore others were sent in search of her sister, but they would stretch out their return to Drekinn for as long as possible. Natan knew her responsibility. She thanked them and left afore first light.

<div align="center">~~~~~ MEANWHILE ~~~~~</div>

The Bog of St Swiftyn's was a few marks flight, or a day's ride a'horseback (on a swift horse) from the Keep of St Swiftyn's. 'Twas a place of marshland amidst Byndynn Forest, naturally heated from the decomposition of the swamp muck, along with some seismic activity deep within the rock under the Bog, which also contained natural caverns. After picking up Kevon, she urged Demonseed to full gallop. They ate up the leagues 'til they reached the Bog late the following evening. Calei's leathers were torn and filthy, her hair still caked with dried mud, sticks and brush stuck in the crisscrossed leather strip, as she brought him to a halt at the edge of the swamp. While the big stallion pawed at the ground, his nostrils flaring, she surveyed the area. Her Sprite vision, mixed with experience, helped her map a foot route well into the deepest and most dangerous stretch. She didn't like what she saw, but 'twould be perilous no matter where 'twas entered, and there seemed no other option. 'Twas a necessary risk.

Choosing her course, she transferred the boy's weight from her body to Demonseed's thick, high-arched neck, then dismounted smoothly, stepping in front of him and placing her hands on either side of his long muzzle. As Kevon groaned softly in near wakefulness, Calei gazed deep into Demonseed's blazing red eyes and instructed in a low voice, "Be calm, my friend. The boy can barely sit up now, you must be still. I shall return."

~~~~~~~~~~

The Summer Solstice would soon be upon them. Graasyn and Bastyen had been traveling for half a winter. Initially, the weather was the single most difficult challenge in their journey home. 'Twas warm now, and hunting was good. Certain of their location at last, they'd thought to gather enough provisions to make a hard march back to Drekinn, and Graasyn had been setting snares all evening, squatting behind a large old growth oak, when she dismounted. While she made her way to the edge of the Bog, the moonlight shone off her long white hair and the glint caught his eye. As he looked up, his jaw dropped at her exquisite beauty, and his heart pounded in his ears. So entranced was he, that barely breathing, he lost his balance and sat hard on the ground, the snare still in his hand. His eyes widened and he held his breath when she suddenly stopped what she was doing and cocked her head as if she'd heard something. The way his heart was pounding, he wouldn't have been surprised if she'd heard that, but realistically, she could have heard him fall. And then she looked straight at him. Her golden eyes burned into his for but a fraction of a candle drip, afore she turned away. They'd been Masked since the Push, yet she'd acted as if she'd seen him for the barest of moments.

~~~~~~~~~~

Calei stepped away from Demonseed and walked cautiously to the edge of the swamp. Although her vision plainly distinguished 'tween the firmer surfaces and the softer ones, she still couldn't see beneath them to know for certain 'twas not going to give way under foot. Her mission would be cut short if she stepped badly, but hazardous nevertheless, and if she failed, she failed Myrrdin, Corbyn, Bryynn, the Highlands, the Sprite Nation, herself, and worst of all, Kevon. She fixed her sight upon her goal, lifted her chin, and then she heard it. Looking around, she thought she saw something o'er by that tree, but her senses picked up nothing evil. 'Twas most likely an animal. She blinked. Was that… no, 'twas her imagination. For just an instant she thought she'd seen a Human. Here? She'd feel if 'twas another Magic bearer, yet she felt nothing, and no Man could have disappeared that fast. She peered intently at the exact spot she'd seen the illusion, and felt something close to desire. Surely not, she decided. Satisfied 'twas truly nothing, she turned back to her task. Entering the Bog.

<div style="text-align:center">~~~~~~~~~~</div>

He couldn't take his eyes off her as she stepped into the marshlands, sure-footed and confident. He didn't know who she was or what she was doing, but he did know he wouldn't let her die out there. But then again, how could he prevent such? The Bog would suck down anything that set foot in the wrong place, to be forever entombed in the muck. Even if he noted the exact location, he knew not how to save her without joining her Beyond. Afraid seeing him would distract her, for she appeared quite focused upon her path, he watched the most beautiful woman he'd ever laid eyes upon, stop and look all around. Awestruck, he saw her hesitate, gazing in his direction again, and then she returned to her task.

Kneeling and removing a large, blood red, glittering egg-shaped object from the saddlebag slung o'er her shoulder, she laid it on the ground at her feet and slowly pushed it forward 'til she could reach no further. Then she sat back on her heels and watched as the Bog accepted her gift with a squelching sound. Once 'twas done, there was no trace the object had ever existed.

Graasyn squinted in curiosity, wondering what she'd just buried in the swamp, as from the appearance of the thing and how 'twas handled, 'twas most valuable. Abruptly, she stood up and turned about, retracing her steps with all haste. But he could not let her go without trying to make contact. At the very least, he had to know if she'd already seen him. Once she reached the edge again, he stepped into clear view, but she looked right through him. Then she reached forth and a sleek black stallion marched out of the trees, snorting his excitement at their reunion. A frail boy sat upon his back, and as she mounted behind him, she glanced o'er her shoulder afore saying something to the horse. As they turned away, the great lathered beast reared up high, his forelegs pawing the air. Once more, he found himself completely breathless. Unable to move a muscle, he watched them race off like the wind itself, disappearing into the tree line on the far side of the Bog. 'Twas a quarter mark later that he finally reset the trap, his mind elsewhere.

<div align="center">~~~~~~~~~~</div>

Calei held the Prince tightly, leaning o'er Demonseed's neck as he raced through the forest, heading further north afore she planned to turn easterly, skirting around the Keep. Bryynn was safe, she was certain there'd been no witnesses, but she was puzzled by what she thought she'd seen at the Bog. She'd sensed no other Magic bearers, she'd never had a Vision afore, and there'd not been any Humans in this area for more than half a century, but there'd been something she couldn't explain. And what in the Flame was that strange feeling of desire? For but an instant, 'twas as if she'd seen into the very soul of the one with whom she was destined to mate. She shook off the notion. She'd been alone all her life, working hard to gain her position, too busy to even think about having a mate. 'Twas the stress of the experience, and nothing more. But, she couldn't stop thinking about what had happened. 'Twould bother her for a very long time.

CHAPTER FIFTEEN

The Empath

THE FOLLOWING DAWN

~~~~~ O'ER SIX MOONS AFTER THE INVASION ~~~~~

Diadranei woke from the nightmare with a start, near falling out of the old growth oak close to the edge of the Bog, in which she'd spent the last evening. Regardless of the vast experience she'd gathered o'er these past many winters sleeping in trees, 'twas still difficult, and sometimes downright dangerous. 'Twas also quite uncomfortable, and if she had any sense she'd set a perimeter guarding Spell and get a proper night's sleep on the ground. She sighed. 'Twould not be much better actually, for the ground was hard as well as cold, and she had not a blanket to spread, and not the strength needed to create one along with the Protection Spell. She couldn't do everything. She had to ration her Magic for emergencies.

She'd arrived long past midnight and was very fatigued, seeking whatever rest she could. But she knew she had to keep moving, and taking a deep breath, she sat up and untangled her clothing from the smaller branches around which she'd tried to anchor herself. The long woolen skirt and cotton blouse she'd been wearing when she left Kaddart had been thin with age, but at least she'd been able to keep them clean and mended while there. Now she was a sight. There was no underskirt left at all, and the top skirt was near threadbare as well as ragged. The dirty gray cloth scarcely covered her long slim legs, and her feet were bare. The apron had been sacrificed to capture her last meal, or more precisely, to bind the one from whom she'd stolen it. She was just a tad unsettled when she became conscious of how easy that had become o'er the winters. She was more upset with the fact that she'd not had time to feed the Warriors and reclaim her meager possessions, afore making her own escape. In fact, as usual, she'd run out into the night with nothing but what she'd been wearing. Would she ever learn?

Moving carefully from branch to branch down the giant trunk, she decided a perimeter Spell wouldn't have done her much good anyway. She'd never had the level of power to Brew the Magic the rest of her Kind could. Or at least, not in the manner in which they did, as her Magic was considered a throwback. She was an Empath, and as yet she'd not found a limit to her abilities in that single-minded focus, while beyond that path she struggled. Even so, she couldn't sustain full power to work within her own Specialty since the Last Holocaust and couldn't restore her full power without returning to the Wyrdritch. All Magic bearers required connecting with their own 'link' to Kadoor. The Highlands had Fire Heart, the Sprites, the Island of Dreams, and who in Hades even knew where the Fay lived, but she was certain they had their Link as well. 'Twas the same for the Elves and the Wyrdritch, returning there unerringly every so many winters, or just never leaving. But for her, returning was wishful thinking. Even if she could find it, she wasn't at all certain she'd be welcome.

Once the flood waters, rock and landslides, and smoke and dust of fires originating from both Dragon and Man, had cleared, the resultant deforestation was horrifying. Still, she'd fully expected to be able to locate her homeland despite topographical changes caused by the upheavals of tsunami, quake, and volcano. Initially, she feared Haven might have become fully exposed to all eyes, but as she walked o'er the land she discovered that although the forests were near decimated, the Wyrdritch remained elusive even to her Elven senses. During the many winters she'd spent actively searching, she came to understand that the Wyrdritch was still there, but the Spell her people had always maintained had somehow morphed, and there was an odd twist that appeared to attach itself to the trees in recovering forests and woodlands 'cross Kadoor, like some fungal infection. The variation affected the Dragons most deeply, and they could not enter or Flame the forests without causing great distress and even pain. As the forests returned, the Dragons withdrew. At first, 'twas good to avoid their Flame, to allow the forests to heal themselves, but in truth, the Spell also affected other Magic bearers, making it difficult for them to navigate what once had been their homes. After some time, she became aware that somehow, she was being diverted away from the Wyrdritch again and again, and she'd finally given up, hoping she'd be Called back with the others.

'Twas only in the past few decades the forests had fully regrown, and were denser and more luxurious than prior to their near obliteration. For so long she'd not dared hope for the return of her people, but since her time in Kaddart, she wondered. If she were right, and the Spell was affecting them all, then the entire Elven Nation would be as lost as was she, and if so, then all Elves were now just as weak, barely able to gain enough strength to sustain their Magic. That meant the Return would have to come from within, from someone who'd stayed behind, while the others scattered to the shadows and Beyond, attempting as did she, to simply survive on what little strength they could manage to Pull from single trees, the shadows of virgin woodlands, and the occasional animal or Human host.

Diadranei knew the plan for Retreat, for she attended the Gathering of the Races in the Last Days. Since Elven Magic was so closely tied to shadows thrown by organics and the Life Force of animals and trees, their survival was the most threatened, and therefore, the Nation scattered. An entire forest was required to sustain them, and as the forests were burned and died out, or simply buried and lost, the Elves sought surviving individual old growth Oak and other ancient trees. Diadranei had not waited around to see the result of the Gathering, knowing 'twould happen as 'twas planned. And although she'd tried to argue they could save the forests and the Nation by standing and fighting with Mankind against the Evil One, she'd met with such ridicule that she abandoned her people in protest. She'd been one of the first to leave. They'd not believed her when she reasoned that if they all stood together with their powers combined, they could fight the evil, they could alter the Spell in such a manner as to cover all the trees, all the land, and the Retreat could be avoided. Instead, expecting all to be lost, the Elves had chosen to strengthen the Spell o'er the Wyrdritch to try to prevent its total decimation, and then leaving the royal family, o'er half the Nation departed, wherever they could find shelter, mostly singly or in pairs or small family groups. The more people to a group, the less likely 'twas their ultimate survival. Many shared tears and last goodbyes as they chose separation to increase their chances that one day, they would all Dance through the Shadows in the Return.

But the Call never came. The forests healed, new growth became old, the light of the sun kissed the world again, enriching and lengthening the shadows that were vital to their health. They should've been able to make the return alone, but none had found their homeland and Haven remained silent. What was wrong? What had happened? Diadranei's senses confirmed she wasn't the only one who could not get back to the Wyrdritch, but she could be the only one who understood why.

Finally reaching the ground from her difficult descent, she jumped the last few feet and landed with a slight thud. Still distracted by her thoughts, she stepped away from the massive trunk, felt something grab her ankle, and lost her balance. Surprised, she barely spun around quickly enough to avoid falling on her face, and sat hard on the leaf litter covering the thick tree roots.

"OH!" The word exploded in the exhalation of her breath as she hit the ground, and with some embarrassment she glanced up quickly to see if anyone had been witness to her clumsiness. No wait, she'd not been simply clumsy, something grabbed hold of her, causing her to trip and fall. Feeling a burning sensation, she tried to stand up, but her foot was held tight, and in the struggle a sharp pain shot through her ankle. Lying back in the leaves she stared up at the branches. "Oh splendid. My Life Force is stretched to the limit and I sprain my ankle," she said disgustedly for whatever creature who might be listening, to hear.

Her bare legs were scratched by the twigs upon which she now laid, and she pushed up onto her elbows, staring down at her feet. Her blouse was torn yet again on the descent through the branches, the neckline so wide now that she tugged and pulled to keep it from falling off one shoulder or the other. Adjusting it once more, she sat upright and scooted her butt toward her foot, which seemed to be fastened somehow to the base of the tree. Pushing the leaf litter aside, she stared in amazement at the snare in which she was caught. Wondering how 'twas avoided last night, she remembered she'd ascended the tree from the opposite side, descending this side, so the snare was probably set all along. But when she tried to loosen it, 'twould only tighten more and more. She stopped struggling and looked closer at the line and the knots. 'Twas made of tightly braided coarse hair, as red as that which adorned the handsome young Warrior back in Kaddart. She closed her eyes as she tried again to untie the clever knots, release the noose, and extricate her ankle, while she allowed her senses to Reach out to the maker.

~~~~~~~~~~

Bastyen was having difficulty keeping his mouth shut. His jaw kept dropping. He watched from the brush a mere few yards from the base of the tree, and couldn't believe his eyes. 'Twas his turn to be out early this morning checking their traps, and he'd found a veritable feast, but this snare surely caught the prize. 'Twas the stunning black-haired girl from the Clear Water Inn. She'd survived! Questions raced through his mind, but he couldn't find his tongue. He observed the girl's struggles, unable to move a muscle for fear of her taking flight, as she reached out and then fell back again in obvious pain. She was injured! He wanted to rush
~~~~~~~~~~

to help, but his body wouldn't respond. At least, most of his body showed no ability to respond. Part of his body was embarrassing him, and given that they'd eaten well since being Pushed here, and in combination with a lot of hard work surviving the harsh climate, his leather pants were a tad snug, and if he stood up now, well... he had to make that stop.

~~~~~~~~~~

Diadranei heard the sharp intake of breath in the underbrush close by, just as she received the empathic image of the young Warrior in her mind, for 'twas his hair and he was here, watching her. She dipped her chin and sat very still, Casting forth to determine if he meant her harm. She learned she had nothing to fear, and yet she was afraid. 'Twas ever thus. Her Magic was not strong in Protection. She had to work her Spells through the 'back door' when most others just charged straight through the front. She'd spent her lifetime avoiding conflict since strong emotion powered one's Magic and she had no one to teach her how to control all that influx. Normally, she'd use the emotions of others to warn her of any rising situations and then she'd simply Dance away. Her blue-black hair and silver-gray eyes were a stark contrast to her pale skin, but she could melt into the shadows as no other. Her solitary lifestyle had honed her methods and she was very good at moving about without being noticed, Suggesting to those around her to become so absorbed in what they were doing, or in some false thought she'd planted, that they wouldn't even see her. 'Twas exceedingly useful, as she knew near everything people were thinking without asking, and some were fearful of her, for they didn't realize she was an Empath. Magical Empathy was extremely rare, even within the Elven Nation. No one recognized her strength, no one understood her Magic. With no one to teach her, everyone assumed she was weak. She'd been a recluse among her own people, not truly welcome anywhere. Living alone after the Last Holocaust had not been all that strange for many winters. But even when she'd been disregarded amongst
~~~~~~~~~~

her own, she'd been near them, and had never been truly alone afore. Her time in Kaddart, although short, made her realize how lonely she'd become. She missed people. She missed her family. She missed the Wyrdritch.

Although, being honest, she had to admit, there was one amongst the Elves who had understood her. If she'd called any one of her Kind 'friend', Diadranei would have said this about the Princess Persephone. She too, had led a solitary existence, but mostly for different reasons. The tall, slender, delicate beauty of the Princess intimidated most of the males of their Kind, and she and her mother were the only females in the royal house. Queen Bryanna had her hands full caring for her demanding and egotistical mate, along with the many duties and expectations of her station, leaving Persephone to help raise her many brothers. This, along with her own rare and powerful Healing Magic, set her far apart from everyone, as what good was a special Healing prowess when Magic bearers had exceptional immunity and usually healed quickly on their own? Although there was need for Skalds, Diadranei knew Persephone's power involved more than that. There was something extraordinary about it, yet they were just children and as such both Diadranei and Persephone were ostracized for their perceived weaknesses, and found solace in each other's company. That is, when the King allowed his second born to leave Haven. Although he refused to acknowledge her Magic, he still kept her under tight rein.

Her thoughts returned to the present situation, as she avoided glancing directly at the brush where the young Warrior now stood. By the look on his face he either no longer cared, or didn't think she could see him. She tucked her chin and clamped her lips shut tight, but she couldn't keep the amusement contained and burst out laughing to the utter surprise of the one staring at her so intently.

Shocked, Bastyen exclaimed, "You can see me!" He and Graasyn had been Masked for so many moons, he just took it for granted that he was invisible to the eyes of others. 'Twas just what he needed to get his feet to move, and he rushed forth to help the girl get out of the snare.

"Of course, I can see you," she giggled as she watched him coming toward her. Embarrassment grew the closer he came, and she anxiously pulled her blouse back up on both shoulders. She bit her lower lip as the handsome youth grasped her ankle gently in his strong hands and finished removing the snare, examining her skin, frowning at the bruising and swelling. Then she wondered at what he'd said, suddenly realizing it hadn't made much sense. "Why would you think yourself invisible?"

"I have been since we left. To everyone but you." Bastyen gazed at her, his fingers still caressing her ankle as if he never wanted to stop touching her. He didn't even bother worrying about security. This beautiful creature held his heart in her hands and there was nothing he wouldn't give her. Trusting her was the most natural thing he'd ever imagined. He'd never felt so right.

<center>~~~~~ SEVERAL MARKS LATER ~~~~~</center>

Bastyen hadn't intended to be gone all morning, but the woman's story was fascinating and she insisted that he shouldn't have recognized her from Kaddart, as she was wearing a type of appearance-altering Magic, called a glamour. As he thought back, he remembered Graasyn saying something about the girl who'd warned them to leave the Clear Water Inn, and he'd joked the old man must be half blind, as her hair was so black 'twas near blue in its highlights, and he'd referred to it as simply brown. Such details were never mistaken in their profession, but he'd not argued the point, as they were on their way out the window, narrowly missing the Agents bursting into their room, and the odd bit of conversation was tucked away for later. Now seemed to be that later. She talked. He listened. He talked. She listened. He'd learned much about Magic in the past few moons, had seen evidence that the LifeBond was successful, knew after having been

Pushed here, that at least one Magic bearer had extraordinary powers, and her appearance alone made him a believer in the other Races. "So, you can feel my emotions and know what I'm thinking? 'Tis as the Link then?" Applying a cool wet compress from a nearby spring and gently massaging her ankle, the swelling reduced significantly. But Bastyen insisted on carrying her back to their campsite, as she still had difficulty weight bearing.

As he walked, she wrapped her slender arms around his neck. His Life Force was strong, and she Drew afore she realized. Although his response was one of pleasure which made her blush, the tiny amount of energy she'd taken satisfied her as though she'd been home. She felt better than she'd felt in ages, and 'twas as if he'd Drawn from her as well. Neither said a word, and the look in his eyes brought her back to the moment. "Not exactly. I can't Hear you thinking, I don't know your thoughts in word form. I know your emotions, which lead me to deduce what you're thinking, 'ask questions' to get confirmation, and I can 'nudge' those emotions, or plant thoughts or feelings in others. I can also sense things that have happened to you, or that might be about to happen, as well as truths and deceptions. Emotions are powerful energies." She felt completely at ease with this man. She wanted to spend the rest of her span of days as close to him as possible, and had no qualms about revealing her specialty. 'Twas still odd that he saw through her glamour, though. Seeking information, the untold truth of one troublesome issue blossomed in her mind, and she burst forth, "You were Masked!" She shook her head. "'Twas not intended to last for long. 'Tis now dissolved."

Her 'specialty' seemed quite powerful, and her words struck from two different directions simultaneously. She knew of the Mask, and they were no longer invisible. 'Twasn't just to her eyes. Battle Lust building in his system, he asked urgently, "How long?"

Reaching forth and running her knuckles gently down his cheek, she felt for the answer. Her brows furrowed and she allowed him to help her stand on her own feet to rest briefly. She still couldn't put all of her weight on her ankle, but his urgency spurred her own, and she hurriedly explained, "I believe 'twas recent... not more than a few dawns. I can't be exact."

Bastyen was now in full Battle Mode. He gathered her into his strong arms and began to run. "We have to get back. Aba doesn't know he can be seen."

CHAPTER SIXTEEN

A Mother's Gift

~~~~~ LATER THAT EVENING ~~~~~

Once Diadranei touched Graasyn in greeting, she understood that the Mask had dissolved slowly from each of them, making their appearance to others somewhat erratic. Explaining this was challenging at first, as the elder Warrior was skeptical. Her ears and accuracy with telling him what he was thinking, finally accomplished that which her words alone, could not. But trying to explain herself to him, was downright amusing. As the evening waned, pondering how to further gain his trust, she finally struck upon the answer to the anomalies she was experiencing in their company. But it still didn't make sense. She'd have to run a test. Standing up, she smiled at Graasyn sitting 'cross the fire. Gesturing for him to look at her, she asked, "Tell me, how do I appear to you?"

Graasyn was still distracted by the similarity 'tween this newcomer to their company and the beautiful woman he'd seen the prior dusk in the Bog. Apart from the color of their hair and eyes, they shared many traits. Pointed ears, ivory pale skin, and their general body build, tall, lean, youthful. He accepted that Elves were real, but were these two women related in some way? And her voice held an amazing musical quality he had difficulty describing, other than something akin to wind chimes. Squatting, he looked up after adding another branch to the fire, studied her briefly, and then replied, "A tall, willowy Elven female, pale skin, long straight black hair, and silver-gray eyes."

Dia then turned her attention to Bastyen. "You? The same?"

Bastyen nodded and replied quizzically, "Yes. The same." 'Twas strange that his father was now describing the girl the way he saw her, and not as he'd described her back in Kaddart.
~~~~~

Dia then drew her hands down her body as if wiping something on or off, without physically touching herself, placing the glamour. Then she returned her attention to the now very startled elder Warrior. "Graasyn? What see you now?"

Unbelievably, he found himself staring at the young girl from the Clear Water Inn. Even her clothing was different. Slowly he stood up and stated, "A human female, tanned skin, brown curly hair, green eyes..."

Dia noted the hesitancy, and questioned him further, "And... what else?"

For the first time ever, he was uncertain of his observations. "There be a slight shimmering effect covering you from head to toe." His brows relaxed, and he continued. "But 'tis something I've seen occasionally throughout my span of days, and has no significance," he concluded stubbornly.

Dia nodded her head more to herself than to them, and turned once more. "Bastyen? What see you?"

"There be no change," he stated a bit shaken, staring at his father. But suddenly beginning to understand, he turned back to her, and after a moment of intense observation he eagerly added, "Wait, I see a minor air disturbance, a rippling outline about you, like a heat mirage. Very faint. I know I've seen this afore, and considered it normal. I thought 'twas what everyone saw. I've ignored this visual phenomenon my entire span of days!"

Graasyn now understood as well, and quickly grasped onto the concept Dia was trying to convey. In agreement with his son, he replied, "As have I. You're saying that I'm actually seeing a 'tell' of the glamour you've placed upon yourself?"

"Yes, that's a good way to describe it. You're seeing the Allure. And Bastyen is seeing through the Allure. 'Tis unheard of. Although 'tis not truly Magic, 'tis remarkable. I know not how you've come by these Gifts, nor do I know of any other possessing such," she stated, shaking her head, her face a study in puzzlement.

~~~~~ THE FOLLOWING NIGHT ~~~~~

After finding suitable spare leathers to replace her old tattered rags, Diadranei and Graasyn spent much time together, staying up all night and well into the next, detailing and testing her Magic. And when the Elf told him of what and whom he'd seen at the Bog, he was finally convinced. 'Twas the Captain of the Elite Guard of the Sprites, with the Heir Apparent, Kevon. The description of the boy's condition concerned her very much and 'twas determined they had to give chase to assist, for Dia knew they were heading to the Wyrdritch and why, and that 'twas a life or death situation. Even though she'd never been on the mainland, Caleichante was well known, her skills legendary throughout Kadoor. But given circumstances, Dia knew the Sprite would need help to find the Wyrdritch. Finally, having come to an understanding of how she'd been repulsed in her searches in the past, she had an idea of how to use her Magic to find that which was somehow there, but not there.

Giving chase was a notion to which Graasyn had no objection. Dia informed them of what happened to Tonn, who's death they'd been sent to Kaddart to investigate. There was nothing they could do now, except inform his brothers of his bravery, and trying to make report to the Commander about Kaddart could wait, for 'twas no Kaddart left. Apparently, they were behind in the current events anyway, and their report would make little difference now. And, if there were other Races abroad, 'twas their duty to recruit them to assist the Clan. Besides, he'd been fascinated with the Sprite, and could not get her image out of his mind. Whether she'd seen him or not, she'd touched his very soul, and he felt close to her in a way he could not comprehend. The father and son Warriors had amassed plenty of supplies and 'twas a perfect set up for the new mission. Adding one more to their travels would barely touch their provisions. Graasyn could see that his son was enamored of the Elf and could find no fault, for Diadranei appeared the perfect match. Intelligent, quick-witted, beautiful, loyal, honest, with an inner strength that made
~~~~~

itself known to those near her, Bastyen had never found a woman with whom he was so intrigued. After breaking down the essentials of camp, Diadranei and Bastyen withdrew to one side of the fire while Graasyn stood watch. They were leaving at first light.

EVANNTYR, THE CASTLE OF THE HIGH KING
~~~~~ THE DUNGEONS KNOWN AS THE PITS OF HADES ~~~~~

The dying man was struggling to breathe, hanging from the wall by his wrists in the iron manacles, his feet unable to reach the stone floor. Coagulated blood oozed from many cuts o'er his naked body, one eye was burned out, several toes cut off, toenails and fingernails long gone, even his genitals had been mutilated, but the executioner had been instructed to refrain from a death cut, and to prevent him from bleeding out too fast. His situation was the result of his own stupidity and big mouth. Taken from his squalid existence in Tupry in the middle of the night by King's Agents and delivered to Evanntyr, now he simply wondered when this pain would end. His body was too broken, he'd never survive. He'd run away so long ago, and now the past had caught up with him. He knew not who had turned him o'er to the Sorcerer, and at this point, he cared not.

The unfortunate male finally gave in, but his positioning and weakness made taking in enough air to speak above a whisper, impossible. He laughed deliriously in his pain-induced madness, and taking frequent shallow breaths, he wheezed, "Yes, yes, 'twas sixteen or seventeen winters past, but I remember it well. We'd guessed the boy you wanted was the First Born, the True King of Kadoor. We'd tracked the strange humans and killed two, along with their huge cat-like animals, but we lost many of our original group and most of the reinforcements you sent. The Dragon remained. The boy was with yet another of the same tribe as those we killed, a young female and her animal. We tracked them all the way to Abysmal Gorge. I'd never seen such an impenetrable wall of vines afore. I had a bad feeling, and I didn't enter the vine wall with the others, for I knew they'd not return. No one had ever entered the abyss and returned. The boy was in there, and he died with the rest. Nothing was ever heard of any of them once that vine wall closed. I backed away from the screams and went home. I've heard those screams in my nightmares since that day. My death will only bring me peace. I speak the truth, for I have nothing to hide but my own cowardice."

'Twould do no good for them to continue, as he believed the man, and frankly, he was getting bored. The aging mercenary was about gone now, and if they waited, he'd Pass on his own, leaving the Sorcerer to miss out on the final insult. Nodding his head for the executioner to proceed, he near drooled, watching in fascination as he slowly slit the man's throat. He so enjoyed a good session in the dungeons, and he wanted to milk every last drop of agony from this one who'd failed him. The mercenary may have believed they'd all died in the Gorge, but he did not. That girl had been clever enough to outwit and out-track the best mercenaries he could buy from Tupry, and he knew who and what she was. Her people were not only extremely reclusive, but also highly intelligent, and ruthless survivalists. If anyone could 'cross the abyss, 'twould be one from her tribe. 'Twas she and the boy who'd forced his Dragon Past the Veil, of this he was now certain. So. The First Born yet lived. And he was with the People of the Talons, the Daggogh. They would pay for their audacity.

The man's strangled cries faded to gurgling as the last of his Life Source dripped from his slashed neck. The many wounds inflicted to extract the ultimate pain for the longest period, were dried, the blood caked upon his limp body and beneath him in a congealed puddle. The Sorcerer smiled. His executioner was near as good as was he. This might have broken his own record for length of time to keep a man alive while being tortured. He turned, his long dark cloak swirling around the stone floor. Ascending the stairs, he was already making his plans to find the Daggogh and destroy them, hopefully, along with the First Born.

MIDSUMMER
ABOUT A MOON AFORE THE BATTLE FOR THE DRAGON CLAN
~~~~~ SOMEWHERE DEEP IN THE RAPTOR'S TALONS ~~~~~

During the chase, Diadranei practiced her Magic at every opportunity, strengthening her ability to Push her message further and with stronger effect, using whomever and whatever was available. The War Horses became exasperated with her efforts, and she turned to her companions, with their consent, although they allowed only a message clearly identifiable, such as using the Link for telepathic communication. 'Twas similar, and therefore became of use to prevent the need to slow down in order to speak to each other, helping them to gain ground upon Caleichante, as Dia used her senses to track the Sprite, guiding the Warriors through the treacherous environment. Physical tracking would have left them further and further behind, and may even have lost the trail, whereas using Dia's Empathy, they stopped only to rest and feed the Horses, and to refill their water skins.

Deep in the Talons, they discovered the People known as the Gordatch. Camping far enough away, Graasyn stayed with the Horses, while Dia and Bastyen walked and then crawled for o'er a mark, to get close enough to observe, unnoticed to those whom they watched.

Settling on a ledge o'erlooking the Gordatch village, they laid side by side. The Elf was bothered by what she saw and nudged Bastyen's shoulder. "Look at that one," she spoke softly. "He is someone of great importance. There's more to him than what appears."

Bastyen stared at the one to whom she pointed for a few moments, and then stated, "What do you mean? I see no glamour."

"No, he's Human, yet when I look at him, I feel something very important."

Bastyen considered her statement. "How important? To the war? To the Clan? He's just a Hunter for the People. What more can there be?"

Dia attempted to explain what she'd 'learned' thus far, in the short time they'd watched. "The People intend to become allies of the Clan. They protect that Hunter. Evil comes to them for such daring. I feel they must be away, to the People of the Razor's Edge. If they don't go soon, many will perish, and that one's destiny will be for naught."

"Do you feel a prophesy? A spy?"

Dia was puzzled and still trying to sort through the information she was getting. Learning to decipher her senses was more difficult than she'd originally thought, but she was improving rapidly. "Mayhap. Yes. I think both."

"Then send them. But 'twould be wise to do so in a dream, so as not to cause suspicion as to how 'twas received."

"'Tis a very good plan, but to whom do I Push such a message?"

Bastyen observed the tribe carefully in their comings and goings for near half a mark. The People were a fascinating human tribe, who covered their skin with tattoos and painted symbols, cut their hair in a multitude of lengths, and plastered sections into colored spikes, leaving the rest in odd braids with feathers and shells. They were expert archers, used a variety of throwing weapons, and partnered with enormous animals for hunting and protection. The Daggogh, who lived in the Razor's Edge, raised and trained the Kahyah, or Night Beasts, huge big cat, wolf-mix creatures, vicious and efficient hunters large enough to ride, while the People of the Raptor's Talons, the Gordatch, bred the Night Wings, enormous, fox-faced, bat-like flying animals with short legs and long fangs, who wrapped their black leathery bodies around their partners, creating the appearance of a humpbacked, two-headed, tailed and winged being that fueled many frightening myths of old. Both were relentless and lethal and it appeared that all Hunters had one or the other.

Evidently a part of a small entourage from the Razor's Edge, 'twas clear that Dia spoke truth in that the Daggogh Hunter called Gabriel, the one she'd identified as special, was being treated with subtle deference by members of both tribes, his presence commanding and unequal to others of his outward status. Yet he did seem close to one. 'Twas a tall female called Gheryh, who shared chieftain status with her mate, Kyrag. Protected from exposure by Dia's Magic, he pointed to her, and stated, "That one."

Dia took a deep breath and then Pushed her message to Gheryh, after which, they withdrew. The female would have a dream this night, and hopefully, she and her companions would be away by dawn. 'Twas good training, and she wasn't sure that she'd accomplished that which she'd attempted, but they couldn't afford the time 'twould take to see the end results. 'Twas all she could manage, each to their own mission. Mayhap one day, they'd know if Gheryh took heed, as well as discovering just who was this Gabriel.

CHAPTER SEVENTEEN

The Strength of Integrity

~~~~~ SOMEWHERE DEEP IN WYNDSYR FOREST ~~~~~

"So you say," the Sorcerer's voice dripped syrupy sweet in Niamia's delicately pointed ears. 'Twas horribly reminiscent of that night long ago, when the Hoard contact with whom she'd met had... even though she thought he'd been under Shift or strong glamour, she could tell. He was staring at her, and she needed to respond. She had to make this good. She'd failed back then, and this one was the worst of the lot. If he understood that she knew... This would be the greatest acting challenge of her span of days.

Nia had Danced her way down to the Darden region, as close to the general location of the Hoard Lair as possible, not knowing precisely where 'twas, and began the process of Calling to the Sorcerer, using the mirror in a painstaking ritual which produced the desired results in a matter of days. She'd abandoned her supplies, as 'twas likely she'd not live long enough to need any of those things again anyway, and the horse would have to take care of himself. During the arduous journey, she'd stolen what food she'd required and slept under trees, using her Magic freely. Trusting the others would accept her terms, she'd not been concerned about them finding her, and was not surprised to observe her sister on her trail. 'Twas good. She'd not really wanted to lose Natan, just keep a few steps ahead, and now she glanced up from the fire into the eyes of the vilest being she'd ever met. Her tongue stuck to the roof of her mouth. She tried to swallow, then swallowed again and licked her dry lips to gain enough moisture to speak. Even as she accomplished these subtle actions, her eyes were hard and boldly focused unblinkingly upon the other.

She needed to finish this. Squinting in preparation for her re-tort, she had a flashback. While trying to decide what to do that dawn after leaving the others, she'd made up her mind and devised a plan. She had not a chance in Hades of killing this one, nor could she just offer the Guard information about the general location of the Lair, for rumors abound and 'twas common knowledge. But she could provide her sister with the names of the other contacts upon the island, if she could fool the Sorcerer into revealing such information. She knew that at least one of them was in the Assembly, but she felt certain there was another, one who was even more dangerous to the Nation. With these names delivered, Amends could be made, and she'd be ready to enter the Beyond.

Even though they'd started in the Darden region, the Sorcerer had refused to meet her there. Now they were in the wilds of southeastern Wyndsyr Forest and Niamia would have to find Natan quickly once the deal was done. 'Twould be necessary, for even the intent to do what she was planning, would force her Past the Veil, and she knew not how long she could stand. Nevertheless, her Suggestion Magic was stronger than most recognized, and she'd had plenty of practice. 'Twould help her in this final effort. She'd been plying the Sorcerer with a story of how the Assemblyman was becoming too reckless, for even she had begun to suspect his identity, and would soon show his hand if left to his own devices. If he told her who the Hoard alliance contacts were, she could protect them, as well as eliminate the Assemblyman's stupidity afore anyone else became wise to their infiltration. She was good. As a Guardsman, she had superior knowledge of how to get away with murder, but she couldn't just kill the entire Assembly to ensure she took care of the threat. If he wanted to maintain control, she needed to know more, and now, for if any of them were found, he'd lose them all. The Elite would not stop 'til every spy was ferreted out, and that included Nia. Then, even her usefulness would be lost to the Black. Her position was something that held weight with the Sorcerer.

She stood up and walked boldly forward. Staring him down, she stated with sarcasm oozing, "Yes. I say. If you don't believe me, then join me in the Blood Oath. I cannot reveal anything to anyone that way, and you'd have nothing more to fear." Sneering, she knew that accusing him of being fearful might push him o'er the edge, and then he'd simply kill her now. But the shock of the emotion she felt emanating from him, the heat of his rage, was necessary to help hide her deception.

The Sorcerer calmed himself, and considered her proposal. 'Twould be impossible to break, and he'd finally have absolute power o'er the strong-willed girl. The Black need know not about such an arrangement. Nia felt his capitulation, and holding out her arm with a smirk on her face, she held her breath, hoping he'd fall for it. He did.

~~~~~~~~~~

The Sorcerer had been angry, and yet excited, when she'd offered herself to him for the Oath. In his eagerness, he'd near cut off her hand, after which of course, he'd Healed her for he couldn't have her bleed to death, but he'd left the pain factor as a reminder of whom she served. Taking his leave, he'd laughed at her pain, oblivious to the truth, and to the Suggestion. Nia rocked back and forth, sitting cross-legged on the ground, holding her arm up against her chest, trying to get past the experience long enough to get moving, but the pain wasn't just in her arm. 'Twas all o'er her body. The Blood Oath had already begun to take her life. She stood up, gulped back the bile, wiped the tears from her cheeks, and looked 'cross the forest. From this ledge, she could see many leagues. Hoping her sister wasn't far behind, she'd need to Dance hard, and find her fast.

~~~~~ NEAR A DAWN LATER ~~~~~

Natanamia loved being a Guardsman, but didn't relish this duty. 'Twas a duty she'd never dreamed to have to fulfill. Even though she'd stated her intent to make Amends, Niamia had also admitted her guilt and she'd accepted the sentence without standing afore the Assembly. She could do naught but respect her sister's last wishes, and act as her executioner. Yet, the chase was anything but normal. How was she planning on making Amends, and where was she going? Natan hoped by their ancestors, that Nia's stated plans were not more lies to fool them into letting her escape. Therefore, she was not deceived by her sister's attempts to lead her. She just hadn't understood why. Her Dance signature was bold enough for an amateur to follow, yet Niamia continued to elude her. 'Twas not by accident, and mayhap 'twas shrouded in Suggestion. For days, Natan Danced warily behind, ready for an ambush that never came.

Suddenly, Niamia appeared so close, she collapsed into Natan's arms. As the sun dawned upon her, Natan cradled her sister and sat in the dirt of the forest floor, backed up to the base of a tall cypress tree. The forest seemed to close in upon them, muting her senses. Niamia gripped her sister's arm so tightly to ward off the pain that her knuckles turned white. She gasped, bloody tears streaking down her cheeks. "Natan, I keep a letter in my boot. Take it and read it after... I wanted you to understand, to forgive me. But I will die afore I can explain, and there is something else I must reveal." She drew an agonizing breath, and shaking uncontrollably, she continued. "You're not alone. There's one more of our lineage. My daughter, Flyrra."

Although a thousand questions ran through her mind with the unexpected announcement, 'twas only one that needed voicing now. Biting back her surprise, she asked, "Where?"

"I know not, she was taken from me at birth, to seal my allegiance. The Black kept her as a personal slave. I saw her but a handful of times. She'd be eight winters by now. Promise you'll try to rescue her. The Sorcerer will feel when I Pass the Veil, and when 'tis reported, they'll kill her. Or worse."

Natan's heart sank. If the Black had taken her niece, she was most likely dead already. Still, Niamia was correct in that there were worse things than death. If there was any chance at all that the child yet lived, she must pursue it. "What does she look like?"

Stuttering with weakness, blood beginning to trickle out of the corners of her mouth as she tried to breathe, she responded, "Half breed, easy to spot. Silver hair. Black eyes."

Natanamia gasped in astonishment, but knowing Nia's Life Force was fading, she could waste no time. "I will find her. She'll know her mother died a champion to the Nation, and to protect her," she promised.

Tears tracks smeared down her once beautiful face as Nia grimaced in pain and struggled for breath. "I love you, Natan."

"And I, you." Natan's voice cracked with emotion as they uttered their final words to each other. Then she squeezed her sister as hard as she could to help her hold on, and lowered her ear to Nia's mouth to hear the wheezed name.

<center>~~~~~ NEAR A MARK LATER ~~~~~</center>

Natanamia wiped her sweaty brow with the back of one filthy hand, and sheathed her blade, grateful to the Fates themselves that she'd not been forced to use it to complete her original mission. She gathered Niamia's weapons, stashing them under the crypt she'd created, afore unfolding the letter retrieved from her boot. Her sister had the most elegant script. She winced. Had. Guilt threatened to swamp her, and she gulped hard to breathe again. There was yet a task to complete afore this mission was done. With the revelation recently obtained, she feared for so much, so many, yet there was one chore left. Read the letter. She held the parchment and stared blindly for a moment, and then as she blinked to clear her vision, she read the hastily scrawled words.

'I am not the only Sprite with ties to the Hoard. They are few now, but insidious in their recruitment, and extremely secretive about their identities. They made it all sound so thrilling, so righteous, so easy, to one of my youth and naïveté. But once I agreed, I found I'd entered a world of abhorrence and abomination, and by the time I realized my mistake, 'twas too late to withdraw. My every transgression led to another. They feed off one's insecurities, one's failures, one's desires. I know what I did was wrong, but I was used. They promised me I'd be a Guardsman one day, but they also controlled me with my offences. If what I'd already done was discovered, I'd never be in the Guard. If I did just one more thing for them, provided one more bit of assistance or information, they could mysteriously right all the wrongs and make my past disappear forever. If I wasn't so encumbered by my family, they said, I could be a Guardsman. And of course, they wanted me in the Elite, they wanted someone higher and deeper, infiltrating the Hold. Someone who had free access, and could travel without notice. And then one night I told them I was done. No matter what they did to me, I would no longer participate, the price was too high, the betrayal already too deep in the House. Their answer? I was raped by my contact, which of course, I could not report. I went home and suffered in silence. In time, I had a child. They helped me through the pregnancy so that no one knew, and Natanamia was already in the Guard so she knew naught, and holds no guilt. Then they kidnapped my little girl and used her life as the threat to maintain control. It seemed there was always another path to getting out, to being a Guardsman, to fulfilling my dreams... and their desires. I blindly followed, for that outcome still beckoned me, and they promised to kill my baby if I didn't. One night they set up a meeting for me with my daughter, and never arrived. 'Twas suggested that I feed from my family, taking enough Life Force that I could leave without waking them, for my own safety as well as theirs. But I became suspicious after a short time, and then horrified by the thought that I'd missed the innuendo, the words spoken time and again... if I was not encumbered by my family... I raced home only to find I was too late, and I'd played a role in the unthinkable. Vampyre. I knew not who'd finished the deed. I tried, but could not discover the guilty party. When I was approached to enter the Guard shortly thereafter, I didn't know if 'twas my own talent or their influence and I no longer cared, for as a Guardsman I had a better chance to rescue my child and discover who'd murdered my family. I never knew who my contacts were, as they were always under cover of foreign Allure, a Magic for which I had no reference. But then, my life had been sheltered, I knew little of the outside world and… '

The letter ended abruptly as if she'd been interrupted, and was never able to finish her tale. Natan faced the fact that she hadn't known her little sister at all. This Sprite was someone she'd never met, someone who struggled in silence against incredible odds and pressure, needing help that never arrived. She wiped the tears from her cheeks with the back of her hand, and vowed that Nia's sacrifice would not be in vain. "You were always the strongest one, Niamia. I teased you when we were little because I may have been first born, but you were their crowning jewel. I was jealous of how pretty you were, your tenacity, your favored status, and I have regretted my behavior since the day I joined the Guard. I ran away from our troubles, and you stayed and faced them all alone. I always wanted to be like you. I forgive you, my sister. I'm so sorry. 'Tis I who must, and cannot, make Amends for how I wronged you. If only you had known… If only…" The tears streamed unchecked once more, washing her grimy face anew.

<p style="text-align:center">~~~~~ A FEW MARKS LATER ~~~~~</p>

Natanamia Danced as never afore. She'd ensured that Nia's remains would be forever enshrined in the wilds of the forest, if she could not return for them. Humans were no problem, as they could not see the remains of Magic bearers without assistance, but she didn't want the Hoard to desecrate her sister's crypt, so she'd placed not a Spell which could be detected, but instead had planted a natural cover of flowery vines surrounded by evergreens, boosting their growth with her own Magic, to the point the crypt was completely, and beautifully, hidden.

She thought she'd been prepared for any revelation of the spy's identity, but 'twas worse than her most horrid nightmares. And yet, 'twas not entirely unexpected. Finding her niece would have to wait. Accusing the one Nia could name out of an implied trio might bring the end of her career as a Guardsman, but she no longer cared, for this one held so much status it could mean the end of the very existence of the Sprite Nation. Conventions be Flamed. Niamia tried to name them all, but was unable to withstand the ferocity of the torture that ravaged her mind and body as she succumbed to the Blood Oath, and so she named the one she determined to have caused, and would continue to cause, the most damage. There was no doubt, for if she'd falsely accused, she'd not have died. Natan had to get to her team afore they left the mainland, or they'd return home and alert the spy.

<p style="text-align:center">~~~~~ THE BLACK'S LAIR ~~~~~</p>

His growl rumbling through the caverns, the Black roared, "Send her to the Talons, feed her to the Pitch!" Spitting his words, thick slimy drool ran down his muzzle and dripped off his yellowed fangs as he clenched his great jaws in anger at losing his favorite slave. He focused his fiery gaze at the Sorcerer, who'd just informed him of Niamia's death. The Sorcerer had to be very careful to conceal how the Guardsman died. If 'twas discovered he'd told her anything, even with such measures to ensure the secret was kept, he'd become a part of the dinner menu without any chance of groveling his way out of that fate this time. However, 'twas a calculated risk, as sharing the knowledge of her death so soon after it occurred was useful to keep up his illusion of having much power to the Black, for he'd made too many mistakes recently.

The child was supposed to have been their hold o'er the Sprite, however, honor held a higher hold, and although it should have been impossible to break the Blood Oath, Niamia managed. He'd once been quite attracted to the maiden, but now he would sacrifice her child, for allowing her to escape or be rescued would send a message of hope throughout Kadoor, and that would never do. Her continued existence also sent that message, and her mother's death sealed her fate. Pleased, he considered such a fate to be fair, for her rejection of his past advances. He'd rather have kept the child for his personal enjoyment, but giving her to the Pitch Elves was just as satisfying, knowing what would become of her there. Young and wiry, but small, he felt nothing for the youth, although mayhap he should. Nevertheless, his heart became stone many winters past, and his lifelong ambition was revenge.

"So be it," the Sorcerer replied, his head bowed as he backed hurriedly away from the Black once again. He never minded having to bow, it kept his master from seeing the expression of repugnance upon his face. Once out of reach, he fled the Lair immediately after informing his subordinates of the order affecting the child's new living arrangements, 'living' being a relative term, as he was quite certain she wouldn't last long.

~~~~~ SOMEWHERE DEEP IN DARKLING FOREST ~~~~~

"Well crap!" Anastasia clung precariously to the tall pine, both arms and legs wrapped tightly around the rough trunk. Plastered against the tree like a battering ram contacting the gates of a castle, she had to think a moment to make certain she was still intact and uninjured. Dancing the 'portals' as she was now referring to her experiment, was a most interesting way to travel, and through the past few moons she'd confirmed 'twasn't using the shadow realm at all, but 'twas similar. She also had decided that Dancing inside wasn't as adversely affected by the movement of the shadows, as 'twas by the appearance of a portal at an inopportune moment in the Dance. She'd been trying to find some consistency in them, so that she could predict or choose her destination, however she wasn't where she'd been the
~~~~~

last time, nor where she'd attempted to go. Honestly, she had to figure it out soon, or the next time she might end up in an even more dangerous situation, like that time she found herself in the Icelands.

Nevertheless, her experiments took a sideline turn with that trip, to see if she could find the lost ones, where they'd been transported, or if they'd died. 'Twas becoming clearer that some of those who'd disappeared and were presumed 'lost', might not have lived through the portals they ended up accidentally taking, and those who survived could have been sent anywhere on Kadoor. Even if they knew what had happened, which she felt was highly unlikely, they'd not have been able to return the way they left, and the Wyrdritch would have repelled them if they'd managed to return a'foot. The departure wasn't too bad, 'twas the destination she needed to learn to manipulate. No, it should've been easier than this, and she was quite certain 'twas something wrong with them, not her.

She sighed and squeezed the trunk tightly, her chin resting on the rough bark as she looked up through the branches. She'd never get enough of that blue sky, 'twas awe inspiring. Wrinkling her nose, she chastised herself. "I should have stepped in a tad sooner." Mayhap if she hadn't hesitated just that candle drip, she'd at least be standing on the ground. Hmmmm. The ground might be very far away at this moment. She peered o'er her shoulder to get a better view of the distance. "Oh, good grief." Relaxing her grip, she stretched out her long legs and stepped away from the tree upon solid footing once more.

CHAPTER EIGHTEEN

The Order of the Eagle

ABOARD THE KRAKKEN

UNDER COVER OF THE MIST

~~~~~ PORT O'DREKINN ~~~~~

Four voices chimed together in protest as new orders were issued. Natanamia raised her hands to silence the outburst. "Yes, yes, if I don't rescue the child, she will die, if they haven't forced her Past already. Her importance is immeasurable, not just because she's the last of my own blood, but because she's a breakthrough. She turns myth into certainty, and makes real the possibility of our Races being reunited. But, I am acting Captain and we are talking about a spy of extraordinary status, one in the upper echelon of our society, one who's influence may decimate us, opening the doorway to a full Hoard invasion of the island. And, we don't know this one's other Hoard contacts. There are mayhap two more of near equal importance, at least one of whom is in the Assembly." She dropped her head in weariness, suddenly o'ercome with the enormity of her responsibilities. The past few moons had been demanding to say the least, and now the future was unfolding as just as difficult. 'Twould be no rest for the Elite Guardsman. Yet she could not be in two places at the same time, regardless of how able she was. She could think of no way around this dilemma. How could she choose life 'tween a child and a Nation?

Natanamia was exhausted after just managing to head them off at the docks of Port O'Drekinn afore they set sail. Now she stood upon the quarterdeck of the Krakken with her Guardsmen. Myrrdin quietly observed, one hip hiked upon the railing as he listened to the exchange, his long black hair loose and lifting in the breeze of the Mist. Clearing his throat in the relative silence of the moment, his clear voice rose o'er the gentle rhythmic lapping of the waters against the hull. "I have a suggestion, if I may?"

LATER

~~~~~ MYRRDIN'S QUARTERS ~~~~~

Myrrdin stood with his arms crossed o'er his chest and his shoulder against the wall, staring at the table. The bottle of Drekinn whiskey still sat in the middle. He'd ensured 'twould not stir from its place of honor come Hades or high water, 'til 'twas set free of his Spell. 'Twould be the day Caleichante returned. Hearing Natanamia's account of their encounter in the forest, he was pleased she was following through with the plan, and apparently doing well, but the mission had just begun. She still faced much, against huge odds. He contemplated the future, and wondered when the Fates would once again bring him news.

~~~~~ THE MAINLAND ~~~~~

Myrrdin had lived with them for so long that he'd become well known amongst the Sprite Nation. His deeds were legendary, his advice respected and highly sought after. As Ship's Master of the Krakken, sailors competed to fill his crew, few ever leaving by choice. His input was greatly appreciated. Natan was not only eager to hear what he had to say, but grateful. Squatting by the small fire, she ate under a canopy of stars surrounded by forest, thinking about their last conversation while plotting her search strategy. Myrrdin pointed out that 'twas certain if she returned to the island 'twould be surmised that she'd succeeded in her mission to execute Niamia, and 'twould not be wise to assume the spy wouldn't think that Nia may have betrayed her other Hoard alliances, since 'twas unclear just how much each of the spies knew of the others. Conversely, her continued absence could easily be explained as still being on the hunt for her sister, when she was now hunting the Hoard and her niece.

Niamia's death would not be reported, to try to avoid back-lash if possible, as well as to give Natan more time to locate and rescue the child. 'Twould mean avoiding overt contact with the spy, for they'd probably be scrutinized upon their arrival and for some time after. Natanamia reconfirmed Aiisabeau as acting Captain, and her Guardsmen were on their way back to the Island of Dreams where they'd watch to prevent further harm, and with any luck uncover the spy's other contacts afore being forced to act. They didn't want to alert the spy too soon, but they could not allow another incident. And they had a duty to protect the ones who were physically close to the spy. 'Twould be an enormous task, but not any more difficult than what Natan now faced. If finding Caleichante was considered a needle in a haystack hunt, this would be far more difficult. Thinking about Calei made her wonder where she was now. She sighed. Worrying was not productive, and Kevon and Bryynn were in the best hands possible. Hearing what had happened to the Heir Apparent, she had to agree with Myrrdin that if anyone could save the Prince, 'twould be the Captain.

<div style="text-align: center">~~~~~ BYNDYNN FOREST ~~~~~</div>

Natan couldn't believe her luck. Having Danced back to South Byndynn in a little o'er one dawn, she was starving and needed to re-energize with a good meal. 'Twas just about midnight when she literally ran into a Warrior as they jostled each other in the narrow doorway of the first tavern in the first village she entered. His reflexes were extraordinary, as he managed to keep her from falling backwards o'er the threshold, which was a tad embarrassing, but the close contact made her aware of his profession, for under that cloak he carried a rather hefty sword. The tall, broad-shouldered man was muscular and obviously of good breeding, as were all Warriors, well-mannered and intelligent, but not one to cross. His skin was a soft brown and matched his eyes, which were generously lined with long lashes. His black hair was course, thick, and had the kind of curls that noble women spent multiple marks trying to duplicate. Natan found herself wanting to reach out and run her fingers through them, and she nervously withdrew her hand when she noticed 'twas lifting of its own accord.

He was traveling to Drekinn under cover, but he couldn't fool her with his subterfuge, and after establishing the fact that she wasn't going to reveal his identity, they struck up a working friendship. Her hearty appetite amused the Warrior, and after eating her fill, he paid the tab for them both, and took her back to his last campsite. The fire was warm and he stood to remove his full cloak, revealing bracers and pads made of multiple layers of feather shaped pieces of heavy leather, tooled in fine detail, giving the appearance of wings upon his forearms and shoulders. During that night, they got to know each other better, two fighters of equal status in their own right, and in their own environments. His respect for the Sprite Guardsman grew with the marks they spent together, and soon 'twas shown that respect was mutual. 'Twas a long day and far into the next night, while Natan explained her mission. As he listened, he sat quietly working with a small dagger to smooth a length of wood he'd carried tucked in his belt. Completing a project that was clearly begun earlier, for 'twas already hollow, he added several holes along the length of one side and notched one end. Several times, Natan wasn't certain if he was listening, but when she became quiet, he'd look up immediately and say something or nod, encouraging her to continue. By late the following night, she'd told him all she knew about the situation, including the only option she could see: to kill the Black.

Natan was delighted, as she ate the rabbit she'd caught and he'd cooked upon the coals, when he pulled forth the wooden flute he'd finally finished to his satisfaction and proceeded to play a series of somber notes, transforming into a hopeful melody that brought peace to her troubled heart. 'Twas her turn to listen now, as the man played and pondered. She'd never heard the song afore, and she could almost feel the story of triumph being told. Music had always helped him organize his thoughts and focus his mind. Soon, he shared those thoughts with Natanamia. He was convinced her mission was a challenge she could not complete alone, and one in which he was eager to participate. He'd heard rumors o'er the past few winters of a young girl of unknown Race being kept as a slave to the Black, traveling with his entourage through the Talons 'tween the Darden region and the Far Northlands, although none could verify. The only reason she was known even as a rumor, was for her highly unusual appearance and unnerving gaze, of which, the Black took full advantage. Although 'twasn't much to go on, 'twas something. Neither he or the Sprite could face the Black alone and walk away, nor together could they openly oppose one who was so well-guarded at all times. In his battle-hardened opinion, this was a mission of extraction: sneak in, sneak out, and keep the stealth. But first they had to find the girl.

Once the plan was made and both in agreement, they decided to split up. Natan would travel southeast back toward the Darden region to follow up on the rumors that 'twas the main Hoard Lair location, while the Warrior would go northeast into the Talons to follow up on similar rumors. To avoid the dangers of local weather shifts, they'd meet midway at the Keep of St Swiftyn's 'tween the end of winter and the Spring Melts, to report of any progress. 'Twould give them each at least five or even six full moons to reconnoiter. They broke camp afore dawn. Bidding her good hunting and taking his leave, he whipped his cloak back o'er his shoulders as he turned, but not afore she caught sight of a large, spread-winged and talon-bearing eagle, tattooed on the back of his left shoulder, half hidden by his own leather wings of protection.

CHAPTER NINETEEN
Elven Vision

Calei had pushed both herself and Demonseed beyond all limits, and exasperated, she recognized she was having trouble staying alert. 'Twas a dangerous passage around this mountain to the canyon beyond, a narrow trail with sheer rock climbing straight up one side of her and falling straight down the other, for at least a league in both directions. Although extremely treacherous, 'twould have been impossible any earlier or later in the season. 'Twas midsummer and even though the winds blew chill at this elevation, the sweat beaded upon her forehead as they made their way cautiously onward, step by step. Having taken the precaution of tying a scarf around the horse's eyes to prevent him from seeing the threat to both sides, she led him, snorting and huffing his displeasure as they shuffled slowly along, Kevon secured to the stallion's back. If there'd been anything organic within reach, she couldn't take advantage, for 'twould leave Demonseed on his own, and Kevon couldn't Dance in his condition, so, one slip and they were all goners.

She stopped and leaned with her hands on her knees as she tried to catch her breath. The extra training was proving invaluable. Kevon spent most of his time near comatose and had begun to moan and cry out in pain often of late. Nothing she did could provide comfort. She cursed Corbyn once again for talking her into dropping the Egg, as Bryynn's proximity was good for the boy, but she also understood 'twas the best plan. The Spell that had eased much of the pain was wearing off as Corbyn had warned, and she must find Persephone and the Wyrdritch soon. She risked this passage for multiple reasons: 'twas so remote it should throw off her followers, and 'twas a more direct route 'cross the Talons, getting them to Darkling Forest quicker. Hopefully 'twas not a huge mistake.

After burying the Egg, she'd chosen to avoid the traveler's pass through the Talons known as the Eye of the Raptor, even though attempting to travel through anywhere else was incredibly dangerous. She'd skirted far north around the Keep of St Swiftyn's, trekked through most of Byndynn Forest, and was now entering some of the roughest parts of the mountain range. Ever watchful to avoid the People of the Talons, the tribe known as the Gordatch, she'd discovered an unlikely party consisting of an Elf and two Warriors with two War Horses, not far behind. Even as she wondered exactly who they were and why they were out there, one of the Warriors drew the focus of her attention. Tall, lean, unbelievably handsome, her palms were sweating as she absently rubbed them down her thigh. The simple action made her warm, and she realized she was becoming aroused. For the first time in her span of days, she felt a strong physical attraction. She'd always been a loner, but there was something about that particular Human. Lying on her belly, resting on her forearms, she couldn't shake the sense of familiarity when she gazed from the ledge down into their camp, but also could not determine a reason. 'Twas as if she'd seen him afore, but surely, she'd remember. Still, she needed to get moving and these three not far behind, their intentions unclear, clinched the decision to tackle the current passage. After traveling non-stop for several days to get here, using every trick to lose the strangers, the lack of sleep and the physically grueling pace was taking its toll. 'Twas amazing that she was still functioning. There were few who could match such a feat. And yet, as she'd started up the steep and winding trail, her pursuers, for she'd determined they were on her trail a'purpose, were only a few marks behind. How could they track her so quickly?

~~~~~~~~~~
~~~~~~~~~~

Taking a brief rest break, Diadranei and Bastyen paired off to the side while Graasyn took watch. Diadranei attempted once again to contact Caleichante, but it seemed her offers were being rejected. That, or they were simply too far away for her to hear the Empathic Call of the Elf. Either way, 'twas concerning. The elder Warrior was pushing them hard, and with the Elf's senses to guide them, they were closing in on their quarry. Nevertheless, Caleichante ran afore them with the skill of a mountain cat and the grace of a gazelle. He could not rest. Diadranei was secretly sharing her strength to keep the Warriors going, and although Graasyn appeared not to notice, she knew otherwise. She could sense his gratitude, but no words were exchanged. Now gazing longingly into her lover's eyes, her slender fingers lingered along one of his ears as she tucked his long red hair behind it. She knew he harbored a certain amount of mixed emotion about his parentage. Mayhap 'twas time to reveal what she'd recently learned. "You wish to know of your past. To know who your true parents are."

He shrugged his shoulders. "I've let that go."

"Don't ever lie to me."

Laughing, he apologized. "Forgive me, 'twas unintentional. Mayhap I was lying to myself. Our coping mechanisms can become such a habit, we begin to believe our own stories, to survive."

Dia nodded her understanding, and then stated, "'Tis Graasyn."

"Yes. He Claimed me. I could ask for no better father of blood."

"No, I mean he is your blood father."

Bastyen was astonished. "What? You must be joking."

'Twas now Dia's turn to laugh. "Please. Me? Joking?"

Incredulously, he asked, "Does he know?"

"Obviously not. He's an honorable man. If he'd known your mother was with child, he would not have left that child."

Bastyen rolled o'er to his back and stared at the forest canopy. "This is going to take a while to sort through."

Sitting up beside him, she looked down at her folded hands. "I know. Sometimes I say too much of what I know."

He rolled back o'er to her, propping himself up on one elbow and placed his free hand on hers. "Not so, Dia, this is wonderful news. I just don't want to hurt Aba, and I fear 'twill. I mean, he'll be devastated at what he missed. Was she a bar maid? A traveler? Mayhap she'd left the area afore she knew she was with child. He's admitted to having a rather healthy sex life in the early days of his Oath, as do many young Warriors. 'Twill be highly unlikely he'd remember which woman was my mother. But then, I was left in the Port District, why did she abandon me? Did they meet elsewhere, and she tried to find him? Mayhap she worked there." Then a revelation came to the young man. "What if she helped raise me? This is mind boggling. You know. You know who she was, don't you?"

"I know not, but I might recognize her if we were in close enough proximity." She felt something straining in the back of her mind and reached out to lightly stroke his ears once again. Touching him brought forth a foreign notion. She squinted as she tried to make sense of the ideas flooding her mind. "You have your father's ears," she stated with puzzlement.

Bastyen sat up beside her so he could watch her face. He knew she was 'learning' something. As a Stealth operative, deduction and attention to details was his forte, and he was becoming very proficient at helping her make her conclusions and leading her onward. He recognized 'twas something of great importance, and so he asked the most obvious question, "Not my mother's?"

Diadranei was suddenly hit with the full knowledge, and she touched her own pointed ear as she said with amazement, "No. Not your mother's."

Eyes wide, his surprised expression now matched hers. "Elven? My mother was Elven? How can that be?"

She had to laugh out loud, for certainly by now he understood that such a pairing wasn't impossible, and near chastised herself for not noting the fact earlier. "Have you not ever wondered from whence your unique Gift came?"

"Dia, must I remind you that we didn't know about that 'til your revelation? But wait... Graasyn shares this Gift. He sees Allure, I see through it. My mother could not have given him this."

With confidence, she replied, "Truth. 'Twas not your mother, nor his, from whom he received such."

"His father! His father was Elven."

She smiled. "Seems Elves found refuge amongst the Humans of Kadoor in greater numbers than I'd imagined. But they could not have stayed, even to raise a child, for such a child would never be accepted by the Royal House of Haven. And with our longer span of days, their continued youthful appearance would become a burden to their safety. Your mother may have been drawn to Graasyn for his Elven blood, mayhap not even realizing such, nevertheless, she wouldn't have known whom you'd favor 'til after your birth, so she would've tried to hide the pregnancy from everyone. And once discovered you took after him, I suspect 'twas why you were left in the Port District. Mayhap your mother was hoping you'd be readily accepted into Human society, as was your father, and reuniting with him may have been orchestrated to some extent."

For a few moments, Bastyen quietly thought about all that had occurred through the past winter. "Well, half breed or not, the way things appear, I'll age and die long afore you, unless I take the 'Bond, but that would separate us just as effectively. Yet, I am a Warrior and we're fighting for the future of Kadoor. I must follow my Oath and fight for the Resistance. I worry that if you stay with me, you'll never be allowed to return to your home." Bastyen stood up, lifted Dia to her feet, then stopped and took a deep breath. Without releasing his grasp, his eyes locked onto hers. "Even knowing such, I must ask. Will you honor me by becoming my lifemate?"

Her face lit up with joy and she could barely breathe the words he'd so longed to hear. "Yes, my love, yes, nothing could make me happier!" Bastyen took her in his arms and kissed her passionately, then pulled back to admire her beauty. She smiled and licked her lips. The taste of him set her on fire with longing, but there was no privacy and they had not the time for celebrations. With her fingers o'er her mouth, she savored the kiss afore continuing her thoughts. "If I'm correct, you have more Elven blood than Human, and may outlive many. Yet no one knows how long they have on this side of the Veil. I have no regrets. I shall never love another as I love you. I am a free Elf and need not the approval of the Royal House, and I've lived outside the Wyrdritch since afore the Retreat. 'Tis no longer home to me, and I shall follow you wherever you go, without looking back."

Bastyen squeezed her hand and brought it to his lips, then held it tightly against his chest as he contemplated his past, his future, his lovely mate. The One had truly blessed him. Then his smile turned upside down as another thought invaded his joy. "Aba is in love with the Sprite we chase," he stated sadly. Then he slapped his open palm to his forehead, in an effort to make light of the seemingly impossible situation. "Wait, what was I thinking? You know everything."

With a lopsided smile, she shrugged her shoulders in acknowledgement, for she didn't know everything. But she did know much. Even from this distance, she sensed Graasyn's feelings were matched, but Calei was an Elite Guardsman, Graasyn a skilled Stealth Warrior, both driven to excel and much needed in this war. 'Twould be no time for them 'til their current mission was complete, and the future was unusually shaded, as with misunderstandings, where those two were concerned. "She intends to return to the island and to her career, and he to his. She will serve the Sprites, he the Clan. I know not how 'twill end."

Graasyn approached them, his jaw set with determination. "Mount up. Let's ride."

CHAPTER TWENTY

Mythical Reality

~~~~~ CROSSING THE CENTRAL PEAKS OF THE TALONS ~~~~~

Two thirds of the distance around the mountain was a treacherous strip of loose rock covering the path as they began their descent. Calei's mind flashed back to Prea, strong-willed and steady, but the big stallion was just as sure-footed, for which she was grateful. After finally reaching the end of the trail, the rock-strewn base opened to a breathtaking canyon meadow surrounded by tall evergreens. Running through the middle, a river of crystal clear water awaited. Demonseed was agitated and Calei wary, but her senses revealed nothing, and his behavior was reasonable given what they'd just endured. Afore she'd allow the horse to drink, however, she reached up and untied Kevon from his back.

'Twas then she felt something amiss. With that sixth sense that raised the hair on the nape of her neck, she dragged the Prince off Demonseed as she spun about swiftly. There wasn't even enough time to draw her sword, her other hand still wrapped securely around the lead rope. She heard the 'zing' of wood and metal splicing through the air and was barely able to step in front of Kevon just afore the spear hit her square in the chest with such force, she lost her footing and was thrown backwards. She grabbed at the shaft of the weapon, and hit the ground in agonizing pain. Unable to breathe as the blackness closed in, frightening shrieks and screams and grunts came from the same direction as had the spear. Kevon slid to the ground somewhere beside her, and with the last of her blurring vision, she watched Demonseed sprinting away, still wearing the scarf around his eyes, the rope now bouncing upon the ground and hitting his
~~~~~

legs, spurring the beast into increasing panic as he disappeared into the forest.

<div align="center">~~~~~ RIGHT BEHIND ~~~~~</div>

Dia rode tandem with Bastyen, while Graasyn's massive Horse carried most of the gear. Despite their great size they were not slow, and given the fierce pace, they covered much ground quickly. They'd spotted Calei and the Prince ahead of them and were close enough to know when they'd entered onto the path. They were going to have to pick it up to catch her now, for she obviously knew they were on her trail, and once she reached the canyon beyond, they'd lose her again. Diadranei was trying, but she couldn't establish contact and they had no choice but to risk a fight to get close enough to reveal their intentions. Bastyen refused to allow her to try to Dance forward, for Dia was no Warrior, and with Calei in full defensive mode, she'd most likely not listen to anything afore skewering the newcomer. Graasyn's temper was on edge as he prayed he'd not have to injure the Sprite afore they could establish that contact. 'Twould be as ripping out his own heart.

Leading the Horses along the path, hot, lathered, and panting, they pushed them for more speed. The huge beasts were not able to take the narrow trail as fast as did the Sprite's horse, and Graasyn fumed as they fell further behind. Just as they rounded the bend at the highest point, they caught a glimpse of the canyon far below and saw them in the distance. Calei stood beside the horse and appeared to be removing the Prince from its back when she suddenly spun around. A gigantic spear flew toward her, but they could see not from whence it came. Graasyn bit his lip gritting his teeth to keep from crying out in alarm, as he watched the spear hit true.

Moments after the stallion raced 'cross the canyon and disappeared into the trees, he saw them. Huge boulders littering the canyon, stood up and unfolded themselves into Trolls. More of the giant creatures ambled forth from the forest, and his entire body shook with Battle Lust as he watched them surround his woman. Tying her and the Prince together by the ankles, they dragged them roughly back into the trees by the leather wraps. 'Twas only at that moment that he realized the spear had hit the saddlebag she wore o'er her left shoulder and 'twas now lying broken on the grass, the tip stuck in the saddlebag. Leather alone would not have prevented penetration. That spear was well aimed and thrown with sufficient force, it should have gone straight through her slender body. Hope renewed, but unable to move any faster, they managed to get to the canyon within a mark and Graasyn raced to grab the saddlebag. Incredulously, the spear tip just pierced the leather and fell to the grass as he picked it up. Opening the bag, he found a fractured sunstone.

<div align="center">~~~~~ INSIDE THE CAVES OF THE BORKAHN ~~~~~</div>

"Do you trust me?" Diadranei whispered to Bastyen, her hand upon his shoulder as he led them deeper and deeper into the mountain. Leaving the War Horses to free graze and hoping they'd not be captured and eaten by the Trolls, the entrance was easy to find simply because the Trolls didn't seem to care if they were tracked and left a wide swath of drag marks behind. Having watched with disbelief while seemingly huge rock formations became living beings, they were leery of their surroundings, but were hoping they could get close enough to find out what happened to the Prince and Calei and effect a rescue by having Dia divert their attention. But 'twas all based upon finding where they were being held, and thus far they'd been miserably unsuccessful. Although, they'd yet to find any of the inhabitants, either.

The Borkahn, more commonly known afore the Last Holocaust as Trolls, were massive humanoid creatures with extremely thick skin that closely resembled rock in color and texture. 'Twas so tough 'twas difficult to penetrate with ordinary weapons wielded with ordinary strength. They could hide in plain sight by squatting and tucking in their bulky hands and feet, raising their heavy shoulders up o'er their necks and covering their faces with their arms, creating the boulder effect. Instantly battle ready, all they had to do was stand up, for full-grown they towered o'er even the tallest Warrior and they had the strength of a dozen men. The males and females were difficult to tell apart, even though they wore minimal coverings. They seemed not to get too hot or cold, their thick skin near all the insulation they required. Their entire bodies had a boxy appearance, with oddly placed deep wrinkles here and there, which gave them an even more convincing 'rock' disguise. Their arms and legs were as hefty as tree trunks, they had no body hair, their eyes were huge and deep set, similar to human but in shades of grays or browns, their noses were flat and wide, their mouths a mere split 'cross their face with heavy ridge-like lips above and below, and they had a small hole within an indentation on either side of their heads for hearing. Humans once told of how they'd kidnap people and steal their horses and herd beasts, and none were ever seen again, presumably due to having been eaten, but 'twas no hard evidence of this. Not much else was known of them for they stayed hidden, their very existence a well-kept secret. No one had proven they were real and most considered them to be little more than myth.

The question startled him and he stopped to look o'er his shoulder. "Now is not the time to ask that question, Dia." Suspiciously he added, "What are you thinking of doing?"

"I just thought 'twould be a good idea to lay down your weapons."

Now he turned to face her with concern. "Why?"

She squinted and shrugged her shoulders as the walls on either side of them began to split apart in sections. Apologetically she replied, "'Twould be an act of good faith. We're surrounded, the Borkahn rarely take prisoners, and the three of us will not survive against such odds. Besides, I sense they won't kill us, if we do it quickly enough."

~~~~~ LATER ~~~~~

Graasyn was more difficult to convince to lay down his weapons than Bastyen, as he'd been near blinded by rage at yet another obstacle to rescuing the Sprite he already considered his woman. Battle Lust was brought under control when Dia explained they need only drop one, as none of their weapons would be sufficient to cause severe injury to the Borkahn, and 'twas a simple declaration of surrender. And, of course, there was the added bonus of being imprisoned in the same cave where even now Calei and the Prince were being held. This was what led to Graasyn's agreement with the plan, for plan 'twas, and they managed to pick up their 'dropped' weapons as well as maintaining control of all the rest of their weaponry, as they were pushed along. The two Warriors considered the entire protocol not only strange, but near ridiculous, as they allowed themselves to be taken captive.

Diadranei spoke extensively to one of them while being led to their holding cell and after pushing in the Warriors, she'd been taken away. Now 'twas Bastyen's turn to seethe, while Graasyn near flew 'cross the hewn-out cave to the far corner where both the other captives lay, still unconscious. He triaged the moaning Prince first and finding nothing apparently amiss, he checked out the Sprite with a fine-tooth comb. Dropping the saddlebag beside her, he unlaced the front of her halter top with trembling hands, and then ran his fingers o'er the silky skin of her chest expecting to find severe injury, but was amazed that although the spear should have pierced her heart, she'd only sustained a wicked bruise, and deduced 'twas the sunstone that took the brunt of the force, deflecting the fatal blow. His eyes distracted by the beauty afore them, his breath stuttered slightly as he slowly looked up into the face of the Sprite Guard, her eyes now open and gleaming as molten gold.
~~~~~

"Wait," he began, but she was faster than he could imagine, and her fingers seized his throat and squeezed on tight. Bastyen turned at the sound and stood with feet planted to the floor, observing without a hint of desire to assist. Graasyn didn't want to hurt her, and with his son 'cross the cell chuckling his enjoyment of the situation, he took advantage of her surprise to break the hold, amazed at her strength. "Please. I'm not going to hurt you. We've been following you for moons, to offer our help. We know what you're trying to do. Diadranei told us...", he stated, and then turned to look for the Elf so that she could confirm his explanation, finally realizing she wasn't with them. Turning his questioning gaze to Bastyen, the young man scowled, and Calei watched first one then the other, in growing bewilderment.

"They took her," Bastyen spat forth 'tween clenched teeth.

CHAPTER TWENTY-ONE
The Borkahn

As Dia approached Gorch, he growled haughtily, "Do not use your Magic on me, Elf. I may not have the same, but I know when 'tis about, and can repel such. You cannot harm me. The Borkahn are stronger than Magic." Then he waited. Saying no more, he watched her closely.

Dia ignored the command and Cast forth her senses, seeking to understand, not to hide or control or sway or alter, sensing his anguish, his anger, his love for his daughter, his disappointment with those who'd turned against him. The whole story burst upon her mind, their warring factions, Roack in league with the Black. She folded her hands and stared at the floor for a moment to collect her own thoughts afore she addressed the Troll. Bluntly, she stated, "If Roack be in league with the Black, he is no longer in charge of his own faction, and will not act in accordance with your expectations. 'Tis why your rescue efforts have failed thus far. Evil twists one's very being, blinds you to reason. If Crytcha yet lives, we must be quick, or the Hoard will simply kill her. If she is with the Pitch, we have even less time."

Gorch was amazed at the accuracy of her statements, and his eyes narrowed with suspicion, as Dia continued. "Search your heart. You know 'tis truth, and would be clear to anyone with eyes to see. And although we were attacked first, we have hurt you not." For several long breaths, the Borkahn leader sat on his simple throne of rock and stared at the Elf, weighing her words. After much time, and certain she'd not attempted to cause harm even if she'd used Magic, he listened as she outlined a daring scheme which included two conditions: release one other of her party to assist her, and promise to release the rest of them, including their

Horses, regardless of the outcome. He altered the bargain, saying he had no way of knowing for certain they weren't spies sent by Roack and so, if they failed, the others would not be released, but would be killed as such. Realizing her control of the situation was tenuous, in desperation, she agreed.

<center>~~~~~ NEAR A MARK LATER ~~~~~</center>

Calei quickly determined there was no ruse 'tween the pair, and she and Graasyn were discussing escape plans by the time Diadranei returned with the Borkahn guards. The journey had been long and hard, and Kevon appeared closer to the Veil by the dawn. The current circumstances were not helping them travel faster, and she'd lost Demonseed. She was more than happy with the unexpected assistance. The pair were at the back of the cell with the Prince, and Bastyen stood up and moved closer as Dia approached, but they didn't open the gate. Instead, the guards stood back and let her come close enough to talk. Bastyen gripped the bars as if he'd rip them from the rock in which they were so deeply embedded, and Dia brushed his hands with her fingertips. 'Twas clear she was to remain distant from them as the simple act brought forth grunts of disapproval. In response, she backed off a step. Calei was now standing at Bastyen's shoulder, Graasyn at the other, as Dia put up her hand for their attention. 'Twas clearly to placate the guards as well.

Speaking slowly so that the Trolls could comprehend, she used a modified, and very flourish, Common Tongue. "I have been in conference with the mighty Gorch, leader of the Borkahn, who has told me of a most disturbing situation," she stated with excess anguish, which seemed to please the Trolls. Turning to them, she said, "I spent near a mark with your glorious leader, 'twill be difficult to communicate our bargain to my companions in a few simple statements. I must speak freely with my team for a short while, so we may choose with wisdom." They conferred amongst themselves briefly and then nodded their blocky heads in affirmation. She turned back to Bastyen and mouthed, 'move away from the gate and bow please', and they all did so as she approached them again. This 'proof' of her leadership had the guards treating her with some respect, and they allowed her to enter and then stood at the open gate to ensure none would leave, as Diadranei reported all that had happened. The guards obviously didn't understand most of what was said and Dia explained that although Gorch spoke heavily accented but fluent Common Tongue, most of the rest of the Borkahn knew only their own language.

<center>~~~~~~~~~~</center>

After explaining that the Borkahn were simple beings, slow and stubborn but not stupid, and how they were naive to most of the inhabitants of Kadoor, 'twas understandable that they required Dia to 'prove' her status to get the others to agree with the bargain, so the facade of her leadership was continued for the sake of their observers. After the Last Holocaust, the Borkahn withdrew, living below in the mountain caverns to escape the destruction. Although reclusive from the outside world, they were not peaceful and had warred amongst themselves for generations. Now came Gorch, who was making the attempt to unite the Borkahn once again under one leader for their own survival against the Black and the Hoard, whose influence was penetrating even their strongholds. O'er the past several decades (for they had a life span of two or three centuries), Gorch had managed to unite most of the different factions under his banner, with only one holdout faction remaining, a group led by Roack. Gorch had long suspected Roack of being in alliance with the Black, and of leading multiple raids against Gorch's people. But now he'd proven such by taking his young daughter, Crytcha, as a bargaining tool. Roack attempted many times to convince his rival to meet with the Black and hear his proposal for 'the good of the Borkahn', but Gorch was not deceived, and after several failed rescue attempts 'twas learned that Roack handed Crytcha o'er to the Pitch.

Dia stopped to take a breath from her narrative. The atmosphere was certainly charged with passion and she was doing her best to remain in control against the assault. Bastyen held her hand as she summed up the bargain. "If we succeed and return with the child, we will be given our release, as well as safe passage all the way through the Talons, and in fact, would end up deep into Darkling. Besides being safer, such an arrangement will get us to the Wyrdritch very quickly, for Gorch remembers the position of the Elven Nation. I and one other, can leave this place to try to rescue Crytcha. The others must stay to ensure our loyalty, and that we'll not only make an honest effort, but will return as promised. If we do not, the others will be executed as spies sent by Roack. We have less than one fortnight."

Bastyen and Graasyn both began to talk o'er each other, but 'twas indicative of their circumstances, and their training, that they were of the same opinion. Dia's Magic would be central to any one of her potential partners, but 'twould be Bastyen to go with her, for although Graasyn's skills were good, his son's skills were better. Growing up in the Port District of Drekinn, he'd become an accomplished burglar, thief, escape artist, and pickpocket. Bastyen wasn't exactly proud of how he'd come by these skills, but they led him into the Stealth profession, for which he was proud. Graasyn would stay. If Bastyen and Dia were gone too long, Graasyn and Calei would make their escape with the Prince. Calei would never have abandoned Kevon anyway, and Graasyn would not have left Calei, so 'twas the only logical plan. Dia finally had to concede and nodded her head in acceptance, a worried frown upon her face. Calei smiled at her and stepped forth from behind Graasyn, her hand on his arm. "'Tis a good plan, Diadranei. I cannot leave Kevon and you know 'tis the only way this can work. If not for Islyth's sunstone, the spear would have sent me Beyond, and I'm still fatigued from my journey thus far. A few days healing and I'll be in top fighting form again. Besides, if they mean what they say, we must accept the risk."

"But what if we fail? They intend to kill you!"

Calei caught the gaze of the tall man standing beside her, and smiled, then returned her attention to the Elf. "I'm in good company, and we'll extend not our stay."

Graasyn then grasped his son's arm. "Return if you're able. Despite our situation, both the women feel no lie, and the Borkahn can get us to Darkling faster and safer than if we're required to travel o'er land. On the other hand, don't get yourselves killed trying to help the Troll, but you must try, for we're bound by the Oath. We'll wait if we can, but the Wyrdritch is our destination and should this bargain go awry, you need seek us in Darkling."

Bastyen set his jaw and nodded afore breaking the grasp and turning away. Taking Dia by the elbow, they left without looking back. Their guards closed ranks behind them and they disappeared out of view, down the darkened passage.

CHAPTER TWENTY-TWO
Perplexing Discoveries

HAVEN

~~~~~ ANA'S QUARTERS ~~~~~

Anastasia lay upon her massive down mattress and gazed at the sheer blue, green, and gold fabric of the canopy gently undulating with the soft breezes from her window, far out of reach. It reminded her of one of the paintings in the library. Of the ocean. 'Twas in one of the paintings…

After scrambling out of bed, hurriedly donning a robe, and running barefoot down the great halls to the library, she searched for the picture. 'Twasn't one of the ocean. Since her accidental trip to the Icelands, the image of the woman a'Dragonback, waving at her just as she turned and dived back into the portal, stuck in the back of her mind, and suddenly she knew why. She'd seen that woman afore. Ana and Coltyn were Alyssa's offspring, but Queen Bryanna was the mother of her other siblings. When Bryanna disappeared, King Jeeryd removed all the paintings with her in them, placing them into a storage room in the back of the library. She'd spent many marks looking at them, teaching herself how to paint. Jeeryd had intended to allow everyone to forget and then destroy them, which was ridiculous, for Elves, as all Magic bearers, lived long life spans and had even longer memories. But he was insane and his lack of insight had him thinking she'd shamed him by disappearing a'purpose, which of course, she hadn't. Ana was convinced she, as well as the rest of the 'lost' had all shared the misfortune of falling through a portal.

She hadn't looked at those paintings in a few winters. Now, where were they? 'Twas no torch in there, but they were kept at the back of the storage room. Had Jeeryd finally managed to destroy them? No! She found them under a pile of old manuscripts and a
~~~~~

thick layer of dust, which was unusual enough to draw one's eye, considering such a mess was easy to clean by Magic. She pushed the top few aside, as she sought the one she needed. Finally, she found it. Queen Bryanna astride a horse, riding toward her in the picture. Waving her hand. 'Twas her, there could be no doubt. The woman she saw riding the Ice Dragon, was Bryanna. But she'd not been able to find the same portal since that night, and she had no proof. Who'd believe her? They'd think she was as insane as the King, and would never trust her again. Not to mention the fact that if Jeeryd discovered her 'experiment', things would get ugly. There was nothing she could do. But could she keep such a secret from her brothers? From Persephone? She needed Myrrdin now, more than ever. The Heir Apparent was the eldest and since he was also considered 'lost', mayhap he'd believe and could do something. Having made the decision to tell only Myrrdin, she returned to her chambers, put her gown back on, and climbed up the step stool to lie on the bed, staring at the shimmering canopy 'til sleep finally closed in on her.

MIDSUMMER

~~~~~ **SOUTHEASTERN BYNDYNN FOREST** ~~~~~

</div>

Ardyth was quite pleased with herself. She'd found a stray horse that had provisions, foreign gear, and weapons of all kinds. By his condition, he'd been abandoned or lost, and had been wandering for a while. Her bounty included a bow, a quiver full of arrows, a sling, leather bracers, camping gear, blades, blankets, and a small chest shield that fit her perfectly. There were runes carved upon the inside of the thick leather shield, possibly a name, but although she'd seen these runes afore, she knew not how to read them. However, from prior experiences, she did know 'twas the language of the Magic bearers. The beast had been packed and ready, but what happened to his rider?

Around first mark, Ardyth sat bolt upright from a sound sleep when she felt the hand upon her shoulder. 'Twas another spirit.
~~~~~

"By the One, am I not allowed to sleep? What could you possibly want?" She hadn't intended to be rude, but she'd been awake half the night for the past few, with several spirits trying to get her attention. Apparently, there'd been many a battle fought here in ancient times. She'd lived alone since she was but eight, traveling through the great forests of Kadoor, rarely going to villages except for supplies she could not provide herself. She'd seen more than most people, had learned well the ways of stealth and deception to survive, although she liked it not. But her lifestyle, combined with her Gift, made her reclusive, and at times, unappreciative of even those who had no other means of communicating.

"I called him Ryndor. It means, 'Swift as the wind,'" the spirit girl told her.

Still a bit groggy, she asked, "Who?"

"The horse you found. He was mine. 'Tis my name spelled out in those runes. I carved them myself."

"Ah. 'Twould explain why he was abandoned, then. I am sorry," Ardyth replied respectfully, but felt she was in for another long night of listening to a spirit tell the story of their demise. Although many of the stories she'd heard were fascinating, and she'd learned much, such as fighting techniques, history (including the many Races of Kadoor), and survival skills, she really needed to get out of this region, at least for a while, or she'd never get a decent night's sleep. But she didn't want to be discourteous, either, especially since she'd just been granted the girl's horse and supplies, which were quite valuable. Mayhap she could get this one to start out by telling her who she was in life, and not just how she'd Passed. "My name is Ardyth. What's yours?"

A crushing sadness enveloped her when the spirit looked up, her almond eyes filled with pain. In the soft, distant voice of the spirit realm, she breathed, "Niamia."

<div align="center">~~~~~ LATER ~~~~~</div>

Ardyth had been correct. 'Twas another long night, but not for listening to the spirit. What she'd learned from the one-time

Sprite Guardsman, had been most disturbing. Requesting she pass along very important information to her sister, who was, apparently, another Guardsman, the spirit disappeared, satisfied that Ardyth could accomplish the task. But the details given, were slim. In her span of days, Ardyth had spoken with many spirits, and she'd come to learn that they thought along an entirely different plane than did those on this side of the Veil, and oft times, attempting to direct the conversation was at the very least, exasperating. However, Niamia had provided three names. Two were spies who could allegedly destroy the Sprite Nation. The third was that of her daughter. Despite the fact that she felt she'd been a bad mother, she'd done everything she could and wanted Ardyth to tell the little girl how much she loved her, but they'd been separated for long periods, and the last time she'd seen her had been winters past.

Fearing she'd forget the names of the spies, Frynbec and Benetyk, she'd written them down and concealed them by sewing them into the chest shield o'er the runes, but the little girl's name would never leave her mind, for the horror of the child's existence, coupled with the agony of her mother's heartbreak, was such to leave a lasting impression. If she could do so, she'd deliver that message. But the other she knew not how to accomplish, for she knew not the name of her sister, nor did she know where the Sprite Nation was located, and while pondering the difficulties of such a task, she realized she knew not the child's location nor even what she looked like. After finally dozing off for a mere few breaths, she'd jerked awake with her mind reeling. Sitting for marks, she watched the fire grow cold, and upon the first light of dawn, she packed up Ryndor, turned his head northward, and rode hard and fast, leaving the region far behind. Sinister happenings did abound, and she needed a change in surroundings. A woman on her own was considered bait.

CHAPTER TWENTY-THREE
An Unexpected Ally

OUTSIDE THE CAVERNS OF THE PITCH

~~~~~ THE RAPTOR'S TALONS ~~~~~

"Dia? What's wrong?" Bastyen immediately felt stupid. What wasn't wrong? He'd been trying to devise a plan, any kind of plan, but their task remained outwardly impossible. Nevertheless, as was the watchword of a Warrior, failure was not an option. He'd rarely been on a mission without his father and was feeling a bit of pressure, but he pushed aside his reservations and stared at his current partner. An Elf. A simply gorgeous Elf who made his heart beat faster every time he looked at her. He shook his head; 'twas no time to lose focus.

Gorch had escorted them to the well-guarded cave entrance, although not the one in which they'd entered, gave them the coordinates to the caves of the Pitch, and then without saying a word, each turned and went their own direction. Gorch went back to his people, Dia and Bastyen to what he thought was their certain death. He had a little hope or he wouldn't have allowed the bargain, but just a little. 'Twas probably bolstered a bit by Dia's Magic, although 'twas interesting to note that Trolls were mostly resistant to Magic. 'Twas theorized that their skin was so thick, Magic near bounced off them, and they had to be completely inundated for it to make any significant difference.

As Gorch saw it, if the Borkahn's attempts to rescue his daughter had failed, he could see no way Magic would help these strangers to succeed, but he was willing to take any chance, however slim. As Bastyen saw the mission, all they had to do was find a way into that cave, locate the girl Troll, and bring her out. Simple enough. He'd spent much of his span of days thus far, getting in and out of places that were considered impossible to
~~~~~

breach without being seen or caught, and this was no different. He paused and glanced yet again 'cross the expanse. Right. They weren't even certain what they faced, after all, who'd heard of the Pitch Elves? Even Dia was stumped, and she WAS an Elf. Sighing and wondering if the Fates owed him any favors, he noticed Dia's eyes scanning through the trees to the side of the gulch, and then move slowly o'erhead 'til she rested her gaze a few trees away. He murmured, "What is it?"

"Shh!"

Sensing something himself now, 'twas not evil, and that, in and of itself, was unusual. The evil was so strong here he could almost smell it, and had to keep his hand on Diadranei's shoulder to keep clear her senses.

"There," she whispered, and he lifted his gaze to where she was now pointing.

A flash of silver was his reward, and then a little girl appeared on a branch just out of reach, as she climbed down from higher up. She perched upon the branch as steady as any bird, and scrutinized them as they did the same to her. Bastyen slowly reached for his blade, but Diadranei stopped him, her hand o'er his. "Tell me what you see," she spoke softly in his ear.

"A young girl, mayhap eight, but small, with matted silver hair, black eyes, filthy, barefoot, torn rags as clothing, no obvious weapons," he whispered in classic Stealth mode, listing the most pertinent details as he saw them.

The report made Diadranei's jaw drop, and he knew she could not see the child through her Allure, but feeling her begin to shake with emotion he wondered if that was all that was going through her mind. "You are certain? Silver hair/black eyes?"

"Yes, so silver it glitters, so black there seems no iris or sclera. I've never seen such a combination in a human. Her ears are covered, but mayhap she's Sprite."

Then Diadranei did something he'd never seen afore. Stepping into the open, gracefully touching her left shoulder with the fingers of her right hand, she swept outward from the opposite hip with her left hand, palm up, and bowed her head. Taking another step, she quickly swept forth her right hand, presenting both palms upward, elbows at her waist as if holding a large platter. He was so surprised by this gesture, he missed seeing the little girl jump lightly to the ground and walk toward them. Afore he could pull his blade, the girl was in front of them and placed her hands palms down on Dia's, then touched her right fingers to her left shoulder and stepped slightly back turning her left-hand palm up, her right matching, in a reversal of Dia's first moves. 'Twas clearly a greeting of peace. While this was happening, he noticed a change in the girl's appearance and recognized that she'd dropped her glamour. Dia's slight intake of breath meant she now saw her as she truly appeared.

<div style="text-align:center">~~~~~ LATER ~~~~~</div>

The child licked the hot juices off her fingers, then handed one of the roasted cave rats she'd just pulled out of the fire by its tail, to Diadranei, who took it appreciatively. Up to three or four times larger than an ordinary rat, they also had longer and sharper claws and teeth, taking speed, quick reflexes, and courage to hunt, providing a good portion of lean meat to the victor. The child didn't even have a weapon, she'd been catching her main staple by chasing the creatures through the tunnels, or reaching quickly into whatever crevice they'd crawled, grabbing them by their thick tails with her bare hands, whipping them out, and bashing them against the rocks afore she could be clawed or bitten. They didn't require much cleaning as did other meals, simply burying them whole in the coals of a fire would burn off the hair and leave most everything ready to eat. The entrails crisped for tossing aside, while the heart, liver, kidneys, and brain (what little there was), were all edible. Their skin was not thick enough for making anything useful, but with a thin layer of fat underneath, 'twas also edible, and roasting made them quite tasty.

Bastyen had just pushed a third one under the coals as he listened to her story. "The Pitch were once Elves who didn't fare well through the War of Chaos. The Black used their weakness and fears against them, made them hate Man, telling them 'twas Man who pushed them out of the Wyrdritch, Man who forced them into starvation and sure extinction. He encouraged feeding from them, turning Vampyre to the point of no longer eating normal food. Now they are no more Elves than am I, but they are completely devoted to the Black, who keeps them in hostages for feeding, and ignorant of the truth. Sadly, the Pitch have grown with the ages, their numbers climbing mostly from inbreeding, with the occasional additions of lost Elves after the Retreat, and they might as well be considered their own Race. They're taught from birth to feed off the Life Force of others, especially Humans, and raised to believe the propaganda and lies of the Hoard. Although they're nothing but bullies, pure evil, killing for pleasure and the control they gain o'er others, as much as for sustenance, their numbers alone, and the viciousness with which they defend themselves and their kind, make them an enemy to be approached with much caution. But they're dimwitted. Inbreeding takes its toll, as does Vampyrism."

~~~~~~~~~~~

As the evening wore on, Diadranei and Bastyen explained their mission to the girl. 'Twas learned that she'd been a captive and had managed to escape, but refused to leave the rest behind, still trying to find a way to help. Her assistance in their mission was vital and would only cost them their assistance in hers, however, she had a much different idea of how they could help, then had Bastyen. "I can get them out of there, of me the Pitch know not. I've never been fed from so they can't detect my presence without a visual. The Warrior was captured trying to rescue me, and has been protecting me ever since. The Pitch Elves either do not recognize individuals, or they do not care. Without hesitation, he stepped ahead of me, shielded me behind his own body at
~~~~~~~~~~~

our first feeding, and did the same for every feeding after. Later, he helped me to escape through the bars, but he and the rest are too big to follow. We've tried to pick the lock from inside and out, but to no avail. I must have the key and 'tis never left alone. If you can but get me the key, I can do the rest. I've been staying in another place and bringing them food and water. 'Tween that and the Warrior's efforts to shield them, they are stronger than they appear. Once the cage is unlocked, I can lead them to my hiding place, where they can heal. When they're ready, they'll make good their final escape on their own. I'll stay with the Warrior. He'll require the most time to heal, for he's protected all the others, and is the most drained. The Warrior and I shall escape together, when he is ready." Her face turned from one to the other during her tale, but 'twas difficult to read their expressions. Now pleading, she continued, "You know I'm right. You cannot complete your own mission if you try to help all of us, too. Most can't go far on their own for now anyway. Please. He cannot last much longer. The key is all the help I need. In exchange, I'll show you how I get in and out, and where they're keeping the Troll. 'Tis all I can do."

Bastyen's brow furrowed. She'd made it clear she wouldn't show them her hiding place, and that this campfire was not her usual accommodations, but that just meant she still didn't trust them completely and was taking high ground on caution. She was a clever child. He also frowned at her description of the Pitch. She'd been in there, had seen them first hand, and spoke as if they were no different than cave rats to hunt and kill. She was strong willed, clear headed, and had a plan. Her stoic face and black eyes gave little indication of emotion, but 'twas apparent she'd lived through much for her winters.

Undoubtedly a half breed, Diadranei could not help but feel excited, for the child's very existence suggested that both the Sprite and Elven Nations survived the Last Holocaust. Mayhap the Wyrdritch had, also. Bastyen, on the other hand, was excited about the Warrior. He could be one of their own who'd been deployed and captured on his way back to Drekinn, or mayhap he was from one of the other War Clans, and could impart vital information on how the rest of them had fared. Were the other Clans attacked as was Dragon? Had anyone survived? But his story would have to wait. The girl was correct in her analysis. He had his own mission, and leaving the Warrior with the girl was the only viable option for now. But once they'd found the Wyrdritch and done what they could for the Prince, he promised himself that he'd return to find the Warrior and his unusual sidekick. Still, 'twould be nice if... "Would you describe this Warrior? What does he look like?"

The girl was silent for a moment and then lifted her head to face him without a word.

Bastyen chewed the inside of his cheek and pondered the meaning of her silence. The Dragon Clan was easily identifiable, for most of them were fair haired and skinned, but the other Clans were not. If she'd told him the Warrior was a redhead or a blonde, 'twould be near positive he was of Dragon. But the child said nothing. He decided to pursue information from a more direct angle. "Do you know his name?"

"No," she responded instantly.

Even Bastyen could feel the deceit in the quick reply, but he pressed on gently. "Does he have any tattoos?"

She hesitated. Should she tell him? She was beginning to trust the one she believed was a Warrior himself. Deciding 'twould not matter, she answered, "Yes. A large eagle on the back of his left shoulder."

Bastyen had trouble not grinning openly with the confirmation of the survival of a Warrior from the Order of the Eagle. Eagle was the second largest War Clan behind Dragon. How had he come to this place? "Thank you. Please take care of him. When we've completed our mission, we'll come back for you both."

Confidently, she replied, "You needn't bother, we shan't be here."

Her expression gave away nothing, and he knew better than to ask where they were going, for either the girl didn't know at present, or wouldn't tell. But 'twould be the wisest move on her part, and he had to admire her spirit. "How old are you?"

Now she appeared uncertain for the first time. Slowly, she stated, "I'm not sure. I think I've seen eight winters now."

Noting her discomfort with the change in questioning, Diadranei asked softly, "Do you have a name?"

The answer seemed harmless enough. What difference would it make for her to tell them what little information she had? "The Black called me many names, none of them do I wish to repeat. My mother is dead, but she called me Flyrra."

CHAPTER TWENTY-FOUR
The Caves of the Pitch

Bastyen and Diadranei crept along the rough passages without a sound, following Flyrra deeper and deeper into the cave. The passage was long, dangerous, rough, and at times narrow and cramped, but circumvented the occupied caverns in the system. Bastyen wasn't certain how she planned on carrying her Warrior through most of it, but then that wasn't his concern. His own difficulty would be similar. He was tall for a Warrior, but the Troll child was likely taller than he, and would have to crawl on all fours through parts of this passage, if she could get through at all. Still, there seemed no other choice.

Eventually, after more than a mark of winding their way into the system, Flyrra stopped and whispered, "From here to the chamber where they keep the key, 'twill be most dangerous. There's no other way to approach except by the same passage as the Pitch, but they don't visit often, just to change the guard. Stay close to the wall, keep to the right, 'twill be around the second turn. Try to stay to the shadows and make no sound. There will be one guard, you must get past him to get the key, and if he sees you or is killed, you have no chance of escape, for they are all Linked. Bring me the key and I'll take you to where they're keeping the Troll. I go no further. If I'm captured or injured, there'll be no one to help the Warrior. I'll wait here for your return. If you're not back in one mark, I'll assume you've been captured, and leave." She shrugged her shoulders. "If you're captured, you'll end up seeing me again, anyway." She stood aside and let them pass, as she pointed into the gloom.

Bastyen climbed down the wall to the floor of the main passage and then helped Diadranei down, placing her on his right and slightly ahead of him against the wall. He wasn't using her as a shield, he was still 'tween her and the enemy, but her forward position was required to allow her to use her full senses. His hand always upon her shoulder, they advanced as he steered her like a skilled dancer leading his partner through an intricate pattern. Dia felt no others in the passage and they continued around the turns, twice rightward as per instructions. Diadranei concentrated, unable to see any reality, leaving the navigation to Bastyen. She would have walked into the wall if not for him. Soon the passage opened into a small chamber lit with torches. They crouched along the wall in the darkness just outside the entrance and tried to avoid casting a shadow from the flickering light as they observed the situation. Dia faced her lover for reassurance. 'Twas exactly as Flyrra described. One guard, torches all around, small chamber, one entrance. The key sat in a niche in the far wall, the guard standing 'tween the key and the entry, a wicked looking scimitar at his hip.

He mouthed the words she needed to hear, "You can do this. I will not leave you."

She nodded her head and took a breath. They'd practiced this very skill throughout the chase and now 'twas time to put such into action. Standing up with Bastyen behind her, they walked straight into the room, her hands crossed above her head as she chanted in a soft, melodic, mesmerizing voice, invoking her Empathy and sending her 'message', "You do not see us, we are not here, 'tis nothing about, that you should fear, 'tis nothing to remember, nothing to recall, nothing to report, nothing at all. You do not see us, we are not here..." Her voice neither rose nor fell, the soft monotone Pushed forth and never ending, droning on as they walked steadily forward, the eyes of the guard lowering as if falling asleep. As they got closer her voice began to falter with insecurity and Bastyen squeezed her shoulder in support. Although she need not vocalize the chant, she believed 'twas stronger if she did, and would last longer. They passed within arm's length of the guard, backed their way to the far wall and grabbed the key, which was simply sitting upon the bare rock of the natural niche. Bastyen shook his head at the lack of security, but this wasn't done. Dia added a slight mix to her Magic chant, "you'll see the key but won't see me…" 'Twould linger after they'd left and prevent the guard from seeing the empty niche afore they changed. The guard hadn't moved and Dia hadn't stopped chanting, but she was getting fatigued, especially with the addition of the extra Push. Nevertheless, they reversed their steps, keeping Dia 'tween the guard and Bastyen, leaving the room and near running 'til they were well out of sight down the passage.

The entire operation took just o'er a quarter mark. Dia near dropped to her knees when she stopped chanting, and Bastyen held her while she caught her breath afore they returned to the girl. When they came to the place they'd left Flyrra, she was delighted to see them again, but leery about how they'd managed to do the deed. She hesitantly took the key, her eyes darting back and forth as if waiting for the punishment, the betrayal. It shouldn't have been this easy. The Elf's Magic must be very strong.

"This is the key," she said in amazement as she turned it o'er in her hand and stared at it as if 'twould turn to ash and blow away at any moment. "I know not how you did this but 'tis clear 'twas not some plan to capture me again, for you've done what you said you would. You truly are a Dragon Warrior. Don't looked so shocked. My friend told me about the Clan. I recognized you right away but had to make certain. If I can't trust you, who can I trust? Come. I'll take you as close as I can, to where they keep the Troll. I can assure you that she's still there, but I can make no such assurance that she yet lives."

~~~~~~~~~~

Flyrra exited the tunnel, crawling out upon a narrow ledge high along the wall of the deepest and largest of the system's caverns, leading her new friends. They found themselves within the great cavern, the entrance off to their left, the main portion
~~~~~~~~~~

spread out to the right. Peering down into the distance, they saw a huge fire burning in the middle of the vast space, providing the only light. Multiple ledges large enough for occupancy and natural rock bridges leading to nowhere, lay along the walls, with vast stalactites and stalagmites throughout. Disturbingly, from most of them were bodies, staked, tied, or hanging in varying degrees of decomposition, and most, but not all, were human. The huge fire was the only thing that kept the stench somewhat at bay. Without torches, the walls were in constant darkness, of which Bastyen heartily approved, as he studied the area in preparation for their task.

Huddled together, the little girl turned and whispered, "I go no further and must give warning. The rescue of my companions will cause you trouble, as the ensuing chaos will end with heightened security. But if I wait, whatever you're doing here will cause me trouble, and I care more about my own, than about that Troll." She pointed to the far end, on the opposite side of the fire, to a tall stalagmite where the Troll was tied. "I have no idea how you intend to free her, but I do wish you luck. And be swift. You have 'til dawn afore they'll find not only the key missing, but the cage empty, and all Hades will break loose. You must have vacated the caves by then, or you stand not a chance of escape yourselves."

<center>~~~~~ MOMENTS LATER ~~~~~</center>

Diadranei huddled behind Bastyen as they crept slowly along the floor of the huge cavern from rock to rock, ever closer to the ring of Pitch. Upon the many ledges o'er head, the Pitch could be seen coming and going. This was the end of the cave system, for there was but one entrance. With her arms tied behind her and head lolling, 'twas no way to determine Crytcha's condition in the flickering shadows, nor to gain her attention. And even if they did, how would she respond? They were strangers to her. The Pitch were milling about, some sitting and staring into the flames of the huge fire, and each one who left the area was replaced by at least two more. 'Twas a place of gathering and they were becoming concerned at the rising number of the evil creatures. The Troll was being kept in the most populated cavern they'd yet seen.

Even though still but a child, she was head and shoulders o'er either of them, obviously weighed more than the two of them together and if she couldn't walk on her own they were in deeper trouble than either could imagine. They'd already determined they couldn't get to her without being seen. They hoped she wasn't Past already. They'd done this once. 'Twas time for a repeat performance.

"But there are so many of them here, the area so large," Diadranei whispered. "I can't Spread the message that far, I don't know if I can do this." She was close to panic, her confidence in their prior success, waning in the realization of the enormity of what they now faced. The key was easy, she just 'blinded' one. This? There must be several dozen Pitch in that cavern, and they moved in and out. The energy 'twould take for her to Push her message to all of them without missing any, was boggling. She swallowed hard.

As a Warrior, Bastyen was not afraid of dying, but he was afraid of failing. He understood Dia's mindset, and recognized the growing panic. Reaching out, he placed his hand on her shoulder, caressing the soft skin on the side of her neck with his thumb. He could feel her Draw from him with near every touch, the skin to skin contact creating a give-and-take Magic, enhancing their love. 'Twas not Vampyrism, for such was crossing the line. She'd explained that what they experienced was normal for her people, 'twas not a draining effect 'tween them, and he trusted her completely. The feel of her had become mutually beneficial as such intimacy calmed her, as well as giving him the strength he required to engage in the impossible. Outlining his plan with assurance, he replied, "We stay in the shadows of the outer wall. We walk tight, keeping your message close, creating a shield of sorts behind which we'll cross the cavern. If we don't attract the attention of those to whom we are nearest, we shall be ignored by the rest. I do not see any of them as particularly alert, and the flickering firelight will work to our advantage. And Flyrra told us they only feed from the Troll at dawn. We should have plenty of time to get 'cross the room to her, afore the sun rises."

Dia licked her dry lips and focused on the plan as another thought occurred to her. "I feel something is not quite right about her, I feel a vigor that isn't showing. But it could be just her spirit, Trolls are known to be very stubborn. What if she can't walk? We can't carry her, she's too big."

"Mayhap what you're feeling is pretense. I'm hoping she's pretending to be in worse condition than she appears, as are those in the cage."

Once again, the emotional assault took its toll upon the Elf. "But this time I must blind them to us, and then blind to her not being there any longer, as well as blind to our leaving. The task becomes more intense as I become more fatigued. What if I can't do this? What if I'm too weak? I've never stretched my Empathy this far afore, and I'm self-taught. What if my Magic fails us?"

Bastyen turned her to face him and stared into her sparkling eyes. He had to make a conscious effort not to allow the physical reaction he had every time he looked at her, to interfere with their mission. "Forget what you were told as a child. Your Magic is not weak. Empathy takes advantage of the strongest energies produced, and you've developed perfect control. This is no different than Pushing your message to Gheryh, that Daggogh leader back in Byndynn Forest, or walking past that guard to get the key. You're no longer alone out there, my love. We work together." He started to kiss her neck, but thought better of it. With any luck, the Fates would allow them time for that later. She nodded her head and lifted her chin. Bastyen stared deeply into her eyes and said, "I want you to Push the message like you used to seek knowledge, or when you covered us in Byndynn. Silent. No spoken words, just Push. 'Twill save your strength by not speaking aloud, and this in turn, decreases what you need to hide." Again, she nodded her head, her eyes bright with concern, but she appeared more confident than just a few moments ago. Although she'd felt 'twas stronger aloud, she had to admit Bastyen was right. Aloud was initially stronger, but drained her quicker, and she'd done well in Byndynn. "Are you ready?" A quick shake of Dia's head, indicated she was.

Taking his initial suggestion of creating a shield of sorts behind which they would walk, she had an idea of her own. With a deep breath, she closed her eyes for but a moment, and then started to focus her Empathy to create a bubble around them. 'Twas not visible from the outside, but like the Shields of Protection the Highlands could create, which gave the illusion of empty space, her shield appeared as a prism from within, the various colors making it seem as if they were inside a giant soap bubble. Once 'twas solid around them, Bastyen began to steer her toward the far end of the cavern, staying close to the edge, careful not to trip or break her concentration as they navigated past wayward Pitch walking about, rock rubble, stalactites and stalagmites, stopping at times in their slow advance for Dia to strengthen the bubble as it began to waver, afore they continued. When they were within reach of the Troll, Dia was sweating profusely and her skin was hot under Bastyen's hand. They had to release the Troll and get her out of there as quickly as possible, but now came the hard part of the journey. Or so it seemed.

Without lifting her head or outwardly moving a muscle, Crytcha whispered, "I see you. You did not come to feed. Who and what are you? If you don't tell me quickly, I will scream."

Dia could not speak and continue the bubble, so Bastyen answered. "We came to rescue you. We are sent by Gorch. Are you able to move? Can you walk?"

"I can walk. I am far stronger than they think. Magic cannot harm the Borkahn. But I do not believe you, and the Borkahn need not your help," she stated with confidence, a slight sneer on her lips.

"Do not hate Magic, for 'tis what can get you out of here alive," replied Bastyen as he sensed the haughty defiance coming from the child. "If you could have escaped by now, you would have. Apparently, you stay by choice. We shall leave you to it, and tell your father you have no need of assistance."

Her eyes widened, and she spit out, "Wait! I cannot escape. I have tried. They beat me. It did not hurt… much. But with so many of them, I could not prevent my own abduction, let alone escape. And they feed from me, although they can take little. Still, I am left to starve, for they feed me not, and I get weaker by the dawn. Very soon, I will be as the rest of the victims here. Please do not leave me. I will do whatever you say."

Bastyen wasted no time. "When Diadranei lowers the shield for you to enter, we will be visible. I have to know if you can break the ties or if I need to cut them."

"I am loose. I broke their pathetic ties long ago. They've never checked them again, since I have moved not."

Dia signaled she was not ready to drop the shield and then pick it back up again just yet. Standing still was giving her a bit of respite, despite the energy drain. Bastyen asked the child, "When was the last time you ate?"

"Not since afore I was kidnapped."

"But that was moons past!"

"The Borkahn do not need sustenance as often as do other Races."

Bastyen noted that Dia was near ready. Mayhap he could give the child something, that would help her gain some energy. Greatly curious, he asked, "What do the Borkahn eat?"

"Rock."

Thinking 'twould be something grisly, he was taken aback. "Rock?"

"You asked."

Bastyen shook his head. The child had to be lying about her diet, but 'twas no time to strike up an in-depth conversation. "Dia is ready. We must coordinate this rapidly. She will lower the shield and you must then step up behind me. Do you need help? You have been motionless for a very long time, and have been starved for longer."

"Pfffft. What's a long time to a Human? 'Twas but a heartbeat for the Borkahn."

He smiled at the child's arrogance, for even though he knew 'twas pure bravado, she was doing her best. "Good. Ready?"

"Ready."

He had to hope the Troll would fit into Dia's shield because his mate was close to her limits now. Scanning the area, he ensured that no one was paying any attention to them at that moment. "Dia?" She nodded and Bastyen squeezed her shoulder.

Several things then happened at once. The bubble dropped, the child swung her arms stiffly away from the post afore stepping toward them, and Bastyen caught sight of a stringy-haired Pitch squatting 'cross the cavern, staring directly at him. The Troll was moving much too slowly, and Bastyen grabbed her. Yanking her behind him and placing her huge hands at his waist, Dia drew the shield back up around them, the Pitch screamed, the echoes sounding like howling wolves reverberating through the cavern, and all eyes were now upon the empty post. To both the child's and Dia's surprise, Bastyen began to jog straight up the middle of the cavern. Although she kept up admirably, Crytcha was in pain and struggling. Dia was having her own difficulty maintaining the shield and traveling at such a pace. As Bastyen hastily shuffled them through a zig zag pattern, the Pitch began to gather in singles and small groups, all heading toward the far end to form a line that crossed the entire cavern, leaving no free space. Advancing toward them swiftly, the filthy beings stood shoulder to shoulder, their arms outstretched, crouched low, moving as one, hoping to fence them in, unaware their quarry was just ahead of them, while more and more reinforcements ran past to join the line seeking the invaders who were taking their current prized possession. As Dia continued to weaken, Crytcha picked her up and carried her, allowing her to focus on her Magic, while Bastyen tried to maintain his grip on them both as they continued up the center of the cavern, streaking past and through the crowded space, evading the enemy.

'Twas nothing short of a gift of the One, that they made it back to the passage from where they'd entered. However, 'twas clear 'twould be impossible for them to climb back up to leave the same way they'd arrived. Barely slowing, Bastyen changed course for the main entrance, and boldly managed to get them through, 'tween incredible numbers of Pitch who were rushing inside in total silence. Apparently understanding what was happening by the Link they shared, the strangeness of the entire operation, combined with the stench, the greasy soot, and the gruesome images forever engraved upon his mind, gave Bastyen gooseflesh, and made him near gag. 'Twas no option now, but to continue 'til they came to the only other entrance to the secret tunnels of which they knew, the one they'd used to get the key. 'Twas as working their way through an angry hornet's nest. Crytcha was exhausted, as were they all, but she valiantly assisted both Bastyen and Dia up the wall into the small opening afore coming to a complete and sudden, stop. The shield dissolved as they separated, and the Troll child was panting hard. If she couldn't climb up by herself, they were done.

Then Diadranei, despite her weakened condition, reached out her hand and touched the Troll, giving her even more of her strength, Sharing positive emotions, the desire to continue, and hope for the future. Crytcha knew what was happening, but was too fatigued to fight it off, and once she accepted the Magic into her system, she was grateful. This was not evil. This was not harmful. This was good. She reached up and took hold of the edge of the opening, and with a grunt, she pulled her heavy body up and slid into the tunnel headfirst. No one had seen them.

O'er the following marks they shuffled, crawled, ran up-right and slid on their bellies through entirely unknown spaces afore they finally reached the outside, where 'twas just dawning. Although they knew not where they were, at least they were heading in the right general direction, for they had to get out of this region fast. Flyrra had warned them they had 'til dawn afore all Hades would break loose. The way their escape went awry, Bastyen wondered if they'd already checked the cage. He could only hope the strange-looking girl and her companions, were free.

They didn't stop running 'til they were well away, and then only for a fleeting rest break. The angry screams of the Pitch echoed through the dawn, but Bastyen could tell from the sound, that they'd not left the caves. 'Twas odd, but then again, everything about this mission had been odd, and if the Pitch had no intention of giving chase, 'twas fine with him.

Once they caught their breath, they continued onward, Crytcha in the lead. They'd exited the caverns in an entirely different area than that in which they'd entered, and after racing into the forest, they were lost. She assured them she knew how to find home again, and was taking them to a shortcut. But they could tell she was hungry, and still in pain. They'd observed the Borkahn and Bastyen could see it in the way she moved, while Diadranei felt it. Even so, the child covered ground quickly. When Crytcha abruptly sat down, her back against a cliff wall, Bastyen caught up to her and asked, "How much further?"

"You must keep walking that way," she stated flatly, her eyes dull and breath short, as she pointed to the east. "Another mark, mayhap two, reach shortcut. Another fortnight back to Gorch, if you miss."

Diadranei was alarmed and kneeled in front of the girl, looking up into her face. "No! You must keep going. You can't give up now."

"Hungry."

Bastyen realized what was happening and became alarmed as well. "I can feed you. What do you eat?"

"Rock," the child repeated.

Dia was confused. "But the Borkahn have no teeth. How do you eat rock?"

'Twas then that Bastyen saw the child really didn't have any teeth and realized that none of the adults had, either. 'Twas not like him to miss such a detail. A flashing notion passed through his mind, of their teeth having been ground down by eating rock, afore the child responded. "Pound it."

Once more, Dia asked, "How? If you're too weak, can we do this for you?"

"Pound it into powder with our fists. Too weak," she stated, staring blankly at the Elf, while shaking her head.

Dia wasn't certain if she was referring to them or herself, but it didn't matter, for none of them could powder rock. They had no hammer, and Crytcha was fading fast. Suddenly, she felt it. And then she smelled it, just as did the child. Looking upward along the cliff wall, they could see the dark brown stain of the sweet sticky substance, dripping down the rock. Desperately, Dia asked her, "And what else? Can you eat anything else?"

Her eyes full of yearning, she replied, "Honey!"

~~~~~~~~~~

In the end, neither Dia or Bastyen could climb up the sheer wall, but the knowledge that the honey lay just above her head, gave Crytcha the strength she needed to climb up by herself. 'Twas a good thing, as even though the hive was not very lively due to the cold, 'twas a massive colony, and the comb was enormous. Crytcha's skin was so thick, the insects could not sting her even if they'd tried, and covered with the bees, she gently reached into the crevice again and again, pulling out huge hunks of honeycomb, dripping the thick golden stuff everywhere as she crammed it into her mouth, while being very careful not to consume any of the insects. The longer she stayed up there, the more
~~~~~~~~~~

energetic she became, and Dia and Bastyen even noted her skin changed from a dirty yellow-gray to a cleaner, lighter color, her eyes clear, her voice bright with hope.

When she finally climbed back down, she'd licked most of the thick golden stuff off her arms and legs, and a nearby creek removed the rest. They all cleaned up in the frigid waters, as the honey had dripped down steadily, and both Bastyen and Dia had gotten their share as well. Warming up with a small fire, they returned to the journey, and reached their destination in just o'er a mark, Crytcha now moving with minimal pain.

In less than a dawn's time from entering the caves, they were back where they'd begun. Gorch met them and was so grateful that he pledged the entire Borkahn kingdom to the Resistance. But, 'twould be after they waged their civil war against those who opposed his leadership and would follow the Black, afore he could send an envoy. He also intended to personally find and destroy, Roack. Bastyen and Graasyn would have stayed to help, but the big Troll understood their mission, having played host to Calei, Graasyn, and the injured boy, while Dia and Bastyen were rescuing his daughter. It seemed that as soon as the rescue party left, the three 'hostages' were moved to 'luxury' quarters, provided with everything they'd required and lived in relative comfort, as Gorch tried to learn how to get along with Humans in preparation for joining the Resistance. But he made good on his promise, by having Crytcha lead them through the Talons into Darkling, where the girl delivered another promise. "My father is the most powerful ruler the Borkahn have seen since the beginning of time. He cannot show you enough gratitude for my rescue, and neither can I. We hope you succeed in your mission to save the boy as you did me, and if you return, Gorch will provide safe passage back through the Talons. You are always welcome in the kingdom of the Borkahn."

The party thanked Crytcha in the way Dia had taught them, with all the formal speech and grandiose wording, and the child's face lit up like the sun shining. Then she pointed to the patch of daylight in front of them less than a quarter mark's walk distant, told them to be careful of the creatures that inhabit Darkling, and then said goodbye, afore she turned and disappeared into the shadows.

CHAPTER TWENTY-FIVE

What Cannot Be Seen

~~~~~~~~~~

Anastasia raced out of the portal as if suddenly appearing from thin air, her long hair flying in braided loops behind her, confidence building in her ability to travel through the barrier even though 'twas getting more difficult. As she ran toward Haven, she thought about what she'd say. Could she make anyone believe her? These last few trips she'd noted the rhythms were becoming more fragile. But she couldn't stop, for she needed more information to prove her theories and to find the lost ones, even though she defied the Fates and faced Passing the Veil with each attempt. Her daring experimentation had taught her much.

Once, many moons past, she'd tried to persuade Persephone that something was wrong with the Spell, but now 'twas evident 'twasn't just wrong. 'Twas failing. And if the Spell failed, the Wyrdritch would simply disappear, for her observations also proved 'twas already shrinking in size, and had been doing so for quite some time. Although she still felt the need to find her brother, she knew 'twasn't his Magic that could save them. 'Twas Persephone's. Her Gift of Healing wasn't for normal illness or injuries to one's physical body, but for Magical calamity, Magical illness. She could right what was wrong with the Spell. But not if she didn't accept the truth. Ana ran to the nearest large oak to Dance back to Haven. She had to convince her sister of her ability, and if she could not, the entire Elven Nation might disappear with the Wyrdritch when the Spell collapsed, and 'twas her firm belief 'twould occur very soon.

<div align="center">

A SHORT TIME LATER

ALONG THE OUTER BORDER OF THE WYRDRITCH

~~~~~ DARKLING ~~~~~

Diadranei Cast forth her senses again, and felt nothing. Not as in, nothing out of the ordinary, no danger, no trouble a'foot, but… nothing. 'Twas like the sensation she'd had not long after the Last Holocaust, when she'd made her first attempt to return home, but now, the feeling was amplified a thousand-fold. And, 'twas a sickness there, deep inside the nothing. She spent near a quarter mark trying to explain it to the others, without success. Caleichante was getting irritated with her inability to locate the Wyrdritch, but 'twas from a sense of personal failure. They'd come so far and Kevon had but days left, if that. Dia felt the strength of their emotions and piled on top of her own, she was losing hope. They'd walked and walked, trying to map the nothing, but this one place was where the strange sensations, or lack thereof, were the strongest, and she was convinced the Wyrdritch should be right in front of them. But how to penetrate the morphed Spell? She'd never felt anything like it, 'twas so foreign she knew not how to proceed.

She'd been at this all night, making little progress, except pinning down this particular area. Casting forth once more, she felt a faint rhythm coming out of the nothing, almost like a heartbeat, but 'twas most irregular. And then several Dragon lengths away, they all saw the pulsing of the air indicating an incoming Dancer, having a very difficult journey pushing through, yet 'twas not a shadow within reach. Even so, expecting someone to approach, they ducked behind the trees a short distance away. Suddenly, out of the nothing, burst a young girl.

~~~~~~~~~~

Anastasia's legs buckled as her feet hit the ground, and she fell face first in the dirt. Pushing up on her hands, she opened her eyes cautiously and glanced o'er her shoulder, her chest heaving as she caught her breath. 'Twas reminiscent of that first trip through and she was no less delighted. She'd done it. She'd escaped the King's guards, and was outside once again. She'd tried to speak with Persephone, but hadn't been allowed to even see
~~~~~~~~~~

her, and then Jeeryd stopped her in the Great Hall. His body-guards were at his side and his questions made clear that he knew what she'd been doing. Unable to explain herself, she'd barely escaped imprisonment, or worse. The light of madness burned in the King's eyes, and his song had become vile. Outrunning the guards, she grabbed the first portal she could find, and here she was.

Spitting pine needles out of her mouth, she sat up, brushing the dirt and leaves off her hands, face and clothing. Looking around, 'twas familiar. This was the western border of the Wyrdritch, and she wasn't far from the barrier. She'd used this same portal several times. If only she could have made Persephone understand. At least she would take the brunt of the punishment to be doled out, if any, and the rest of the brood, including her sister and Coltyn, would be safe. Well, they'd be safe for as long as the Spell lasted. Horrified at the implications, she leaped to her feet and turned sharply toward the barrier. She had to go back, she had to try again. But how to get to Persephone? She spun around once more when she heard the voice coming from o'er her shoulder.

"I believe we can help you," Diadranei stated with gentle persuasion, Reaching out to the youth, embracing her in tranquility and courage.

Anastasia felt something surround her, and all fear melted away as she also embraced something about herself that she'd always known, but hadn't understood. She could tell what the other was thinking, 'twas not the Link as she heard not actual speech. No. She felt her thoughts. She knew this one could teach her much.

<center>~~~~~ DARKLING BASE CAMP ~~~~~</center>

Bastyen, Caleichante, Diadranei, and Graasyn had been alone together for some time. Ana was concerned they were arguing o'er her presence, and if she'd not promised to sit here 'til they returned, she'd be long gone by now. They'd talked by the fire for about a quarter mark when she first arrived, but when Diadranei's hand touched hers, she'd had the strangest look on her face. Making Ana promise to stay, she'd signaled for the rest of them to follow her inside the tent. Diadranei's voice could be heard in disagreement with the rest, but finally 'twas evident they'd come to an impasse, and Diadranei spoke up loudly enough for Ana to hear through the hides of the tent in which Kevon slept fitfully. "Let me do this my own way. 'Tis going to be a shock to her, no matter how 'tis presented. I will tell her. Please."

Ana's eyes followed them as they filed out of the tent and sat on the logs surrounding the fire. Diadranei sat next to her, and placing her hand on Ana's arm, she spoke with urgency. "'Tis my belief that you are an Elf of great power, with Empathy rising, and whatever this musical hearing talent is, increasing your senses and strength exponentially. Once tutored and you come into your own, 'twill far surpass my Magic. Even so, I would agree to become your mentor, should you accept such an arrangement." She cast her gaze around the fire, afore she continued. Taking a deep breath, she stated, "But for the moment, we have more pressing needs than tutoring. Your brother Myrrdin understood Persephone's Magic, for he's the one who sent Calei with Kevon for her help. Surely, he knew she could Heal such." She took another deep breath and continued. "And if he knew, then someone else must have known as well." She stared at the young Princess, willing her to understand and accept the horrible truth.

Anastasia's eyes grew wide as her senses grasped what the other was saying. Indignantly, she stated, "The King. He knew all this time. He kept her submissive to his will, bound her to his side constantly, so she could never explore her Magic for herself. He used her to his own advantage, taking from her without her knowledge. He'd have Passed by now, had it not been for her 'ministrations'." Sighing, her anger subsided as wisdom grew. "And yet, if he'd fully acknowledged and allowed her to grow, mayhap she could have Healed him of his insanity. How very sad.

How deceitful, devious, selfish, can one be? Tell me, is Kadoor like the Wyrdritch? I mean, are there others like my father? And did my mother know?"

Dia was proud of her, and of the way she'd taken the information thrust upon her. "Sadly, yes, there are others like your father. Many others. The worst gather to the Black and are called the Hoard. The rest of us are known as the Resistance, and we fight them and the evil they spread. But there are still those who claim no side, allowing evil to persist and remaining ignorant by choice. This is how the Last Holocaust occurred. As children, I knew Alyssa, and 'tis clear she's had her hands full trying to do what she felt was right. 'Tis also very sad to hear that Queen Bryanna is one of the lost. She was much loved, and her children good Elves. Mayhap with your Magic you can find her, as you've tried to find the others." Dia felt a slight jolt from Ana with her words, but there was no time to pursue. For certain, 'twas not something that mattered now. "But back to your other question. Did your mother know. 'Twould take an amazing woman, strong and independent, juggling a submission she felt not, with a determination to rule fairly, while hiding her actions from Jeeryd. I sense your mother knew not about her stepdaughter's Magic, but did know about the King and his past deceptions, and she would have had to hide such knowledge to keep safe her stepchildren, and you and your little brother."

"Your Magic is strong indeed. I wish to learn from you."

"I promise to teach you all I know, but after this is done. For now, we must hurry.

CHAPTER TWENTY-SIX

Healer of Magic

~~~~~ **INSIDE HAVEN** ~~~~~

Persephone had just returned to her quarters to clean up for last meal when she saw her little sister stepping out of the dressing room. "Anastasia! I thought they'd taken you!" She was so distraught, her eyes glistened with tears as she reached forth to gather Ana into her arms. Only then did she see the other standing behind her. Shocked, she stammered, "Diadranei? But, where have you been? I thought everyone was gone. How… how did you get back inside?" She turned her questioning gaze to Ana once more, and as the sun dawned upon her, she understood that Ana had been correct all along, and the Wyrdritch, along with what was left of the Elven Nation, was in mortal danger.

Their reunion cut short, Diadranei quickly outlined their mission, and her belief about the Spell, a belief that Ana shared.

Persephone's brow furrowed, a look of bafflement upon her face. "But I can do nothing about such."

Diadranei pleaded with her. "Persephone, everyone recognizes your strengths, Corbyn, even Myrrdin. Jeeryd has kept you ignorant and insecure, the knowledge of your powers a secret, to satisfy his own greed and lust for control. He was insane afore I left! Surely, he's in no better condition after all this time."

Persephone hung her head. 'Twas much information to digest, and she felt so tired. She was always tired. 'Twas as if she were being suffocated, constantly drained of all energy. She peered at her friend, trying to comprehend what she was being told.

Diadranei felt her confusion, and something else she couldn't quite place her finger on. But there was little more she could say. "'Tis simple really. Kevon is near death. The Wyrdritch is near death. We dared not attempt to bring him inside. Please,
~~~~~

Persephone, please come with me. You refused to come with me afore the Retreat, you stood with your family and your duty, and I accept that. But this time, if you refuse, we all perish."

Persephone struggled with the fatigue. 'Twas as if a living fog surrounded her at all times. When she answered, her voice cracked with emotion. "After you left, Dia, I was all alone. No one understood me as did you. We were children, but we were untutored, and our Magics unrecognized. I knew not how to stand against my father. I was not as strong as you."

With sudden insight, the picture became clear. "Dragon dung! My dear friend, there's more to you than you know. Look at what you've accomplished! Without you, the King would've Passed long ago, and you must have been reinforcing the Spell for eons. No wonder you have no energy! But even though he's not a good man, he is your father and you couldn't leave him to suffer. Even unconsciously, you exude your Magic to the betterment of those around you."

"Mayhap you are correct."

"Of course, I'm correct! I always am!" She and Persephone giggled like little girls once again. For just that moment, 'twas as if time circled back to their childhood.

Now that she understood, Persephone was no longer indecisive, and her fatigue lifted slightly. She was not a Warrior, but her will was strong and her Magic, stronger. "The King will notice if I leave. He's quite attuned to my presence. I'll temporarily neutralize that threat first. We can't be gone long, for I must stabilize the Spell as soon as possible. 'Twill take much, but for now, just a little. No one will notice and we can then leave. Once I see the Prince and decide how to perform his Healing, I can return and finish my work on the Spell." With all seriousness, she added, "I know not how difficult Healing either shall be, but Kevon must come first. Wait here, I'll return shortly."

Persephone went directly to the King's chambers and with a flick of her hand, put him and his surrounding guards into a deep slumber, and again, she felt a surge of energy, the constant fatigue lessoning a little more. They'd not awaken for several dawns, nor did his personal guard change for that length of time; however, she couldn't put the entire castle to sleep, and they had to be careful to avoid being caught. She backed out of the room and locked the huge doors behind her. Telling the maidservants not to disturb the King's rest, she quickly returned to her own chambers.

Having slipped into Haven via Diadranei's Magic, Anastasia had a better idea for their return. "I know how to get us all to the barrier without being seen," she said, as she beckoned them through the adjoining door to her chambers. "Follow me!" Excitedly, she disappeared into her dressing room. Puzzled, they looked one to the other, then barged in after her.

NEAR A SENNIGHT LATER

~~~~~ BASE CAMP ~~~~~

</div>

Anastasia stared at the sleeping Prince. He was an attractive young man, her own age. He'd appeared so frail, so helpless, so close to the Veil, when they'd finally reached Persephone. Gathering, drawing, pulling, and finally encapsulating and extracting the poison from his system, she'd done what no other had ever done afore; Healed someone from the evil of the Spell Sword. The incredulous deed took o'er three days, and only Dia was allowed in the tent during the process. Calei was initially livid with the restriction, but Graasyn kept her calm and held onto her shoulder to prevent her from tearing down the entire tent with every moan, groan, or scream of pain they were forced to endure. Truth be told, no one was certain just who was doing the screaming and moaning, the boy or the Healer, and occasionally they heard two voices together. Dia came out multiple times in the first two days, answering not their questions other than to say, "Won't be long, now," or, "Persephone shall prevail!" Then she'd race off and return shortly with one thing or another, a rare herb, a certain root, a twig from a specific tree, water drawn from
~~~~~

the place where two creeks joined into one, collectively considered an odd assortment of items that left them all shaking their heads and squinting.

After the first day, Calei sat cross-legged with her back braced against a nearby tree. Ready for action in a heartbeat, she fingered her blade, keeping her eyes focused upon the tent, taking sustenance from Graasyn and speaking only to him. Upon the third day, 'twas quiet as a tomb on the other side of the hides, and Dia did not venture forth. They'd all paced about with worried frowns 'til at last they heard one very long and agonized moan, and the entire tent lit up as if set on fire inside, an effect which promptly disappeared. They'd all leaped forth, when unexpectedly the flap opened and there stood Diadranei near holding up Persephone. The slight figure of the Princess now appeared as frail as was the Prince just a few dawns past, and Caleichante jumped in to assist. Dia accepted her help gratefully, nodding her head toward the tent and saying only, "He lives," as they walked past. The two of them took the Princess to Dia's bedroll where she fell asleep immediately, and then they all dashed back to find Kevon was also sleeping soundly upon his furs. Dia had not said a word and as she walked in behind Calei after seeing to her friend, 'twas clear they all thought him dead, he was so peaceful at last.

"Yes, he lives, of this I am certain. But make no mistake, he's still very weak and 'twill take many moons afore he completely recovers. The poison is gone from his system, but did considerable damage, and 'twill be as an injured Warrior recovering from a serious battle wound. And although the Healing near killed Persephone, she was the victor in the end. Now 'tis up to us to help the Prince recuperate and reclaim his strength. Persephone needs only a few marks sleep for her own recovery, followed by a good meal."

Resting again, Ana sat and recalled all that had happened since they took flight from Haven near a sennight past. 'Twas as a life span. When her sister finally accepted her calling, her Magic took o'er and grew beyond even Ana's expectations. Skeptical when they reached the barrier, she was skeptical no more, as their trip through the portal told the story. Persephone was aghast that her little sister had taken such a risk, but then she was more than thankful, for she too, felt the sickness. She'd worked on the boy, Healing him in the crudely constructed tent, and now 'twould take time. Time the Elven Nation didn't have. After waking, she'd attempted to Heal the Spell, but it soon became clear that she'd have to work from the inside. With Ana's assistance, she'd learned how to find and use the portals and stepped freely through, leaving Ana and the others behind. Kevon was out of imminent danger, but if Persephone couldn't stabilize the Spell, the Wyrdritch, along with everyone therein, was doomed. She'd promised to return within a dawn from this very day. Ana wasn't sure the Wyrdritch had another dawn. Persephone had never broken a promise, but she knew in her heart, there was always a first time.

She'd sat with the Prince since her sister left, waiting and watching. And whenever he stirred enough to eat or drink, she'd been there to help, getting very little down him and not certain he was aware of his surroundings, but was told that he'd not eaten this much in moons. He'd even called her Calei once, mumbling his thanks for her help. The real Calei made frequent visits to check on his progress and to report Persephone had yet to return, but otherwise, Ana knew nothing of what they were doing. She cared not. Kevon needed her. Calei brought her everything she wanted, or for which she asked. She'd barely set foot outside.

Greatly curious, Ana reached forward and pushed Kevon's white blonde hair off his face. She was captivated with the feel of it. Silky soft and yet strong, thick, wavy and… suddenly, he fully opened his eyes and she was speechless. They were the color of the sky itself, the perfect shade of blue, the color she'd come to love. She'd never seen light colored hair or eyes afore. 'Twas breathtaking. Astonished, she watched him turn his head and squint at her in confusion.

His eyes felt like sandpaper and he had to blink several times afore he caught Ana's gaze again. His first attempt to speak failed and he cleared his throat, which only sent him into a coughing fit. Finally, Ana, who'd been so engaged by his appearance, shook her head and came to her senses. Grabbing the water bag, she leaned o'er the boy, lifted his head, and helped him to take a sip. "Not so fast, Kevon," she scolded.

Kevon wasn't used to anyone but Calei calling him by his given name, let alone scolding him, and he was taken aback. After a mere candle drip, he propped himself up on his elbows and squeaked, "Who are you?" His initial question led to another, and then another. His voice grew stronger and more noble with each word. "And where's my blade?" He cleared his throat and continued. "And where's my Captain? And by the 7th Egg, where am I," he demanded to know.

Princess Anastasia of the Elven Nation was quite used to giving orders she expected to be carried out forthwith and without question. She sat back on her heels and began to laugh, just as Caleichante, Bastyen, and Graasyn all tried to push their way through the entry flap at the same time. Leaving the introductions to another, for she'd never announced herself, she looked quizzically to Bastyen. "Where's Diadranei?"

The young man appeared quite agitated, as for the second time in just a few moons, he was separated from his mate, and powerless to assist. "She went with Persephone two dawns past. They're inside the Wyrdritch."

Ana was shocked that her new mentor had made so much progress Dancing the portals, and shocked she'd not come to see her afore leaving. Then the gravity of the situation hit, while Kevon simply stared from one to the other 'til his gaze landed upon his trainer and Captain of his Elite Guard.

Calei nodded for permission to speak, afore making formal introductions. He was already beginning to fade with exhaustion. "Your Highness, I promise to tell you everything that has happened since you were wounded, but you need rest."

"First, I need to know what's wrong here. 'Tis not me, for whom you're all concerned right now." Kevon had always been highly astute. But everyone seemed reluctant to explain.

Suddenly, Ana tilted her ear toward the entry, then leaped up and exclaimed joyously, "They return!" Beaming, she looked back o'er her shoulder, but the Prince had nodded off once again.

<p style="text-align:center">~~~~~ TWO DAWNS PRIOR ~~~~~</p>

Diadranei had just been to the creek for water, when she turned away and found Persephone standing at the edge. 'Twas evident something was very wrong, for her friend seemed not to even know where she was, let alone what she was doing. When had she returned through the portal? "What's wrong?"

With a flat expression, and wide eyes that appeared not to see, Persephone stated, "He's dead."

Diadranei recognized the shock under which her friend was now operating, and with alarm she replied, "Who's dead? The Prince? No, he lives! I just left him, though he still sleeps."

"Not the Prince. I speak of the King. Jeeryd is no more."

'Twas obvious that Persephone felt the weight of his Passing and Dia hugged her, guiding her to a fallen log to sit. After a careful check, Dia was assured her friend was not injured, but now that the shock was wearing off, the heaviness of exhaustion took its place. Dia needed to know what had happened. She needed to know if the Wyrdritch and the rest of the royals were safe. Touching her gave more information and gave it faster than just being in close proximity, and after touching Persephone's arm, she saw what was bothering her friend so much. "By your hand?"

Vacantly, she replied, "I don't honestly know."

Persephone finally made eye contact, and Dia was relieved. "Tell me what happened."

The Elven Princess folded her hands in her lap and stared at them briefly afore she raised her sight once more. Her voice was now steady and sure, but guilt still held her in its grasp. "When I returned to Haven, I sought audience with Alyssa and my brothers, calling them together in secret. Alyssa had discovered that I was missing and she found the King and his guards asleep, but attempted to keep their condition undisclosed. However, they'd all awakened when I returned. I told them everything I knew because I had to neutralize Jeeryd's interference to free myself to Heal the Wyrdritch. Although I should have, I knew none of this, believe me. I was surprised with what I learned. I've been so naive. My brothers, even Alyssa, admitted they'd always known but could not prove, that Jeeryd had a hand in the deaths of King Lucien and his sons, and that he was in league with the Black. Myrrdin confronted him, and this argument was what precipitated his self-exile following his escape. He left to save his brothers, whom Jeeryd threatened if he returned or told them anything. They were young, Myrrdin was Heir Apparent, he felt the weight of duty. And then Bryanna disappeared. Alyssa knew more than I, but not all, and became incensed at the danger we'd faced without even knowing. Jeeryd had even threatened her life. So, they waited for Myrrdin's return or for something to happen to give them clear direction. This new information, did just that. We confronted Jeeryd, flanking Alyssa with our weapons drawn, and prepared to fight the entire King's Guard if he refused to step down. But he only sneered and laughed, and ordered his men to kill us. They hesitated. He became angered, and approached us with his own blade drawn. His men gathered behind him but took no offensive action and… it all happened so fast. Afore my brothers and the King could engage, afore Jeeryd could swing sword against my family, I stepped in front of Alyssa and tore myself away from him. 'Twas as if my Magic had encased him like a cocoon. 'Twas a horrible sensation, as if we'd been physically attached and suddenly ripped asunder. I just stood there with my mouth open, as he dropped in agony to the floor and died as insane as he'd ever been. By then, my brothers had surrounded us to protect us from his Guard, as I stood stock-still and gaped for what seemed an eternity. Out of the ensuing silence, to a man, the Guard laid down their weapons and kneeled to swear fealty to the Queen." Persephone was silent for a moment afore finishing her tale. "Alyssa appointed me Heir Apparent 'til Myrrdin returns or relinquishes."

For several heartbeats, Dia waited to make certain Persephone had no more to say. She could hear the birds singing their wake-up songs, the gentle breezes ruffling through the tree branches far above. She knew what Persephone needed to hear. "You've been through much. But you didn't kill him."

The anguish of the Princess, shone in her eyes. "I am a Healer. I am not so certain."

"You acted not against him," Dia emphasized.

Turning to face her once again, she stated with uncertainty, "He Passed the Veil by my actions."

Now Diadranei was angry, but not with her friend. The many decades of exile, mixed with the events of the past winter, bubbled inside her as an erupting volcano, and she stood up and firmly stated, "No. He lived all these winters, by your actions. You acted not against him, you simply stopped. He died. 'Twas long o'erdue, and many more would have Passed had you not done what you did. This is war, Persephone. 'Tis no telling how much more damage his allegiance with the Black may have done to the Nation. 'Tis time we all make our stand."

Persephone nodded, sitting quietly while she absorbed the truth of her friend's convictions. Then she unlaced her fingers and stood up to face Dia. Now for what she'd come to ask. She spoke softly, but with her new-found faith. "I need your help once more, Diadranei. I've tried to stabilize the Spell, but there's still much work to be done, and 'twill take more than I can do on my own. 'Tis much bigger than I, and I'm still learning all this. And the Spell has been morphing for centuries. I need your Empathy to show me the pathways of the illness so I can complete the Healing. And once 'tis done, the Wyrdritch safe and things have normalized inside once again, I need your help to redesign the Spell; make it ours, make it secure, and reproduce it. Alyssa wants the Elven Nation to join in alliance with the Dragon Clan. She wants to offer the Spell to the Battle Commander, to secure the Lair of the Resistance against the onslaught of the Hoard."

"'Twould appear that Queen Alyssa has made her stand, as intelligent and shrewd as her daughter and stepdaughter."

"I do not think we would be speaking today, if not for Ana's bravery and perseverance. And do not forget my brothers, who stood firm as well," she replied, shyly.

"And your Magic! Take some credit for yourself!"

Persephone laughed, but the seriousness of the situation returned. "Then you'll come? 'Tis not yet stable, and can collapse at any time, but Alyssa and my brothers have refused to leave Haven, to flee to safety through the portals. They've placed much faith in me. I cannot let them down."

"Nothing can keep me away."

"Afore you make such a pledge, I feel you must consider another. Even I can sense the strength of the love your lifemate holds for you in his heart. Are you certain you can risk such for the Wyrdritch?"

"I risk such for you, and for the Nation. We've all been asked to make sacrifices and we must succeed, to bring the Elves back to the effort. We need good allies. Come, afore 'tis too late," Dia encouraged. Then taking Persephone by the hand, they grabbed the closest portal, Dancing away in the blink of an eye, leaving behind the bucket of water at the edge of the creek. When Bastyen found it later that morning, he knew what had happened, for she'd told him to expect such. Still, 'twas no easier than if he'd not been made aware.

CHAPTER TWENTY-SEVEN

By Royal Decree

~~~~~ LATER ~~~~~

After Dia and Persephone told their story to the rest of the group, 'twas decided they'd all return inside the Wyrdritch to allow Kevon to recuperate afore they began the long and dangerous journey back to the island. While there, Alyssa insisted they stay in Haven. Bastyen and Dia, and Graasyn and Calei, each stayed in separate but adjoining guest chambers, with Kevon in the King's chambers. Alyssa stayed in the Queens' chambers, Persephone and Ana in their own. 'Twas a good arrangement for all her guests.

A new age had begun for the Elven Nation, and Alyssa was wise. Joy filled the castle as in times of old. For the first few sennights, Dia and Persephone spent much time together, working on the completion of the Healing of the Spell Dome (the name they'd chosen), and to fulfill the Queen's wishes to create one to use as a gift to King Gabriel and the Resistance. She'd sent out scouts immediately, and yes, now that the truth was known, now that the Wyrdritch was Healed, now that the inside was normalizing, the reports from outside flowed in daily. Alyssa spent most of her time sifting through a flood of information, catching up with what they'd missed, to determine the status of Kadoor. Now things were beginning to slow down enough for her to breathe. Nevertheless, there remained a growing mountain of tasks at which she must chip away.

'Twas in the last few dawns that Alyssa had made some momentous decisions. 'Twas not only her wish to join the Resistance, but 'twas her desire to join the Elven and Sprite Nations back together, at least as allies, if nothing else. This was precipitated by Kevon and Calei's presence. The two Sprites were honorable and straightforward, also desiring an alliance 'tween their Races. But
~~~~~

how to seal such? After much heart-wrenching consideration, Alyssa brought Ana to her chambers for a discussion. When Ana professed agreement with her plan, she called for Kevon. Although the Sprite Prince blushed profusely with his acceptance, he admitted to having been afraid of being forced to an arranged pledge once he returned home, and since he and Ana had become near inseparable, he was quite pleased with the arrangement. Now the test of that friendship, and of their noble commitment, would begin. 'Twould take a Royal Decree, and that would mean she had to have a celebration, complete with a formal dinner of numerous courses, along with much grandeur. This was the part of being Queen she really didn't want or appreciate, but 'twas necessary. Which was why she was elated to learn about the couples. Bastyen and Diadranei already considered themselves mated, but for an Elf, 'twas not a fact without the Royal Decree.

With Bastyen and Graasyn both bearers of Elven blood, and Dia full Elven, she had a perfect excuse for a triple ceremony, and 'twould make the one less painful. After all, she was sending her daughter into the wilds of Kadoor, and with the way things were going, who knew when, or even if, they'd get to see each other again. Separately, she'd brought both couples into her office after she'd spoken to her daughter and Kevon. Dia was quite interested, and her mate was pleased to accept. Then she called in Graasyn and Caleichante. "I know of your half breed status, but this is a new age. Elven blood is Elven blood, and I wish to offer you the opportunity to accept your mate by Royal Decree in the ceremony, along with your son and Diadranei." She'd expected the same happiness that she'd seen in the younger pair, but Graasyn hesitated. She furrowed her brows, and not for the first time, wished she had access to the Link, as did the Highlands.

Graasyn tried to get his tongue to unstick from the back of his throat, but his mouth was suddenly too dry. Glancing at his heart's desire, the look on her face was one of disappointment. With him? With the question? He hadn't asked her to be his mate, to take vows. He'd not known what she'd say. Mayhap 'twas not what she wanted. She was fiercely independent and he could not tie her down. Would she accept? He swallowed hard and tried to form the question, but with his elongating silence came the Sprite Captain's response. To get them both out of the awkward situation, she stated, "Although Graasyn is a half breed, you offer him the chance to take a mate by Royal Decree. This is an extraordinarily gracious offer, but I think I speak for both of us, in that we'd not want to interfere with Diadranei's joy." Calei caught Graasyn's eyes again. In the immediate instant of the offer, her heart expanded and she'd had to catch her breath, for she'd seen his reluctance upon his face. Mayhap he was not ready, or he wasn't certain of his feelings for her. She had no such qualms. She shook her head to avoid displaying the disappointment she felt. "Besides, I am Sprite, and this event should be for the Elves and the Nation.". Graasyn put his hand possessively upon the small of her back and nodded his agreement. His own disappointment was palpable. Alyssa could feel the misunderstandings, but she had too much on her plate now, to attempt to counsel the pair. She'd nodded and dismissed them, hoping they'd eventually work out their issues, and appearing dejected, they left.

<div align="center">~~~~~ LATER ~~~~~</div>

As it turned out, the mating ceremony was majestic and beautiful. Mayhap not as grand as such events were in the old days, but Diadranei was near o'erwhelmed, and Bastyen thought he'd never get her feet to touch the ground again. Guests from all o'er the Wyrdritch attended, many of whom Diadranei remembered from childhood, and Alyssa realized that a census would have to be completed, adding that to her lengthening list. The Elves filled Haven to standing room only, spilling to the grounds beyond. Alyssa gave her royal approval, presiding in the Grand Ballroom, which hadn't been utilized in many a winter, and had been completely transformed for the occasion. After dinner, there was an ensemble and would be dancing, with wine and mead free-flowing from a waterfall which had been created in the middle of the huge marble and granite room. One would have thought 'twas a royal mating ceremony. Well, as all the guests soon learned, 'twas.

Afore the frivolities, and after Bastyen and Diadranei's mating decree was made public, Alyssa called again, for everyone's attention. She'd needed a good excuse to get so many here, for this was the true reason behind the event. She declared her intent to seek an alliance with the Resistance, and to ally themselves with the Sprite Nation once more. To do so, she was offering her youngest daughter, Anastasia, as promised to the Sprite Heir Apparent, Kevon, who was visiting, seeking such an alliance from the Island of Dreams. Everyone knew the story by now, and understood that 'twas not exactly truth, but 'twas close enough, and only accentuated that the Black had returned. If Ana traveled all the way to the Sprite Nation, she would not be turned away, as Kevon's acceptance of the decree, along with the approval of the Captain of his Elite Guard, was all the protection she required. They all agreed with the Queen about developing their new alliances. 'Twas simple logic. Who knew how many Elves were still spread out o'er Kadoor, needing to be Called back for their own good, as well as for the Nation. They had not the power they once enjoyed, and could be conquered without strong allies. The Hoard was spreading their brutality from shore to shore, and even far beyond.

Ana and Kevon stood at the Queen's side and accepted the Promise Decree, as was their duty, afore managing to sneak to the back of the crowd and then to an outside hallway, within half a mark after the dancing and revelry began. As Ana pulled the ornate picks from her elaborate hairstyle, allowing it to flow loose down her back, she studied the boy Prince. He was cute. Did he think she was pretty? Actually, did it matter? The entire decree was but a protocol to bring the cousin Races back together again, and if they never fulfilled it, 'twould not make much difference.

She was just being afforded the opportunity of a lifetime, to leave the Wyrdritch and see Kadoor. And mayhap she could begin her search for the lost ones again, for now that the Spell was Healed, 'twas no way to continue the search from inside. She sighed. She'd rather be anywhere right now, than here. Shrugging her shoulders, she said, "Let's go to the creek. There are lots of baby frogs hopping about, and we can catch them with our hands!"

Kevon's entire face lit up. He'd been looking at the young Princess. She was very pretty. For a girl. And she came up with the best ideas. Since he'd been inside the Wyrdritch, they'd spent all their time together, training, building their strength, and increasing their skills by learning the portals, and regardless of what the adults thought or wanted, they were becoming devoted friends. "Sounds great!"

Suddenly, they heard a squeak nearby, and Coltyn came out from behind Ana's billowing skirt to stand in their way, little arms outstretched, preventing them from leaving. His face a mask of disbelief, he spoke, "But, you can't leave me here! I haven't done anything wrong in like, forever!"

Ana was confused, and looked around to see if anyone was watching. Up 'til now, they'd been pretty much front and center, and after finally getting into the clear, she just wanted to make a quick getaway while they had the chance. "What?"

Coltyn looked so pitiful. "I've been good, why do I have to stay here?"

Kevon elbowed Ana, and winked to let her know he understood. "Right. Staying through all this, would be considered punishment by any sane person. C'mon, you can go with us, but be quiet!" Taking her little brother by the hand, the three children snuck out the back hallway, and then raced off to the creek.

~~~~~ THE GRAND BALLROOM ~~~~~

Graasyn was an accomplished dancer and led Caleichante around the floor, spinning, swirling her full-skirted gown o'er
~~~~~

the marble, her high heels sparkling with huge diamond, sapphire, and emerald shoe clips. He hadn't had so much fun since just after he'd taken the Oath, when all the new Warriors were presented to the Brotherhood and the Clan. He always seemed to be out of the Den on some operation or other, whenever there was such an event afterwards.

Alyssa had ensured their guests were properly attired for the event, and he wore a black long-tailed silk jacket and matching slacks with white lace-front shirt, in a style reminiscent of times long afore the Last Holocaust. He hadn't worn anything but leathers since the night of his Oath at the Dragon's Den, and Calei had confided that she'd never worn such as this. Her silk dress had a full gathered skirt, the color changing with the lighting from shimmering purples to blues, greens to golds, as they made their way around the floor. The bodice was snug and laced up the front, leaving the top open and plenty of cleavage visible. The ruffled cap sleeves were designed to appear like wings as they trailed down the dress, and she had a long train attached by jeweled brooches at the shoulders. Her snow-white hair was braided and piled upon her head in long loops, displaying her sensually pointed ears. She was so beautiful. "I love you," he breathed. Graasyn stared into Caleichante's golden eyes, and marveled at his good fortune. He never wanted to lose her, yet he felt beneath her somehow. She deserved all this pomp and circumstance, but although he was well paid for a Warrior, he could never afford this back at the Den on his wages. Sadly, he continued, "I would pledge myself to you in such as this, if I but could. But I am a Warrior and have no other status to offer."

"Diadranei has no more status than do I. All this was to soften the loss for the Queen and to avoid resistance to her decrees. She was able, through this event, to ensure her people were distracted, excited, and willing to accept. If she'd just attempted to present such to them after all the recent changes and revelations, 'twould have been a different story than the one told this night.

She is quite brilliant." Then Calei dared to speak that which she'd felt since she'd first sensed him at the Bog. "I love you, too."

"You do?" Graasyn was surprised. For some reason, he didn't think himself worthy of a Magic bearer.

"With all my heart."

Graasyn dropped eye contact, and they continued to glide around the dance floor afore they both required a rest break. Filling their glasses, they stood side-by-side, chatting with the Elves, each pondering what had, and had not, been said aloud. He was an honorable man, a good Warrior, and took his Oath seriously. 'Twas a lifelong commitment. Could he offer her enough to make her want him as much as he wanted her? But he had to remain with the Resistance, had to serve the Battle Commander, and he couldn't strip her of her position as an Elite Guardsman, he'd never do that. There seemed no middle ground, but he wished with all his heart that she would stay with him, forever.

She knew he was honest in his declaration of love, and he'd come so close, just stopping short of asking for her pledge to vows. Calei could feel his indecision once more. 'Twasn't the first time they'd had this near discussion. She sighed. Mayhap this relationship was not meant to be. If only he'd ask. Her answer was upon the tip of her tongue, and would be easily given. But she wouldn't strip him of his freedom, or burden his Stealth Ops position. If he felt he must remain single and could not bear a lifemate, then she would respect that. But she could never love another. So close. He'd come so close to asking her this time. 'Twas with envy that she gazed 'cross the great marble expanse at Bastyen and Diadranei, an emotion for which she felt shame.

He noted the change of expression and asked uncertainly, "Calei? Are you well?"

Calei cast her gaze to the floor, giving her an instant to brighten her expression afore she caught Graasyn's eyes. "I'm fine," she said, but Graasyn wasn't fooled. Preventing him from pursuing his line of thought, she grabbed his drink, and placing both glasses upon a nearby table, she laughed merrily, enthusiastically dragging him back to the dance floor, where all seemed forgotten. Again.

THE RUINS OF DREKINN VILLAGE
~~~~~ THE DRAGON'S DEN ~~~~~

O'er one full winter past, the smallest Dragon and the most massively muscled Warrior in the Brotherhood, had taken the 'Bond. Initially, Darque wondered how 'twould work out, but through the following moons she discovered that Axyl and his petite Green, Haniyyah, were perfectly matched, as were all the 'Bonded. Their unique attributes made them highly valuable, for with Haniyyah's diminutive size came her ability to simply walk about the Den with Axyl, and seemingly without effort and without notice, fit into the normal hustle and bustle. The Clansmen and staff all came to love the little Dragon, leading Darque to assign them as the resident Team, and unbeknownst to all, task them with sleuthing for the spy. They were very near successful, which made them a prime target.

And then things had taken a turn for the worse, and nothing could have prevented the cascade of events that drew them into the midst of an ambush, just a few dawns afore the Battle for the Dragon Clan. 'Twas calculated and took advantage of their size difference, the fact that Haniyyah, of all the Dragons, was unable to launch with her partner from a dead stop, requiring sufficient height or a lengthy run to attain flight. 'Twas brutal, Axyl receiving severe head and internal injuries early in the fight, yet o'er the course of several marks of defensive maneuvering, Haniyyah finally won against their three attackers. But they were as close to the Veil as any had ever been, and if not for the feisty Green's tenacious hold, both would have been lost. Darque and Gunnarr had arrived just in time to assist with her final effort, Storrm, Mystynn and the rest of the Teams, arriving shortly after. They'd flown the pair via slings, back to Shayla and the Den, and using her salve made with Blood Crystal, they'd been able to Heal from their near fatal wounds, but 'twas touch and go for most of the night.

Still recuperating, they'd been too weak to participate in the big battle that followed, but since they were already in the hospital wing, they assisted the Healer and her Apprentices as they could, as well as helping keep the refugees moving along to the dungeon where Fryya and Walkyr took them through the Spell Door, into the caverns of the lair below. 'Twas a process that could not be accomplished quickly, as only three or four at a time could walk through what appeared to them as a solid rock wall, holding skin to skin with Fryya, having seen eight winters now, the youngest of Darque's sisters, with the boy Seer, Walkyr, at seven, instructing them in the process and keeping them in line.

The big battle occurred near two moons past, and yet, Axyl felt he was getting worse rather than better, and after helping for several marks in the continuing rescue and salvage efforts about Drekinn, Darque noted their weakened condition and sent them to the Healer along with several others who'd just managed to live through their own serious battle wounds. Now the pair were resting in their cave. The burly Warrior was aggravated. The others had been wounded in the Battle for the Dragon Clan, and Axyl couldn't get past what he saw as a huge difference. He'd been injured near afore their fight began, knocked off Haniyyah's back to fall unconscious to the ground where he remained 'til Darque shook him when 'twas all o'er, seeking information. He'd missed not only that battle, but the big one as well, and felt he'd let down his 'Bond partner, his Warrior brothers and sisters, and the Clan. His self-identity was one of personal strength, valor, and the ability to protect others. He was raised and trained as a Warrior and he'd never turned away from, or lost, a righteous fight. 'Twas humiliating, and the big man was quiet in reflection.

Haniyyah was concerned. Her partner was confident, robust and outgoing, a stark contrast to her more reserved and shy nature, but since their injuries, he hardly said a word to anyone, and avoided contact with the others. She didn't want to pry, but she felt 'twas time she knew the real reason behind his change. Although his injuries were completely Healed, his physical prowess returning with his endurance, something was still wrong and she decided she had to use the Link to seek an answer. 'Twas an unspoken rule that one did not invade the privacy of another's thoughts, even your own LifeBond partner, without invitation or good reason. What she discovered there surprised her, and in astonishment she gasped, "Oh!"

Axyl immediately came to her side, asking her solicitously, "Are you still hurting? What can I do for you?" He'd completely missed her foray through the Link, so distracted by his own thoughts. His concern and love for his partner had not wavered, but his personality had made a significant reversal. The handsome Warrior, who was usually surrounded by many friends and beautiful women, had become a recluse. Haniyyah could feel the others' misunderstanding of his refusal to socialize, but then, she also felt their compassion. Now she knew his loss was greater than she'd believed. 'Twas not just the fact that he'd been unable to participate in the fight, but his entire body, from the crown of his head to his toes, was covered with scars. A few would mayhap disappear eventually, but most were big and angry red, and would never change. Her Healing power had been so weakened by the time they'd been delivered to Shayla, that they would have Passed the Veil if not for the Healer's special salve. But the severity of their wounds, the length of time 'twas, from when they'd been wounded to when they'd managed to release her Healing, left his Human skin a map of the battle he hadn't even known raged all around him. Although Haniyyah had made a valiant effort to shield him, talon slashes, fang tears, and Flame burns, were all clear to the eye. Axyl was not vain, but he was popular with the females of his Kind. Warriors lived hard and played hard because they knew they'd probably Pass the Veil hard one day, and he'd been no exception. Recently, of the few occasions someone made direct contact with them, she'd felt only sadness for what their friend had suffered, but Axyl translated such feelings to pity, an emotion he didn't want or need, and which made him bitter. He could not forgive himself for being unable to even lift his sword to protect his 'Bond, and he could not believe any woman would want him now. In his mind, others thought him ugly, as well as a coward.

Haniyyah knew without saying, that an apology for not being able to alter the scars upon his skin, would not alter the deeply embedded scars upon his soul. He needed something stronger than her Magic, even stronger than their 'Bond. He needed true love. 'Twould require a good Human female, one who saw beyond the physical scars, to help him heal the emotional ones. Someone he could trust as he did her, someone who could give him back his identity. She wondered if such a female existed.

CHAPTER TWENTY-EIGHT

So Much to Hide

~~~~~ THE BATTLE OF ICE MIST FALLS ~~~~~

Ardyth melted into the rocky cliffs near the falls, thick strands of algae draped o'er her long auburn hair and down her shoulders. 'Twasn't really necessary, as her hair was dark enough, especially wet, not to be noticed in the shadows of her hiding place, but she didn't want to take any chances. Besides, not only did she feel the need to avoid the red glint that sometimes caught in the rays of sunshine, she was pale, and her skin, even tanned, was not that hard to spot amongst the foliage. She watched enraptured while a fierce battle waged o'er head, Dragons of all colors facing off, their screams of pain, defiance, and rage near deafening. Torrents of blood fell upon the region, staining the icy waters and flowing downstream to who knew where. She hadn't explored far in that direction, after all, she hadn't been here very long. But when she'd stumbled upon the area she'd instantly felt at peace and decided this was 'home'. Now look at it!

She tried not to move as she was aware of the enhanced vision of those flying humans, not to mention the vision of their Dragons, and she'd had enough of people for her entire span of days. Could she not just be left alone? Find a quiet, out-of-the-way place to live and be happy?

She'd figured out this war, having been in many a tavern since she'd fled that oracle in Tupry as a child. She knew about the LifeBond, and of course her own early education included, as did everyone's, the many prophesies of Kadoor. Those of which she'd not been aware, she'd heard in late night gaming sessions while earning enough to purchase precious supplies including salt, pieces of heavy leather, boots, bow strings, buckles, steel blades and other items to replenish her weapons cache, afore moving on.
~~~~~

And there was the frequent communication with the dead wherever she went, that gave her significant news. Therefore, she knew enough to avoid the Hoard, and she'd also heard about the Battle for the Dragon Clan and the growing Resistance. She'd been tempted to seek them out, but honestly, what did she have to offer? Everything she knew about fighting she'd learned from her many siblings, or from her encounters with the dead (and look where that got them), so, self-taught, and although effective, not very flashy. She was still petite but her lifestyle built muscle, and while she was strong, she was considered curvaceous and had been tying down her breasts with a width of leather since puberty. She could use a blade, spear, or sling with lethal ease, throwing or handling. But a sword? Never had one, never could afford one, and as a loner out in the wilderness, she never saw the need. An excellent swimmer, she was also an excellent hunter, and given enough time she could devise a trap to capture anything. She could kill anything. Or anyone. No qualms. She'd had to defend herself often (especially since she'd developed those curves) and now didn't want to have anything to do with towns. Or men. Well.... except for one. The man in her dreams lately. 'Twas always the same one, a huge, masculine, savage fighter, but quiet, loving, and gentle with his little green Dragon. He was covered from head to toe with wicked scars from massive injuries, and by the looks of it, he should no longer inhabit this side of the Veil. Yet she found him quite enthralling, even ruggedly handsome, and watching his hand caress that Dragon's snout, she'd shiver with desire, wanting him to look at her, to touch her. She sighed. She was dreaming about a Dragon Clan Warrior in 'Bond. She wasn't certain 'twas just her imagination, but of all the ridiculous notions... to think a man of his position would ever be interested in the likes of her. Mayhap 'twas because she was lonely and of all the War Clans, Dragon had the rowdiest reputation. But even though she enjoyed her independence, her heart ached for the companionship and intimacy only the man in her dreams could provide.

Her attention returned to the battle. Thinking back to her last communications with others she realized everyone she'd met, pretty much believed the Dragon Clan had been obliterated in the big battle. Nevertheless, as she stood squinting, her hand shading her eyes, she was certain those were LifeBond Teams up there fighting Hoard Dragons. If the Clan yet lived, there was still hope. Not just for Kadoor, but for her.

MEANWHILE

~~~~~ DREKINN LAIR ~~~~~

</div>

Shayla, not only Darque's aunt, but Healer for the Dragon Clan, and up 'til shortly after the first LifeBond, the only Healer, had her hands full that night. After the big battle, she'd taken her two best Healer Apprentices, Lowah and Kelsey, having trained since they'd arrived at Drekinn as refugees, and promoting them both to full Healer status, she'd stationed Lowah at the Bog, keeping Kelsey with her at the Den. The decision hadn't been too difficult, but she'd never reveal her real reasons to either of them. Lowah was a quick learner, hard worker, and showed great promise. But with amazing perception, Kelsey seemed to absorb her lessons as if she'd already known everything afore she was taught. Both their patients fared well, but somehow, Kelsey had a gift she couldn't describe.

With such extraordinary talent, she felt comfortable with either of them working alone, but her senses told her there was more to Kelsey than she'd revealed and she wanted her at the Den where she could keep an eye on her. Kelsey had never given anyone any reason to doubt her allegiance to the Clan or the Resistance, but there was something odd about the slight girl who stood at least two fingers shorter than Darque, and not being near as muscular, weighed far less. But when she thought no one was looking, the girl appeared near as strong as the Battle Commander herself. There was an air of deception about Kelsey, but she'd never been caught in a lie. However, this was war. They had to be watchful
~~~~~

for spies. Everyone had to be careful, but her brother had grown increasingly paranoid using the Blood Elixir that extended their lives and changed their DNA, and although she'd used an altered product of her own creation, now called the Blood Crystal, following a slightly different evolution than did he, she hoped she'd recognize the same pattern in herself, if such occurred.

With the Battle of Ice Mist Falls underway, she prepared her apprentices for possible incoming, although she knew that the Bog was closer to the fighting, and prayed Lowah could handle what would most likely be the most seriously injured coming her way. At least she had her young apprentice, Chynnar, to assist. Shayla directed reorganizing some supplies, and smiled as she thought of the gangly young orphaned girl who'd leaped at the chance to learn the profession, following them around since the day she'd arrived as a refugee of a particularly gruesome attack, near a winter past. 'Twas close to the beginning of the war, not long after the 'Bond, and shortly after Lowah's own arrival.

She thought back. Kelsey had arrived just o'er two moons later, having joined another group traveling to Drekinn, whom Darque had helped when their subsistence farm was destroyed by Flame. They had two of the most beautiful Mastiffs with them, and she'd wondered how those dogs had survived their wounds, after doing a thorough examination upon their arrival. Darque kept a water bag of Gunnarr's saliva, smelling and looking like fine aged whiskey, which is what happens o'er a period of time, beginning the moment the thick clear fluid hit the air, the result of the Magical Healing properties fading but still very powerful. She'd provided it to use on their wounds, unbeknownst to them, but 'twould have taken more than that to heal those dogs. She hadn't considered Kelsey's association at that time. Mayhap she should have.

Just then, Kelsey's voice rang out from the adjoining room, bringing the Healer back from her reverie. "Shayla?" Kelsey stopped abruptly and cleared her throat, peeking covertly from under her long dark lashes at the others, to see if they were now looking at her, afore she swallowed and continued, her voice now slightly altered. "Where do you want these extra racks?" The others were bustling about and showed no signs of noting anything out of the ordinary, for which she was grateful. She'd couldn't afford to be careless. Mayhap she'd stayed too long. But how long was too long? Every day, no matter where she awakened, 'twas a tightrope she walked.

~~~~~~~~~~

Throughout the night, Shayla received updates on the battle through Haniyyah's Link. She and Axyl were recovering well from the Ambush of Byndynn, two days afore the Battle of Evanntyr, followed the next dawn by the Battle for the Dragon Clan. 'Twas a horrible sequence of events from which, in Shayla's opinion, the Clan had survived against all odds, and by the skills and tenacity of her nieces, Darque and Storrm, now Battle Commander and her Second Fighter. With all the activity, she lost sight of Kelsey.

~~~~~~~~~~

Kelsey hoped that Shayla hadn't observed her exit from the clinic as soon as things were under control, seeking the only place she could let down her guard. The kennel was her favorite sanctuary. The slim young woman with perfect pale skin, long, brown, curly hair, and large brown eyes, looked like she'd blow away in a stiff breeze, and was smaller than half the children with whom she'd dealt o'er the past winter. The almond shape of her eyes, along with the pointed uplift of her ears, and the wind chime echo of her voice, she tried to keep under tight glamour, but the effort was becoming ever more draining with the increasing distractions and stress of the war. She'd never been so surrounded by Humans. Having no way to return to the Wyrdritch, just living day to day was becoming exhausting.

Near a winter past, her father was killed in a ruthless Hoard attack upon their subsistence farm in the Outlands, where they'd lived since shortly after the Retreat. He'd been a Skald of the Elven Nation, one of excellent repute, who hated Humans and blamed them for the Last Holocaust. Forced to leave the Wyrdritch, he took his only daughter and made their way outside, surviving not only that devastation, but the many ages since, upon their farm, teaching her all he knew as a Skald. Only once had they tried to return home, but unable to find it and believing the Wyrdritch was no more, they'd returned to the home of their own creation, her father more embittered than ever.

Now, everything they'd created, everything they'd owned, had been lost to the Hoard. Despite the prejudice with which she'd been raised, she'd recognized her chances of survival were reduced by being alone. There was only one other family of farmers within a few days' walk, and working her way there, she'd encountered the body of their daughter in the woods, not far from the remains of their barn. They'd been attacked as well. If not for her Elven vision and senses, the girl's blooded and mutilated body might never have been found. Sneaking in closer, she discovered the girl's parents had gathered together what they could, loading it upon a small, pieced together cart, but had not left, still searching for the girl. Taking the chance, she placed her glamour and played her role.

They'd traveled a few days, heading toward Drekinn Village, but the mother died afore they encountered another small group of refugees. Kelsey attempted to intervene, but with her energies ever-low, and the woman so distraught o'er their plight, she could not be helped. Re-building their carts together, they used their horse to pull it, replacing the others' lost cow. Pooling their resources, they continued toward Drekinn. The others had two of the best-looking Mastiffs she'd ever seen and although they had Dragon saliva they were using as a salve given them by the Dragon-riding girl who'd helped them along their way, the dogs would not survive long. The salve would not heal their lungs, nor help heal their closed fractures. She'd grown quite attached to the dogs on their journey, especially Bullaga, the younger one. Using her Skald skills, with a touch of Elven Magic, she'd boosted their healing. Though 'twas not a given, both dogs survived, but not her 'father', as he, too, lost his will to live after his mate Passed, and they buried him along the way. Once more, 'twas nothing Kelsey could do, to prevent such. When they reached Drekinn, now alone again, she dropped most of her glamour, saving about half the energy, and faded into the crowds.

Shortly after, Shayla renewed her call for Apprentices, and several of the refugees, along with a handful of villagers, answered. Mayhap she should have avoided such, but she had nowhere to go, and her skill was in the healing arts. So, she accepted an Apprenticeship. Training began immediately and was hands-on from the first day. She'd tried to be cautious, avoiding Grifynn, the Battle Commander, and his Second, Darque. She could not reveal her prior knowledge, for how would she explain? Healers in the Human world knew of and about each other, and 'twould raise suspicion. During her stay, and in the following moons, she learned that a spy had infiltrated the Clan, and when Bensyn, the other dog that traveled with them, was butchered, she increased her efforts to hide her origins, for surely, they'd think 'twas her if 'twas discovered she was not Human, and they'd probably kill her afore she could convince them otherwise. It seemed the Humans didn't know anything about Elves, even though they'd lived amongst them for ages, and they seemed to think that any Magic bearer was allied to the Evil One.

She visited Bullaga often after his friend was killed by the spy, stepping up both her glamour and her paranoia of being discovered, for once Darque took o'er as Commander, she'd ordered Axyl and Haniyyah to the task of ferreting out said spy. Nevertheless, even avoiding confrontations, her healing ability was gaining unwanted attention. Every spare moment she asked herself the question, should she stay or should she leave?

The kennels were considerably less occupied now, housing only the breeders and pups along with the elder Dogs, or whose handlers had Passed. The others were out with their Humans again, now that they'd been taught some strategies on how to assist in fighting Dragons, and how to avoid Flame. She'd helped them accomplish that. For, although she now went by the more Human name of Kelsey, she was an Elf. Her real name was Kelseacyr, and her innate sense of communication with animals had her rather fond of the big War Horses, but she'd become enamored of Bullaga and 'twas to him she'd return for respite from the stresses of her life.

CHAPTER TWENTY-NINE

Parting Ways

DARKLING FOREST

~~~~~ BASE CAMP ~~~~~

</div>

Late winter/early spring was the most unpredictable of the seasons, and spawned the most dangerous weather patterns in the mountains, oft times spreading its havoc even to the plains of Kadoor. The party had spent the heart of this winter within the Wyrdritch, the weather regulated by Magic, so 'twas a surprise to return to the bitter cold and frost of Darkling. But with a strong sense of the future, they knew they had to leave now. 'Twas near dusk, and Diadranei walked arm-in-arm with Persephone toward the barrier. She was going back to continue her work on the damage caused by the Spell, and to assist Alyssa to Call the Elves in the Return.

Anastasia had already said her goodbyes afore they'd left Haven. Kissing Coltyn on the forehead, he'd wrinkled up his nose and then ran off to the creek to catch tadpoles. He'd been fascinated with the baby frogs she and the Sprite Prince caught, and wanted to see the entire process. And he had his many brothers to play with, as they came often to Haven now, although no one had the heart to mention Leisalarr. Things were already changing for the better.

The two friends stopped at the barrier and listened for the portal to be opened. No longer a weak and random event, 'twas directed and could be called forth, opened to allow in someone from outside, or used to repel those who did not belong. Although being thrust through a portal to another place would not kill, 'twould confuse, and those who'd been so pushed, would not recall how they'd traveled, or even that they had. 'Twould be as if their destination could not be found, or did not exist. 'Twas
~~~~~

how they'd decided to design the new Spell, so that the Resistance could use it to protect their Lair from the Hoard. Outnumbered for now, they needed all the help they could get, to defeat the Evil One.

After working side-by-side, each using their specialties to the maximum to Heal the Spell, alter the way it worked, and Brew the gift, they'd not had much time to talk about what had happened since they last saw each other. Dia pursed her lips. The war, and their diplomatic mission, would not wait, for Kevon and Ana would soon be added to the Hoard's most-wanted list. 'Twould be their next meeting afore they could catch up, and that meeting wasn't promised, for first they must find Darque, offer the pledge of the Elven Nation to join in alliance with the Resistance, unveil their gift of protection, and then work on the Sprite Nation to join. That meant they also had to escort Kevon and Ana safely back to the island. As if that wasn't enough, Dia had become Ana's mentor and knowing their time together, was short, her lessons were hard, her expectations, high. Now, their Empathic senses told them something horrible was on the horizon, and without their help, 'twould prove devastating.

Dia sighed. Words failed her, and so she encased her friend in love and fellowship. Persephone was full of heartbreak, but also resolution in her mission as a specialty Healer, a Healer of broken Magics, for 'twas much damage caused by the failing Spell and 'twould take time to manage, including the fungal-like spread affecting the forests and the Highlands. She was also the official Heir Apparent and of this news, Persephone was not particularly happy, for after hearing more about her brother's current lifestyle, she had a feeling Myrrdin would not return, and she'd be stuck with a status she did not want.

Silently, Diadranei watched her childhood friend turn and step into thin air, disappearing instantly. 'Twas still a wonder when she saw it happen for 'twas not through shadow and seemed completely impossible, even after having worked on it together.

Her fingers o'er her mouth to quell her quivering lip, she stood for a short while 'til she felt a strong hand upon her shoulder, warm knuckles brushing her other cheek. Lowering her head, she twisted into Bastyen's arms and let him hold her tight. Bastyen lifted her chin and catching her gaze, he slid his hands onto either side of her face. Pulling her lips to his, he held her fast to deepen the kiss, afore reluctantly breaking the moment, eyes still closed, his forehead resting against hers. Slowly they turned and walked hand-in-hand, back to the warmth of the campfire. There'd be no time for more intimacy for many moons to come. Dia and Ana had been keeping tabs on the 'feel' and the 'sound' of an incoming storm that seemed to be building into something quite impressive, and in which they could not afford to allow themselves to be caught. They had to get out of Darkling. They had to get to the Keep, where they could winter o'er in safety, afore traveling on to Drekinn, the last known place the Queen's reports showed Darque. They'd be leaving at dawn.

<div align="center">~~~~~ THE KEEP OF ST SWIFTYN'S ~~~~~</div>

Darque stood yet again upon the ramparts of the Keep, staring into the light downfall of sleet, scattered with huge flakes of glistening white snow. Even under the cover of the guard stand, her long red hair was damp, the braids plastered to her back, her eyelashes stuck together with the frozen flakes. She rubbed them in fatigue with the heel of one hand, then crossed her leather braced arms back in front of her chest, afore continuing her vigil. Off and on for marks, she'd been discussing the past, the present, and the future of the war, with her namesake, the shade of her ancestor, Darque Abriya D'Rienne, known as the First Warrior. Having been dragged from the Beyond along with her father, former Battle Commander Grifynn, during the recent ceremony in the bowels of the Keep, the spirit was full Rashei and could tell the future. Not as did a Seer, but 'twas similar. Seers had Visions, the Rashei, or 'witch women', were scholars and Mystics.

Prescience, clairvoyance, and prophecies were their way of life, but they specialized in scrying, a method of Seeing that involved water. From the First Warrior's sight, Darque learned that a convergence was approaching the Keep. Both good and evil were coming their way and they needed to be prepared. The incoming blizzard atop heavier than usual snowfall, would strengthen as it crossed the peaks, and would arrive too soon. Blizzards such as this one, could build for sennights and rage o'er a moon, and all travel, including Dragon flight, would be impossible for an unknown length of time.

Awaiting reinforcements from the Lair of the Resistance currently housed at the Bog of St Swiftyn's just a few marks' flight away, they didn't have many upon whom to call, and she knew they'd be hard pressed to protect the Keep adequately from the kind of battle of which she'd been warned. But the Teams living in Drekinn Lair, established afore the entire village was destroyed in the Battle for the Dragon Clan, were needed to protect the Clan still living there. Through her Communications Officers, Rolf and his 'Bond, Nalwynn, who had the strongest control o'er the Link with others, able to Send and Receive consistently o'er the furthest distances with all the Races, she'd ordered them to hold steady 'til after the storm abated.

With the vision of a raptor, her sharp eyes roved from the east, from whence the Shade told her would come 'help', towards the west, from whence her reinforcements would be coming, and finally to the south, from whence would come the evil of the Black. She didn't know whether to hope for more snow to stop the Hoard for now or not, for more snow would also hinder the journey of their expected guests. The First Warrior was adamant that this party of travelers would bring with them the solution she so desperately needed, to protect her people and the growing Resistance, and they must be rescued and brought into the Keep at all costs, for the next thing of which she was certain was the coming of the Hoard upon the heels of the storm.

She chewed her bottom lip and pondered the logistics. What the Shade reported of the future was not to be doubted, but the future was not set in stone. A miasma of possibilities, like trying to see what was at the bottom of a murky river, the flowing water churned as did time itself. So, although 'twas clear the travelers brought with them the solution, 'twas not clear just what that solution could be, nor how much time they had afore the attack, nor even how long this storm would last, and these uncertainties frustrated the Battle Commander. Still, she couldn't ignore the warning, but they couldn't just fly blindly into the storm soon to be rolling in like a tsunami, either. The party coming sure as Hades better be ahead of that, or 'twas little chance of their survival.

She contemplated her options. Her own hybrid insight gave her confidence that they had some time, 'twasn't all going to occur within marks, and she was fairly certain 'twouldn't occur within a few days, either. Mayhap a moon? If the Fates were generous, mayhap more. Her gut instincts also told her they'd get but one chance on the rescue, and 'twould be to go out as late as possible to search for the party. If they were within a day's flight, they could be brought in ahead of the storm, if not, they'd have to hunker down and hope for the best. She kept Rolf and Nalwynn, assisted by Axyl and Haniyyah, busy through the Link, reporting on any action from Evanntyr, but there'd been nothing since Gabriel had been proven as the True King. Impatiently, she also waited to Hear anything from Brannyn, her contact within the Hoard, but thus far, there was naught but silence from the Fay, who had achieved a most high promotion, that of Right to Second of the Black himself. There was but one other 'tween them now. The Destroyer.

Gunnarr perched upon the wall in his usual majestic pose, as close to her as he could get, his powerful wings tucked up tightly to his flanks, long tail wrapped around his feet, head bowed slightly to avoid getting hit directly in the face by the cold wet flakes. He hated snow. Although 'twas coming down slowly, 'twas wet and sticking together. Shaking once again, great lumps of the soft white stuff fell from his massive head and shoulders, his blue scales glistening with the moisture. He pouted and squinted his huge crystalline eyes, closing the thin inner lid to give them some protection, while still allowing him to see. Cold didn't stop a Highland Dragon, but it did make them cranky, and wasn't particularly comfortable. Darque wouldn't allow fires on the wall as 'twould be too visible o'er long distances, but he'd give anything if she'd let him heat the stone under his butt, just a little. Yet, the Magic expended would be just as visible for leagues, even through the heavy curtain of a storm, and right now they couldn't afford that chance, as well as needing to maintain his Magic at the highest achievable levels in preparation for the expected battle. The only good thing about this situation was that, however badly it made the Dragons of the Resistance feel, 'twas mirrored for the Dragons of the Hoard, putting them all on even fighting ground.

~~~~~ SOMEWHERE IN THE WESTERN
REGION OF BYNDYNN FOREST ~~~~~

</div>

The Sorcerer stood on the ledge looking o'er the forest canopy. He'd already been waiting far too long for that stupid Dragon to return from his mission, afore sensing his death. Having re-discovered the Eoche, the massive and lethal insect brought to him by the fishermen so many winters prior and then razing their village after killing the brothers who delivered it, he'd been inspired. He had the Dragon drop the rusted iron cage housing the insect, into the expansive ward of the Keep of St Swiftyn's, where he was quite certain Aalanna had the spirit of Grifynn anchored. He would enslave Grifynn's spirit so that he could force him to reveal the secrets of his Dragon-Human hybrid bloodline, to give him Darque's weaknesses, some way to defeat the prophesy.
~~~~~

Even though Aalanna should have been alone in the vast Keep, 'twould be nowhere in the entire mountain for her to hide, for the Eoche hunted by vibration, and she'd die a most hideous death. But somehow, the plan had gone awry, and the Dragon was killed. He knew not if he'd completed the mission, but he'd reported that the Keep appeared occupied, just afore all Communication ceased as he was forced Past the Veil in an attack o'er the Bog. He was sick of his plans being diverted. It seemed this one was a failure as well. So. The survivors of the Clan must have taken o'er the Keep and/or the Bog. And if they were at St Swiftyn's, they were surely still at Drekinn, for the contingent he'd sent there to find Fryya and Gabriel, had disappeared. Could they not have the decency to just die already? When he returned to Evanntyr, 'twould be Flame to pay. 'Twas time to mount another attack, and this time, he'd hit the Clan with everything they had.

CHAPTER THIRTY

The 7ᵗʰ Prince and the Pearl Diver

ABOUT A SENNIGHT LATER

~~~~~ ICE MIST FALLS ~~~~~

Ardyth slept late that morning, snuggled in her furs, for the weather was threatening to come in hard from the northeast, leaving the skies dark and cloudy, and Ice Mist would be inundated once again. She looked forward to seeing more of the falls' namesake frozen mists as they floated through the region, dissipating when they finally touched the ground or the surface of one of the many lakes. The mists coming off the falls would freeze into the silhouettes of animals or birds, and sometimes she thought she could see people and entire battles, appearing as if living things, as they moved slowly groundward. 'Twas eerie, but 'twas also captivatingly beautiful.

She'd worked hard yesterday, gathering sufficient wood to fuel her fire if she was snowbound for any length of time. 'Twas a rare, late season storm, and those were always the worst in the mountains, some hanging on for more than a couple of moons. She looked outside. Instead of a cabin with a bay window, her chosen home was made of rock and had an open view, the falls behind which she'd settled so many moons prior, providing a heavy, but most beautiful curtain, as well as providing insulation, her cave remaining a steady and comfortable temperature throughout the seasons. Ryndor didn't mind, and had his own area in the back, but she'd taught him to come and go as he pleased, never fearing for his safety or that he'd not return, for the beast seemed quite attached to her.
~~~~~

She'd never tired of the sound of the water, nor did she lament the humidity, which she controlled by the fire, for she was water born and 'twas her element. Besides, the falls afforded her the most security she'd ever known, for although she could see out through the running waters, no one could see in through the same. 'Twas a trick of the light, and she'd learned that even with her fire lit, she was safe, and she and Ryndor's presence would go undetected. Using her remarkable breath control, taught to her as a small child along with the rest of her village, she could stand under the running water of the falls and breathe, as long as 'twasn't a solid wall. She'd even taught the horse to stand with his head nearly 'tween his front legs, as they remained still for up to a quarter mark or more, allowing the water to run o'er them, spitting out what trickled into their mouths. This feat had taken her several moons to accomplish with the horse, but he'd learned to stand perfectly still and calm, tolerating the falling water surrounding them, hidden from all view. The trick might come in handy in the future. One could never be too prepared, and with such training the horse had come to trust her completely, and never panicked despite cause.

After stretching and rekindling the coals, she dressed and considered her chores for the day. 'Twas just then that the frantic noises coming from the lake beyond had her scrambling outside, racing around the falling waters and rocky outcroppings to discover the source. She had no idea what she'd gotten herself into after rounding the bend of the falls just as a large winged creature floating on what appeared to be a raft, tipped o'er and began to bob up and down helplessly. Tearing off her heavy layers of clothing on the run, she pushed off from the grassy edge with both feet, stretching forth her body with every muscle taut, legs together and arms reaching out in a shallow dive that took her far into the icy waters to make the rescue. 'Twas not difficult, and after carrying her new friend onto the shore, she shivered but carefully checked the little Dragon for injury afore setting him down on the sands so she could dress once again. "I've never seen a baby Dragon afore," she puffed from the cold, not from fatigue, trying to make conversation to distract the little one from panic at his near drowning experience.

But Bryynn wasn't one to panic. Instead, he pouted. "I'm near a sennight hatched. I'm not a baby. I'm just not full grown." He shook off the remaining water and waddled up closer to the girl as she sat on the rocks hugging herself, trying to warm up. "And what about you? You're a baby Human, or not full grown either." He sounded contrite, but his actions were concerned and grateful. Touching her bare ankle with one sharp stubby talon, she felt the instant tingling and most welcome warmth spread throughout her body, and she stopped shivering. Magic could be a wonderful thing.

Ardyth smiled. "Where did you come from?"

"I was buried at the Bog of St Swiftyn's, but I wasn't sure if I was supposed to hatch yet. Only, if I didn't, I would've suffocated. My egg cracked when I was helping my brothers in the Battle of Ice Mist Falls about six moons past, and I struggled for a long time afore I had to break out." He looked around. "This is Ice Mist Falls, correct? I only saw it through their eyes, but I felt drawn here."

She nodded. From his story and watching his earlier antics, he'd had a rough time thus far, and could probably use some help. "Yes, you've arrived at your intended destination. 'Tis obvious you can't swim... can you fly?"

Sulking, Bryynn stated, "Not yet. I was trying to learn."

She bit her tongue. Near drowning wasn't the best method for learning how to swim, let alone how to fly, but she could follow his reasoning. Swimming would strengthen his wings for flying, but he really couldn't do that alone, without already knowing how to swim. However, after such a harrowing experience, she didn't want to criticize. She'd already deduced the youngster wasn't strong enough, and 'twas dangerous for him to be out there on the water at this point. Even though they'd just met, there was a growing connection 'tween them and she knew he had a good heart. "You're alone. I understand. There are just some things one needs help to learn." Looking around, she asked, "Where did that raft of yours go?"

"It sunk. 'Tis not really a raft. I found it o'er there in the shallows," he pointed. "The Warriors call it a Thumper. 'Tis a Clan shield covered with Dragon scales. One of them must have lost it during the battle. But it did float upside down, I just couldn't steer, and when I tried to use my wings to paddle, it tipped, and I fell off."

The poor little thing looked so lost, to bolster his confidence she stated enthusiastically, "Well, using your wings in such a manner is an excellent way to strengthen them. Good thinking." Her smile was so bright, his frown melted away. "So, do you know how Dragons usually learn to swim? I believe I can help you with that part, and we can figure out how to get to the flying lessons later."

Bryynn was excited, but solemn, as he accessed his Memories to reply. "Our parents teach us. Or siblings, if they're around. We sit on their backs as they swim, using our wings and legs as they go deeper, 'til we're swimming on our own. Same with flying practice. We fly tandem, 'til we're on our own. It doesn't take long, a few moons or so, as we grow rapidly. But I thought I could do it myself."

"I suppose you're an orphan, as am I."

"You're an orphan?" Even though to his knowledge he was not, Bryynn's entire expression relayed his sorrow for the girl. But then another Memory teased him, and quizzically, he snuggled against her. She was being honest and meant him no harm, and there was something else... a pull, an attraction. He stared at her blouse. 'Twas coming from there. In a subconscious response, the Human reached up and took hold of something 'tween her breasts, hanging under the fabric.

Ardyth was struck by a memory from her own past... her grandmother telling her about the Dragon's Eye, that 'twas the 'color of her destiny'. She gaped at the little one now resting his chin on her knees. She'd not noticed his color when she'd first seen him, as he'd appeared rather dark when wet, but now he was dry, and his blood red scales sparkled. He stood about mid-thigh, but then she wasn't very tall. Leaning forward, she pulled the Eye from the neckline of her blouse, and dangled it in front of him. His astonished gaze swept back and forth 'tween it and her, his own color and that of the Eye matching perfectly. "Where did you get that," he stammered.

"My grandmother gave it to me as a child. 'Twas the only thing left intact when..."

"...your village was destroyed," he finished her statement. "She told you 'twas the color of your destiny', correct?"

"How did you know that?"

"Because, I am your destiny. You are the reason I couldn't hatch when all the rest did. You are the one for whom I have waited. You are MY destiny."

<center>~~~~~ LATER THAT AFTERNOON ~~~~~</center>

After Bryynn helped her prepare for the incoming storm, she, gathering firewood, and he, using his nose and his talons, finding and digging up many edible roots and fungi she'd missed, she decided 'twas no time like the present, especially since her new friend had eased her workload, and all her chores were done early. She didn't expect the storm to hit for several days, if not a full sennight, yet 'twas getting very cold and the flurries were wet. Bryynn's Magic prevented her from succumbing to hypothermia as Ardyth stripped down, and with the little Dragon perched upon her back, she waded into the icy waters of one of the lesser bodies at the base of one of the smaller waterfalls. When 'twas deep enough, she ducked under and stretched out, as Bryynn shifted his weight for the swim 'cross. 'Twould still take near a mark to get to the other side, and from there, they could walk back to her cave. After his prior experience, he'd been none too happy about the plan, but his new friend had convinced him of her skill, and he crouched low to keep his balance as if surfing the ocean waves. Soon, he was dragging the tips of his wings through the water. Even with a passenger, Ardyth was a strong swimmer and he quickly lost all fear, splashing in the water as she continued with long smooth strokes, both arms pulling about shoulder width apart, then tucking her elbows forcefully to her sides, she pushed great volumes of water behind them afore bringing her hands around and back together to extend forward again, her legs completing a coordinated whip kick maintaining their forward speed. He was excited and confident enough to lay upon his belly, using his wings stretched out as far as he could, paddling along as if she wasn't just underneath him.

Ardyth could feel the little Dragon becoming less dependent upon her, could sense the increasing strength of his wings pulling through the waters, and was amazed at how quickly he learned and adapted to the rigorous workout. Within half a mark they'd entered very deep water in the middle of the pool and he was fully engaged, using his wings and even his back feet to push and paddle. She adjusted her pattern so that the water covered her back leaving him semi-floating while he continued to paddle along near on his own, even using his front legs to help him adjust his balance just afore they reached the other side. Spitting as she crawled along the shallow bottom, she wiped the water from her eyes and helped him off her back, and then pushed him up o'er the edge of the shoreline where they sat and eyed their trip.

Ardyth didn't quite know what to say. She was mystified. "'Twas clear you'd not been a swimmer when we began, and yet your strength and coordination grew at an astounding rate. 'Twould have taken a human child several moons to make the gains you showed in just this one attempt. How can that be? Did you use Magic? But why not simply use it to learn how to swim in the first place?"

Just as mystified, Bryynn stated, "Magic doesn't work like that." His head kept turning 'tween her and 'cross the pool where they started. Pondering, figuring, deducing, the little Dragon's mind was awhirl, and all the events of his life since he was laid, came together as clues. Clues to his 'special Magic'. 'Twas something unique for every 7th Prince of a 7th Prince, aside from their normal share. While still in the Egg, he'd often wondered just what his might be, or even if he'd break the mold, so to speak, since he and Gunnarr had switched birthrights, leaving him with nothing special at all. He'd Reached out to his brother Gunnarr, drawing his attention to the Bog where he'd been buried, he'd even helped when Gunnarr tossed his Egg o'er the Sea of Dreams to their cousins, the Water Dragons. There was more, so much more. And suddenly, he understood. He was an Amplifier. And, he'd benefitted from her ability, just as he could amplify other's abilities, making them richer, stronger, quicker, better. He could also reverse that, as when he interfered with the Hoard Dragons' Healing during the battle six moons prior, and blocked the Spell Sword from killing the Prince. It appeared as if he could draw from, or to, anyone. He'd caused Haniyyah's Flame to be bigger, longer, stronger than any she or any other Highland, had ever belched, saving her life and the life of her 'Bond, the Warrior Axyl. Apparently, he somehow absorbed Ardyth's swimming skills, just as he manipulated Magical skills. 'Twas boggling.

The possibilities suddenly seemed endless. And of course, 'twould be a given that the Hoard would want him. If only he could use his Magic to grow faster! However, just because he had such a Gift, meant not that he could use it effectively. Magic was not only finite, needing to be refueled, 'twas delicate and strong as steel at the same time, and required finesse, physical and spiritual strength, and practice or experience, to excel. Magic could wax or wane with one's emotions, which was why strong emotion was so powerful, and adding blood to the mix, such as the Blood Call for the LifeBond, gave it ultimate power. But each Magic bearer varied in all these factors, and so Magic had no balance, and without Mankind to provide such, Kadoor would simply implode from all the unrestrained energy. 'Twas the dilemma which led to the Highlands' decision to stay behind at the time of the Retreat just afore the Last Holocaust, to help Mankind survive. 'Twas during that time that Gunnarr had tossed his Egg to the Water Dragons, for his own protection.

And now the circle was closing. His destiny was this Human female. They had much to do together. Learning to swim was but the beginning. She had given him a gift, and he had something to give to her. For near a quarter mark, he pondered what that was, while they sat on the shore. Then Ardyth, who was also quietly reflecting, stood up. "I can sense your fatigue and hunger, and with such, comes the cold! Follow me. We can warm up at my fire and you can rest. But afore all that, can you help me keep warm enough to dive for that shield? I can't leave something that valuable."

<center>~~~~~ LATER THAT EVENING ~~~~~</center>

Everything Ardyth owned, was functional and served a purpose in her survival, although some of her tools and weapons were carved, scrimshawed or inlaid, to make them more aesthetically pleasing. 'Twasn't that she didn't like things, or that she wasn't creative, 'twas simply because she hadn't the means to travel with much, and had been on the run since she'd made her escape from the Oracle, never finding a place to settle. And near everything could be bartered for something else. She'd even traded Ryndor's saddle not long after his 'acquisition' when 'twas discovered she was more comfortable riding bareback, and Ryndor didn't seem to like the constriction of the saddle, anyway. Yet she'd kept the pearls. Having shown them to no one in her entire span of days, she felt compelled to share with Bryynn. He marveled at the multi-colored assortment when she dumped them out, the flickering firelight reflecting off them and making them even prettier. Drawing his talon through the huge pile in fascination, she sat cross-legged. "I've kept them all this time. I could never sell one without revealing my riches, so I just hid them. Occasionally I take them out, sort them by size or color, admire their beauty, play games with them. I couldn't bring myself to part with them, and I'm not sure why. Memories, I suppose."

"The pearls saved you from the same fate as the rest of your village. Mayhap you felt the need to save them in return."

Ardyth considered his words for a bit, then continued, "'Twas my hope they'd be put to good use one day, as was my original intent."

"Mayhap they will be put to better use than your original intent. Giving them to Shytin would never have achieved the honorable goal you'd set."

Nodding her head, for she could say nothing, she realized that she felt her grandmother most strongly whenever she pulled out the pearls, and this time her grandmother whispered in her ear, telling her to put her trust in the little Dragon.

<center>~~~~~ A FEW MARKS LATER ~~~~~</center>

As the evening wore on, Bryynn taught Ardyth how to use the Eye to 'see'. Reluctantly, she'd admitted to having never attempted to utilize what she'd heard about the mythological powers of the Dragon's Eye, and had always just worn it concealed under her blouse. Along with the pearls, they constituted her own private fortune. Following his instructions, she wrapped a piece of leather in a cone around the Eye, stitching it closed like a funnel, to create a type of spyglass known as a monocular. Once she achieved a higher level of expertise, the funnel would not be needed, but for now, 'twould help her focus. Peering through for the first time, she Saw a cave near the Bog, the final base camp used by the Warriors Graasyn and Bastyen. Then she Saw the Warrior. Her sudden intake of breath jarred Bryynn and his stare made Ardyth blush, for by the little Dragon's expression, he knew her thoughts.

<center>~~~~~~~~~~</center>

Ardyth practiced with the Eye 'til near dawn. The constant soft roar of the waterfall was interrupted by Bryynn's voice as he wakened. Without preamble, he asked, "Are you coming with me, or shall I make the journey alone?"

'Twas not what she'd expected her new friend to say first thing in the morning, and she was puzzled. "What do you mean? What journey?"

"As of now, you and Corbyn the Fay are the only ones who are aware that I've hatched. 'Tis time I made my presence known, and joined the Resistance. Even though I still need to learn to fly, I have much to offer. We are not 'Bonded, although we're certain to take if we enter the Magic, but we do share a special Link of sorts. 'Tis not uncommon amongst our Kinds."

"Where do you go?"

"To the Keep. 'Tis where I feel my brother, Gunnarr. He and I have much to discuss. His Magic as High Prince and mine as 7th Prince, are entwined as no other, ever. He was last laid, first hatched, and I, first laid, last hatched. I know not why this anomaly occurred, but I shall forever be left in the dark if I make no attempt to discover my true calling. At the same time, I know you and I are destined to be together. I hope by the Ancients, you decide to join me, but I cannot force you to do so, and I feel an increasingly strong pull to go."

"You realize the storm is building, and that we'd be traveling directly into it?"

"You can carry me under your cloak, while I keep us warm."

"Right. That's a great plan."

"I knew you'd agree!"

Ardyth had to laugh at the expression on his face. She shook her head and then got up to rekindle the fire, and while she dressed, Bryynn made plans. Although she'd been reluctant to leave her home, she'd never stayed so long in one place afore, and her restlessness was augmented by the fact that the Warrior Axyl was out there somewhere, and even though she had little hope of ever meeting him, 'twas certain she never would, by staying here. Packing her things, including her latest acquisition, the Thumper she'd recovered from the lake, she and Bryynn decided to make the Warrior's last base camp the first stop on their way to the Keep. 'Twould provide marginal safety from both the weather and the unknown, surrounding the region.

CHAPTER THIRTY-ONE

The Pledge Fulfilled

~~~~~ DARKLING ~~~~~

The party traveled as fast as they could a'foot, but they were slowed by Kevon's lack of endurance. They could only hope the Borkahn would keep their word about meeting them and taking them back through the Talons underground, for if not, they'd never beat this storm and 'twould be impossible to survive without cover. Add to that, the fact that they'd lost Demonseed and both their War Horses, 'twould take many more moons to get o'er the mountains, and they needed to return as soon as possible. They'd been searching for days for the same place where they'd entered the forest from the caves of the Trolls, but 'twas well camouflaged, and even the enhanced vision of the Elves and Sprites did nothing to assist them.

Allowing a brief respite from the hard pace, Graasyn opened his mouth to say they had to find shelter to weather the storm, when into their midst walked Crytcha. Without formal greeting, in her thick Common accent she flatly stated, "The boy lives. You succeeded."

Kevon was the only one of them who had no real idea of the appearance of a Troll, having slept through most of their journey, and standing up, he couldn't take his eyes off the female. Crytcha laughed, as the boy no older than she, and yet quite a bit smaller, stepped back and looked to the others for enlightenment, as well as confirmation of their safety.

Graasyn walked forward, taking the offered arm of the Troll in a warm embrace of friendship, for he couldn't have been happier to see her. "'Tis the excellent timing of the Borkahn, to find us at this very moment, my friend. I take it by your appearance, that this is no happenstance."
~~~~~

Shaking her head, she replied, "No happenstance. While the mighty Gorch continues in his annihilation of the evil faction led by Roack, I meet you to fulfill the promise of Gorch, to return you safely to the western side of the Talons. I am most happy to have the opportunity to do so, for this means you lived through your mission. 'Twas a difficult one, indeed." Crytcha noticed Anastasia while speaking, her eyes narrowing in uncertainty.

Dia came forward to greet the girl with a hug, from which Crytcha held back, so as not to cause damage to the slim woman's body. Her gentle touch was charming, and reminded Diadranei of the way she'd handled the bees, despite extreme hunger. "Crytcha! I am so glad to see you again! Please, allow me to introduce you properly to the Prince of the Sprite Nation, Kevon, along with the Princess of the Elven Nation, Anastasia, who travels with us now."

Once everyone was acquainted, Crytcha stated, "Come. I have a surprise for you," afore she turned around and began walking away from them, while they scrambled to follow.

~~~~~~~~~~

After entering the caverns, they all stuck closely to Crycha, for to lose sight of her, was to get lost in the vast mountainous system. Without access to view the stars, they knew not how long the trip took, but only slept twice along the way and were provided with food that the Borkahn had brought in just for them, having learned their preferences and needs from those left behind during the rescue. They met many others of the Borkahn, all of whom showed great deference to the girl Troll, and all of whom seemed prepared for battle, although they had no weapons that anyone could see. They had to wonder how they fought, and once again, they wondered just what they ate. They knew the Borkahn loved honey, and while traveling, they noted they kept their own hives, harvesting the honey and the combs. 'Twas incongruent watching the huge beings taking most reverent care of the tiny insects. But when they'd asked, 'rock', was what Crytcha had replied.
~~~~~~~~~~

Since they'd eaten only that which was offered, and Crycha didn't eat anything that they could see, Dia broached the subject as they continued. "Crycha, I see that the Borkahn are beekeepers, and that you eat honey. Is there anything else you can eat? You mentioned that you eat rock."

"Berries."

"Berries?"

"We mash them, eat them like honey, dip the rock."

Dia could not make sense out of the surrounding feelings. "Could you show us? I'm quite interested."

Waving her hand in a gesture meant for them to follow, she stated, "Come with me."

Deep down a side corridor, they heard the rhythmic pounding of what sounded like stone against stone. As they came closer, they watched several Trolls of all ages, taking rubble from a huge pile at the end of a tunnel, placing it upon a rock, and using only their fists, smashing the rock into powder. 'Twas as if they were creating music as well as food as they seemed to coordinate their actions. And for the first time, they were made fully aware of the awesome power wielded by the Borkahn, as their huge fists crashed down upon solid stone, pulverizing it in an instant.

Watching for some time, they noted others taking baskets of the powdered rock, and Crytcha took them to see what happened next. The baskets of powder were delivered to several more Trolls, again of all ages, who scooped up a handful of the powder and used their saliva to moisten it, kneading it to a paste, spitting as was required 'til they had a flattened patty about the size of their hand. This they carefully layered into another basket, which was taken to yet another area. Seeing them spit in the rock powder, and knowing this would be eaten, had everyone's brows raised, but they were very curious by now and they followed again, wanting to see the end result.

Entering a heated area, they saw several large flat rocks in a circle, with Trolls surrounding them along the outside edge.

While some kept the coals blazing around all the flat rocks, the others took the patties from the baskets and laid them on the hot rocks 'til they changed color, at which time they were completely dried. These cooked patties were turned and removed by hand, for no tools could they see. Once dried, they were rolled and packed into another basket and sent off yet again. Dia speculated that the pliability of the cooked patties must have had something to do with the saliva with which they were made.

Crytcha then led them to what the party referred to as 'the dining room', where the rolled rock patties were made available to everyone, and many Trolls milled about, socializing. There were plenty of large bowls made of granite, marble, or wood, filled with either honey or mashed berries, in which many of the Borkahn would dip their rolls afore eating them. 'Twas a group dining place and they came and went as they wanted. Crytcha was pleased with their approval of the system, and stated proudly, "Told you I eat rock. You believed not."

"We believed you, my friend, 'twas just that we didn't understand how. We don't eat rock, and we now see how does the Borkahn."

"We all make food. We all eat. Everyone shares. Don't make food, don't eat."

Diadranei nodded her approval. "'Tis good. And we do appreciate the tour, but I have another question."

"Ask."

"You mentioned having a surprise for us. What is it?"

With a smile upon her face she announced, "We found your big horses. We cared for them while you were gone. They wait for you on other side. Follow me." Although Calei wondered about Demonseed, 'twas no more information coming from the child.

O'ER A FORTNIGHT AFTER BRYNN HATCHED

~~~~~ THE KEEP ~~~~~

</div>
~~~~~

After the Eoche incident, Darque and Gunnarr had stayed at the Keep, along with Walkyr and Fryya. When the standing watch sent word that there was someone approaching, the Battle Commander threw on her leathers and hurried to the guard station. Even though covered in a fur lined, full length leather cloak, similar to that which Darque was now wearing, 'twas clear the one currently stumbling along the bridge toward the gates of the Keep was tall and slim, and when she slipped on the ice, landing face down with a splat, her hood fell away, revealing long blonde hair. Certain she was alone, the children standing watch ran out to discover a young woman armed with a vast array of foreign weaponry, including a bow and several blades. 'Twas just afore dusk, and Darque had the bruised and bleeding woman carried in and taken to Chynnar's clinic.

Hypothermic and delirious from hard travel through the building storm, 'twas no use trying to get any information from the female Gunnarr identified as a Sprite. Chynnar made her drink an herbal concoction to reduce the fever and help her sleep through the night, although it took three of them to get it down her, afore she could care for what turned out to be relatively minor wounds. Being a'foot, Darque was truly amazed the woman managed to survive. Curiosity peaked to know not only who she was but why she was so driven, for 'twould have taken much motivation to make such a journey. Her concern that the Hoard knew the Keep was occupied, strengthened, but then again, was this woman a part of the party whom they needed to rescue? She bit her lip, her fingers straying to the Dragon scar on her thigh, then turned and left the stranger in Chynnar's clinic to sleep off the drugs. 'Twould be morning afore she had any answers.

<center>~~~~~ AFORE THE FOLLOWING DAWN ~~~~~</center>

Still groggy, the Sprite's first question was, "Who are you?" Chynnar had been watching their new guest throughout the night and immediately directed her sleepy assistants to fetch the Commander. The concoction wore off earlier than expected, but Darque walked into the clinic just as the children were running out, near falling o'er them in the doorway. If her senses hadn't been enhanced, someone would have been injured, and she wasn't pleased.

Harshly, she began, "I thought she would sleep longer," and then stopped midsentence. Apologizing for her foul mood to the children and then to Chynnar, she faced the Sprite with a sigh. "We have no plans to harm you, but I believe 'twould be wise for you to identify yourself first. After all, you came here with the prospect of finding something. Or someone. Mayhap we can help you."

The Sprite sensed she was in no imminent danger and that the woman was not lying. 'Twas evident she was in charge, despite her appearance. Although striking, and decently armed, she was Human, and, well... short. She jerked with a painful twinge coming from her forehead, and bringing her hand to her face, she felt the scrape from a recent fall. Where was she? The journey had taken much from her, she'd failed to find the Black's Lair, and she was still exhausted. "My name is Natanamia. I am First Mate of the Elite Guard. And I came here to meet a Warrior."

Darque wasn't sure what she'd expected to hear, but 'twasn't that, and puzzled she asked, "A Warrior? Any one in particular?" But there came no response, for the Sprite was once again, unconscious.

<div align="center">~~~~~ LATER ~~~~~</div>

Half the Teams of Second Flight who were stationed at the Bog, had arrived just after dawn, and now Darque faced them to present her final orders afore they flew out on their mission. Astraa and her 'Bond, the Quad Prince Kaygynn, Tannah and the Fifth Prince Synddarr, Tiyya and Shasynn the Sixth Prince, along with Thorrn and his 'Bond, Taniyyah, had been briefed and were prepared to do whatever was necessary. Darque and

Gunnarr would lead the rescue, and would require three of the Teams as backup, leaving behind Astraa and Kaygynn to guard the Keep. 'Twould be the most dangerous mission they'd yet encountered. Ice cared not about the sharpness of a Warrior's weapons or the skill with which they were wielded, nor for the strength of their Dragon partners. No, ice was relentless, would beat them, blind them, deplete their Magic to prevent hypothermia, drive them down to the ground and bury them without mercy, and there was nothing they could do, to fight against the onslaught. The very notion of attempting to go forth in such a storm gave the average Dragon and Man nightmares. 'Twould take the help of the Fates, along with polished flight skills and much daring, to complete this mission.

"We've held back longer than I'd wanted, because of circumstances beyond my control, but we can wait no longer. We have little intel, only that there is a party traveling toward us from the east, who must be found and brought into the safety of the Keep afore this storm buries them, and mayhap, us. They have in their possession, that which will repel the Hoard coming upon the heels of this blizzard. Without this information, that attack could very well be our last stand, and this I will not allow. Push not too hard, check your speed to conserve your strength, as we fly directly into the building storm against gale force winds, and therefore, I expect not to be able to fly more than a few leagues afore we must return. But these travelers have the information we need, and I intend for it to be mine." Grave faces surrounded her and they all nodded acceptance of their orders. Into the blizzard would they fly, to the Veil and beyond, to complete their mission and support their Commander. Launching one by one, long leathery wings beat down upon the battlements, while Tyrza and the children covered their faces against the furious wind, as the massive beasts, with their riders, disappeared into the thickening white curtain.

~~~~~~~~~~
~~~~~~~~~~

'Twas nothing less than a miracle of the One True Liege, when, as they rose o'er the mountains, they saw two things simultaneously. The first was a spray of heavy snow erupting toward the sky o'er the far side of the jagged peaks, indicating the blizzard was building furiously and would soon break o'er this side of the mountains, blanketing the entire ridge in a total white-out within a mark. 'Twas a very bad sign and meant they had to turn around immediately, abandoning the rescue, as 'twould chase them all the way back to the Keep. The second was what appeared from on high as eight large boulders dotting the mountain. 'Twas strange. They'd scouted this ridge thoroughly o'er the past several moons, and no such rock formations existed.

As they approached, the boulders stood up and unfolded themselves into living beings. Trolls! They were real! Flying closer, the giant creatures reached down for something they'd been shielding. The Teams were already so close that if the Trolls had been reaching for weapons, they could have done nothing to prevent a battle, but Darque could see each of the eight Trolls as they lifted their six people and two War Horses, offering them to the Teams, high enough that no Dragon need land upon the deepening wet mess from which they'd not be able to launch again. Darque feared for those left behind, for the backbeat of Dragon wings might cause avalanche which could certainly force them Past the Veil, but 'twas no way to accomplish the rescues by gliding through the gusting winds. With practiced precision, each of the party were picked up in massive talons, and carried back toward the Keep.

They knew. Somehow, the Trolls knew of their mission and assisted the Teams, as well as keeping safe their charges from the incoming weather while they waited. So many questions she wanted to ask, but the blizzard exploded o'er the ridge and began to barrel down toward them. She wanted to help the Trolls, but they couldn't stay. As the last to leave, she looked back o'er her shoulder, but no trace of them could be seen upon the white ridge. By the One, let them be safe, she thought.

~~~~~~~~~~

After a rapid debriefing in which Darque was given the short version of their travels, the pledge from the Elven Nation of their alliance with the Resistance, along with the offered Spell, she had quarters found for their War Horses, and then sent them all to Chynnar to be checked out. She'd spoken quickly to them, but hadn't really had time to socialize with her long missing Stealth Team, except to order them back again as soon as they'd eaten and received a clean bill of health from the Healer, and now, standing in front of her was Natanamia, who had already spoken with the newcomers.

Darque understood the two children were to travel back to the Sprite Nation and that Caleichante had handed them o'er to her First Mate, but somehow, this hadn't set well with Natanamia, and she'd arrived just a few moments prior, so unsure of her position that she could not give voice to her thoughts. Darque nudged her a tad, by saying, "You know your mission is not complete without providing safe passage for the Prince and Princess, back to the Island of Dreams."

The door was opened and instantly, Natan found her voice again. "But my mission was to find my niece and meet the Warrior here!"

"According to the information I received, the Eagle Warrior found her and 'tis thought they have escaped the Pitch. Have faith. If they yet live, he will bring her here, as per your agreement. And if he returns prior to your return, she will be safe. I pledge her protection, and she will be treated as an equal. The children of the Clan will accept her as one of their own."

"You are very confident."

"I know my people. And you know I speak the truth. You understand, as do I, there is not a chance in Hades of finding her now. Let the Warrior do what he does best. Your mission has altered. Even though I cannot command you, for you have not sworn fealty to the crown of King Gabriel, I can make sugges-
~~~~~~~~~~

tions. I believe you will see the right path and make the appropriate decision."

Natan had to agree that the Commander was correct. She was the only one for the mission. Kevon and Ana must be ushered safely to the island and protected there, 'til the spy was neutralized, if not already done. Much to her surprise, Caleichante had, with the blessings of the Prince, rescinded her position of Captain of his Elite Guard, choosing to join the Resistance and stay with the Warrior, Graasyn. She felt 'twould not be long afore they were mated. After the discovery that the Resistance had not one, but three separate Lairs, Calei had handed o'er the Prince and Princess to her former First Mate and best friend, effectively taking them all out of the coming battle, because she felt 'twas even more important to stay and help Diadranei Draw down the Spell Domes o'er the Lairs, for the Elf would not be able to do so alone. 'Twas, as would be expected, a valiant decision for the former Captain. Although Natan was torn, for she wanted to wait for the Warrior and Flyrra, there was no knowing how long that might take, and she might as well do something more productive in the meantime.

She dropped her gaze for a moment and then lifted her chin and assumed battle ready stance to address the Commander. "Although I do not currently recognize your authority o'er the Sprite Nation, I have little doubt 'twill not be long afore we are allies. And I must admit that your strategy is the only one that makes any sense. The quicker we get them back to the island, the quicker we can take care of our own threats, and then join the Resistance outright, if such course is determined by Lord Rohar. I know you are aware that the three of us could Dance 'cross country, 'twould be no cake walk in this storm, but it could be managed as safely as a'Dragonback, and you have no Dragons to spare. The Krakken can pick us up if we Call ahead, or if we can get Corbyn, or even your Communication Team, to relay such need. If we encounter any of the enemy, we will have to fight our way out, but such an encounter will be less likely traveling our way, and leaving quickly."

Darque was highly insightful, and as she listened to this summary she realized 'twas something more the First Mate was trying to convey. She chose not to interrupt her, waiting as patiently as she could, simply observing. Natanamia was not distressed, she was determined, and divided in her need to stay and help in the fight, mayhap being there when the Warrior returned with her niece, and to take the Prince and Princess safely back to Dream Hold. Abruptly, Darque realized a third possibility, and she watched this struggle in the Sprite's glittering eyes. She nodded to encourage her to continue, for 'twas more to tell, and if she were correct, the Guardsman was about to offer...

Natanamia took a deep breath. Her status as First Mate would be forfeit if she failed, but much worse could be lost, for once again she faced a decision 'tween the lives of children and the existence of a nation. She had to offer her plan, for to stop the Hoard was everyone's responsibility and the Lairs of the Resistance must be protected in order to keep fighting. All three Lairs. If the Resistance fell, the Hoard would soon be upon the island and 'twould be no stopping them. She knew the Commander was trying to work out a relay team with Caleichante and Diadranei, to split the Spell and then Draw o'er first the Keep, followed by the Bog, and then return and Draw down o'er Drekinn Lair, each in succession. But such a plan had little hope of success. They would have no strength left to make a third Brew 'tween the two of them, and 'twould take too long afore they could manage such. And aside from the length of time 'twould take to split the Spell, and to manage them all individually, once the Bog and the Keep 'disappeared', especially if either happened mid-battle, Drekinn Lair would be attacked in full force. The Lair under the Dragon's Den was currently protected by an Illusory Spell held by six Free Dragons who'd volunteered for the duty shortly after the Battle for the Dragon Clan, and would fail with a pressured attack, sending the Six, as they were known, Beyond at last, to join their already fallen lifemates. But they'd not give up easily, for 'twould leave the Lair completely at the mercy of the enemy invaders. 'Twas their sworn duty to Hold their protection o'er Drekinn 'til they fold or were released, for the remainder of the Clan's adult survivors were there, along with half the surviving Teams, several Free Dragons, and o'er a hundred Free Warriors still stationed there to protect them. There'd been no time to bring everyone to the Keep, and 'twas not considered necessary initially. There were few adults here, for 'twas an experiment, colonized by the children along with three Warriors, one of whom, Torstynn, had been badly injured in the Battle of Ice Mist Falls and was recovering, his girlfriend Raynah, his twin brother Tyrrsyn, Aalanna (Darque's mother), Master Tyrza, and Chynnar. Aside from Darque and Gunnarr, currently also at the Keep were Walkyr the Clan Seer, and Fryya, both accomplished and proven fighters. The rest of the children were all in training and would take up bow, sword, blade, or whatever was at hand, and fight to the Veil should need arise.

But still, the Spell must Draw down o'er all three Lairs at the same time, to provide the maximum protection and to confuse the enemy. 'Twould take many winters, if ever, for the Hoard to figure out what had happened if 'twas done at once, and she was confident they'd never break the Spell, even if 'twas understood. If Natan, the young Prince, and the Princess, stayed, the three of them could help Brew the extra strength 'twould take for full coverage much quicker, creating three separate spheres of Magic out of the original, providing one for each of the Lairs. As 'twas her opinion that St Swiftyn's was too much for just one Magic bearer, 'twould take both Dia and Calei to cover the massive Keep. Then Kevon and Ana could Draw down o'er the Bog, and she could handle Drekinn Lair alone. This plan would also keep her charges safer than if they were with her there, for at the Bog, they'd be surrounded by LifeBond Teams, Free Dragons, and

Warriors, and in a defensible, and yet unknown, Lair. Once the Spell was stable they could leave, but 'twould be far more danger-ous than if they took their leave now. Kevon and Ana would be as vulnerable then, as were the children of the Clan now.

CHAPTER THIRTY-TWO

Intel Feast

~~~~~ O'ER A MARK LATER ~~~~~

Darque stormed out of the library where she'd been in conference with her predecessor for the past half mark, ignoring the other ghostly spirits filling the hallway, pushing through their essence in frustration as if walking through clouds of mist, unfelt. With the exception of the spirit of Grifynn, who refused to leave the Altar Room where Aalanna had brought him through the Veil, for fear of Shytin or the Sorcerer gaining control, and the spirit of the First Warrior, who seemed to have no fear of anyone or anything but was extremely irritated that she also had no ability to hold a sword and little ability to affect the physical world this side of the Veil, both of whom could communicate with all of them, the Keep was full of ghostly forms of men, women and children who appeared to not even know they were spirits or that anyone else was there. For them, there was no way to communicate in either direction, and seeing them had become a normal part of their everyday lives.

The first sightings were by the children who lived here with Master Educator Tyrza, who'd proposed this settlement after the destruction of Drekinn, and which now housed the pride of the Clan, o'er three hundred no older than thirteen winters, the entire surviving population of children from the big battle. But even they'd stopped wondering about the spirits, for try as they might, the spirits gave them no notice. No one knew who they were, and they'd all just accepted the fact that the Keep was haunted. Oddly enough, the First Warrior and Grifynn were not visible to others unless they chose to make it so. Darque, Storrm and Fryya could see them both, as could the Dragons, and Aalanna could see Grifynn regardless, but apparently, the dead were not easily
~~~~~

viewed or spoken to by just anyone. So, she had to wonder why so many could see the other spirits. 'Twas puzzling.

Darque and Abriya had been discussing the feasibility of Brewing a third LifeBond afore the coming invasion, but the secret the First Warrior inadvertently revealed, had her namesake spitting Flame. How could they have ignored the danger, waiting so long to fight back? The Black might have been defeated then, the Hoard in its beginning, and none of this would've happened. She cared not for the obvious implication that her own existence would be in question. Millions, billions of people were murdered during the War of Chaos and then again by the Hoard when they came back into power afore, during, and after the Last Holocaust, near destroying Kadoor. The Magic bearing Races were forced into retreating to survive, Mankind was near obliterated, and 'twas beginning once more. As a seasoned and skilled Warrior in command of the Brotherhood, the Dragon Clan, and the Resistance, obscene negligence wasn't strong enough terminology for their ancestors' lack of action.

The tautly muscled blue Dragon met his little Flame Spitter at the entry to their private quarters, with a large mug of mead. Wordlessly he handed it to her as she strode past. Although she rolled her eyes she didn't refuse the proffered peace offering, for which he was thankful. He knew of what she'd just discovered. 'Twas something she'd suspected for a long time but he'd been very careful to avoid thinking. Even though her anger wasn't directed specifically at him, 'twas directed toward his ancestors and his Race and therefore he felt the brunt of her emotions. Silence reigned for near a quarter mark while Darque sat and chewed her bottom lip.

When the heat had lessoned somewhat, he broke the hush. You could hear a pin drop afore Gunnarr spoke, sounding almost apologetic. "'Twas for good reason that the Matriarch, Maahayyel's Ancestor, refrained from the creation of the LifeBond Magic at the beginning of the War of Chaos."

Darque slammed the mug down on the desk, mead sloshing o'er the sides as she exploded in her response: "And what possible reason could she have had, to evade the chance to kill the Black? To destroy the Hoard in its infancy?"

Gunnarr wasn't known for his patience any more than his lovely mate, but 'twas clearly finesse required at this moment. He took a deep breath. The legendary cat was already out of the bag, and if anyone needed to know the truth, 'twas the Battle Commander. The First Warrior had done him a favor in her slip of the tongue. Quietly he replied, his words slow and clear. "Because, for the Magic to be as powerful as 'twas required, it had to affect all Highlands."

Darque was still angry, and her words spit forth. "So?" She hung her head in embarrassment at the outburst, and wiped the mead from the corner of her mouth with the back of her hand, as she reigned in her emotions.

He could tell she didn't understand. Not really wanting to increase her ire, as she truly had a redhead's passion, he softly reiterated. "All of them."

Darque had already regained her composure. Gunnarr had to give her credit, no matter how pissed off she became, she could quickly recover her focus, and upon the battlefield, none could best his woman. Curiously now, she asked, "Every Highland?"

"Yes. The entire Race."

Her hands up in the air, she shrugged her shoulders, squinted and repeated her earlier question with more control. "So?"

Gunnarr sat back on his haunches, cocked his head, and responded saucily: "Oh c'mon sweet cheeks. Think about it."

Darque furrowed her brows. "What possible difference, " she began, and then the sun dawned upon her, and with widened eyes she sputtered, "NO!"

Gunnarr sighed and crossed his forelegs o'er his scaled chest. 'Twas a subject to which he'd given much thought afore encouraging his mother to take the plunge once again. Still, he felt justified in rekindling the Ancient Magic. "The Black would never try to take the 'Bond, but he, or any of his Hoard are susceptible. Even knowing 'twould make no difference, they avoid the Cut and the ceremony, for they fear the lack of control, which is ironic, for the Black controls them all. However, 'tis possible that one we offer could Reach out to one of the Hoard. Or even the Black himself. 'Twould be tragic."

"Indeed," Darque stated reflectively. "We must choose our candidates carefully."

"Even so…"

"Then we depend on the idea that evil is not inborn, and that 'tis the choices one makes that sets one's fate." Darque sat quietly for a few moments, sipping her mead. "Do you think 'tis possible that if a Hoard Dragon took the 'Bond, the Warrior could help them pull free of Evil?"

"All things are possible. But we cannot assume 'twould be the Dragon to change. Evil is a strong influence, and might even undermine the Warrior."

Leaning her elbow on the desk, she stared at her mug and pondered how this information might affect future ceremonies. She didn't want to accept they could lose a Warrior, not to mention how difficult such a loss would be to accomplish, for the Highlands were the hardest to kill, and a human in 'Bond shared his Magical Healing. And to make that tragedy even worse, 'twould be one of her own. Could she do it? She thought about Rakkah and Mikkal, and was saddened once again.

Gunnarr stepped closer and with one talon, lifted her chin upwards, so he could see her piercing blue eyes. Reluctantly, he stated, "There's more, my sweet."

Unease filled those eyes. "More? How much more? All Highlands and…?"

"All Mankind."

Darque's mouth dropped open and she sat back hard in the chair. Speechless for several heartbeats, she weighed her options.

'Twas possible that any gutter snipe, liar, or thief, could take advantage of the 'Bond. 'Twas no wonder why the Magic had been kept such a secret and why 'twas venomously opposed when 'twas invoked.

Abruptly, she heard a commotion coming down the passage near their quarters, and she and Gunnarr stood up and looked toward the door as it burst open. There stood Tyrza, and unbeknownst to the Master, the First Warrior was at her shoulder. With Darque's gaze flitting 'tween them, 'twas Tyrza who, completely out of breath, spoke up excitedly. "I know who the spirits are!"

Darque squinted. "Which ones?"

The First Warrior peeked around Tyrza, and both voices flatly replied in unison, "All of them."

<div align="center">~~~~~ LATER ~~~~~</div>

Master Educator Tyrza was a highly intelligent woman who'd been one of the first, along with the youngest of the children, to see the spirits of the Keep. Since that time, she'd relentlessly researched to discover their origins, and with the help of the First Warrior, who led her in the right direction, she hit on the truth. What was known about the Keep was that 'twas abandoned o'er half a century earlier, and the Rashei were the last residents. This 'abandonment' was not o'er a period of time, but occurred in a single instant in which the entire society simply disappeared. It seemed they too, had their Hoard spy, and evil had infiltrated the Keep. Abriya told Darque that despite appearances, they were not dead, and she believed the Rashei knew not what had happened to them, even after all this time. 'Twas why the 'spirits' of the Keep could be seen by so many.

Darque took a deep breath, her gaze shifting from the floor to her mate. The Brew had begun, but 'twould take an unknown length of time to prepare. The Spell Dome would provide the protection they needed, but at the least might make it impossible to bring the 'spirits' back, and at the worst, cause them difficulty with their continued existence. There was still time to stop the Brew. Should she? Searching Gunnarr's eyes, she queried, "Do I destroy them, then? We need the Rashei. The Resistance needs their Gifts. And 'tis an entire society here. As many, if not more, than the survivors of the Clan."

He knew the weight of the decisions she made daily. Her maturity surprised those who saw only the youthful face of the Battle Commander, yet he understood the toll her duties took and allowed her to vent her frustrations, for in the end, she would make the right decision with or without his involvement. Therefore, he simply summarized what she felt. "You know not if the Spell Dome will cause them any harm, or if 'twill doom them to an eternity of their otherworldly existence."

She rolled her eyes and shook her head. "Oh thanks. Not exactly the kind of inspiration I'd expected to hear."

"'Tis not always good news, my delight, yet your decision remains the same. You had a plan prior to this knowledge, and the needs of those for whom this plan benefits, have not changed with such knowledge. After much observation, even the First Warrior cannot state for certain if the Rashei are aware of their own existence. 'Twould be tragic indeed to lose them forever, but they've been lost o'er half a century already, and 'tis not known how to bring them back, or even if they can be brought back. For Abriya has determined that 'twas the use of the Book of the Conqueror that created this state of being, and no one knows where the Book is now."

~~~~~ **IN A CAVE NEAR THE BOG OF ST SWIFTYN'S** ~~~~~

They'd traveled hard and fast to get here and Bryynn had been forced to use much Magic, not only to provide safe passage, but to keep them all from freezing. Ryndor had sniffed the little Dragon, licking his nose in friendship and accepting the warm tingle of Allure without issue. They'd returned to the Bog from
~~~~~

whence Bryynn had hatched, in less than a dawn. The effort was exhausting.

She'd brought plenty of provisions, and Bryynn had eaten most of them upon arrival, making up for the expended energy. Now he clutched onto her waist, wrapping his tail around her for a secure hold. She'd created a blanket sling of soft leather, that allowed him to sleep in this position while she could work hands-free. She busied herself preparing a fire. 'Twas already set up, and except for lacking food stuffs, 'twas an abundance of supplies. Beds were made, there was a pile of dried grass in the back for Ryndor, plenty of firewood, and the pit was rock lined. The Warriors had vacated in a hurry, taking only that which they'd required for hard, fast travel, leaving everything else behind. She even found snares ready to use, which were most welcome, since they'd need to resupply afore they made the final push to the Keep. In good weather that trip should only take a day's hard ride, but 'twas not good weather, and she didn't want to wait too long. The snow was falling slowly but steadily, and 'twould be worsening toward St Swiftyn's. Being caught without food, was not wise.

Keeping Bryynn tucked under her cloak hugged against her skin, she knew where he was so she didn't inadvertently step on him, and they both stayed warm without the use of Magic. She'd cautioned him not to use anymore on anything that wasn't absolutely necessary, for they'd soon face much need, a plan with which he approved. Although his Magic was strong, he was newly hatched, and 'twould take several moons and much growth, to build up his endurance.

Once settled, Ardyth stood at the entry of the cave, to practice using the Eye. Peering through, she was surprised to see Axyl. The Warrior of her dreams. He appeared so suddenly and so close, she was startled and near dropped the Eye, stepping back as if about to run into the man. Bryynn stirred and poked his nose out from the sling, his eyes hooded. But she could tell he wasn't very appreciative of having been jerked awake. "Sorry," she murmured to the little Dragon, then took up the device once again. This time, she saw the Bog outside their cave. But 'twas not covered with snow, she could not tell if 'twas a vision of the past or the future, but 'twas mid-fall. Then came many Dragons, bearing many humans, and Darque met them. They were creating a Lair under the Bog! She was perplexed, and blurted aloud, "But, is this past, or future?"

Bryynn poked his nose out again, and mumbled, "Past, obviously. I am still there. That's where my Egg was/is buried." He reached out one talon and pointed, then pushed the leather off his muzzle. Scowling peevishly, he stated, "I didn't know they were underneath me! If I'd known, I wouldn't have left. But then, if I'd not left, I wouldn't have met you." Having made his grumpy statement, he burrowed back into the sling, for Highland Dragons do not like being cold.

Trying once more, she saw nothing but the Eye's astonishing beauty. She sighed, tucked it back into her blouse and put the leather wrap in Ryndor's saddlebag afore stretching out for the night.

~~~~~~~~~~

In the morning, she and Bryynn made the decision they would not openly approach the Bog Lair, for they knew not the current situation, nor did they know the location of the entrance, or of any Protection Spells or traps that might be about, particularly after he related the story of his hatching and the fight 'tween the Hoard Dragon and his brother, Mystynn, in the air above them. 'Twould be wiser to wait and watch.

The journey had been hard, especially on Ryndor, but using Bryynn's Magic, they'd pushed through as if time had no meaning, and now they were both fatigued and hungry. Even the little Dragon was astonished at the feat, and wondered how 'twas done. He was convinced he'd created a timefold of some sort, through which they'd traveled, but couldn't explain how.
~~~~~~~~~~

Venturing out to lay a few snares, Ardyth wondered what they were going to do from here. Moving from bush to bush, Bryynn stirred awake as she thought about how the Eye had helped them. They'd discovered much; this cave, the Bog Lair, even the fact that her dream Warrior was not only real, but alive. Every time she saw him, he was stunning. And then they discovered something that stunned them both.

Ardyth kneeled near a large pine to set one of the snares. Suddenly, Bryynn yanked the edge of the sling away from his head, near afore Ardyth registered the spirit racing toward her through the trees. As Ardyth swiftly stood up, the little Dragon seemed to grow twofold, his short wings flapping free of the sling, his body 'tween her and the spirit like a shield, as he roared indignantly, "YOU WILL NOT LAY HAND UPON THIS HUMAN, FOR THE 7TH PRINCE PROTECTS HER!" His ferocity shocked Ardyth, and she stepped back a distance, cradling him defensively as he settled back down, scanning this way and that, for the danger. But the spirit was now, nowhere to be seen.

Her eyes wide and ready for a fight, she questioned, "What just happened? And why?"

Bryynn was still agitated and on high alert as well. "'Twas a spirit intent on using your Gifts to his own benefit. 'Twas not good. I had to stop him."

Ardyth had never had reason to be afraid of a spirit. Bored, agitated, frustrated, yes, but not afraid. "What benefit?"

"He wanted to use your body as his own. He wanted you to channel his spirit. 'Twould give him control o'er your physical presence, the ability to do what he could when he was yet alive."

Ardyth was confused. "But how? And how did you know what he intended?"

"Seems we are connected on a deeper level than I initially thought. Ardyth, do you not understand that you are special? Have you not ever spoken with the dead? Touched them?"

"Many times. I see them, I can touch them, more so than others. I've learned that the spirits must expend much energy to manifest sufficiently for anyone else to see them or touch them, but not with me. Yet, they've never attempted to force themselves upon me, or cause me harm, other than mischief to gain attention. I knew not that such could happen."

Disheartened but determined, Bryynn concluded, "I think 'tis my fault. My Magic is combining with your Gifts. I don't know how to prevent such. I am too inexperienced. But know this: from now on, we must be very careful. Now that we are together, the evil spirits will begin to seek you out. And if a spirit wished for you to channel him or her, you are able. You will need to learn how to prevent being forced to such, or you will lose your will, and very likely, your life."

Ardyth considered the snippets of conversations of which she'd heard at the Keep while using the Eye, and had the sensation that her expanding Gift could help the Resistance somehow. To join in the fight had been her desire for many winters, but now she saw potential. Now she might have something to offer. "This could be helpful, as well as harmful. Can you teach me how to channel safely, and how to protect myself?"

"Channeling, yes, but preventing if forced? I know not even if a Human is capable of such ability. But you are a descendent of the Rashei, and although this Gift was rare, 'twas not unheard of amongst them in the Ancient days. Mayhap at the Keep, we shall find information on how to protect yourself. In the meantime, we must not be separated. Ever."

<center>~~~~~~~~~~</center>

Ultimately, the weather prevented them from setting any more snares, and after retreating to the cave, they discussed what had happened, along with their next move. O'er the following day Bryynn explained how to channel a spirit. 'Twould be as living underwater and trying not to panic by the fact that you weren't breathing, but you didn't need to, for only one would need to breathe at a time for both to live, if the spirit didn't get you killed. Ardyth couldn't see how that information was useful, but kept her opinion to herself.

Her nightly ritual since Bryynn had come into her life, was to practice using the Eye. She'd taken to shamelessly watching 'her' Warrior, following his every move, admiring his looks, his stance, the way he walked, how he held himself. She noted the cut of his jaw, the color of his eyes, the size of his hands, and her skin warmed, the pink rush of blood coursing through her body from the roots of her hair to the tips of her toes.

Ardyth had been awake most of the night, and leaning on one elbow, she pulled the Eye out of her blouse, making another attempt to 'see' without the funnel. She was getting much better at it, and once more, she watched Axyl as he sat awake on his rack, the little Green stretched out on the floor beside him, snoring softly.

Bryynn's muffled voice came from within the blanket bundle, as he flatly stated, "You like him."

Indignantly, she asked, "Have you been listening to my thoughts?"

"Did you tell me to refrain from such?"

"You little sneak!"

"I resent that. I am not little."

"Oh please. You're the smallest Dragon I've ever seen, let alone of which I've heard."

Now he uncovered his head and peeked out from the blanket. "I've barely begun to grow. Besides, there is one who will be smaller."

"Oh! Then you have noticed the Green! And by the sheepish look upon your face, you like her."

"Matters not to whom I'm attracted. It matters to whom YOU'RE attracted. I wish happiness for you, and I feel what you feel. And what you feel, is a strong attraction to the LifeBond partner of 'the Green'. So, stop trying to redirect."

Ardyth sat upright, her legs crisscrossed, and gathered Bryynn into her lap. "Does my attraction affect yours?"

"No. Well, yes and no. 'Tis complicated. But 'twould be convenient if we shared partners when we choose mates."

The statement caught her by surprise. "Mates? Aren't you a little young to be thinking along those lines?"

"Dragons are aware when laid, and I have already felt the connection with my future mate. And you're redirecting again."

"But he's a Warrior! I doubt he'd even notice me. What am I to him? Nothing. I have no status, no family, and consider not the pearls. They count not as wealth. I'm not like them, anyway. I'm not polished, I'm not pretty, I'm not a pearl. He can have any woman he wants. Why would he want me?"

"Why wouldn't he? You're beautiful! You're also talented, strong, an excellent swimmer and teacher, and highly skilled with a multitude of weapons including spears, daggers, slings, and bows."

"I am not, but I won't argue with you. Besides, a Warrior's primary weapon is a sword, and I can't even lift one."

"We all have our strengths, and can choose whether to use them."

Ardyth sighed. He was correct, but she was shy, had no social experience whatsoever, not counting the gaming she'd done in various villages, and unless the big Warrior noticed her, she had no chance.

Their snares were empty and by the end of their second day, they'd decided 'twould be the lack of food to force the issue, but afore they abandoned their new home and made the trek to the Keep, they prepared as best they could, using the Eye. Their attention focused toward their destination, and since Ardyth was improving with every use, she was able to direct the 'sight' and discovered much. She 'saw' the Battle Commander, tried to listen as she addressed her Warriors and her lifemate, and was quite interested in the fact that the Keep was haunted by many spirits. She was most interested in one.

Afore she fell asleep, Bryynn asked her what she'd learned from the Commander. "Something about twins," she'd replied warily. Bryynn pondered for many marks.

<center>~~~~~ MEANWHILE, AT THE KEEP ~~~~~</center>

Patience was not her forte. Darque had always hated waiting. But there was nothing she could do to help in the Brewing of the Spell. Battle plans were made, her Teams were watching, her Communications Officers were relaying information keeping everyone in the loop, even the children were prepared. The Brew was complicated, as she'd learned were all Greater Magic Spells, and appeared 'twould take as much as another full moon, with all of the Magic bearers working full time together creating the three glowing spheres. 'Twas obvious they'd not have succeeded without the additional help, and if they were lucky, they'd be ready to set in motion afore the Hoard attacked. But the weather wouldn't hold forever, and once the snow quit falling and the thick layers of ice began to melt, 'twould be nothing left to stop them. Still, she knew not the timing of the expected attack, and her forces had no news to report toward such knowledge. Mayhap 'twould not occur afore the running of the Spring Melts? She could but hope. Nevertheless, if the weather was in their favor, so 'twas for the enemy.

She looked up from her desk in the office they'd arranged for her at the Keep, when she heard the pounding of boots coming closer, as the familiar masculine voices echoed in the hallway, yelling, "Darque!" Within a fraction of a candle drip, in burst Graasyn, with Bastyen right behind. Her eyes lit up with pleasure at seeing her long-time friends and most skilled Stealth Team once again, having thought they were Past the Veil for many moons, hoping by the One, they were not. Their briefing upon arrival had been short, and afterwards they'd all been busy. Now she jumped up and ran to them as she would have just a few winters past, then tried to stop herself afore leaping into his arms for a hug. But Graasyn would have none of that, and stepped forward far enough to grab her up while she was still moving, and held on tight as in times of old. When he finally put her down on her feet again, Bastyen came forward and hugged her as well, although not quite as enthusiastically, but all grins faded with the confirmation of the meaning of this meeting.

Graasyn took a half step back, his son at this side, both assuming Battle Ease, a position that felt strange to them now, it had been so long. "'Tis true then."

Darque nodded her head, then stood as tall as she could, and catching his eye she replied sadly, but with confidence, "Yes, 'tis true. I am Commander now."

The Warrior had always thought the girl would make a fine replacement for Grifynn one day. He just hadn't expected it to be this soon, but he had no issue with her promotion, and wanted to correct what she might be thinking. "I'm not sorry to serve under you, Sir, I just wish I could have seen him again, to complete our last mission on his order, to make report one more time. We've never failed him afore. I like it not."

Darque shrugged her shoulders nonchalantly. "You can still make that report."

Bastyen cocked his head and asked, "Sir?"

Darque appeared to be talking to someone at their shoulder, while both men turned around in bewilderment. "Abriya, will you manifest long enough to escort them? Don't forget to pick up Aalanna on the way, so they can see Grifynn." Then she continued, addressing the much-puzzled men. "The First Warrior will provide escort to the Altar Room, where you can give your report, and finalize your mission. Then, return to make your initial report to me." She flipped one hand away from her, saying, "I'll be around here somewhere."

Graasyn and Bastyen showed little surprise when Abriya manifested, for they'd been warned about the spirits of the Keep, but they were surprised by the way this one looked. Barefoot, wearing a full-length, white-pearled, funeral pyre gown, with her long red hair sweeping the floor and blue eyes flashing, she was the spitting image of Darque herself. With the revelation of their new-found Gifts, they'd worked out a silent language of signals so that each could share their knowledge with the other, with no one the wiser. With such, they determined there was no glamour being used. This spirit was real, and Bastyen couldn't contain his thoughts. "She could be your twin!" Darque smiled slightly, as she certainly felt the same. She and Abriya could be twins. Then she frowned. As could King Gabriel and his half-brother, and now permanently stationed Warrior bodyguard, Rakkah, currently living at the Bog. Nodding to their new Commander, they took their leave in silence, following the spirit readily, as Darque's eyes glazed o'er, trying to recall some distant memory.

<center>~~~~~ LATER ~~~~~</center>

Gunnarr had encouraged his lovely mate to play a game with him, to help her make her decision. He knew what she must do, for he knew her well. An offensive fighter, she did not like waiting for the enemy, and defensive positioning was not to her advantage. But he would never force his opinion upon her, and looking up from the chess board, he stated, "'Tis your honor."

"My what?"

"The game..." stated Gunnarr quietly, one brow ridge raised as he attempted to draw her attention to the board on the desk 'tween them.

"The what?" She repeated, her mind elsewhere. Waiting was difficult. She was oft times too impatient and such made her falter in her decision-making.

"Chess. First move. 'Tis yours," he stated with his great head cocked to one side, his gaze now boring into hers.

"Chess? I can't play now, Gunnarr, I need to come up with a strategy!" She shook her head. Could be only a matter of marks afore the expected attack, and the Spell was certain to take longer to be effective. She had to defend the Bog and the Keep, and mayhap even the Lair of Drekinn for as long as that took, with a mere handful of Teams and Frees. 'Twould be a slaughter. This could end up being their last stand.

"But, my charm, chess is a game of war, of strategy, and you're one of the best players I've ever known." He sat back on his haunches. His blue scales glistened even in their quarters, the scar pattern on his upper left chest declaring his rank, the only 'defect' to be noted. General Gunnarr was a fine war strategist on his own, matching his lifemate's skills on the battle field, but even though he'd heard not the prophesy of old, he knew what she must do, and he couldn't let down his mate. 'Twas mutual respect in their relationship, no ego to be bruised 'tween them, with no one's status higher than the other. Yet, he would abide by her Command, as the Humans saw her above him, even though the Highlands saw things otherwise. 'Twas his duty and pleasure to uphold their mated status, to satisfy her completely in all ways, and to protect her and stand beside her in the war effort as her most trusted advisor, and most skilled officer. Gently, he urged, "'Tis still your move."

Leaning o'er the chess board, she squinted and licked her full red lips. Something about this situation was familiar. Her mind sought the prophesy she'd heard so very long ago. Murmuring aloud, she said, "A chess move shall lead the feint. To win the battle, you must use your twins of power, twins of fate." Gunnarr looked curiously at her, knowing she was working out something perplexing. The twins part had always been a mystery, but now she understood. And chess. Of course! This was all about the setup, and first move was hers to take. Her eyes shining with sudden inspiration, Gunnarr wrinkled his leathery snout into a broad, satisfied grin. He would fight Past the Veil with his beautiful mate at his back. Excitement filled the air as she stood up and exclaimed, "'Tis indeed!"

CHAPTER THIRTY-THREE

A Working Strategy

~~~~~ LATER ~~~~~

Now she had a plan. Well, part of a plan. She still had to figure out how her 'twin' held a weapon, for the Vision surely showed Abriya and her Dragon Sword, astride Gunnarr's broad back, and the Shade could not manifest solidly enough to do that, nor could she leave the Keep. Rakkah could double the King, and 'twas already part of his duty to do so. Their Dragon 'Bonds had practiced with them both. Petrayyah could now function with Gabriel, as could Daynahmyn with Rakkah, even though they'd each Pass the Veil as per their 'Bonded status. But 'twas still a piece of this puzzle, missing. Did she have time for all the pieces to come together?

Suddenly, she Heard Brannyn's voice, coming from afar. *"Beware the rage of the Sorcerer. He will pay well, for the destruction of all."* She held her breath, for he must have been whispering. Hoping he'd repeat, or clarify, or even add to his warning, after several long moments, she had to admit there'd be no more information from the Predator. Even when she could clearly Hear them, his words rarely made sense 'til after the fact. No, he didn't lie to her, but 'twas always that double meaning. 'The destruction of all?' All what? Dragon dung! Why did he have to be so aloof? Could he not be more specific? She groaned in acceptance. She did appreciate any assistance from the Fay, as he was risking his life with every breath he took inside the Hoard, let alone by sending her information. Given their history, she reasoned Brannyn was confirming her concern that the Hoard knew they held more than one Lair.

Just then, Graasyn entered the room with Bastyen at his shoulder. They'd been down to check on the Spell progress. The
~~~~~

two had been assisting Tyrza, Torstynn, Tyrrsyn, and Raynah with organizing the children for the expected siege, and came with news as soon as 'twas Heard. "Commander? The Hoard have begun to move. They head straight for the Great Plains of Drekinn."

"Not toward us? What's their ETA?"

"'Twould appear that they're still within the Talons, not long out of King's Gate. The Dragons lead the King's Agents who travel a'foot, and they are avoiding the Cut."

Darque had stationed Daxx and Linayyah, and Apryya and Dannyrkyn at the Cut to attempt setting up an ambush to reduce their numbers, but now that option was out. And by avoiding the Cut and heading straight north, their route would take them past Drekinn afore veering toward the Keep. Optimistically, she replied, "Drekinn could be in their flight pattern from Evanntyr. How many?"

"Reports are coming from the Daggogh to Ethynn and Makayyd, and then through Nalwynn and Rolf, counting a full contingent of Dragons, along with o'er two thousand Agents, Sir."

She chewed her bottom lip and focused to slow her Battle Lust. Control was needed at this point. She couldn't allow the Lust to run rampant o'er her senses so long afore the battle. However, two thousand was but spit in the sands of the Dragon's Breath for King Shytin. Although 'twould be difficult to defend from such numbers, for she now commanded a mere 300 Warriors split 'tween the Bog and Drekinn, along with the surviving Clansmen, he had many more troops available to him. Where were they?

After sharing their own adventures, the Stealth Team were briefed o'er all the details of the past winter, and they'd heard much of the situation while guests of Queen Alyssa. If those forces continued on this path, they'd hit Drekinn within the next fortnight. Graasyn was frustrated. "If they change not their course and attack the barrier, 'twould be more than enough to break down the Spell." He shook his head while Bastyen nodded. They both understood the ramifications, but 'twas Bastyen who stated the obvious, "The Six won't have a chance."

Darque knew the odds of the survival of the Six through such a battle. 'Twould be their end. She never ruled out anything, not even that the Hoard should not know about them at any of the locations, however, since the Eoche incident and given Abriya's warning, as well as Brannyn's recent revelation, she'd expected the Hoard to make the Keep their primary target, and mayhap ignore the Bog completely. But Drekinn? Only to finish their demolition, and after the fact. 'Twould be her own strategy to apply her forces first to the heaviest expected target so as not to weary or lose them afore they hit the most opposition. But she was not the Black, nor was she the Sorcerer or King Shytin, all of whom seemed Hades-bent on being completely stupid. Not to mention, but she would, that the Spell Dome was still being Brewed. Natanamia, Caleichante, Kevon, Anastasia, and Diadranei were even now working to split the original into three portions, each needing to be strong enough for their intended use, to protect all three Lairs of the Resistance. Had she made a mistake, taking the extra time to do such? Her mind flashed back to the big battle. They'd lost so many. Tannyr, Kaahayyel, Ariel, Zaydarr, Loryyn, Krynnarr, Barynn, Shraadarr, Flynn and Shanndynn. The list went on and on. No. She would not abandon anyone again. This time, they would all stand, or they would all perish. She'd had enough.

Darque left the Warriors and went directly to the Altar Room, where the Elves and Sprites worked the Brew. The room was enormous, like the Grand Ballroom of the Dragon's Den, with the multi-leveled bowls arranged along the far wall from ceiling to floor in a cascade, where the spirits of both Grifynn and Abriya had been pulled from Beyond. Abriya floated about the Keep at will, but Grifynn's spirit was in a tug-of-war with the Sorcerer, who sought to catch him in a weakened moment and snatch him away from his anchor, Aalanna. Since the Sorcerer had obtained the former Battle Commander's hair and a tiny drop of blood, 'twould be possible. Therefore, Grifynn chose to stay in the Altar Room, even to remain floating about the bowl of water where he'd originally been drawn, to avoid any unnecessary confrontations.

The room was beautifully decorated, with intricate mosaics everywhere, even covering the bowls inside and out. Graduated in size, they were aligned with a spring that constantly fed them, creating a gently flowing waterfall from near the gold domed ceiling. As they watched, the five Elves and Sprites stood in the far corner forming a circle, each with their hands stretched forward, not quite touching three glowing and growing spheres of light floating in the middle of them, about chest high, as they chanted in what appeared to be a state of near catatonia. Their hands moved as if they were pulling or drawing the spheres into larger ones, adding the visible threads of energy weaving through the room, gathering from outside toward the glowing balls of light. Ana and Kevon shared one of the new spheres, Natan and Calei shared another, and Dia had one of her own, upon which she was concentrating.

Darque was a tad confused. She'd originally been told that Natan was creating the sphere for Drekinn, and Dia was working with Calei. What had happened, she wondered? Having received the rundown of Diadranei's Empathic senses, 'twas possible the change in line-up had something to do with perceived need. If so, mayhap Drekinn would be the primary target? Or mayhap 'twas another kind of need, something that only Diadranei would recognize. She popped her knuckles. She could attempt to second guess all she wanted, 'twould get her nowhere, and 'twas impossible now, to clarify. There'd be no speaking to the Spell bearers 'til after the deed was done. However, 'twould be like the Elf, to put herself in the most dangerous position, something that would create havoc with Bastyen. Whispering, so as not to disturb the process, Darque spoke to Gunnarr o'er her shoulder. "How do they do this for days on end? Do they not need to eat, or… anything else?" She furrowed her brow.

In his deep rumbling voice, Gunnarr responded, "When in the Brew, Magic bearers know not time in the same manner as do we, so, no, they require not food or… anything else." Grinning, he then retorted, "And you need not whisper, jewel of my heart, for little can disturb this process, as long as they move not out of the circle of power within they began."

"So, as long as we manage to prevent the breach of this room, they will be able to finish, and Draw down the Spell Dome?"

"Correct, in that they will be able to finish the Brew. But 'twill be necessary to transport them to the open, to Draw down o'er all the Lairs, for it cannot be done under cover. And they will be completely vulnerable during this process. 'Twill also require each has the strength to handle the energies they Draw, which is why I believe Diadranei was wise in choosing partners. Kevon and Anastasia together, are strong enough to control the power of their sphere, as are Caleichante and Natanamia handling much more power for theirs. Nor will Dia's sphere require more than she can handle alone. But, do not misunderstand. 'Tis not an easy Brew, and is taking much from each of them. They will need our protection, for not only can they not defend themselves during this process, they will be weakened for some time after."

So, she thought, 'twould be wise to change up the original guard duty, and have Graasyn and Bastyen deliver Dia to Drekinn and protect her as she Drew down the Spell. But Graasyn would want to be with Calei. She shook her head, this was no time to make such distinctions. They were all Warriors and would take their assignments and do their duty as she ordered. Still, she made a mental notation to rearrange the guards, afore she recalled the last LifeBond in which they near lost Daayn and Kashiyann, taking the unexpected 'Bond of Tannyr and the Ancient, Kaahayyel, to prevent. All because the Ancient had lost control, having been weakened by prior Brews. Would there be any chance of them finding a solution to such a loss with this Brew? She wondered. "And what of Kevon? Is he strong enough? What would happen to them if he fails? If any of them fail to handle the energies they Draw?"

"Although the sphere for the Bog will require both the Prince and the Princess to create and set, 'twill be up to Anastasia to prevent Kevon's weakening, by balancing the Brew with her own strength. However, if she fails in her efforts to assist the Prince, or if any of them fail, I believe 'twould be best described as something akin to a volcanic eruption."

~~~~~~~~~~~

The occupants of the room continued their work oblivious to their audience, as Darque turned and silently took her leave, Gunnarr at her side. His assertion wasn't exactly that for which she'd hoped. She was trained as a Warrior and there was always an option, a tactic, a solution, a feint. 'Twas just a matter of preparation. But this time, she could see none, and questioned not, her partner. Striding briskly through the cavernous hallways, she focused on her battle strategies. Tension radiated off her skin as the heat off the sands of the Dragon's Breath, something that usually aroused the Mighty Blue, but the situation was in constant flux and his lady liked it not. How was she to lead into such chaos, and have any chance of victory? They were sorely outnumbered, they were currently spread out in three different Lairs, and 'til she could understand how her Vision would come about, all they could do was wait for the battle to come to them, for they knew not where 'twould begin. And where, by the Hades of the Fade, was Corbyn? He usually stayed close to Storrm, but her sister had reported the Raven was mysteriously absent.

Grumbling under her breath by the time they returned to their combination office and private quarters, Darque plopped into the chair beside the dining table serving as a makeshift work desk, and glared at her lifemate. "Can this get any more compli-
~~~~~~~~~~~

cated? I am besieged with new information! 'Tis rushing o'er me like the Spring Melts, and twists all my plans!"

Gunnarr glanced around in feigned apprehension, teasing her. "Don't ask such aloud, you may temp the Fates."

But although he was always successful in toning her mood, she was still concerned. Nonetheless, she grudgingly countered with sarcasm, near afore he finished his statement. "And if I am forced to start taking notes, we're up the creek. You know my script is barely legible. I can scarcely read it!"

The mood had definitely altered as Abriya floated into the room. "You didn't get that from me. My script is quite lovely."

"Right. You can't even hold a quill," Darque refuted with a smirk.

"Rub it in. See how far it gets us." Abriya crossed her arms and scowled at her namesake.

But Darque could not maintain the façade of lightheartedness, and stood up, exclaiming, "I AM A WARRIOR! And a Flaming good one!" Settling herself, she continued, willing to admit only to Gunnarr and the Shade, that which irked her most, "But my Sword helps me not, to handle this flood. I'm drowning here. 'Tis absurd."

Gunnarr's eyes glazed o'er, momentarily in Link with another, afore he Replied, his voice unexpectedly full of mystery and excitement. *"We have a new visitor above. A traveler was just brought into the Keep by Storrm and Mystynn. They eagerly await your arrival in Chynnar's lab."*

Mystified, she Stated, *"Another one? In this weather? Who?"*

"I think this is something you should see for yourself."

<center>~~~~~ THE CLINIC ~~~~~</center>

As they all hustled to the clinic, Abriya bringing up the rear, Darque had to push her way through a growing crowd of excited children blocking the hallway afore she near tripped o'er Mystynn's thick tail, coming face to face with his huge, green-scaled backside, where he'd plopped his rump in the middle of the entry, protecting the clinic's new occupants from said children. Peeking around him was Storrm, an impish grin on her face. When they moved aside, allowing her free access, there stood a short woman in a full cloak made from the hide of an ellka. The Teams involved with the rescue efforts were all standing guard topside, but Chynnar and Tyrza, along with Graasyn, Bastyen, Tyrrsyn, Torstynn, and Raynah, flanked the newcomer, their expressions reflecting mischievous reluctance to miss out on this experience.

Pulling back her hood and unlacing the cloak, the woman tossed it on one of the examination tables. The visitor had a similar build and height to the Commander, with long, thick, red hair, remarkably reminiscent of Darque's own. 'Twas clear to all that if one didn't look too closely, they could double each other. The woman was carrying what appeared to be a baby in her arms, and as she caught Darque's gaze, a tiny, blood red, leathery scaled Dragon, peeked out from the sling in which he was being supported, under a metal studded leather chest shield of Sprite design. The baby Dragon blinked his eyes as if just waking, having been clutched around the woman's waist.

Abriya was astonished. "You can see me, hear me." Floating closer, she tentatively reached forth her hand, placing it upon the woman's shoulder. "I can touch you."

Darque was as astonished as was the First Warrior, for even she had not felt the hand of her ancestor as more than a slight pressure, a puff of air against her skin, and knew how much effort Abriya expended, just allowing others, even herself, to see her ethereal presence, let alone talk. Abriya was so emotional, if she could cry, tears would have glistened in her eyes, threatening to spill o'er her cheeks. Darque was speechless.

"'Tis our belief that you can do much more," said Ardyth to the First Warrior, as Bryynn wrinkled his large, wide-set nostrils in curiosity at all the new smells, the back of his head pressed firmly 'tween her breasts, as he stretched his neck toward the ceiling.

~~~~~ THE BATTLE COMMANDER'S OFFICE ~~~~~

Darque could feel all the puzzle pieces coming together. After a detailed planning session in which Ardyth and Bryynn explained the channeling process, she dismissed all her Warriors, and then her Seconds in Command, Mystynn and Storrm, with a half-hearted reprimand. They'd flown off alone, hadn't told anyone, and secured no backup, leaving the King with less protection at the Bog. But given the situation, they'd felt their actions were justified. Mystynn had sensed the presence of his youngest brother, and convinced Storrm they must venture forth into the snow, currently showing signs of slackening. Storrm agreed they had to take the chance, and without telling Darque, they'd left just a few marks earlier. Once airborne, Bryynn directed them on their perilous rescue and protected them on their flight, afore Mystynn Called to Gunnarr, alerting them of their arrival with the prize of a lifetime.

The woman's horse was put up with Graasyn and Bastyen's War Horses, in an alcove off the main ward of the Keep, sheltered from the weather and provided with sufficient grain to supplement what was left of the dried grasses brought along by both Ardyth and the Warriors, 'til he could be provided with something else. The horse was amazing, had barely flinched when Mystynn flew by and picked them all up in his strong talons, the girl and her 'baby' with one leg, the horse in the other. Lifting the beast's hooves out of the deepening snow, his legs dangling as they soared through the air to the Keep, he was then dropped a short distance to the ward. He'd staggered a bit, but was not injured, as Mystynn set the woman and her 'baby' down with a bit more finesse, afore they were escorted to the clinic.

After a very short family reunion, both Gunnarr and Mystynn Alerted the Third Prince, Ragnyrr, Third Fighter along
~~~~~

with his 'Bond, Kydra, stationed at Drekinn, and then Ragnyrr Told Kaygynn, Synddarr, and Shasynn, and their 'Bonds, who were currently in the ward above. All this took less than a mark, and after their meeting, Storrm and Mystynn returned to the Bog. 'Twould be their duty to deliver Darque's orders to King Gabriel and his bodyguard, Rakkah, and to ensure Rakkah and Petrayyah understood their upcoming roles.

In the meantime, Ardyth, Bryynn, Chynnar, and Abriya, were meeting in one of the smaller altar rooms to the side of the main chamber currently being used by the Spell brewers. They had much to discuss. The attempt to channel the First Warrior would be dangerous for both parties, but 'twould essentially bring Abriya back, allowing her to fight as if she were alive again. Since Ardyth had no prior experience, Bryynn would have to teach her to accept the spirit, and Abriya would have to learn how to join with, and not smother, Ardyth. They had little time for such a learning experience, so 'twould take Bryynn's Magic as well, combined with Ardyth's Gift and the Dragon's Eye. 'Twas not exactly a Magic Brew, even though 'twould involve some Magic to make the channel most effective, giving Abriya full use of the physical body she would inhabit and to combine with Ardyth's fighting knowledge and experience. 'Twas not a Spell, 'twas more like an exercise, learning a new dance, or perfecting a sword combination.

Nonetheless, 'twas just as complicated as anything Darque had heard of thus far, and 'twas divulged that if Ardyth was killed away from the Keep where Abriya had been conjured, 'twould doom them both to the Fade. But she would send them on this mission, anyway. Abriya's skills were needed, as well as the fact that she would be her 'twin', to lure the Hoard attackers to the Great Plains of Drekinn to fight, allowing the Spell Brewers time to Draw down o'er all the Lairs. As far as she was concerned, once the Domes were successfully Drawn, her Teams and all the fighters would go into full retreat. She didn't want to lose any more than necessary, to get the job done. If this was successful, they'd have the time they needed to fight back effectively in the future.

Meanwhile, the Teams, the Frees, King Gabriel, the Clan, the children, all the Races allied with the Resistance, and even her own ancestor, the 7th Prince, and the newcomer, depended on her making the right decisions. She hardened her heart, for such was her destiny, affecting the lives of all. But now 'twould even affect the spirits under her command. She prayed that her Legend Song would be one of triumph.

CHAPTER THIRTY-FOUR
And So, It Begins

As Darque walked to the mess hall, she remembered the first moment she'd laid eyes upon the Magic bearers. They possessed such physical beauty that 'twas difficult to see them as ordinary people. And then she spent some time with them. Enlightened, intelligent, passionate, with customs and values that seemed very different, and yet, were very much the same as those of the Clan. When Diadranei reached into her shoulder bag and stepped forth from the others, Darque was instantly on alert. And then the Elf pulled forth a ball. 'Twas an ordinary looking ball, about the size of the balls with which the children played, around which one could just spread their fingers using both hands. 'Twas nothing unusual about it in any way, not even in color, as 'twas a drab yellow/beige. After being told these people would bring her the 'solution' to protect the Clan and the Lairs, Darque was expecting something a bit more impressive. Her disappointment must have shown on her face, as Diadranei smiled and held the ball out toward the Commander. Afore Darque could reach forth to accept it, not really understanding that which she was accepting, the Elf lowered her hands, and the ball stayed afloat. By itself. 'Twas then that she noted the slight pulsing as if it had its own heartbeat, and from within shone a barely noticeable light. Dia nodded her head, 'suggesting' that she hold her hand close, but not touching, the ball. She'd done as she was 'told' and could feel the emanating warmth. 'Twas as a living thing.

Gunnarr met her at the mess hall for a bite to eat. He'd had his supper, having just returned from a recognizance mission that turned into a local hunt, but he could always have more. "Yes, my sweet. The weather is clearing throughout the Talons. The storm has abated."

"I could sense it. Still, we are near ready."

"'Tis one more thing you need do, afore the Spell bearers leave on their mission."

Tilting her head, she caught his gaze and stated, "I won't be pleased about this, will I?"

They were surrounded by children in the huge mess hall, and the few adults not actively participating in the Brew, were also present. Grimacing, he Spoke. *"When the Spell is completed o'er each of the Lairs, 'twill be an explosive surge of light, lasting but a candle drip. Every Human, large animal, and Magic bearer within range, will be obliterated, while the trees, the plants, the most delicate blade of grass, will remain untouched. Being underground will provide adequate protection for all. I would suggest there be at most, but two or three protectors for each Spell bearer, for they must all be touching that one at the time of the surge."*

Darque could not believe what she was Hearing. She was close to reaching her limit, and without thinking, she responded aloud, turning about and near stamping her foot. "What do you mean by that?" Suddenly, she realized the entire mess hall had gone silent, and all eyes were upon her and the Mighty Blue, who sat back on his haunches with his shoulders elevated and his eyes looking everywhere but at his lovely mate. Shifting to their Link, she continued, *"Two or three protectors? I was planning on having the entire Clan out there! Every available Warrior! Just what are you trying to tell me? How explosive? How hot? And if they're not touching? What happens?"*

"'Twill not be safe for anyone but the chosen few to be topside at any of the Lairs during the Draw, 'til done. Two or three might be close enough to manage touching the Spell bearer to survive the surge, but no more than that, for 'twould be a stretch for them to protect more. 'Twill be as a hundred lightning bolts striking all in the same place, at the same time."

Gathering her thoughts and adjusting her plans yet again, she repeated herself, seeking confirmation. *"What exactly will happen to those not touching, or underground?"*

"Instant charcoal."

Darque took a breath. *"How did you know this, and why did you not tell me afore?"*

"My little Flame Spitter, I was sworn to secrecy by the Spell bearers. They were afraid you would not allow them to complete the Brew."

"They knew this afore they agreed to the split? They all knew they would have so little protection if they participated? Even the children?"

"They knew."

Darque scowled. But afore she could turn aside, Gunnarr stayed her with his paw upon her shoulder. "Don't say it," she said. "Just don't."

"There's one more thing."

"No. You just told me the 'one more thing'!"

Spitting forth his last bit of information, he squinted with the expectation of the backlash of her temper. "Flame will interfere with the completion of the Domes."

"WHAT?"

"You were just thinking about protecting them from the air. You can't. The Teams in the air will have to keep Flame far above and away from the Lairs. 'Twill interfere if within the perimeter."

Darque scowled again, and without saying another word, they walked into the mess hall. But she couldn't eat. She was Relaying her change of commands to all the Teams.

A FEW MARKS LATER

~~~~~ DREKINN LAIR ~~~~~

</div>

The Battle Commander had ordered everyone to the caves, including the War Dogs and Horses. Since the rescue and salvage teams had broken through to the lower level of the Port District,
~~~~~

they had more than one way to get to the Lair below the Den, no longer requiring one of the Dragons or Aalanna Grifynn siblings, to walk them through the Spell Door in the dungeons, although that was still the only way through that door. Having the new entry/exit was convenient, since Darque, Storrm, and Fryya were currently elsewhere, and the Dragons were few, and busy.

As a Healer, Kelsey knew well how to get around the labyrinth of the Lair, and as soon as she could sneak away from the others, she went straight to where they were keeping the Dogs, hiding in the shadows of the corners, out of sight. They'd just received warning of incoming, and her heart raced. For the past moon, they'd thought that the Keep would be the initial target, but now it appeared 'twas Drekinn. They'd been gearing up for the wounded to arrive, but had thought they'd be coming in from somewhere else. Drekinn would not survive the coming assault, and with all she'd done already, she owed these Humans nothing. Besides, she was using too much energy for her glamour, there were too many people around her, as well as Haniyyah, Nalwynn, and a handful of other Highlands, and since the big battle there was nothing large enough from which to Draw energy, all the trees had been Flamed. Although she was constantly brushing up against someone, she dared not Draw from them. With the scrutiny she was now enduring, they'd soon see her for who she was, and they'd never believe she was not a spy. She had to get out of here, go back to the Outlands, live alone. But she couldn't leave Bullaga.

She stood very still and tried to slow her breathing. 'Twas hard to think anymore. Her father's teachings and the unexpected acceptance, kindness, and compassion she'd encountered, clashed in her mind. 'Twas sheer confusion. She'd been keeping her weapons strapped on her person of late, and was glad. She'd purchased the short sword and boot blade from Alric the Weapons Master, using her own pay. Her own pay and her own weapons were things she'd never had afore, and of which she was proud. Along with the martial arts she'd been taught by her father, she'd spent many marks training with the new weapons with the Warriors and others, in the Pits and below, spending every spare moment to become proficient in their use. She was no Warrior, but she felt confident she could give the Hoard some trouble. If she met up with them.

She could see no others near, as she snuck around the corner. And then her brow furrowed. The War Dog Kennels of the Den were spacious, the dogs well trained, obedient, and naturally intelligent, and Bullaga always lounged at the far end. He only moved to eat or drink or when she came to visit, as he'd missed his friend, Bensyn. In the last few moons, no one else seemed to have any time for the big boy. Now 'twas a crowd of huge dogs within a relatively small space, lying all o'er each other, along the far wall. Where was he? "Bull," she whispered, Pushing her voice deep into the space. The massive beast's head immediately lifted above the others in the giant pile of mostly fawn colored fur, his flop ears perked, his eyes shining. He stood up, stretched, yawned, and began lumbering toward her, jostling his way through the crowd. Kelsey was afraid someone would see him, but as she thought this, his big brown eyes scanned the area from side to side. Then he stared right at her, and once in the clear, began to lope.

Moments later, she knelt and hugged him hard, her arms too short to reach all the way around, his deep chest pressing against her shoulder, his huge head o'er her back. His paws were bigger than both her hands put together, his skin thick, heavy, loose but strong (making it difficult for an attacker to get a firm hold), and his dense, double layer, short apricot coat, was soft as velvet on his ears. However, the reunion was short by necessity. Her mission was urgent and Bullaga recognized such, following her out of the make-shift kennel and through the maze of cavern tunnels toward the Port District entrance. Everyone was on the other side of the caves, preparing for the battle. Would they think her a coward? If everyone was dead, would it matter? The children were gone, so they were safe, with only the adults left below. They'd put up a fight, but the end was inevitable, for they were absurdly outnumbered. Even the Six could not keep out what was coming. At least her one and only friend would survive. If she had anything to say about it.

<center>~~~~~ THE BOG ~~~~~</center>

Rakkah stood, his heavily muscled arms crossed o'er his chest, his sea green eyes boring defiantly into the matching eyes of King Gabriel. They were the spitting image of each other. Gabriel's hair had grown and he no longer wore the paint of a Hunter of the Daggogh. Since he'd been crowned and now led the Resistance, he'd been working out with Rakkah, who had taken on the permanent duty station of personal bodyguard and double for the King. Yet, their unique history led them to share a unique rapport. Rakkah, being only less than one moon elder, not o'er a winter as everyone thought, tended to keep a tight rein on his 'little brother' because he took his duty seriously, and, because Gabriel had made him swear that if anything happened to him, Rakkah would have to take his rightful position as King. 'Twas a promise he would do anything and everything in his power to prevent having to fulfill, and that meant he had to keep his brother alive.

The King glared at Rakkah and stated, "I should make you my Jongleur, instead of my bodyguard, as 'tis surely jest that you think to stay here and prevent me from doing what I can, to help."

"We can discuss my promotion when 'tis done," Rakkah bit forth.

Gabriel was not amused. "You must go. Being my double is part of your position. If you don't do this, I will. The Hoard must think they have me in their sights, to draw their attention away from the Lairs, allowing the Spells to be completed."

"You threaten me? I will throw your scrawny ass on the ground and sit on you 'til this is all o'er. Your protection is my duty."

Gabriel snorted at this description, for his physique was closer to matching his Warrior brother by the day. He backed off, and said in a calm voice, "Your duty is the protection of what I represent."

Rakkah started to retort, but could not find sufficient words. He huffed. His brows furrowed in concern. The brothers loved each other. This mission would be their first real test, and Rakkah did not want to lose another brother. Both had already done that, and 'twas still fresh in each of their minds. Instead, he changed the subject. "Is Daynahmyn battle-ready?"

"She is."

Expecting a less than positive answer, he tried once more. "You will stay below with the others 'til the Spell is Drawn."

"To Hades, with that! I will protect the Spell bearer. Fear not, for I know my limits, and although I am still a better archer than you, as are all the People, 'tis not so with a sword. However, you have taught me much. I can hold my own at this point, nonetheless, 'tis you who are adept at fighting a'Dragonback, and 'tis you who must do so. But if you try to keep me out of the ground fight, I will call upon my authority."

Rakkah opened his mouth and then shut it, for Gabriel was the King regardless of how close they were, and if he 'called upon his authority', 'twould be nothing he could do, to keep him safe. Still, he attempted once more, with a slightly different approach. "I will go, but I insist you stay here, your Highness, for your own protection. Your loss so soon after taking the crown would disrupt the prophesies, and make many lose hope. Promise me that you will stay below, for you are the True King, the First Born." At this reference, Gabriel smiled and winked, and Rakkah stopped talking.

Taking Rakkah arm-to-arm in a Warrior's embrace, Gabriel showed his brother the benefit of the added marks of hard work, and slapping his shoulder, he grinned broadly. "I promise you nothing, except that I will tell you not what I did, unless you ask.

After all, you won't be here!" They broke grasps and as Rakkah walked off down the corridor, he stated softly, "I will make you proud."

"Just don't make me unemployed," said Rakkah o'er his shoulder, without slowing down.

<div align="center">~~~~~ THE KEEP ~~~~~</div>

They'd barely had a few marks rest in their own room and now Ardyth was resolute, as she quickly dressed in Darque's borrowed Warrior leathers, which fit her very well, and made ready for the channeling process. She had to hurry, for the Hoard would be upon Drekinn soon. Although fighting would be required, 'twas not their primary mission. Pretending to be the Battle Commander, she and the First Warrior would distract them away from Drekinn and keep them engaged so Diadranei could place the Spell, and then they were to enter whatever Dome to which they were closest, and stay put 'til they could return to the Keep.

Dia would be transported to Drekinn Lair by Rakkah and Daynahmyn, impersonating the King. General Gunnarr would take her, along with Bastyen and Graasyn. Once delivered, they would join in the air o'er the Great Plains of Drekinn, as bait. Storrm and Mystynn had returned to the Bog, but as the big Green provided air support, Storrm would be on the ground with King Gabriel, to protect the Prince and Princess, while the rest of the Teams of Second Flight, Daylyn and Makyyan, Hannah and Izayyah, and Daayn and Kashiyann, would join any aerial battle that formed. Darque and the recently mated Warrior Team, Torstynn and Raynah, would stay at the Keep, protecting Calei and Natan. Torstynn was healing well from the wounds he'd received in the Battle of Ice Mist Falls, and had regained much of his skills during the incident with the Eoche. His twin brother, Tyrrsyn, admonished him to stay close to the Spell bearers throughout the fight and not to wait 'til the final moments, as his gait was still too slow. Torstynn could fight, as long as he didn't have to move fast or far, and with a grin, he'd promised not to do either, while Raynah promised he'd keep his promise. Tyrrsyn, Master Tyrza, Chynnar, Fryya, and Walkyr were preparing the children to take in wounded, and to fight any invaders who got past the protectors. As had all the humans been warned to stay below ground, all Dragons had been warned to stay clear of the Lairs, 'til after the Spells completed. Even the War Horses and Ryndor were now below.

Bryynn would be with Ardyth, and Abriya would arm them once the channel was complete. Cradling the little Dragon, she marveled at how heavy he was becoming, how fast he was growing. As she adjusted the chest shield, she fretted that it made her look pregnant. Bryynn winked at her and trying to alter her mood, said, "Not so soon, my dear! But do not be concerned, for I will 'hide' myself."

The comment went unnoted, and Ardyth returned to her original concern, stating sternly, "You will not tell them. I suspected such, but we can do nothing else. Abriya must be able to fight! I can't swing a sword. I can't ride a Dragon. I don't have the experience, and we don't have time to learn, nor do we want to learn in the heat of battle."

The little Dragon's jovial mood altered. He was quite upset. He'd not expected this complication of which he'd discovered, and he did not want to lose his partner. She was his destiny, and if this went wrong, his destiny would be very short-lived. Besides, he felt responsible. He'd gotten her into this, after all. Yet, he could think of nothing useful to say. Miserably, he replied, "Please believe me, I knew not that you would have no control o'er such."

"Of course, I believe you! I place my future in your hands, Bryynn. If Abriya chooses not to vacate my body, or is unable to do so when the time comes, I expect you to do what is right. She is much more valuable to the war effort than am I. I've been on the run my entire span of days. Mayhap 'twas for such a time as this. You will stay with her, as you have stayed with me. She will take good care of you." She paused, swallowed hard to regain her voice, and then turned, "We have to go now, promise me, you will say nothing afore the channeling process."

Bryynn had tears welling up in his huge dark eyes, and the added moisture made them glitter all the more. He pouted. "I promise." But in his heart, he could not promise to allow the spirit to possess her forever. Having her own body again would be addicting, and the longer she was channeled within Ardyth, the harder 'twould be to let go, even for someone as honorable as Abriya. He wasn't even certain she could. Hugging her, the chest plate o'er his sling providing a modicum of protection for both the 7th Prince and the First Warrior, they left for Darque's quarters, where Darque, Abriya, and Chynnar awaited them.

TRIPPING THE LIGHT. FANTASTIC

(THAT'S DARQUE'S SARCASM. SHE MADE ME PUT THAT IN HERE.)

~~~~~ THE ALTAR ROOM ~~~~~

</div>

'Twas complete. Darque watched the Magic bearers as they separated, each 'carrying' their sphere of light. The once drab balls were now glowing enough to light up the entire room, making them difficult to look at directly. They floated just above the hands of their bearers, following about chest height. Stepping back from each other, they parted, pulling their spheres with them, the partners maintaining control together, Dia alone. All was going smoothly, and then, just as they stepped back out of the circle of power, Kevon tripped. Darque's enhanced reflexes had her near 'cross the room afore Gunnarr stopped her, one talon upon her shoulder, as Ana reached out with one hand and assisted Kevon to regain his balance afore he fell. The ball of light they shared bounced precariously about while everyone seemed to hold their breath, but the pair recovered and the ball settled back into its place, moving smoothly along with them.
~~~~~

His stumble seemed more associated with fatigue, than with a misstep. Could he do this? Kevon's face was a study in concentration, his sky-blue eyes focused solely upon his partner and their shared sphere, as if he could see nothing else. Anastasia maintained a somber self-assurance that matched that of the adults. Despite what could have happened had they lost control o'er their sphere, her concentration was unflustered by Kevon's slip, and they continued to move backwards. Once outside the circle, they all paused afore turning gracefully, balancing the spheres. As they faced the Commander, Gunnarr thought he heard Diadranei speaking, as she Pushed her feelings to the big Dragon. Then Darque understood, too. 'Twas not the Link, but she was beyond pleased to have confirmation of their ability to communicate, on any level.

'Let's do this,' was the feeling Pushed forth. Dia was a good Empath, as was Ana, therefore, they'd be the best communicators during this process. That left Natan and Calei, without voice. 'Twas no matter. Darque felt that 'tween her own senses, and those of the High Prince, they'd be fine at the Keep, for the Hoard were still headed to Drekinn. She was grateful the Prince and Princess would be able to communicate at the Bog, as well as Dia out there alone. But she liked it not, for they'd be away from her direct supervision, and possibly under attack. As Natanamia, and then the rest had emphasized, the best-case scenario was for all three Domes to complete afore the Hoard 'crossed the Plains. Worst case? She didn't want to think about it. At least they hadn't been attacked afore the Brew was complete.

<div align="center">~~~~~ DARQUE'S QUARTERS ~~~~~</div>

Darque watched Ardyth and Abriya merge. Standing facing the Shade, she took one last breath, then the First Warrior stepped forth to embrace Ardyth as they became one. As Abriya disappeared, Ardyth took a startled breath, looking around as if she'd never seen anyone there afore. She now appeared exactly as the Battle Commander. The channeling made subtle changes that completed the transformation as they melded together, and even Storrm and Fryya, her own blood, would be astonished at the likeness. Her movements were initially stilted but soon became fluid, as the First Warrior drew breath after breath, blinking her eyes to regain her living focus. Then with determination, she reached forth her hand and in a voice that would be mistaken for Darque's own, commanded, "Come."

Inside the shared body, the two communicated. As Abriya entered, Ardyth felt a fullness, then a suffocation which she'd expected and therefore attempted to ignore, but she could only hold her breath so long. 'Twas much more difficult than anticipated. She'd never panicked afore, but 'twas unnerving.

Ardyth: I can't breathe. I need air!

Abriya: Take your breath with mine. Your lungs breathe for us, your eyes see for us, your heart beats for us. We live together. We shall not fail.

Suddenly, Bryynn told Ardyth to use her breath control, as if swimming. Organizing 'her' breathing with Abriya's just as she would with the ocean waves through which she'd been swimming all her life, calm abruptly prevailed, and the rising panic was denied.

Ardyth: Yes, I can do this. I have done harder things in my span of days. But, Abriya, I've never fought with a sword.

Abriya: You need not have such experience, for your body is strong, your reflexes are quick, and we are built alike. We will use our combined talents. Just allow it to flow, and let me command the sword.

Puzzled, Ardyth answered: I have no sword.

Abriya: I Call to mine.

A moment passed, and then Ardyth/Abriya frowned. Their communications took place in the blink of an eye, yet she had Called to her Dragon Sword, and 'twas not forthcoming. Darque wasted no time, and stepping forth, she pulled her own Dragon Sword from the scabbard she carried. She'd expected this, and they'd discussed the consequences. If the First Warrior's Sword did not come when she Called forth from a living body, 'twas most likely where it could not answer, or was too far away, for a Dragon Sword could not be destroyed. Gunnarr had reluctantly agreed that Ardyth/Abriya would require the Sword to complete the 'twin' diversion, since a Dragon Sword was created by Magic, imbued with the essence of the bearer, and could slice through scale, making it possible to kill a Highland more quickly and with any strike, not just via the sweet spots. Yet 'twould leave Darque without her primary weapon. Darque had argued that she could fight with any sword, had in fact, made their first kill with a boot blade, and their intel told them that the Keep would be the last to be attacked, which was good, since 'twould take the longest to Draw the Spell o'er the Keep. Gunnarr was still not pleased, for not only would she be without her Sword, she'd be without him, and 'twas only the fact that Abriya was in 'Bond with his great grandfather, Solvyngarr, that they'd be able to function as a 'Bonded pair.

Ardyth/Abriya knelt and bowed her head as she reverently held out her hands to accept the Sword being offered. The question now was, would Darque's Sword allow such, while she yet lived? They'd attempted this afore the channeling, but the Sword would not settle in Ardyth's hand. Abriya's spirit would have to make the difference, or she'd be at a distinct disadvantage in the aerial battle to come.

As Darque handed the Sword to the First Warrior, she felt it resist. She stopped and held firm as the resistance diminished o'er the space of a few heartbeats, and she then placed it in the others' hands. The Sword had chosen to allow the transfer. After all, 'twas her 'twin', her namesake, her ancestor. Even if 'twas theoretically temporary, Darque Abriya D'Rienne had returned to the fight, as was told long ago.

~~~~~ **FLIGHT TO DREKINN LAIR** ~~~~~

Ardyth/Abriya was disappointed that she'd not recovered her own Sword, but was pleased with the one provided. 'Twas perfectly balanced, fitting her small hands as if custom made, as was her own. She'd taken it with trepidation in her heart, for surely 'twould be Flame to pay. But nothing happened, and standing up, she'd swung the blade through an ancient cadence, getting the feel for it once more, teaching Ardyth to let go and allow Abriya to control their reflexes. Her heart beat again, pumping the Life Source through her body, fueling the Battle Lust once more. She cradled Bryynn, reassuring him of her intent to vacate as soon as the mission was done, and as her vision began to turn crimson, she faced her namesake. Grasping arm-to-arm, they nodded grimly to each other, and she was off. Gunnarr waited in the open ward with Diadranei, along with Rakkah and Daynahmyn, here to pick up Bastyen and Graasyn. They would join them in the long flight to Drekinn.

Darque had chosen the feint attack, baiting the Hoard from all three Lairs to the Great Plains, but timing was an issue due to the distance 'tween. Darque knew Abriya had a plan to achieve what was required, however, they'd had no time for details. The plan's execution was left in the First Warrior's capable hands. Abriya was not concerned, for the Dragons had access to their ancestor's Memories, and Gunnarr was her 'Bond's grandson. Solvyngarr would be proud indeed. The General was a strapping big Blue, intelligent, swift, vicious, solid, and yet he possessed an uncanny wit, mixed with common sense. Much like Sol.

During the flight, Abriya Spoke with both Gunnarr and Daynahmyn, *"We must be swifter than ever afore, my friends. Drekinn will be hit first, as Darque said in your briefing, and we must get there in time to allow the Elf to complete the Spell. 'Tis my opinion that the hold o'er Drekinn will fight the new Spell, for the Six have no true awareness, and any attempt to dismantle, will be*
~~~~~

seen as an attack. Therefore, the new Spell will be more difficult than the others, to Draw down."

Daynahmyn saw this spirit channeling in a Human, as a poor representative of their Battle Commander, and with little faith in her heart, she Replied afore General Gunnarr could. *"I feel you have a plan. Something we have not tried or known of afore? A new trick, mayhap?"*

The sarcasm was thick, but afore Gunnarr could rebuke her, Abriya Replied. *"Yes, I do. Remember Daynahmyn, Lord Solvyngarr and I, fought in the War of Chaos. I am the First Warrior."*

Day did not answer. General Gunnarr had to bring them together, or they'd not survive this fight, and faith in each other's skills and commitment, was required. He Spoke sternly to them both. *"We all fight the same Evil, whether the atrocities we have witnessed and in which we have participated, are recent, or ancient."* 'Twas perfectly stated and received, and Abriya and Daynahmyn released their issues, as Gunnarr continued. *"Tell me, Abriya, what you have in mind."*

"We need to get to Drekinn Lair quickly. And, we need to return just as quickly. We have not several days to do this, nor a whole day, for we must drop off these, and then return to the Lairs from which we just came, to bait the Hoard. Darque and I sense they will stage their attack upon all the Lairs at the same time. In this way, we can bring all the Hoard Dragons to the Great Plains, leaving the Spell bearers to do their work. Sol and I learned as we fought. We experimented, pushed the boundaries, threw everything we had at the enemy, for there was but one of us, one LifeBond pair. Early in the war, we took advantage of the Magic of the Highlands. Particularly, your ability to enlarge spaces."

Gunnarr was most intrigued. He understood the plan and had wondered how Darque would work around the timing. *"I see not how this could be an advantage during the fight. Tell me more."*

Now Rakkah could Hear the conversation, as Day relayed through the Link. *"Do you recall when the Ancients first came to Drekinn? There were twenty, and you all fit into the Lodge?"*

"I know how 'twas done, I understand the Magic. I use it often. We pushed the walls away from us. I lifted the ceiling of Darque's room so I wouldn't hit my head when I first laid talon upon her. 'Tis how I fit through the caverns of the Lair under Drekinn. As we did at the Lodge, I pushed the walls of stone, outward."

"Yes, but did you realize how you oft times came out afore her, through those caverns?"

Gunnarr had never given it much thought. His Magic was a part of him, the consequences usually went unnoted. Now, as his strong wings beat, his mind went back to the times he and his mate frolicked through the caves, chasing her into the narrow passages, and then waiting for her on the ledge as she came behind. She'd wondered how he'd done such, and he'd always shrugged it off as being faster than she, but was it just that? He pondered. Then he understood. *"When I push aside the physical, the stone, ground, and wood, the space in which I then move has its own properties of existence, its own effects of time. But how was this helpful? The Hoard must have learned the trick, and nullified the advantage."*

"'Tis a LifeBond benefit. 'Tis only achievable with a 'Bond partner. Sol and I surmised 'twas the result of the Human Balance Effect."

Even as Bryynn remembered how they'd traveled from Ice Mist to the Bog, he listened to Abriya's reply with fascination, for he'd accomplished this same phenomenon with Ardyth and her horse. Gunnarr was getting excited. Since the Last Holocaust, the Highlands had been solitary, reclusive, and without a war to fight, they'd not been very creative, nor pushed their Magics to any length, for there was no need. Now, he could see a new possibility, a different twist on his Magic, and 'twould be of enormous benefit for First and Second Flights, to increase their advantage.

Clarifying what he hoped she was saying, he added, *"Then if I Push aside the airspace with which we are surrounded, I can create the same effect. We can then move at a speed unimaginable. We can attack and fall back, at will, as long as our energies are equal to the task."*

"Yes. We can."

"And you have done this?"

"Yes, I have!"

Daynahmyn cast her glance to Gunnarr, and then they both stretched out their long necks and Pushed. 'Twas a feeling they'd experienced afore, but never at this level. Even though Day and Rakkah were not actually in 'Bond with each other, and Gunnarr and Ardyth/Abriya were in the same situation, they were able, through their shared similarities, to use the effect to fly faster than either of them had ever flown afore. And remarkably, while they flew through the timefold, they could clearly see what was around them. 'Twas as if everything outside of the 'fold' was traveling in slow motion, instead of speeding along as were they, making their intended destinations easily managed with pin-prick accuracy. Gunnarr recalled when he and Darque had approached this speed on their own, without understanding how 'twas accomplished, and he knew that Storrm and Mystynn had been taking advantage of the same phenomenon. Still, each Dragon and each Human partner would produce their own effect, each differing as they differed, and so, Gunnarr had to slow down to keep Daynahmyn within defensive range. Even so, the journey to Drekinn was made in less than half a mark. As they approached, they could see the Hoard in the distance, mere specks in the skies above ants upon the ground, as they left the foothills of the Edge and began to cross the Great Plains. 'Twas not much time left.

<div style="text-align:center">~~~~~ MEANWHILE, BACK AT THE KEEP ~~~~~</div>

'Twas a tricky process, but with her 'Bond's assistance, Storrm managed to get both Kevon and Anastasia aboard the big Green sitting just behind her without losing their sphere, and they flew back to the Bog with all haste. The snows were no longer falling, but the winds were cold, and Mystynn had to use much Magic. Since the Hoard were coming anyway, and this Spell was their last hope, 'twould make no difference if they were seen, and Mystynn spared nothing to make the trip safe and quick. He'd gathered ample energy in the past moon to fuel his Healing for the expected battle, but if the Spell worked, 'twould be a short one. He and Storrm had to succeed in this mission or the Resistance was lost, and so they'd already agreed their lives were forfeit to their ultimate success. 'Twas an unspoken order of the Commander and all knew what they faced. No one backed down.

<div align="center">~~~~~ THE RUINS OF DREKINN ~~~~~</div>

Kelsey paused to catch her breath amid the rubble close to the main gate of the Den, her hand signal staying Bullaga at her side. They'd have to make a long dash through the rest of the village ruins, then work their way to the barrier without anyone seeing either of them. As her heart rate slowed she gazed southward and could see the Hoard in the distance, their Dragons flying high above the King's Agents marching upon the ground. There were too many, the reports were correct. The barrier would not last long once they arrived, and then what would she do? She and Bullaga had to get out afore they came, afore the barrier fell apart.

She turned around sharply at the beating of Dragon wings. This close already? Looking up, her Elven vision identified both King Gabriel and the Battle Commander, just afore they dropped below the ramparts. They were bringing someone to the Den. She shook her head. Too little. Too late. A few more swords and two Dragons, would not turn the battle in their favor. Bullaga sat down and gazed at her, his long tongue hanging out of his muzzle as he panted. They'd been running all the way from the caves, non-stop, climbing uphill through the debris, and he'd not had such a workout in a very long time. Her eyes flickered from the huge Dog, to the Dragons landing in the Pits. What could Darque be up to?

Curiosity got the better of her, and altering her plans, she palmed her blade, slid it back into her belt, ensured the sword was in her hip scabbard, and began to make her way into the Den, aiming for the Training Pits, as Bullaga followed closely behind. 'Twas no one to hide from, and she moved swiftly to her destination, only to see the impossible happening. There upon the sands, a tall slim Elf dismounted from behind Commander Darque on General Gunnarr, with the help of two Warriors who'd just dismounted from behind King Gabriel riding Daynahmyn, slipping to the sands, floating a Spell sphere. But after watching the LifeBond Teams fly away, she was even more mystified. What in Hades were they doing? Leaving the tall Elven girl with two Humans, made no sense. Unless… of course! That must be a Protection Spell, and for them to try to Draw down now, had to mean 'twas much stronger and more effective than the Illusory Spell held by the Six. 'Twould be a slow process, but mayhap they'd be done by the time the Hoard arrived. But why wasn't everyone out there helping to protect her in this Brew? Why order everyone below? Darque must suspect a spy. She had to leave.

But she couldn't take her eyes off the Elf who'd already begun to chant, the Warriors flanking her, battle ready. She shook her head. That Elf looked familiar. She'd been so young when she'd left the Wyrdritch with her father. Had she known that girl? And how did an Elf come openly to the Humans? So many thoughts ran through her mind, the familiarity of the girl, the release of the Six, the protection of the Lair. However, if they succeeded, the current barrier would disappear, and she had no clue as to how she'd get away then.

~~~~~~~~~~
~~~~~~~~~~

Diadranei began chanting as soon as she stepped to the middle of the vast Pits. They'd thought to bring all the Spell Domes down at once, but 'twasn't feasible to coordinate the timing, and Drekinn had to be completed as soon as possible. Each of the Spells would be done when they were done. She could only hope by the Fates, 'twould be sufficient. Being a powerful Empath, she knew the others had already begun, and could feel her mate and his father standing close by, ready for battle. They would protect her 'til their last heartbeat, and she hoped by the 7th Egg, 'twould be long enough. If Bastyen was forced Past the Veil, she wanted to follow, however, she would not abandon her task.

And then she felt it. Another presence. No! She'd expected Drekinn to be the first attacked, and 'twould also come an event that would require her presence to avoid catastrophe, although she knew not what 'twas, but this was too soon! She paused. Even as she continued to chant, her senses told her the presence was not evil. 'Twas another Elf. One who's curiosity was peaked in misunderstanding. Regardless of her Race, she should have been below in the Lair, unless she came from outside. Who was she, why was she here, and had she no idea of the danger?

<center>~~~~~~~~~~</center>

Kelsey made her decision. 'Twould make no difference if she stayed, for she could not help other than to martyr herself, something her father would have found appalling. Hurrying now, she and Bullaga left the Den, working their way from place to place, hiding so as not to draw attention from either side, for both Daynahmyn and Gunnarr had vanished soon after dropping off their passengers, and she knew not where they'd gone. After a mark, the barrier became clear to her vision, long, narrow, open gaps appearing near the ground as if shredding, indicating the new Spell was close to complete. She decided to make a final dash and push through, but she was horrified as she approached the failing barrier, for so too, had a small group of King's Agents, apparently forging ahead of the others. As she watched, mayhap twenty of the invaders pushed their way through the weakening Spell as through a broken fence, stumbling, falling on their faces and each other, swearing, untangling their weapons, and then regrouping. Kelsey understood the new Spell must be exceptionally powerful, as 'twas taking a long time to become effective, but even if it dropped right now, these men would still be inside, and those in the Pits would not be able to see the enemy sneaking up upon them. 'Twould be no one to assist, for they were all in the Lair below, and if the Elf was killed afore the Spell was complete, Drekinn would be unprotected. What should she do?

~~~~~~~~~~~

The King's Agents sprawled inside the failing barrier after having pushed through the pain it caused them, for if they failed, they were doomed to the dungeons, and the executioner. They cared not that the Dragons were still behind them and they'd be without their Flame as backup on this mission, for they had to get inside this barrier and find out what was going on in the Dragon's Den. Besides, working around the beasts was risky, with many of their comrades having been Flamed 'accidentally', so 'twas far safer to fight without them.

They'd received inside information that not only was there a Spell o'er Drekinn, hiding the fact that the Clan had survived, but that a new and stronger one was being Brewed, and they were to stop it afore 'twas complete. King Shytin, along with his personal advisor, the Sorcerer, commanded they attack three separate locations, and Drekinn was but one. The other two were probably already under attack, for those had traveled longer than the faction from which these Agents came, and they'd deliberately traveled slowly and without cover, to divert attention from the other two contingents.

The Agents had seen the Dragons flying in, they'd seen them leave. They'd left three people in the Pits of the Dragon's Den, and 'twas an eerie glow rising from the area. 'Twas Magic happening now, and drawing their weapons, they ran toward the castle.
~~~~~~~~~~~

<center>~~~~~ AT THE BOG ~~~~~</center>

Kevon and Anastasia arrived at the Bog aboard Mystynn, using full Magic to not only keep them warm, but keep them seated through the strong winds of flight, as their hands were otherwise occupied. The battle was coming upon the heels of the storm, just as the First Warrior predicted, but 'twas anticipated this location would not see any action. The Prince and Princess stood near the entrance to the Bog Lair, as close to the middle of the treacherous region as possible, upon a large pile of rock that lifted them up to the highest level they could reach. Facing each other, they began immediately. Chanting softly, they seemed to be in a dreamlike state as if they knew not where they were, but they obviously knew what they were doing. Each focused upon the sphere, their musical voices harmonizing, as King Gabriel and Storrm flanked the pair upon the ground, swords drawn. The rest of the Teams were already in flight scanning for incoming, and would defend from above. They had to hold their positions. If the Hoard came, they must protect the Prince and Princess at all costs. The two youngsters chanted on, and slowly, the ball of light began to brighten, pulse, and grow as if alive, becoming a miniature sun with a tiny ray of light shooting forth toward the sky.

<center>~~~~~ THE WARD OF THE KEEP ~~~~~</center>

Circling the pair, Torstynn, Raynah, and Darque stood ready to fight. Fryya and Walkyr were sharing command duties with Tyrrsyn and Master Tyrza below. Of all the children, and Master Tyrza, too, they had the best fighting skills and swordsmanship, and were battle-hardened. Although Tyrza was not a Warrior and hadn't even lifted a sword since Early Childhood Training, she was a remarkable blade thrower, and had saved them all by killing the Eoche that recently 'dropped in' to visit. Chynnar managed to harvest the Eoche venom, and the People, led by Gheryh and her mate, Kyrag, were even now tipping their arrowheads made from Dragon teeth. The People stationed at Drekinn would be using the poison they'd created and brought with them, a combination of the vine sap of the wall from Abysmal Gorge, and the Veil Grit. This vine sap poison had already been field tested with good results. Although neither of the poisons would kill on contact, the Dragon could be finished once he'd dropped to the ground.

Darque swallowed hard to push aside the devastating feeling of loss which filled her whenever she and Gunnarr were separated. She had to depend on Abriya to protect her 'Bond and lifemate, and 'twas a notion near painful. Nonetheless, there was a job to do here and now, and Gunnarr and the First Warrior would do theirs. She focused her attention upon Caleichante and Natanamia, standing in the center of the huge ward, their growing sphere floating 'tween them as they chanted softly in a language Darque recognized as Ancient Tongue, of which she knew enough to decipher. They called forth the forces of nature, the energies of organics, the tenacity of the Good and Righteous, and the strength of the Ancients, to set forth the Spell. In her mind, she added a plea to the One True Liege, to help them in their efforts. The Draw of the Domes had begun.

<div align="center">~~~~~ DREKINN LAIR ~~~~~</div>

Kelsey spared no effort, for the Agents would not, and as she raced back to the Den, Bullaga loped along covering her back. She made it in plenty of time, her Elven speed and reflexes better than the Humans following, but Bullaga was slower. She told him to keep coming, and not to turn about for the kills. The Agents saw the slight girl enter the Den, but huffing and puffing, they had to stop to rest by the time they got to the main gate.

Everything happened at once as she entered the Training Pits, and she could scarcely believe 'twas her, taking this stand. Bullaga would enter soon, and should still be ahead of the Agents, but in the meantime, she had to convince the pair that she was not a spy. She ran toward them, trying to explain who she was and that she was there to help. Yelling about the Agents chasing, her words stuck in her dry throat and 'twas harder to run through the sands.

Graasyn saw her as soon as did Bastyen, quickly determining that although she appeared human, she was wearing a glamour hiding Elven features. Was she a spy? Why was she here? Still, they would take no chances, for even though the Elves had sworn allegiance to the Resistance, not all Elves knew of this agreement yet, and no one was getting close to Dia.

As the tiny Elf approached, Bastyen and Graasyn stood battle ready, swords resting on their forearms ready to fight. The Elf was yelling, and as she ran closer, they could hear 'twas something about King's Agents. Dia's chant was getting louder, the light was getting brighter, the Elf was getting nearer, and they prepared to strike. Then they saw Bullaga running past the girl, and as he took his stand in front of her, she ducked thinking they were about to swing, and the War Dog gathered himself to leap forth to protect her, when suddenly they Heard Dia pushing forth a name. 'KELSEACYR!'

Bullaga sat down. Kelsey stood upright. Quizzically, she asked, "Diadranei?"

Just as bewildered as was the Elf, Bastyen stayed his arm and that of his father, asking, "You know her?" He wasn't certain to whom he'd addressed the question. Either could answer, and he'd feel less confused.

Catching her breath, Kelsey explained with urgency, "You must trust me. Diadranei is my friend from the Wyrdritch. Childhood. Please believe me, she can no longer Push forth her feelings, for she is too far into the Brew. I'm surprised she could impress upon you, my name." Kelsey looked first to the men, then to the Dog, and then to the entrances of the Pits. "There are at least twenty, mayhap more, ahead of the main force. The Six fail. They come to kill Dia, and prevent the Draw. I can help you!"

Bastyen snorted, and then opened his mouth to ask if the child was jesting, when the first of the Agents broke through the heavy oak doors. As they sauntered into the Pits, swords in hand, they sneered at what they faced. One War Dog, two little girls, one of whom was occupied and could not join in the fight, and two slim Warriors. Probably Stealth Ops, and no good with a sword. 'Twould be a walk in the park. The Sorcerer would be pleased. While most of them stood waiting along the perimeter of the Pits as they filed inside, three broke ranks, targeting the girl.

The two Warriors looked skeptically at the tiny Elven maiden, and in response, with a wicked grin she dropped her glamour and pulled her sword and dagger. Bullaga's attention was now upon the approaching enemy, and they all stood ready to fight to the Veil to protect Diadranei.

MEANWHILE

~~~~~ IN THE LAIR BENEATH THE DEN ~~~~~

</div>

Master Craftsman Cathay was startled when Regynn grabbed her from behind and turned her about, for his mission was to join in the aerial battle. Knowing him well, she quickly asked, "What did you forget?"

Pulling her close and kissing her soundly, he laughed, turned about and yelled o'er his shoulder as he jogged down the corridor, "To tell you, I love you!"

Cathay watched her Warrior rush out of the caverns to mount his big green, Sydrayyah, on the ledge, afore she returned to helping the People with their arrowheads. 'Twas understood that the defenders of the Lair would hold 'til they'd all Passed the Veil, for the Hoard would take no prisoners. As she hurried to prepare the arrows to the prescribed specs, she prayed for the safety of her adopted people, the Dragon Clan, and for Regynn, her soon-to-be mate. 'Twould be sad if after all they'd been through, they were denied their pledge to vows.
~~~~~

~~~~~ IN THE SKIES ABOVE THE WARD OF ST SWIFTYN'S ~~~~~

As the multitude of Hoard Dragons flew closer, ready to lower themselves far enough so as not to injure the Agents as they dropped from the long ropes into the ward, they checked their Flame. 'Twould not do to injure the Men they were bringing with them, and 'twas not in their orders to do so. None had the desire to argue with the Sorcerer, and simply did what they were told. The 'no-Flame' order, and the 'do not injure' order, would hold 'til they'd all dropped their Human cargo. They did, however, notice the two Dragons flying in from the south, who back-winged hard, and then took off again as if afraid. 'Twas Darque and Gabriel! Both the Sorcerer and the Black, would pay well for their capture. Quickly dropping their Humans, most of them flew southward following the pair, leaving behind a few, as Resistance Dragons appeared from nowhere, and protecting the Men below, the Hoard met Flame with Flame, as the aerial battle began.

~~~~~ O'ER DREKINN LAIR ~~~~~

Regynn barely mounted and launched from the cliffs when he saw the incoming Dragons of the Hoard. But what in Hades were they carrying? 'Twas as if they were dragging along a heavy curtain hanging beneath them. 'Twas as some kind of enormous net.

Sydrayyah Answered, *"Men! They bring Agents on nets made of ropes. They plan to attach them to the cliffs, or free-swing them into the caves! There must be hundreds of them!"*

The plan was a good one. The caves could not be reached from above or below without much effort, however, they could be flown in. But the Dragons of the Hoard were not in 'Bond, and the Agents could not Hear them. Most did not ride, either. Therefore, the men would not be able to relay information of what they faced, or seek rescue. Clearly, they expected to win through surprise and sheer numbers. As they turned their attention toward the Plains, the Six were losing strength as hundreds more Agents still a'foot, began to push through the barrier, marching hard toward the Den. They could be upon the Spell bearer within a half mark.

Unexpectedly, they saw Gunnarr with Darque, and Daynahmyn with King Gabriel. Regynn had been a Warrior for many winters and knew a scam when he saw one, but he shook his head wondering how 'twas accomplished. As the Agents were flown toward the cliffs, Sydrayyah and Regynn flew directly into the curtain of men. 'Tween her Flame and his sword, many fell to their deaths into the rocks or the churning sea below. But they kept coming. And very soon, Sydrayyah had to begin defensive maneuvering as those Dragons who were now free of their cargo, attacked. Suddenly Axyl and Haniyyah joined them, the handful of Free Dragons still holding the caves with their Human allies.

From inside flew arrows and spears, Star Wings and daggers. Men died, Dragons Flamed, and the Clan withdrew behind their rock shields, drawing bows again. For every arrow shot, a Hoard Dragon fell, but the Healing kept them from death, and since they fell into the sea, no one could finish them off. Still, the poison was slowing them down and preventing them from Flaming more. If an Agent made it into a cave, his body came back out quickly, pierced by sword, torn asunder by the Night Beasts, or blooded by the Wings who'd stayed with their Hunters, to feed the inhabitants of the sea below, the crashing surf stained pink with their Life Source. But, they would soon run short on ammunition, and even though many died, there were many to replace them. 'Twas only a matter of time afore they'd be inundated. Their only hope was the completion of the Dome.

Gunnarr Spoke to the Teams, Telling them to retreat to the Plains, to leave the Lair to their own defenses. With his woman inside, Regynn had an issue with that, but he obeyed orders, and once he saw the Free Dragons who'd stayed in the Lair, Flaming the incoming quite successfully, he felt a bit better. Yet, 'twas still difficult to watch. He wondered what the Commander's plan was, for surely, she had one, and why she'd allow the King to fight so openly. He noted when the Hoard finally saw the King and the Commander, fighting o'er the Plains. They'd baited the Hoard Dragons from the other Lairs to give chase, 'til both Gunnarr and Daynahmyn turned to fight. Now they Called to the other Teams for backup. So openly. Of course! Regynn tossed his dark blonde hair o'er his shoulder with a muscled, leather braced arm, and then directed Syd toward the Plains, hoping he was correct in what he was thinking, praying they could give Diadranei enough time.

<center>~~~~~ INSIDE THE KEEP ~~~~~</center>

Darque had remained under cover 'til the feint was complete. Now she rushed out to help. Watching the unbelievable number of Agents raining down into the ward dropped by dozens of Hoard Dragons, Tyrrsyn stood ready at one of the gates into the Keep, a large group of heavily armed Clan children, his backup. All had a look of determination upon their faces, all were prepared for the attack. Lined up with the oldest in front of the youngest, they were to hold this entrance, preventing any of the Agents from seeking shelter when the Spell Dome was completed. However, they'd not truly expected these numbers, and as a trained Warrior, he recognized that his new girlfriend was not a fighter, only extremely talented with throwing weapons, having killed the Eoche with his twin brother's dagger, saving them all from a most hideous demise.

But these would be her first human kills, as 'twould be for the children, and he'd been worried about how she'd handle this offensive 'til he'd heard her instructing her charges in self-defense, taking advantage of every life experience to teach as per her Mastery level, as well as to keep the children functioning without panic, for panic would get them all killed. He'd heard the wide-eyed little blonde girl ask, "Master Tyrza, should we be scared?" Tyrza recognized Kryn was near her limit after her near-death experience with the Eoche just a couple of moons past, and needed reassurance. Without missing a throw, she answered, "Keep me supplied, and they die as they lived. If they get past our Dragons and the Warriors, then you start throwing. You throw everything you can get your hands on, you pull your weapons, you hit, you kick, you scream, poke out their eyes, bite, scratch, you try and you keep trying, for you are a Warrior-in-training, a defender of the righteous, and those of the Hoard will burn without ceremony, like the garbage they've become." Her instructions were extremely inspiring to all those within earshot, and she'd made sure that was plenty far.

Little Kryn was very serious, but no longer fearful, when next she asked, "'Tis a good day to die, then, Master Tyrza?"

Tyrza smiled, exclaiming with conviction, "'Tis only a good day to die, once you are Past that Veil. We're not even close! Now go find something for me to throw!"

But Bynner noted the look on Master Tyrza's face. She ducked behind the heavy door to catch her breath, and considered the odds. More and more Agents were being dropped in the Ward, and if they managed to kill Natanamia and Caleichante afore they completed the Spell, 'twould be impossible to hold the Keep. She pulled Bynner closer. "Take your sister and hide. Go deep, and don't come out. Do you hear me?"

Wide-eyed, the young boy stammered, "Yessum."

"Go!"

The boy grabbed his little sister's hand and off they raced down the corridors that would take them into the bowels of the Keep.

But Kryn had other ideas, and pulling out of his grasp she ran in another direction, near as soon as they were out of the Master's sight.

Chasing close behind, he cried, "Kryn! Where are you going?"

"Mess Hall! C'mon! Master Tyrza needs more to throw!"

Bynner shook his head and trailed behind. Rounding the corner of the open arched doorway, he saw his little sister dragging knives, forks, glasses, and drinking bottles out of the kitchen, stacking them in the middle of a nearby table.

"What are you doing?"

Grabbing and carrying as much as she could in each armload, she explained, "She can throw this stuff."

Now he understood. Still trying to fulfill the Master's directive, he stated, "Kryn, she can't throw eating utensils and bottles, let's go, we'll have to find something else."

Stubbornly, she replied, "These are knives, the forks stick in the tables, and glass cuts when broken."

Bynner saw the determination upon his little sister's face, and with new respect he helped her gather armloads of bottles, glasses and all the eating utensils they could find, piling them onto the tables. Even if the Master couldn't throw these things, they could be used in hand-to-hand combat. Swiftly wrapping them into the cloths, they hurried back up to the ward, dragging their offering.

Master Tyrza was hurling more conventional weapons so fast she was running out, while the ward was being o'er run with the enemy. Even the People had seen her accuracy and speed, and they'd given her most of their own Star Wings, Fans, and throwing knives, to keep her in action. The children dragged their loads through those flanking the Master, but there were no weapons left to hand her. Reaching back, she hadn't even noticed their plight, when she felt something odd placed in her open hand. 'Twas a fork. Doing a double take, she looked at both Bynner, who had an anguished expression upon his youthful face, and Kryn, who seemed pleased as she could be, afore she smiled, turned about, and threw. Down went another Agent, the fork sticking out from the side of his thick neck, just as he was about to strike Walkyr from behind as the boy was engaged with another. Incensed, she yelled at the Seer. "Walkyr! What in Flame are you doing out there?"

"Training to be a Warrior when I grow up," he quipped o'er his shoulder, and then blocked and struck the other Agent, fell-ing him afore he could reach the Spell bearers. Working his way toward Torstynn, they began to fight back to back, making a lethal duo. Hitting it against the wall, Tyrza broke the bottom of the bottle Bynner handed her, and continued to throw, but her eyes darted toward one of the other entrances to the Keep 'cross the ward, where the boy Seer should have been. Another arrow flew from that opening, striking down an Agent. The People still held the entry, but if Walkyr was out there in the ward, where was Fryya?

Tyrrsyn and the children at his gate were battling Agents, as well. Her boyfriend was an elegant swordsman, and Tyrza could see his blade as it streaked through the air, the sunlight glinting off Clan steel. He struck and stabbed, time and again. Impaled front to back, two Agents went down as one. She threw another fork and then a dinner blade, taking out two more of the enemy. But, wait. She shouldn't be able to see Tyrrsyn fighting. He should be inside that gate, not entering the ward. The huge oaken door was closing behind him, as all alone, the Warrior pushed back the enemy from the entrance. 'Twas now closed, and the children were even now locking it from the inside, the People moving to another entrance. 'Twould have been on his orders. Gooseflesh rising on her arms, she returned her focus to defending her gate, while he battled his way out to stand with Walkyr, Darque, Raynah and his twin brother. Losing sight of Tyrrsyn, the ward was crawling with the enemy, and she had yet to locate Fryya. Reaching back, nothing was placed in her hand and dropping her eyes to the floor, the tablecloths were near empty. Grabbing several items, she threw with both hands, accurately and efficiently killing one Agent at a time.

Abruptly, she noted Kryn had gone missing once more, and just saw her brother's backside, chasing after her. "Where are you going?" She wasn't certain, but she thought she heard the little girl yelling something about the Master Craftsman's quarters. Near whispering to herself, she pleaded to the One, "Please help us. We just need a little more time!"

~~~~~~~~~~

All the Lairs were struck with remarkably similar timing, the Hoard Dragons fearing the retribution of the spirits of St Swiftyn's and unwilling to Flame, using the excuse of not wanting to harm their Human cargo, and fearing to Flame the Bog because of the surrounding forest. Carrying several Agents upon each of many ropes, they dropped them off as close to their targets as possible, leaving them at Drekinn and outside the Bog to march in, or to rush into battle in the ward of the Keep, while they chased what they perceived as personal gain, flying swiftly in pursuit of the King and Darque. Soaring in with the appearance of being caught off-guard, they'd played their roles well, and 'twas up to the defenders on the ground, to protect Calei and Natan as they began to turn in a synchronized pattern, the sphere now huge, glowing as brightly as did the sun itself, rising upwards while flattening, as a shaft of light shot toward the skies, widened and then began to slowly arc down. 'Twould encompass the entire mountain of St Swiftyn's. High o'er head, the few Dragons who'd not taken the bait were being met with equal force by Mystynn, Astraa and Kaygynn, Tannah and Synddarr, and Daylyn and Makyyan. Hannah and Izayyah, and Daayn and Kashiyann, had followed the feint to assist in the battle o'er the Plains. They would be joined by most of the Hoard Dragons, along with Gunnarr and Ardyth/Abriya, Rakkah and Daynahmyn, Kydra and Ragnyrr, Axyl and Haniyyah, Daxx and Linayyah, Yanais and Shykiyyah, Rolf and Nalwynn, and Tyndall and Fyndarr, while Apryya and Dannyrkyn, Zoe and Kyrlayyn, and Ethynn and Makayyd, found themselves defending the Bog.

Although the sight was awe inspiring, Tyrrsyn's attention returned to the ward. Once the Spell reached the ground, they were all toast. Their lives mattered not, they had to protect the Spell bearers, but he must try to get Darque's little sister and the boy Seer back inside. Leaving the People with the children and
~~~~~~~~~~

Tyrza, he was struck by the sure knowledge that Drekinn and the Bog were even now engaged as were they, as he raced forth into the thick of battle, sword drawn, to join Darque, Fryya, Walkyr, Torstynn and Raynah. The Spell bearers continued their slow turning in the midst of the chaos, heads back, eyes blind to their surroundings, oblivious to the raging battle around them.

<center>~~~~~ THE BOG ~~~~~</center>

The Prince and Princess chanted on, the sphere expanding into a huge ball of light, as Storrm and King Gabriel held off the Agents attempting to cross the marshland. Those who didn't sink into the muck, were met with sword on sword. Yet, even though many were lost to the Bog's own natural defenses, there were so many more that the continuous stream of Agents following began to run 'cross the human bridges of the bodies of those who had the misfortune of being in the lead and were slowly sucked down, allowing the rest to reach the center where stood the defenders of the Spell bearers.

Amidst the fighting, occasional dead Hoardsmen caught Storrm's eye. Their heads were crushed. No weapon they used would have caused such damage, but she had no time to consider further such a mystery. Storrm was a dynamic swordsman, but the King was not. Although he'd been training hard, 'twas the first time he'd used a sword in battle, and his skills were adequate at best, compared to a Warrior. Seeing him struggle against the Agents with whom he fought, she yelled, "Use that which you know!" A satisfied smirk spread 'cross her face as Gabriel did just that. Leaving his sword in the abdomen of the last Agent he confronted, he swiftly drew his bow from his shoulder and began to peel off arrow after arrow, killing so many with such speed, he was even able to help reduce the crowd with which Storrm was now surrounded. The arrows were tipped with Dragon teeth and were so sharp, each sliced through and killed several at a time afore finally reaching their limit. 'Tween arrows, his Star Wings flew 'cross the Bog in rapid succession from his hip and along his ribcage, using both hands at once, forcing ever more Past the Veil. He was, after all, trained by the People.

<center>~~~~~ ABOVE THE BOG ~~~~~</center>

Looking up from the Bog so far below, the Hoard Dragons caught sight of Rakkah and Ardyth/Abriya as they seemingly abandoned the distant Keep, racing toward the south. Giving chase, they near drooled with their good fortune. They were not in 'Bond with their Human cargo, not able to Hear them, and had no respect for such trash or anything they might say, at any rate. Humans were constantly screwing up everything the Sorcerer ordered, always in their way, and oft times causing them to suffer the consequences of the resultant failures. Seeing the tiny forms from on high, mayhap so many of them could infiltrate both Lairs and end the Spell without their assistance. They cared not for what those Spells might be trying to accomplish. The King and Darque were finally within reach, and they'd be paid well for such treasure. The Humans were on their own.

<center>~~~~~ O'ER THE GREAT PLAINS OF DREKINN ~~~~~</center>

Gunnarr and Daynahmyn flashed 'tween the Plains and Byndynn Forest, baiting the Hoard away from the Bog and the Keep, bringing as many as they could with them, while Axyl and Haniyyah, and Regynn and Sydrayyah, led the intensifying battle o'er the Plains in their absence. 'Twas insanely unnerving for the Hoard Dragons, losing sight of Gunnarr and Daynahmyn as if they'd just disappeared. With Bryynn enhancing their Magic, they raced onward, leaving the others behind while they returned to Drekinn, luring the Hoard Dragons away from the cliffs. Briefing the other Teams on the new strategy, they Pushed past the enemy, appearing on their backs or under their bellies, or even right in front of them, slashing, cutting, ripping, tearing. The First Warrior took advantage of her Sword, to slice through thick Dragon necks, decapitating the vile creatures, one of the ways they could be forced Past the Veil. Reaching her Sword high o'er head as Gunnarr appeared under yet another of their enemy, she sliced him stem to stern, his entrails spilling toward the Plains like steaming spaghetti, afore he could attempt to engage his Healing. 'Twas not in their orders to kill, just to keep them occupied 'til the Domes were complete, but every dead Hoard Dragon was one less with whom they'd have to contend in the future, and after all this time, 'twas good to be back in the fight.

Regynn could see everything outside of their timefold as they swiftly maneuvered around. Abruptly in position, he took his cue from Ardyth/Abriya and stood upon Sydrayyah's shoulders. Ferociously stabbing his sword straight up through the belly and into the chest cavity, he struck the heart of the Dragon under which they appeared, Syd Flaming full stream to cover him from the surrounding enemy, afore they vanished again. One after another of the vile creatures crashed to the Plains below, as the Teams of First and Second Flight played their deadly game of hide and seek. The Hoard Dragons knew not where they'd gone, when or even where they'd materialize again, but instead of withdrawing, they became so maniacal that they were being bested by so few Dragons, they lost all reason, and continued to try to fight what was clearly a losing battle.

<center>~~~~~ THE TRAINING PITS ~~~~~</center>

As the three Agents raced for Kelsey, she crouched low, keeping her eyes upon them. Bullaga, sensing she had no need for him here, watched for more to approach. Using the training she'd received as a child, she waited for just the right moment. Springing forward she caught the first man's sword with her own in a clash of steel on steel, then twisted it out of his grasp with blinding speed. Undercutting it with the dagger to provide added boost, the sword flew upwards, followed by the man's astonished eyes. Kelsey took advantage of his lapse of attention to plunge the dagger to the hilt into his chest, pushing him backwards right in front of the Agent who was running up behind to assist. This one was too slow to stop his forward momentum and he tripped o'er the dead Agent, falling flat on his face in the sands at Kelsey's feet, while she gracefully stepped back a few paces. The third man was getting closer and he looked up, catching her gaze. Prepared for what was about to happen, her eyes fixed upon the Human, the fallen Agent pushed up on his hands and tried to get his legs under him, just as the sword came down and buried itself through his chest and into the sands, nailing him in place. Kelsey didn't hesitate as the third man was now close enough to regret his chosen target and tried to stop, his face reflecting his terror. The Elf took one step, then leaped, and using the sword's cross guard as a spring board, she hurtled through the air, kicking his weapon out of his hand and landing with both feet in his chest. Afore he even hit the ground, she brought down her short sword, impaling the last of the trio. Quickly, she turned, ready for more, but they were still surrounding them, filling the perimeter of the area, and the action had taken place in just a few heartbeats. Their comrades' deaths had yet to even register to the others.

Graasyn's brows raised, and he looked at his son with tilted head, trying not to laugh out loud. Bastyen was amazed, for even though he was mated to one, Diadranei had never shown him the martial arts of the Elves. "She just killed three of them! Afore I could even think how to help her!"

The elder Warrior chuckled at this reaction. "I don't think she needs our help, son. And I believe we are now three behind in the count!"

As the remaining Agents began their charge from all directions, his vision crimson in the Lust, Bastyen shouted just afore his sword met that of an incoming Agent with a solid, jarring clang, "Soon to be rectified!"

At that point, 'twas full Battle Mode for the odd foursome, for even without training, Bullaga was a War Dog, and as swords reverberated through the Pits, he plowed into the enemy, knocking them down, locking his jaws upon their sword arms and their necks, rendering them unable to swing and then, unable to breathe. Leaving them drowning in their own blood, he didn't take the time to finish them afore his next attack, ignoring the wounds inflicted upon his body.

As Diadranei continued her chant, she began turning, her head back and arms outstretched as the sphere grew and rose above her, the light growing brighter, reaching toward the sky and beginning to widen like a blooming flower that would cover several square leagues, the distant edges starting to curve downward in a massive arc.

<center>~~~~~ THE WARD OF THE KEEP ~~~~~</center>

Fryya parried and stabbed the Hoardsman who'd just run up to her, then drew back her short sword, and without turning around, jabbed it past her hip, stabbing the one coming up behind, afore slipping her grip and swinging wide and forward, near beheading yet another. Joining the battle as soon as they'd seen how many they fought, she led her best friend, Walkyr, to aid Darque and the others. Their War Dogs, Drys and Horace, who were now bigger than were they, had also entered the fight, fiercely protecting their young handlers, and were themselves being protected by the huge Night Wings of the People. 'Twas quickly learned that the Agents feared the Dog and Wing combinations near as much as they feared the Sorcerer, and sensing this, they all took full advantage. The Night Beasts had been protecting the People inside the gates, along with the children, but had also joined the open fighting in the ward. Near double the size of the War Dogs, the Agents they attacked, stood not a chance.

Arrows had been flying fast and heavy, but 'twould seem they'd run short on supplies, for even Tyrza's signature method of killing was now noticeably absent. Fryya had been struck by more than one glancing blow of sword or dagger, yet she still stood and fought, while bodies were piled upon bodies, dozens impaled with an odd assortment of knitting needles, hair picks, broken bottles, and eating utensils, which she knew must have been kiped from the Warrior's personal quarters, the Master Craftsman's quarters, and the Mess Hall. She was certain 'twas a story behind that, and hoped 'twould be one she'd live long enough to hear. The piles of bodies had helped the defenders by providing cover, and making it more difficult for the rest of the enemy to approach. Scanning quickly around, she noted the sphere had grown enormous, flattening and rising high above the Keep, creating a shimmering arc of light encircling the mountain, curving down and falling fast. Desperately, she called for Walkyr, and then for Drys and Horace, knowing they had but moments left them to get to shelter, for the Spell bearers could not protect so many.

Spinning around searching, the Night Wings and Beasts who'd been fighting had disappeared, probably, hopefully, already safe inside. Then the Dogs bolted past, near knocking her feet out from under her, just afore she felt Walkyr's hand grab her by the elbow as he carried her into his own momentum. Sprinting for the gates, the children inside opened the huge doors, and the Dogs preceded them as they dove headfirst into the shadows just as a flash of light made everything disappear. As she lost all vision, Fryya wondered if this was how 'twas to Pass the Veil.

<div align="center">~~~~~ MOMENTS PRIOR ~~~~~</div>

Raynah noted the children heading for the entry, and fought her way toward her mate. She and Torstynn managed to get back to Natanamia, Tyrrsyn was closing in on Caleichante and would be safe within a heartbeat, and thank the One for the Lust, for all of them were bleeding from wounds inflicted in the battle, but they were still on their feet. Suddenly, one hand on the Sprite, she wondered, where was Darque?

<div align="center">~~~~~~~~~~</div>

Darque's Clan sword was not as effective as her Dragon Sword, which would have sliced through everything in its path as a hot knife through a brick of butter, but she quickly adjusted and stacked up so many bodies, she'd lost count long ago. Now, as the surrounding light became near painful to her enhanced vision, she sought out the others, and realized she was the only one not within reach of the Spell bearers. 'Twas a situation she'd best rectify immediately.

<center>~~~~~ THE DRAGON'S DEN ~~~~~</center>

The Agents were dead, but more would soon arrive. Kelsey kneeled beside the fallen War Dog, blood covering her hands and face. She wasn't certain if 'twas his or from all those she'd assisted Past the Veil.

Graasyn yelled at her, "C'mon, girl, there's no time!"

"Bullaga is injured! He can't get up!"

Bastyen attempted to reason with her. "You have to be in contact with Dia afore the Spell completes!"

But Elves could be a stubborn lot, as the Warriors were learning. Shaking her head, all she would say is, "I won't leave him!"

Graasyn and Bastyen threw a fleeting glance toward each other. They could not, would not, leave another warrior down. And so, they ran. The War Dog outweighed the girl by more than triple, and although she was trying to drag him, even her greater strength gained her little ground. The beast could barely lift his own head, and the tears were streaking down Kelsey's face as she continued to strain. The Warriors grabbed around his chest and his hind quarters, lifting him off the sands, and with Kelsey's assist, they ran as fast as possible, back to Dia. With the Spell falling around them, Graasyn said his silent goodbyes to the woman he'd left behind, wishing with all his heart that he'd shared vows with her when he'd had the chance. More Agents began to pour into the Pits racing toward them, and his mind drifted through the chaotic din while they near dragged the big Dog toward

Diadranei. By the One, he thought, if I survive this, I will not let that chance slip past me again.

<center>~~~~~ A FEW MOMENTS LATER ~~~~~</center>

Just as the Spell Dome completed o'er Drekinn, 'twas heard a faint whispering of six Dragon Voices, and they felt the powerful beating of spirit wings pushing them along, speeding them to Diadranei as the Six were released. At the same time, Dia managed to stretch forth her hand as Bastyen, Graasyn and Kelsey strained to make contact. With the help of the Six, all of them made it, including the injured Bullaga, as with great effort he lifted his massive head and sniffed at the hand reaching out, his wet nose just touching Dia's fingertips. 'Twas followed instantly by an explosion of massive proportions, of scorching heat and blinding light that burned everyone within the range of the new Dome to mere ash in a heartbeat, Agents and Dragons alike. And then, Drekinn Lair simply disappeared. It didn't leave a visible void, it just wasn't where 'twas. And no one would be able to 'find' it, unless the Gatekeepers chose to bring them inside. After which, still within the glow of the settling Dome, Dia pulled in those Teams and Frees who'd been fighting upon the Great Plains.

<center>~~~~~ THE BOG ~~~~~</center>

As the Dome completed o'er the Keep, Mystynn raced back to the Bog to assist Storrm. What he saw made his heart grow cold, for he knew he'd be too late. His wings beating powerfully, he Screamed, *"Storrm! Get to the Spell bearers! NOW!"* His hopes sank, seeing how far away she'd traveled from the pair, and she was still fighting off so many. She had but a few candle drips.

Storrm Heard Mystynn's cry, and realizing her position, she hammered the Agent in front of her on the top of his head with the hilt of her Sword, dropping him instantly to the ground at her feet, afore slicing the next one in half. Then she turned, and with her enhanced speed, fled for safety. But, Mystynn was in danger! *"Get back! You'll be wedged in the path of the Dome!"*

Gabriel had worked his way back to Anastasia, and grasping her ankle with one hand, he reached forth the other, yelling, "C'mon, c'mon, c'mon!" He couldn't believe what was happening. Storrm leaped up on a boulder attempting to dive closer, but even with her enhanced strength and speed, she wasn't going to make it. Suddenly, he felt a suggestion coming from the Princess. 'Drag her to us, Hunter!' 'Twas a suggestion he didn't understand 'til he saw the boulder rise, and with blocky arms Crytcha pushed Storrm by her feet, launching her head first toward Gabriel in an astonishing acrobatic move. Wild-eyed, he watched her dive through the air, but given their elevated position, she'd still be too far away, and pulling his bolo from his hip pouch, he threw in the space of a breath, catching the Second in Command by her outstretched arm, and yanking her the final distance toward him just as a blinding light exploded o'er the Bog.

Mystynn had been so focused upon his 'Bond, that he'd underestimated the Spell borders. As soon as he Heard her, he back-winged harder and faster than he'd ever done afore, using every muscle in his huge body to stop his forward movement so he could retreat, unable to take advantage of the new strategy to use the timefold. And then, he felt it crash down in front of him. Like a net caught on the scales of his chest, it dragged him to the ground just afore he saw, and felt, a hot burst of light.

CHAPTER THIRTY-FIVE

The Aftermath

SHAYLA'S CLINIC

~~~~~ DREKINN LAIR ~~~~~

Shayla wiped her sweaty brow with one forearm, and then finished wrapping Bullaga's chest and shoulder. His heart had been nicked by the sword, but 'twas a glancing blow diverted by his sternum, preventing it from being split in half. Early treatment, along with a bit of Magic to keep his Life Source from draining and his heart pumping, had made the difference 'tween life and death for the big boy. Using her Blood Crystal, the chest wound was well on the way toward closure, and she expected the big War Dog to make a complete recovery by full summer. She smiled at Kelsey, whom she now knew as Kelseacyr, and believed she was even prettier without the glamour. The Elf would not allow the treatment of her own wounds 'til after she was certain Bullaga would live. Shayla reassured the girl that she'd be permitted to Claim Bullaga, after she was given full rights as a Clansman, if 'twas what she wanted. Kelsey immediately accepted both offers.

'Cross the room, Ardyth/Abriya glanced up, just as the bloody, muscle-bound Warrior stepped through the doorway, afore allowing his little 'Bond, Haniyyah, to enter. Ardyth's heart jumped, and Abriya raised her eyebrows. Axyl had received relatively minor wounds in the battle and Haniyyah's Healing took care of them, but Han insisted he let Shayla check him out. The Warrior was on the other side of the clinic, and Shayla had warned the pair to stay clear of everyone, for they needed to leave afore the questions started. After all, every Clansman was aware of what Darque looked like, and all the Warriors and Dragons knew her personally. Knowing the Commander was still at the Keep, there'd be no mistaking the resemblance. 'Twas an issue
~~~~~

that Darque could not have addressed prior to the attack, but was planning on addressing soon.

Abriya: That is the Warrior of whom I sensed in your heart?

Able to think of nothing else to say, Ardyth shyly responded: Yes.

Abriya teasingly replied: I think if 'twas you in control of our voice, we'd be tongue-tied! He is quite handsome, and 'tis evident he is both fierce and brave, as well. A perfect match!

Ardyth was horrified: What are you going to do?

Abriya merely shrugged their shoulders, intent on getting his attention, but afore she could introduce herself to the big man, she faltered. Puzzled, she asked: Who are we?

~~~~~~~~~~

Shayla was Darque's aunt and had her own hybrid history, including Rashei lineage, and she sensed the quandary. 'Twasn't all that difficult, considering their expression. Darque had briefed her on the channeling, so she stepped 'tween them and Axyl, as soon as she noted the developing situation, preventing the First Warrior from saying anything, and giving them a reason to leave. They'd been checked out, their wounds dressed. They needed to be on their way back to the Keep. Darque had warned her the channel had to be ended as quickly as possible, but it had to occur at St Swiftyn's.

As Ardyth/Abriya left the triage area, Axyl stared, baffled, for he was certain of two things. That was not the Battle Commander, no matter how much they looked alike, and something had just been averted. Something that involved him.

His voice hadn't been heard often of late, and it surprised Shayla. "Who was that woman? And where is she going?"

"A new arrival at the Keep. I'm sure Darque will be holding a briefing for everyone very soon."

Axyl turned and nodded to Haniyyah, who stepped up behind him as he stated o'er his shoulder, "I'm leaving."
~~~~~~~~~~

Shayla was confused, and hurrying after, she leaned out the door, and asked, "But, where are you going?"

She could just hear his answer, rumbling down the hall as he aimed for the Pits, from where Han could launch. "The Keep. I want that briefing now."

~~~~~~~~~~

Since only the Spell bearers could govern the portals initially, teaching the Gatekeepers was at the top of the need-to-do-now list. As soon as the Domes contacted the ground, the Magic bearers at each location pulled in all their fighters, which would have appeared to any witnesses as if they were killed in a huge explosion. Thanks to Ardyth/Abriya's timefolding trick, they'd lost not a man or Dragon in the aerial battles. Dia knew what was about to occur, and allowed Han and Axyl to leave the Dome shortly after bringing them inside. Participating in the battle had been good for the big Warrior, but what was soon to take place, would truly help. It pleased her much.

At the Bog, Mystynn had just managed to survive at the edge of the Dome as 'twas completed, and although he had some burned scales, his Healing covered them. Storrm had finally deduced how the Hoardsmen had died with crushed skulls, and knew at least one friendly Troll was out there somewhere during the battle. When Crytcha stood up and launched her toward the Magic bearers, she'd not been too surprised. As a Troll, Crytcha had crouched to avoid the Dome completion, and suffered only a burn 'cross her back such as would occur on Humans with too much time out in the sun. But 'twas a new experience for the child, and delighting in the caverns under the Bog, she'd freely wandered after Lowah treated her with salve. She'd been sent by her father to join the Resistance to represent the Borkahn while he continued his war against Roack, and had only just arrived when the fighting began. But Darque soon learned that 'twas also to protect the child after yet another abduction attempt, and she was accepted into the Clan with gratitude.
~~~~~~~~~~

At the Keep, Darque was the last to reach the Spell bearers, just managing to touch Caleichante, as the Sprite reached forth her hand to grab her. The defenders in all the Lairs were amazed as the light softened to normal, their vision clearing to see that every one of the attackers within the Domes had simply turned to dust that blew swiftly away in the lightest breeze. Although they could see outside the Domes, 'twas quickly accepted that no one could see inside. 'Twas an eerie phenomenon that took most a few moons to learn to completely ignore.

Immediately after, the Healers went to work, while the Magic bearers hit the mess hall, just afore they hit the racks. Within the first sennight, the chosen Gatekeepers were proficient at all three Lairs. In the many briefings held, Natanamia recognized her sister's chest shield, gifting it, along with the rest of Nia's gear to her, after Ardyth gave her the names of the spies upon the island. Both Assemblymen, Natan was livid, for neither would she have suspected of betrayal. Soon after, Kevon, Anastasia, and Natanamia bid farewell per their prior agreement with the Battle Commander, for 'twould be too dangerous if they didn't get out now, and they'd already gone above and beyond. Dancing their way cautiously 'cross Byndynn Forest, then south along the coast to Port O'Teliv, they caught the Krakken, and sailed home. After all they'd been through o'er the past winter, the trip was somewhat less than eventful. Myrrdin was quite delighted to meet his little sister, but was just as disappointed that Caleichante had not come with them. The ex-Captain made Natan deliver her promise that 'twould be soon. The bottle of Drekinn whiskey awaited her arrival, and she expected to have celebratory news when next they saw each other. Having heard about Graasyn, Bastyen, and Diadranei, this announcement had him lifting his dark brows in curiosity.

Using the timefold, Axyl and Haniyyah had arrived at the Keep within a half mark of the battle, despite orders to stay where they were, Ardyth/Abriya and Gunnarr just ahead of them. But instead of rebuking the pair, Darque was grateful, for the First Warrior and Ardyth were having difficulty separating. It seemed that since they were channeled for so long, not only did Abriya yearn to stay, but she was becoming confused and didn't know how to separate them, and Ardyth wasn't certain she could breathe on her own again. But once Abriya set their eyes upon the hulk of a Warrior with the multiple scars, feeling Ardyth's heart leap with joy along with Bryynn's when he saw the little Green, she'd forced the separation, near ripping them apart, leaving her tears in Ardyth's eyes, after which, she simply disappeared. 'Twasn't long afore Axyl and Ardyth were seen sitting together in the mess hall, Haniyyah walking with Bryynn, who was growing so fast he could no longer fit in the sling. Seeing the big Warrior's return to his prior robust and boisterous self was heartwarming, but seeing the look on his face and in his eyes when he gazed at Ardyth, was even more so.

Shayla would remain at the Den as the official Senior Healer of the Resistance, continuing her work on Dragon anatomy and healing in the field. She made permanent the duty station of Senior Healer Lowah at the Bog Lair, and opted to send Kelseacyr to the Keep, with Bullaga, to work alongside Chynnar. The Keep was where most of the Magic bearers joining the Resistance would be taking up quarters and spending most of their time, and they would need a knowledgeable Skald. A bonus for Bullaga was that Fryya's female, Drys, and Walkyr's male, Horace, were at the Keep with their young handlers, as well.

Chynnar, the child Apprentice Healer, was given full promotion after the battle, and although she'd yet to see a full fourteen winters, Kelsey, being the elder by far and the most experienced, chose to promote Chynnar as the Senior Healer, rather than taking that position herself. She would continue to mentor the girl, teaching her the differences in Humans and Magic bearers, but she was satisfied to be second to the youngster, who had worked hard to achieve her status, and was quite the natural. After seeing what she'd done with the poison she'd harvested from the Eoche entirely on her own initiative, using only her instincts and a fine sense of deduction, as nothing like that had she been taught prior, the Elf was impressed. Kelsey was certain they'd show little gap in knowledge and skills 'tween them, within a few winters.

CHAPTER THIRTY-SIX

The Island of Dreams

Immediately upon their arrival, Natanamia gave orders to watch the spies. The first of whom they'd learned, was the most dangerous and would be the most difficult to take down, and if there were others, they had to know. Unsure how to proceed, for they had no real proof, 'twould be up to the Guard to gather such evidence as would be required.

Anastasia could feel the animosity emanating from the Lady the moment they met. She'd found it difficult to stand too close, let alone touch her, during their formal introductions. 'Twas disturbingly similar to when in her father's presence, and how she felt the air prickle when he and her mother were in the same room, her skin itching with the discordant sounds. But then, 'twas also something irregular Heard around all the Guardsmen since they'd returned with Natan. Just what that was about, she knew not, and 'twas most aggravating to the little sleuth.

'Twas a mere few dawns since their arrival, and while walking with Lord Rohar along the balcony, the conversation took a turn toward Kevon and Calei. Anastasia was not one to mince words and oft times too honest for her own good, so if her friend, Kevon, had issues with his mother and father, she wanted to know just who was lying, for someone was, and she needed to be certain 'twas not the Lord. Calei knew there was a spy upon the island, and with the invasion she knew 'twas deceit within the royal house. She'd begun to think the Lady might be involved, warning Kevon to avoid discussing such with his mother upon his return. If her senses were correct, both she and Kevon were in real danger, but could she trust Rohar? 'Twould be prudent to confirm.

Choosing to push the issue at that moment, she casually mentioned that during their journey, she'd uncovered a disturbing discrepancy 'tween Kevon and Calei's knowledge of how Kevon came to study with Calei, the Captain disclosing she'd received a secret command from the Lady, and that Lord Rohar had not wanted the boy, nor had he wanted Kevon to be trained.

Suddenly Anastasia realized Rohar was staring at her as if she were evil incarnate, and without thinking, she blurted forth the truth as she Heard it. "She's quite mad, you know."

But the truth had not the anticipated effect, and Rohar's song plunged into such disorder, it near made Ana cringe. "What did you say?" His voice was harsh, his eyes flashing.

Anastasia was perplexed, but she could sense his anger was not directed toward her. Still, she wasn't certain just what she HAD said to cause such a fuss. Was it what she'd said about the Lord, Kevon, Calei, or the Lady? Her sister's warning to keep her special knowledge to herself 'til she knew better the people with whom she'd be living, came back to mind. She hoped she'd not just destroyed a blossoming relationship, as well as her future, and feeling the need to explain, while still trying to ferret out the truth, she made her apology. "Forgive me, m'Lord Rohar. I thought you were aware. I often forget that others cannot Hear as do I. Mayhap I misspoke."

His expression now reflecting the confirmation of past doubts, he stated firmly, "No, my child. You spoke truth as no other. 'Twasn't Tialani who wanted the boy. Nay. 'Twasn't her who wanted to ensure his fighting skills, either."

'Twas all she needed to Hear. Rohar was being truthful.

Taking long swift strides back into the Hold with Ana following behind, keeping up as best she could, he faced his Guard, standing nervously glancing at each other afore seeking out Natanamia, as he bellowed, "Bring me the Lady Tialani! NOW."

To a man, the Guard glanced first to Natan who gave a barely noticeable nod of her head, afore they spun about and hurried to fulfill their mission.

<center>~~~~~ O'ER THREE MARKS LATER ~~~~~</center>

Lord Rohar sat restlessly upon his throne, Natanamia slightly behind and to his right with Anastasia at her side, when the Guard returned… alone. Rohar's eyes roved from one to the other, as he attempted to get any of them to meet his gaze. "Where is she?"

This wasn't exactly how they'd planned on 'taking down' the Lady, but mayhap the situation could still be salvaged. Kalisadei was first to step forth, and stated respectfully, "M'Lord. We have terrible news to impart."

"What say you?"

"The Lady has been located. When we approached her in the Royal Gardens she turned and fled toward the cliffs. Her body is being retrieved from the rocks below."

"An accident?" As Rohar stood up and stepped forward on the platform, Natan stepped closer, Ana in tow. He could not help but notice how his Guardsmen's eyes flickered to Natanamia afore answering. They knew more than they were saying. 'Twas something happening of which he was unaware, and must cease. He glared pointedly at his First Mate afore returning attention to his Guard.

Naftaleah sensed they must speak the truth, at least part of it. She stepped forward and cleared her throat. "My apologies, m'Lord. 'Twas no accident. When 'twas evident there was nowhere to run, she ignored our attempts at reasoning, afore stepping off the edge on her own." Kali's eyes dropped to the floor as Naftaleah finished her report, and she stepped back in line with the rest of the Guard.

Ana elbowed the First Mate. Natanamia took one look at her face and realized the Guardsmen still weren't telling the whole story, and 'twasn't to do with her being a spy. She shook her head to silence the question, but Rohar noted the exchange. Gritting his teeth, he stared at the girl with furrowed brow. Ana held his gaze, her beautiful brown eyes a'glitter with Allure, and something else. Understanding? So much turmoil since her arrival. What more could she offer? Solace, or pain? Mayhap truth? After several heartbeats, he walked o'er to the Elf, and reached forth his hand. Ana took it. All eyes were upon the pair, a slight gasp from some for the act. Except for Myrrdin, no Sprite had touched Elf since the Separation. Kneeling afore her, eye to eye, he roared o'er his shoulder for all to hear, "There shall be no more intolerance, lies, hidden truths, rumors, betrayals, or fear to speak one's mind, in this house!" Standing and turning to the Guardsmen, he cleared his throat, tightened his jaw, and furrowed his brows in anticipation of much heartache, afore he lowered his voice and asked, "And what did she say afore she leaped to her death? What were her last words?"

Anastasia was proud of the man who would be her father-by-vows in the not too distant future. He not only understood, he acted with courage. Knowing the female was in league with the Hoard, had betrayed him to the death of his sons, and to the near death of the Heir Apparent, and that even his Guardsmen had attempted to protect him from such, 'twas likely her last words were cruel, as well as irrational.

"We were too distant," began Lyrianei nervously, wanting not to cause her Lord more distress than that which he already suffered.

Aiisabeau stepped boldly forth from amongst the others, shaking off hands attempting to hold her back. "No. We were not too distant. Her last words were clear, m'Lord." Bolstered by their foreign visitor and his changing attitude, 'twas still considered treason to speak badly of the royals. Having to admit Lady Tialani committed suicide, let alone that she was the one Niamia named as a conspirator with the Hoard, was closer than most of them wanted to get to that line. She lifted her chin and voiced the thoughts they'd all shared for many winters. "She was no Lady. She was a Hoard spy, a traitor to the royal house, her own blood, and the Sprite Nation." She fixed her eyes upon the Lord and waited to see what he'd do about her insolence.

He dragged his gaze away from her and stared at the floor for a moment, as Ana tightened her grip on his hand. Looking first at her, he felt her calm acceptance of the scandalous events and was encouraged. The revelation of Tialani's deception wasn't surprising to him either, and he was ashamed that he'd turned a blind eye to his doubts, unable to break with tradition and decorum to openly admit the facts afore... He shook his head. 'Twas time for new rules, new policies. New blood. Quietly, he questioned the one standing boldly afore him. "And those words were?"

Now her heart began to pound out a rhythm of fear, as sweat beaded on her forehead. But she'd waded in hip deep and might as well continue, as there was no going back. Still, her voice held no condemnation, only the blunt factual narrative of what they'd all heard. "She yelled for us to hear above the crashing of the surf. 'Twas no doubt of the content. 'I have lain with the Hoard,' she screamed, 'and liked it. I have become drunk on the elixir of Life, and craved more.'" Despite her resolve, she cringed at the hateful words she must now retell, afore spitting them forth. "'You tell that heathen bastard that he took away from me, not only my youth and my lover, but the treasures of my womb, my sons. Their deaths shall be on his head forever.' And then she jumped, m'Lord." Licking her dry lips, she stood ready for anything, her heart still pounding in her chest.

His knees buckled, and he sat on the floor in the most outward display of emotion he'd ever shown. Anastasia stepped forward to kneel beside him, her eyes glittering with concern for the man whom she'd begun to like very much. Her own father was a weak man as different from his Queens as were the poles of Kadoor, who'd never made a decent decision, had stolen the crown, and was suddenly thrust into the Last Holocaust. Buried under the weight of change, insecurity, and regrets, sanity failed him. Even though her brothers were all good men, clever and wise and tough, taking after their maternal ancestors and far surpassing their sire, she'd still hoped for a real father figure in her life. But she was strong on her own and could make it through without. However, 'twould be nice... "She never loved you. You are not at fault for something, simply because someone claims you are. No one here blames you for what she did. She admitted to acting as Vampyre, for nothing more than pleasure. You didn't encourage her to seek out evil, to turn spy and betray the Nation. You didn't push her o'er the edge." Ana stood up and shrugged her shoulders as she finished. "She chose."

Lord Rohar stared at Anastasia, as he sorted through a multitude of emotions and history and expectations. Standing up with the assist of her proffered hand, he stated, "You are wise beyond your winters, my child. Come, I have many decisions and preparations to make. I believe your... unique insight... will be most welcome." Ana was well pleased with the harmonious melody beginning inside him.

<center>~~~~~ EVANNTYR ~~~~~</center>

There'd been Flame to pay when the attacks failed to produce Gabriel, Darque, Storrm, Fryya, Walkyr, or any of the others on their growing list of most-wanted, while losing so many troops and Dragons for naught. But the Sorcerer had argued that at least the Lairs were destroyed, for no trace could be found. The explosions that occurred during the battles must have demolished all three locations, as well as everyone within. They'd seen the same blaze of light at each of the suspected Lairs, and none of the fighters from either side who'd been close to the blaze, had returned. 'Twas likely Darque set up suicide blasts, to prevent the capture and torture of her precious Clan, and all three locations were obliterated. Nevertheless, he knew in his cold heart that Darque was highly intelligent and the Clan might yet have survived.

Proof of that possibility came soon thereafter, and he knew that somehow, his plans had failed yet again. The Sorcerer maintained a connection with all his spies, and when he felt Tialani Pass so quickly after losing Niamia, there was no doubt about what happened there. Now all his contacts upon the island were sure to be compromised, and along with losing the Clan, the work of many ages was gone. Without those contacts, the Island of Dreams, and the Sprite Nation, was untouchable. He shook with emotion, his eye twitched, and he grit his teeth so hard, his mouth filled with the metallic taste of blood. Corbyn the Raven would pay, even if he was not directly responsible, for in his mind, every ill-fated step he took could be traced back and attributed to the Heir Apparent. His old nemeses would feel the wrath of the Sorcerer. He roared in fury, the sound of pure malice echoing through the castle.

A FEW DAWNS LATER

~~~~~ DREAM HOLD ~~~~~

</div>

Lord Rohar had declared his intent to seek an alliance with the rising Resistance, led by Battle Commander Darque, with the True King, Gabriel, in her protection. His old Captain had chosen to remain at the Keep, and the Lord had agreed with his son's decision to grant Caleichante her wish to leave the Guard and stay with her new lifemate, making her ineligible for his purposes. Asking for volunteers to report to him in one dawn, he would choose a representative from the Sprite Nation. Allowing them plenty of time to give serious consideration to the proposal, the one he chose would have to travel to St Swiftyn's, negotiate the alliance with a people who knew little to nothing about their existence afore meeting Natan and Calei, become their liaison to the Battle Commander, and fight shoulder-to-shoulder with the Humans and their other allies, as such events transpired. The mission would take the Sprite away from home and family for who knew how long. Mayhap forever.
~~~~~

From their reports, the Elven Nation, now led by Queen Alyssa, would soon be sending their own representative, and Natanamia, in days' past, would have been one of the first to volunteer. But since Niamia's death, she'd been considering leaving the Guard entirely, her thoughts wavering from her own personal demons, to the needs of the Nation. 'Twas in her mind that the Sprites should send more than one representative to the Battle Commander. They needed a full team to help in the war effort. Her leadership experience told her that one Sprite Guardsman was just not enough to get the job done effectively, as just one would end up acting as a diplomat and none of the Elite were particularly gifted in diplomacy. What the Resistance needed, was good fighters. Still, if she weren't going to remain a Guardsman herself, why even bother making such a suggestion? The past weighed heavily upon her, she'd lost her sister, still hadn't found her niece, and tormented by doubt, depression was rapidly gaining a grip. Standing on the third-floor balcony of Dream Hold, she stared unseeing at the many exotic flowers and plants filling the Royal Gardens below, inhaled their rich fragrances, knew she'd miss all of it, but she had to leave. Everything about the island brought back painful memories, distracting her from fulfilling her duty. Yet, she was a fighter, and evil must be fought by all. Her indecision was palpable.

Anastasia was taking a break from playing piano for Kevon, who had finally fallen asleep. Although he'd made considerable progress, the Brew of the Spell Dome took much from his already depleted energies, and he was still recovering. While he rested, she explored Dream Hold. As she walked, she saw Natanamia at the balcony railing. She'd told her how the chase team knew the Lady was the spy, and the fact that Ana had helped to reveal such in her own way, was the most effective scenario that could have occurred. They'd not quite known how to go about it without resistance from the Lord, and therefore, Ana had done exactly what she should have, and in perfect timing. All of them were grateful for the intervention of the Elven Princess. But 'twas something else on her friend's mind at this moment, and sliding in beside Natan, Ana stood quietly leaning on the railing for a while afore she spoke. Since their arrival on the island, she'd noted how distant the Guardsman had become. 'Twould not have taken her Empathy to understand the other's turmoil. "Natan? What your sister did, had nothing to do with you. You're a good Guardsman."

In her heart, she felt that she'd failed everyone she'd ever loved. She hung her head and then nodded to the young Elf. "I thank you, my dear one," was all she could think to say.

"Don't quit," Ana implored her.

Shaking her head, she replied, "I can't stay."

"I know, but we still need you. We need your skills and dedication. And you need to go back to the Keep, to wait for the Warrior and Flyrra."

Natanamia stood gazing out o'er the gardens, reflecting upon the other's faith in her. She hadn't discussed her idea with anyone, and wondered what the little Princess would think. Oft times, she'd discovered much wisdom came from the child. She began hesitantly, "I was thinking..."

Ana didn't hesitate in her response, not even allowing her friend to finish. "'Twould be a worthy undertaking. Speak to him."

She chuckled under her breath. "Your Empathic abilities are somewhat... "

"Distracting? Disturbing? Odd?" Ana crossed her eyes and flashed a quirky smile that made Natan laugh out loud.

"I was going to say precocious, but any of those would do. You keep taking my thoughts out of my mind afore I even finish thinking them!"

"Your thoughts are clear in your heart. We've traveled far together, and I know of what you've experienced. But I also know that you're much stronger than you give yourself credit. You have not reached your breaking point, despite what you've been through. 'Tis most telling for one in your position. In these times of war, we need such leadership."

She hung her head. The praise was difficult to take, considering all the happenings of the past winter. Returning to her plan, she asked, "Do you think Lord Rohar would agree?"

"Yes, I do. You know as well as I, that the Sprites must send more than one representative. I believe you should discuss your plan to send a squad of fighters to the Resistance. And why not you, to lead them? 'Twould give you good reason to wait there for the Warrior as well, and if word comes of him, you can help more readily from there, than from here."

Natanamia didn't miss Ana's comment about her waiting for the Warrior. She wondered just how much the girl knew about her feelings for the dark-skinned Human. 'Twas her memories of their time together that soothed her at night, and thinking about him made her heartbeat quicken. Choosing to ignore the remark, she replied, "'Twould require I be promoted to Captain first, you know I was only acting Captain on the chase." She sighed. "I'll wait to hear his appointments."

But Anastasia stubbornly continued. "No. Go to him. He seeks his emissary now. Make your recommendations. Ask to lead the team. He will not turn you down. Trust me."

Natanamia glanced up, and grinned. "Are you saying this as an Elven Princess, or as the future Lady of the Sprites?"

Ana's expression changed, but she didn't blush as she had with such teasing in the past. Instead, her expression was one of wisdom, as the young Elf stepped closer to place her hand upon the other's arm. "No. I am saying this as your friend. The past is past and you must move on. And the change would do you good. 'Tis true, staying here might be difficult and depressing and your skills might falter. 'Tis not likely, but 'tis possible, and 'twould not be safe for any of us. But you are a good leader, Natanamia, and your experience on the chase transformed you into a good

Captain. I wish you to continue in that capacity. Serving the Sprite Nation. Serving Lord Rohar and Prince Kevon."

"And Princess Anastasia," Natan added with a courtly bow. Sighing once more, she nodded her head in affirmation of the plan, but she still had her doubts about openly approaching the Lord. "I promise to seek an audience with Lord Rohar, as soon as he can spare the time."

At precisely that moment, a handsome man walked energetically onto the balcony, turning his head this way and that. Lord Rohar had obviously been searching for someone, and when he heard the end of their conversation, he asked, "Who seeks my audience?"

Surprised and pleased by his robust entrance, for the First Mate had not seen him looking so confidently spirited in many a winter, she exclaimed, "M'Lord!"

"Oh, good, Natanamia! I've been looking for you. I understand you have a plan to propose, which will require a special appointment. And, have I mentioned that I approved your promotion to Captain?"

Natanamia glanced suspiciously at the Princess, questioning in a bare breath out of the corner of her mouth, "When did I ask for that?"

"Matters not. 'Twas granted," Ana whispered back, with an expression of pure innocence, while the mystified Lord glanced from one to the other.

<div align="center">~~~~~ A FEW DAWNS LATER ~~~~~</div>

The Royal Great Hall was filled to capacity. Standing front and center, Captain Natanamia saluted Lord Rohar, Prince Kevon, and Princess Anastasia, with her right fist to her chest and a nod of her head, afore turning about and striding 'tween her team of Sprite Elite Guard, each turning and folding in behind her as they filed out of the Hold. 'Twas much fanfare from the island's citizens lining the path, as they made their way to the docks to board the Norryn, which would take them to the mainland. From there, Natan, with her newly appointed First Mate, Aiisabeau, along with Kalisadei, Lyrianei, sisters Datyniah and Dalakiah, and brothers Kryllyn and Ardryyn, would Dance swiftly to the Keep. Word was sent earlier to the Battle Commander to be expecting them. She'd replied that they were most welcome. Since the newcomers to the team had never been on the mainland, the former chase team members had fun teasing them during the trip. Nevertheless, they had to move carefully to avoid the Hoard. The only former member of their team who wasn't making this transition, aside from Niamia, was Naftaleah, who had, reluctantly, stayed behind as newly appointed Captain of the Guard, to protect the royals. She would be busy indeed, since the other Hoard contacts had yet to be neutralized, but 'twas felt they were closing in and 'twould not be long. Naftaleah was not only a good fighter, but extremely perceptive, and had already begun to gather evidence against them, to prove their deceit. Rohar had agreed to say nothing, so as not to lose their opportunity to find the guilty, but had placed the children under intense guard.

As Ana watched her friend sail forth from the Island of Dreams, standing at the same balcony where they'd discussed this very situation, she thought about how much her own life had changed in the past winter. She couldn't help but wonder what Lord Rohar would do when Kevon took the throne. She'd be a part of that, whether they mated as per the decree, or not. Although 'twas expected, 'twould not be forced, and Anastasia could still rule side-by-side with the Sprite Prince. 'Twas solidly engraved into the future, if she chose to accept.

She looked around and admired the beauty of the Hold, and of the island. She was truly falling in love with her new home. Then she looked again at Rohar. He was quite a handsome man. Now that the burden of evil was lifted from his shoulders, he also appeared much younger than when they'd first met. Her quick mind flew from one thought to the next and settled upon her mother, now ruling alone in the Wyrdritch. Rohar was alone. They were both excellent rulers, and their people needed to be brought back together. 'Twas why she was here in the first place. Why not have the adults pitch in their share? She grinned and ran off to find Kevon. Although they had time, there'd be much work to do, to encourage such a relationship.

An Uncertain State of Affairs

Kayarr sat crossed-legged upon a large rock on the edge of the beautiful canyon meadow at the base of the mountain in which he and the child found themselves after descending a rather treacherous path. He'd just been entertaining her with some notes he could produce holding his hands cupped together, the hole o'er which he blew controlled by his thumbs to alter the sounds, a feat the little girl was trying to match, to no avail, causing much laughter. Her laughter was contagious, for 'twas now joyous and carefree, a sound as musical as that produced by clear crystal, and somewhat mesmerizing.

Although he'd had his doubts initially, this child should have no trouble making friends, once she was introduced into a proper environment. Kayarr knew she'd never been around other children, never had a normal existence, but considering her skittish and untrusting nature when he'd first found her compared to now, he was well pleased with her progress. She seemed to be blossoming. Yet he could not help but feel some anxiety for her future. Raised in the caves of the Black's Lair, surrounded by evil, struggling to survive, doing anything and everything necessary, despite what that may have involved, she would soon be thrust into an entirely different life. 'Twould be a life of honor, of education, of expectations to which she'd never been exposed and in which she'd be far behind her peers. 'Twas a life of training and discipline, near luxurious by her prior standards, but 'twas also a time of war in which all would be required to make a stand. Without adult guidance, would she survive such a change, or would she be ostracized for not only her odd appearance, but for her strange ways? He hated to think of the possibility that the new life awaiting would be harder for her than that from which she'd been rescued, forcing her to seek refuge by returning to what she understood.

He watched her with increasing respect, squatting in her usual posture, her bony knees and long legs surrounding her arms, leaving only her feet touching the stone, as she continued to struggle with the new experience, repeatedly trying to duplicate the sounds he'd produced by blowing o'er his hands. Her face a study in concentration, brows furrowed, tongue sticking out, she'd try again and again. He couldn't fault her persistence. But could she use such an attribute for her own benefit, to adjust? Could she adapt to not having to steal, to having someone to help her, to needing to be loyal to another? He wasn't even sure she could adapt to wearing shoes and appropriate clothes, although he had taught her proper hygiene. And he could sense the lingering feeling of abandonment she held about her mother, which would probably carry o'er to the entire Sprite Nation, who might see her as an outsider for her half-breed status. Yet she was extremely loyal to him. But he'd been the first in her life who'd placed her needs above his own. He near felt guilty they'd developed such strong ties, for she'd be a stranger to her own blood.

As these thoughts warred with one another in his mind, he saw something out of the corner of his eye. 'Twas dark and moving fast, and the child suddenly leaped up and raced off. Quickly following, he yelled at her to come back, but the burst of adrenaline did more harm than good. Coughing, he gripped his chest with one hand. Breathless, he was forced to stop and lean o'er, balancing himself with the other hand braced upon his knee. 'Twas annoying, really, that his recovery was so slow. He'd heard rumors of being drained of one's Life Force, which led him to believe 'twould be highly arousing, not painful. However, the Pitch had not been trying to mate with him, returning near daily, pushing him closer to the Veil with each feeding, the length of time 'tween, not enough to fully recover afore the next, 'til he could not have recovered had they fed again. When the child arrived with the key, 'twas barely in time to prevent his Passing. But the pain still made his eyes water when he had to put forth much effort, and although originally 'twas as if every rib had been carved from his body and then shoved back inside, backwards, 'twas improving. Clearing his throat, he yelled again, his voice gravelly, "Flyrra! Stop! That horse could kill you!" But this warning, as had the last, was evidently ignored by his black-eyed companion, and he watched helplessly as she became a sparkling dot in the distance, her silver hair reflecting the sun's rays like a mirror.

After their escape, the skinny child had single-handedly dragged him through the vast tunnel network of the caverns, to freedom and beyond. Although the others straggled away o'er the span of a few sennights as they regained their health, she stayed, caring for him for several moons as he continued to convalesce. The Pitch hadn't been interested in their attire, leaving him with his leathers, cloak, and boots intact, but they had divested him of his weapons, a loss he felt most strongly through the harsh winter which bogged down their travel. Flyrra had managed to locate a curved short sword of fair quality (meaning she stole it from one of the Pitch, a daring feat for which he was not happy, but was grudgingly grateful), which helped them obtain sufficient food, and gave him a sense of security previously lacking.

Once the Spring Melts had run, they'd tried walking towards the Keep of St Swiftyn's, for that was the rendezvous point arranged with the Sprite so long ago. But despite his confidence in knowing the general location of the Keep, they'd had some difficulty navigating, which he'd shrugged off as being in unfamiliar territory. He was truly baffled when they'd first arrived in this canyon, as 'twas obvious they were now traveling in the wrong direction, and he wasn't even certain how they'd gotten here, however, it did afford them pleasant respite, and he was confident there was another way out of the canyon, along the river, further north. While they were very late, he knew not how else to get the child back to her aunt, and prayed to the One, she'd managed to survive and was still waiting.

Sweet fantasies invaded his mind whenever he thought about the Guardsman, thick silky blonde hair spilling o'er creamy white shoulders, pale green eyes to melt one's soul. His body began to respond, a warm sensation gathering, blood rushing. He shook his head to clear those thoughts. He had a mission to complete. He needed to forget about her, and focus on the plan. Once 'twas done, he'd probably never see the Sprite again anyway, for she'd be off to do whatever 'twas she was doing, and he'd resume his original task. His fellow survivors separated, each traveling to a different Clan to reconnoiter. His chosen destination was Drekinn Village, his task to discover the fate of the Warriors of the Brotherhood, and try to make report to Grifynn, the Battle Commander. His Clan had been devastated in a surprise aerial attack by the Hoard, which appeared calculated and must have had some inside assistance. Unexpectedly, several Free Dragons came to fight with the Order of the Eagle Clan, but they were forced Past the Veil assisting a mere dozen Eagle Warriors to escape with their lives. Without their sacrifice, all would've been lost. But soon after his journey started, he heard rumors that the Dragon Clan, as well as other Clans, had also been attacked upon the same dawn, and no word had been forthcoming since.

However, that obstinate child was his charge for the time being, for which he didn't know whether to be grateful or totally frustrated. "Flyrra!" But she was out of sight in the distant tall pines. He dared not call any louder, for even though they were far from the original caves, he knew not the territory reigned o'er by the Pitch, and there were always the humans Flyrra had told him about, the Gordatch. 'Twas no telling what others inhabited the Talons. So far, if any knew of their presence, they'd remained out of sight. He sighed and stared at the stark contrast 'tween the grasses of the meadow and the boulders that dotted the area, and then as the pain diminished he caught his breath and stood up again. He needn't worry so about that child, for she was very capable of taking care of herself, and actually, he wasn't at all certain just who was taking care of whom. Still, he found himself caring very much about her and her future, and if things were different… There she was! And wonder of wonders, she'd caught the horse and was leading it back now.

'Twas a gorgeous ink black stallion of exceptional breeding. Sleek, fast, thick muscled, outwardly intelligent, but without tack or anything that could be used for identification, he was dragging a frayed rope and had a torn scarf tangled in his long mane, that might have been tied around his eyes at one time. The beast was in need of a good grooming and he'd obviously survived alone for many moons, but the grass in this expansive meadow was rich in nutrients, the river running through the middle, crystal clear. Although his legs and flanks showed evidence of a fight or two against clawed predators, evidently, he'd been the victor. Not even winded from the chase, Flyrra was all grins as she proudly handed the rope to the Warrior. "Now you can ride," she declared in that strange voice of hers that matched her aunt's. He likened it to wind chimes, the musical quality of which he'd never grow tired.

"Now we both ride," he answered with a broad grin, his eyes sparkling hazel with amusement as he took the rope from her tiny hand. Turning the beast's head to remove the scarf, the stallion's deep red eyes flared like lit coals, and he was initially taken aback. With furrowed brow, he asked, "More of your Magic?" The use of such might attract other Magic bearers to them, and he'd spent much time trying to impress restraint upon her.

Standing about waist high to the Warrior, she looked up and innocently stated, "I did nothing but calm his panic." Fearing his disapproval, not that he'd ever shown such toward her, she searched his eyes for change, for 'twas certain the color denoted his emotional status, as she'd seen evidence of this o'er their many moons together. Noting they remained their green to hazel appearance, a positive sign, she continued with enthusiasm, "He's of Sprite breeding, I believe. But he's quite confused and has lost his owner."

Kayarr knew the girl had a connection with animals, and accepted her report at face value. He was saddened by the emotional scars left upon the little girl, which led her to fear his disapproval. No, 'twas not that she feared. Since finding her with the Pitch, he'd not known a braver person of any age or sex. But, 'twould take much to heal the results of such horrific abuse as the child had endured. Gratefully, he replied, "I know not how such bounty was granted us, but his loss is our gain, little one." To ease his mount, he walked the horse to the closest of the boulders scattered about, then reached down for the girl as she scrambled up to sit behind him. Loping off toward the west, and St Swiftyn's, he declared, "To the Keep!"

Flyrra wrapped her small arms as far as she could reach around the Warrior, and chimed in, "To the Keep!"

MEANWHILE

~~~~~ ST SWIFTYN'S ~~~~~

</div>

'Twas difficult to gain much information from the First Warrior, as her time was short when she could manifest sufficiently to speak, and 'twas always a surprise to see her of late. Abriya had disappeared for near a moon after the battle, without explanation, although Darque suspected 'twas the trauma of the experience, and though she was now beginning to return, her visits were brief. Darque felt there was much she was missing, but didn't know quite where to begin. This afternoon, she chose to bring up the most basic of their needs, as the spirit abruptly appeared, sitting on her desk. 'Twas a question they'd all had since they'd first explored the Keep. "Abriya, I really don't know what to do. We're starving here. We don't have adequate farmland. How did you grow enough food for your society?"
~~~~~

"You aren't starving, your people have been extremely resourceful using the Dragon's…uh…fertilizer. And, creating that garden area in the ward was quite inspired."

"But I intend to bring the entire Clan here. Or what's left of it. Besides, the Resistance will continue to rise, and even though we've been farming around the Den under the Spell Dome, we need more. Far more. 'Twill need to be closer as well, for we can't continue to depend on deliveries. Drekinn will remain as a Lair and will only need to feed the Teams and Frees who take up residence, along with whatever workers will be required for maintenance. The Den will be quarters for officers, guests, and for what staff will be required, as well as continuing as a training facility."

The First Warrior reflected for a moment, then stated matter-of-factly, "Then you should reopen Shahanalaa."

"Shahanalaa?"

"Long afore the Last Holocaust 'twas known by many other names as well. Shangri-La, Shambhala, Agartha, Paradise. The Rashei knew it as Shahanalaa. 'Twas shrouded in myth. Our history teaches that 'twas created as a 'burp' in the conception of Kadoor, occurring in the beginning of Time itself. Some claim 'twas due to the chaos of the miasma of Magic struggling to settle, and they believed that once Mankind arrived, the balance was gained. There are many stories, but the one truth is that Shahanalaa survived the Beginning, the War of Chaos, and the Last Holocaust. 'Tis breathtaking, and spread o'er several square leagues, full of caverns, hills, cliffs, meadows, forests, lakes, rivers, waterfalls, a veritable smorgasbord of landscapes, some not seen anywhere else. 'Tis as the Oasis to the Dragon's Breath, but set in the middle of the Talons. The weather is controlled there, never getting too cold or too hot. 'Tis where we obtained the bulk of our food throughout the many winters of our residency."

Darque no longer questioned what was once considered myth. She'd read about these places in her Early Childhood Training.

Abriya was not only claiming they existed, but that they were all the same. She could not understand how 'twas kept such a secret however, and asked, "And this is where?"

"'Tis only accessed through the Keep. 'Twas one of the reasons the Rashei settled here after the ruin of Rienne."

Darque was exasperated. "Abriya, you mean to say that you've known all along there was a farming region with access through the Keep? Why didn't you tell me?"

The spirit shrugged her shoulders. "Why would I think of telling you? I don't eat. Technically, I don't even breathe."

Darque slapped her open palm to her forehead and took a deep breath, afore she looked up again and replied, "Granted, there is some logic to be found there somewhere. But if not you, then why didn't Ama tell me about this?"

Unabashed by Darque's response, Abriya explained, "Your mother was very young when she was taken from the Keep, and mayhap she never worked there. And Corbyn merely untethered her memories so they are now triggered by events, or by what she sees from her past. She cannot see Shahanalaa, as the gateway is hidden by a powerful Spell created by the Fay during the War of Chaos to shield it from the Hoard, the 'key' then granted to the Rashei along with their duties as caretakers of the Book, and later the Fangs of Solvyngarr, and my Dragon Sword, all of which are missing." Abriya's face took on a puzzled look. "Darque, although I believe the Book was stolen by the one who orchestrated their disappearance, and we still don't know about the Fangs, the thought occurs to me, we've looked everywhere for my Sword, and it has yet to answer my Call. 'Twould still be trying to come to my hand, even though I am back in spirit form. Mayhap Myriam hid it there."

Every time the Fangs were mentioned, Darque felt a strange tingle urging her toward some discovery. It seemed at the tip of her fingers. She rubbed her eyes. Although the Highlands shared their Memories, able to access those of their ancestors, 'twas as a giant library available at their whim, but still needed to be searched. Therefore, neither could she blame any of the Highlands now, for not revealing this region. But recalling their time was short, she merely stated, "Good point."

Abriya was beginning to fade. "There's another one. Evidence shows that the disappearance, the event that took the Rashei, occurred in the early morning. If so, there would have been a detail working in Shahanalaa. Those people may not have been affected, and if not, they could still be living there, unable to leave."

Abriya's voice faded as did her image, and as she disappeared, Darque listened to the whisper coming from the distance, 'til she could hear no more. She sighed and shook her head, frustrated with the limited time in which they could hold such discussions. 'Twould be no forthcoming information 'til Abriya returned, yet from what the Shade had said, 'twould take some kind of key to open this new region, and the Fates alone knew what or where that might be now. She wondered how it went undetected even from above, how it maintained its weather conditions (although those two questions could have the same answer), and how they'd break in, for finding and opening Shahanalaa was not an option, 'twas an obligation. And she didn't even want to think about how difficult it might be to find the Book of the Conqueror and the Fangs of Solvyngarr. If they'd fallen into Hoard hands, 'twas paramount they know, and wherever they were, the priceless treasures must be recovered. She needed more information. Mayhap 'twas time to have Ardyth channel the First Warrior once again.

THUS ENDS SEARCH FOR THE WYRDRITCH

Look for Further Adventures, and Answers, in:
The Battle of Winter's Edge, Darque Legends Book 4

Long Live Darque and the Dragon Clan!

Author's Bio

Born in Connecticut and raised in the Midwest, Derrien Relyea grew up fascinated with mythology, Viking lore and Dragons. Her vivid imagination was kindled by her highly creative family, encouraging a love of writing and fantasy. She worked her way through Oklahoma City Community College with degrees in Occupational Therapy and Therapeutic Recreation, and later graduated from The University of Oklahoma Health Sciences Center with a degree in Physical Therapy.

Taking her cue from an exciting genealogical history and such authors as Anne McCaffrey, Edgar Rice Burroughs, Jules Verne, and Sir Arthur Conan Doyle, she has embarked upon a new adventure in her life. Please join her at:

http://thedragonwarrior.com

Kudos and credit to my friend and accomplished artist, Lisa Dixon:

http://www.lisadixonart.com